The Girl in the BOX

The
Girl
in the
BOX

SHEILA DALTON

DUNDURN
TORONTO

Editor: Allister Thompson
Design: Jennifer Scott
Printer: Webcom

Library and Archives Canada Cataloguing in Publication

Dalton, Sheila
The girl in the box / Sheila Dalton.

ISBN 978-1-926607-26-9

I. Title.

PS8557.A4724G57 2011   C813'.54   C2011-900553-0

1   2   3   4   5   15   14   13   12   11

We acknowledge the support of the **Canada Council for the Arts** and the **Ontario Arts Council** for our publishing program. We also acknowledge the financial support of the **Government of Canada** through the **Canada Book Fund** and **Livres Canada Books**, and the **Government of Ontario** through the **Ontario Book Publishing Tax Credit** and the **Ontario Media Development Corporation**.

Care has been taken to trace the ownership of copyright material used in this book. The author and the publisher welcome any information enabling them to rectify any references or credits in subsequent editions.

J. Kirk Howard, President

Printed and bound in Canada.
www.dundurn.com

Poem on page 309 is "As Kingfishers Catch Fire, Dragonflies Draw Flame" by Gerard Manley Hopkins.

Poem on page 310 is "anyone lived in a pretty how town" by e.e. cummings.

Dundurn	Gazelle Book Services Limited	Dundurn
3 Church Street, Suite 500	White Cross Mills	2250 Military Road
Toronto, Ontario, Canada	High Town, Lancaster, England	Tonawanda, NY
M5E 1M2	LA1 4XS	U.S.A. 14150

———

*For Carol Pazitka, with whom I travelled
to Guatemala in the seventies.
Her inside knowledge of Guatemala's political struggles,
her love for that country and its Mayan people,
were one of the main inspirations for this book.*

———

Chapter One

Jerry

Guatemala, Feb., 1983

The smell was thick as sludge, and rancid. It forced an intake of breath, and Jerry wanted to pinch his nostrils shut and run out of the hut.

He struggled to ignore it, but the stench dropped into his throat and lodged there. When he tried to swallow, he coughed instead.

"*Agua?*" He turned to the Mayan behind him. "*Por favor?*"

The man nodded while continuing to talk to his wife.

Jerry leaned into his arms on the rough-hewn table and stared at the crucifixes on the wall.

There were five hand-carved wooden Messiahs in front of him, each more lurid than the last. One strained so far outwards from his cross that Jerry thought he looked like he could tear himself off and change religious history. Painted blood ran from the hands, feet, and sides of all five, and hung in gobs from a number of wounded knees. It cascaded over one Christ's body in vermilion stripes, ending in a single dangling blob at the bottom of the cross.

The murmur behind Jerry grew louder. He swivelled around. The couple dropped their eyes and lowered their voices simultaneously, as though performing a duet.

"*Agua?*" he pleaded, a hand to his throat.

"*Si, señor.*" This time, the man shooed his wife behind a ragged curtain then followed her out of sight.

Jerry concentrated on the pictures on the wall, colourful renditions of what he thought must be Mayan deities, interspersed with rumpled copies of paintings of Catholic saints. An abundance of spiritualities, where he himself had none.

He frowned at the uplifted eyes and sweet, secretive smiles of the saints. Multicoloured woollen frames bordered each blissful face — red, orange, bright yellow, the kind of blues and greens that oceans radiate and skies sometimes faintly reflect — colours out of a child's fantasy, woven together with tufts and tassels and thick, knotted fringes that infused the pictures with the kind of robust good cheer he'd come to admire in Latin Americans themselves.

His spirits lifted. But there was that unhealthy smell, and a filthy blanket hanging heavily over the doorway, blocking air and light.

He'd met the couple while riding the bus to the village of Panajachel, on the way back from the market in Chichicastenanga.

Baskets were everywhere, and lunches wrapped in banana leaves, redolent with spices. Chickens clucked beside their owners on the seats. The women's feet were bare and dusty, the ribbons in their thick braids vibrant against the dark coils of their hair.

As Jerry admired both ribbons and braids, the woman in the seat directly across the aisle from him leaned forward and vomited in a thin stream onto the floor, then moaned and nestled back against her male companion.

The macho drivers and the hair-raising roads made travel sickness so common here that no one except Jerry reacted. He sat forward in his seat, frowning at the ashen grey of the woman's face, a stark contrast to her blue, red, and orange *huipil* and the vivid *rebozo* clutched tightly to her mouth.

She groaned again, loudly, and Jerry's frown deepened. The man, who, despite his healthy brown face, looked dull and pedestrian beside her in his faded T-shirt and polyester pants tied with string, pressed a hand to her forehead.

Jerry leaned across the narrow aisle and spoke haltingly. "The *señora* is ... ill? Sick? *Yo soy* ... doctor," he added when he saw the fear in the couple's eyes. He hoped to reassure them; his Spanish was limited, and it was the best he could do. "From Canada. Don't be afraid."

He addressed the woman, punctuating his speech with hand gestures and smiles. "Do you have stomach pain? A headache? Where do you hurt?"

It was the husband who answered in a thin, uncertain voice. "*No es nada, no es nada.*"

Meanwhile, his wife struggled to sit upright. She looked at Jerry through narrowed eyes, then she turned to her husband and said something urgently in a language Jerry assumed was Mayan.

The man replied in a rapid burst, shaking his head vigorously. She countered with something short and sharp that made him look down at his broad, dusty hands, still shaking his head, but more gently.

Again the woman spoke to him. Jerry heard the word *Canada* but could understand nothing else. The man set his lips, frowning, then turned to Jerry. "Canada ...?"

Jerry nodded. "*Si*. From Canada." He pointed to the maple leaf on his backpack.

The man frowned, obviously wrestling with the language. "You please … come to my home?" His forehead knotted.

Jerry stumbled to find an answer.

"*Por favor*." The voice was now pleading. Both the man and his wife were gazing fixedly at Jerry.

"For your wife?" Jerry said. "You need a local doctor. I'm not a … doctor for the body. I help with people's … minds." He tapped his forehead.

The man blinked and said, "For … mind?" touching his own head.

"*Si*," said Jerry.

The man's face came alive. "We like … you … visit. You. Come. Visit?" He was pointing back and forth, to himself, to Jerry, agitated, eager.

Just for a visit? Jerry had found the Maya gracious and a little shy outside their marketplaces, but he was not convinced the "visit" would be other than a hard sell, or even something more sinister. The country was at war with itself, had been for decades. Being from Canada was a plus, he knew, better than being American in the eyes of the Indians, but even so…. What had excited the man about him being a "mind doctor"? Had he misunderstood?

Likely he'd interpreted Jerry's words and gestures as meaning he could help with headaches or head pain. Jerry wished he could tell the man he'd said "doctor" only because his Spanish was bad and it seemed a way to offer reassurance.

He didn't want to spurn their hospitality, though, if that's what it was. His Guatemalan friend Jacinta, who was half-Mayan, had told him it was an honour for a *gringo* to be a guest in a traditional Mayan home. He was due back in Toronto in less than a week and had spent his time, apart from these trips on the local buses, at the usual tourist haunts, where the indigenous people were like props or background music, he thought. Hospitality to a *gringo* in these troubled times was rare.

The irony of it. He wants my help as a doctor, when I came here hoping to learn from a Guatemalan shaman. A tour he'd hoped to take, on which he would meet shamans and be introduced to some of the psychotropic plants they used, had fallen through because of the political situation. His friend Jacinta knew an *H'men* but had told him it was impossible to arrange a meeting in the current climate, even for a Canadian doctor.

He nodded curtly. "Yes. *Gracias,*" he said. "Is it far?"

"No far," the man replied quickly, but his downward glance gave his words the lie, and again Jerry wondered what he was in for, and why.

They travelled for a while in silence, Jerry gazing absently out the back window at the stinking grey scarf of diesel fumes trailing behind the bus.

Just outside Panajachel, the Mayan man waved his hands in the air excitedly and pointed to the front of the vehicle. Understanding they had arrived at their stop, Jerry gathered his things and followed the couple off the bus.

White, red, pink, and blue houses reminded Jerry of the pastel candy hearts kids gave out on Valentine's Day back home. Tiles of reddish-brown clay pipe curved on the rooftops, and fences of corrugated scrap metal divided one tiny yard from another.

The man pointed towards them, and Jerry assumed that was where the couple lived, "no far" after all.

But the man walked past the crowded dwellings, into the trees beyond.

Here it was all fat, leathery leaves, spiralling vines, and densely packed trees in a blind climb for the light. You couldn't see the sky. The air glowed green through the foliage. Jerry tasted sweat on his lips and swatted at the insects blurring his vision.

After about half an hour, the trees began to thin. Jerry followed the couple down a sharp incline, crackling through the dry underbrush, before heading up another steep slope, crowned again by trees.

The man glanced at Jerry's weary face. "No far," he said anxiously.

Jerry forced a smile and kept walking. If the man's sick wife could do it, so could he, he thought, though his stomach hurt as well as his head. So far, he had escaped an attack of *turista*, and he hoped his luck wasn't about to give out.

There were only small, scrubby bushes around them now, no trees. The brilliant sky was patterned with clouds, and he squinted up at them, grateful they were thick enough in places to block the worst of the midday sun.

After a climb that made his legs ache and his heart thump in his chest, they reached the top of the hill, and over the rise was a house. Or at least, a dwelling — patchwork walls, a doorway covered in a length of greasy-looking cloth, and a roof of what looked like warped bark, but was more likely corrugated cardboard.

These people have nothing at all. Jerry looked around him, rubbing his forehead hard with his thumb. *Nothing.*

Close to the hut's doorway, a large wooden cross wrapped in a ratty swatch of lace leaned sideways at a lopsided angle.

To the left of the cross lay a small vegetable patch, staked with tree branches, guarded by a tattered scarecrow of potato sacks and old plastic bags. An assortment of squash sat in a broken basket nearby. Produce from the garden?

The air bore down heavily and sweat rolled into the corners of Jerry's eyes. The silence, punctuated only by the warm hum of insects, the static whir of their wings, began its own buzz inside his aching head.

"Home?" he said to the man beside him, his throat thick.

"*Si.*"

Jerry managed a sickly smile then looked away.

The woman pulled aside the stained curtain and ushered them inside.

And now, here in their small dark house, with his head pulsing and the gory crucifixes seeming to throb in sympathy, he wiped his brow with his shirtsleeve and nervously licked his lips. He thought suddenly of Caitlin, his long-time lover. If anything happened here, if he could not get away, she would sound the alarm. But he wasn't due back for days yet, and besides, what good would it do?

The back of his throat tasted of salt. His stomach lurched. He put his face in his hands for a moment, and when he looked up, they were standing across from him, their shoulders touching, staring. The man's eyes looked like they could ignite wood, Jerry thought; the woman's were more fearful.

She held out a chipped cup. It felt warm in his cradled hands. Inside he saw a yellowish liquid. Tea? He drank greedily, emptying the cup before registering the mouldy aftertaste.

"We lose *cinco* … five … children, *señor.*"

Jerry jerked his head up and gripped the mug more tightly.

The man was explaining something in an awkward blend of English, Spanish, and what had to be his own dialect. Jerry couldn't understand a word until the man repeated in a soft voice, "We lose *cinco* children."

Desperation was now a fourth presence in the room. Jerry looked at the woman with pity. She seemed too young to have so many children. The heat and darkness and smell …

"We have still one child." The man clasped and unclasped his fingers, lowering his eyes. "Inez." His lips trembled. When he looked up, he directed his gaze towards his wife, as if seeking her permission to go on.

She nodded almost imperceptibly, her own eyes furtive. When her husband began speaking again, she held a hand to her forehead.

"She ill, very ill," the man was saying, and for a moment Jerry was confused. He thought the man was referring to his wife.

"Please. Come. Look at her. *Por favor.*"

"Of course. Though, you understand, I am not a —"

The man shifted his feet and stammered, "Is no our fault ..."

Jerry froze. That phrase or ones like it — he'd heard them so many times in the emergency wards — *"It's not our fault." "We didn't mean to hurt him." "She fell."*

Automatically, he murmured a soothing, "No, no, of course not," all the while thinking, *Oh god, have they done something awful to this child?*

"Can you take me to her?" he said, swallowing to dislodge the unpleasant taste in his mouth. *This isn't Canada,* he cautioned himself. *They've lost their children to disease or famine, not abuse, and they wouldn't be so concerned about this girl if they didn't love her.*

"*Si.*" The man steadied himself against the table for a moment. "Come," he said and headed out the door. His wife followed him through the entranceway with Jerry close behind.

They led him in the direction of a small stand of trees beyond the market garden.

As they approached, scrabbling noises and low moaning, almost a *mooing* sound, made Jerry's chest constrict.

A little farther into the trees sat a box.

A patchwork wooden rectangle, about Jerry's height, about three quarters that in width. No windows. Jerry thought of shipping crates, of luggage trunks, and shuddered. The door was tied shut with a length of rusted chain and a metal padlock. *Oh, god, no.* He licked his top lip and drew in a slow breath, hoping to quiet the beating of his heart, now loud enough to interfere with his hearing.

The thumping from the hut was interspersed with grunts. Jerry shut his eyes as the man fiddled with the lock. When he opened them, the door, too, was open.

She came out into the daylight, thin and straight, dragging a length of chain behind her. She was squinting and looking away from the sun. He noted the delicate bone structure of her face, the fullness of her mouth.

Then she raised her face to the light and extended her hands in an expansive gesture as though releasing a flock of birds.

Jerry felt time slow down, and everything around him grow big. The scene became a separate world hanging in space. The girl looked directly at him, and he swam in the spaces created by her gaze, while the freed birds flew up and away. She had the most unusual eyes he had ever seen, an exaggerated hazel, he thought later, the light ring round the inky iris more gold than brown, glowing inside the rust-coloured pupil like a starry topaz jewel. The intimacy he felt, along with the horror of her circumstances, was so unexpected, it shocked him.

The chain was ludicrous. She looked fragile, almost elfin, standing quietly and at ease even as her expression turned fierce. Out of this stillness, she took a slow step his way, holding his eyes.

When she looked away from him towards her parents, hands hanging loosely at her sides, he watched closely, puzzled. He was thinking how unafraid she seemed, almost languid, wondering if that meant her parents hadn't abused her, despite appearances, or whether she was numb, or mentally slow, or full of despair, or something he could not even guess at.

He was so absorbed in watching her, he had to rouse himself to observe her parents. He needed to see how they were responding.

They were gazing at her, unsmiling, almost transfixed, it seemed to him, not at all the way he would expect parents to look at their child. Perplexed by what their expressions might mean, he tried to link them to cases he'd seen in the past. But he could think only of the children he'd worked with at a psychiatric clinic early in his career. Inez reminded him most of a young boy there, an autistic child with an angelic face who'd been physically and emotionally abused. Was that the story here? Then why did her parents seem both awed and afraid?

They began talking to each other in low voices, ignoring him and Inez.

The girl slowly looked him up and down. Perhaps she was mimicking his appraisal of her. Some of the disturbed or autistic children he'd treated mimicked the behaviour of others. There was something unnatural in her gaze, he thought, though he could not be sure, given that her eyes were so unusual. Her skin was tawny. Many of the Mayans Jerry had encountered had dusty-looking skin, but hers reflected the sunlight.

She was absorbed, but it was as if she were looking at him from a great distance. He'd known kids in the autistic spectrum who looked at people as if they were observing alien objects. If this girl did suffer from autism, it could go some way towards explaining her parents' attitude. He'd seen cases where parents completely rejected their autistic children, out of ignorance and fear.

Her hair was long, so tangled and matted it stood out from her head in a wild rasta halo that dwarfed the delicate features of her face. She was short, like her parents, but so slender and fine-boned that she conjured gazelles, blue herons, graceful, long-limbed creatures that appeared tall. Despite the ragged shift that barely reached mid-thigh, she held herself with dignity.

She looked perhaps thirteen or fourteen years old.

"Your daughter?" Jerry's voice cracked.

"*Si*."

The woman was crying.

"Why is she chained?" Indignation made his voice harsh.

"She ... bad," said the woman at last, lowering her head.

"*Loca*," the man intoned softly.

"Unchain her. Please." *Don't jump to conclusions*, he cautioned himself once more. But what could ever excuse keeping a child in a wooden box, on a chain?

When they hesitated, he went on, "I am a — I work with those who are ... *loco*. I —"

"She run away —" began the woman, waving her hands.

Words froze in Jerry's throat. He didn't want her to run away. "Let me talk to her a minute," he said softly.

"No talk. Inez."

Jerry turned abruptly away from the couple to avoid saying something he might later regret. As he slowly moved towards the girl, he tried to recapture her gaze, but she was looking down at her bare feet, hands behind her back.

"Inez," he said when he came within a few feet of her.

She peered at him, a deep line forming between her eyes.

"Inez, I am a doctor. I am here to help you."

She didn't move, but he heard her sigh.

"May I come closer?" He said all this in broken Spanish, not knowing if she knew anything but her own dialect. She did not respond.

He moved forward again.

"Sit. Would you like to sit?" He lowered himself into a squat and gently patted the earth beside him.

He was startled at first when she sat, not next to him, but across from him, her chain clattering briefly then coming to rest, coiled, beside her. He'd expected to coax her for a long time before she'd even approach.

Sweat prickled his underarms. "Are you a good girl, Inez?" he said softly, because what her mother had said about her had made him both angry and sad.

Her nostrils flared, and Jerry tensed. When she grunted like a contented animal, he let his breath out softly and rested more comfortably back on his haunches.

Inez began to twist her head from side to side. Her lips were parted and her eyes closed. Jerry noticed how unusually long her lashes were, shadowy against her cheeks.

"Inez, you are good," he said quietly.

She stopped turning her head and opened what seemed to him intelligent eyes.

"Yes," he said, "you are."

She hunched her shoulders up near her ears, her eyes never leaving his face. Only when he stood up slowly, still looking down at her, did she lower her head. Then she began digging with one finger into the dirt between her feet.

Jerry looked at her helplessly for a moment then strode over to the couple. "Why have you locked her up like this?"

Her parents stood in mute resistance.

"Why do you call her bad?"

The woman looked beseechingly at her husband. When he said nothing, she spoke to Jerry in broken phrases. "She ..." She clutched her *rebozo* to her throat. "She ..." Then she twisted the shawl in her hands. "She ... like ... animal ..." The woman began again to cry.

"In what way?"

"Scream." The man was waving his arms around his head.

"Scream *loud*." His hands over his ears. "And ... tear. Uh ... brak ... *break*. Everything." He was stamping about now, his face contorted into some personal approximation of anger, picking up branches and snapping them in two, baring his teeth, throwing stones. "Like ... that," he said, stopping.

"How long have you had her in here?"

The man shrugged helplessly. "Since —" and held his hand out, palm down, at mid-chest.

She could have been at most twelve, and likely even younger when they locked her up, Jerry guessed as a rush of saliva flooded his back teeth. He swallowed. "How often do you let her out?"

The woman shook her head.

Her husband shot her a glance. "Sometimes. On chain." Then he launched into an incomprehensible monologue, gesturing energetically.

Jerry stared. How was he ever going to find out what had happened to this girl?

Inez, meanwhile, was standing up, looking warily at her parents from narrowed eyes, her head tilted towards one raised shoulder.

"We must talk," he said to the couple. "In the house. Bring Inez."

"No, *señor*," the man answered. "I cannot."

"Evil," he thought he heard the woman mumble into the *rebozo* clasped to her mouth.

Oh god, oh god. Jerry took a deep breath. "All right. Just come to the house."

He watched the man guide his daughter back to the box. When she resisted, he pushed her and spoke in a commanding voice.

Instantly, the hunted look left the girl's face, and she spat at her father as she retreated backwards into the darkness.

The man fastened the padlock. "*Loca*," he muttered, shaking his head and wiping at his cheeks as he led the procession back to their home.

Once inside, Jerry began to talk purely out of frustration, knowing he wouldn't be understood. But the man broke through his wall of words.

"You. Take her," he said. "You — doctor. You take her. To … your … country."

Jerry felt as if several pieces of machinery had come loose in his head. He sat down hard, nearly bringing the wobbly chair with him. Why did they want him to take her? Nothing made sense. Did they just want to be rid of her?

Only one thing was clear: whatever their motives, there was no way he was going to take the girl. Too many complications, too much responsibility…. He tried to read their faces, wondering if they were trying to read his.

The man seemed determined. He jutted his chin forward. The woman again held her gaily coloured shawl to her lips, the eyes staring over it, stark with — what? Desperation?

Jerry thought of the unguarded brown glow of Inez's eyes, the way she had observed him, distant then uncannily near, before her parents had intervened. That, and the horror of her circumstances.

Perhaps there was something he could do for her here in Guatemala.

"Help us." The woman lowered her *rebozo* and held her hands palms-up from her chest as though in supplication or despair. To Jerry, it was a hideous mockery of her daughter's earlier gesture of giving and release.

When he didn't respond, the woman disappeared behind the curtain veiling one corner of the room. She reappeared holding a small grubby cloth bag that she pressed into his hand. It felt soft and prickly at the same time, like cat fur roughened with burrs; sticky, too. He pushed it back towards her. "No, no ... I ..."

The man stepped between them. "*Por favor.*" His voice was as pleading as his wife's eyes, the *por favor* sounding to Jerry more like "for pity's sake" than "please."

Jerry held up one hand in surrender, stuffed the sticky pouch into his pants pocket, and backed away.

They followed him, speaking in raised voices. He couldn't understand a word, but their intent was clear.

"I can't —" he began. "I can't! No!" He shouted it, raising both arms, then strode across the clearing, praying they wouldn't follow, and into the trees, welcoming them now for the barrier they provided against this nightmare couple and the nightmare of their lives.

That evening, back in Panajachel and exhausted, he walked along the dark shore of Lake Atitlan, his head down, his hands stuffed into the pockets of his shorts. The girl's situation was so desperate ... Maybe he could go back and give the family money? But that might not change *her* circumstances.

There were many reasons why taking her away was not a viable option. Apart from anything else, how could he explain it to Caitlin? They'd met here in Panajachel, twelve years ago. What was he to say? "*I found this strange kid in a box in Guatemala. She may be autistic, or schizophrenic. Or dangerous. I'm bringing her home. With luck, she won't kill us.*"

Hell, no. Sarcasm wouldn't cut it. He shook his head, sat down a few yards from the shoreline, and stared blankly over the lake.

"*Caitlin, I've come across this case of the most terrible child abuse ... a young girl, between thirteen and fifteen, I think, locked up for years in a shed no bigger than a box. Caitlin, I can't just leave her there ..."*

Yes. If he let Cat hear the problem just as it was, unembellished by his inchoate feelings, she'd be able to deal with it. He almost knew what she'd say.

She'd encourage him to bring the child to Canada. She was kind-hearted, caring. She would also resent the imposition. And why not? Even though they didn't live together, the impact of Inez on their relationship would be huge. No, he couldn't do it. It was impossible.

He wondered briefly what would have happened had Caitlin come with him on this trip. He'd wanted her to, but when the plan included what she called "drug tourism," she'd declined. She'd never shared his interest in entheogens, and the one ayahuasca trip he'd persuaded her to take had been something of a disaster.

"You forget I grew up with musicians. I've seen too much shit related to drugs," she'd said. "I don't even like you when you're on them." She was referring to his few research experiments with LSD. "You get all pompous and crazy, like you've seen the light or something, when you've only seen the inside of your head with all the connectors in the wrong plugs. If you want to see what *is*, you should meditate."

When he'd launched a defence, she'd interrupted him. "It's no good, Jerry, I tried LSD when it was legal. It gave me insight, but the insight disappeared along with the high, and besides, it wasn't true insight. I thought a lamppost was worthy of deep respect, for god's sake. Anyway, I thought you hated those tourist things."

"I do. But it's the only way to go right now. There aren't even very many of them any more. I only got in because of Doherty."

She'd thrown her hands up in the air and walked out of the room. He should have known better than to mention Doherty. Caitlin couldn't stand him.

When the tour was cancelled, it was too late for Caitlin to reconsider. He'd already booked his flight and arranged vacation time. "I'll go anyway," he said to her. "Just for a holiday. Why don't you come, too?"

"I can't afford the time. Besides, isn't the situation there dangerous right now?"

He remembered answering that, from what he'd heard, if you were Canadian and were careful not to get involved in politics, you'd be okay.

"Well, I'm not sure how I'd feel, being there in the middle of it," she said, and when he remonstrated that when they'd met twelve years ago in Panajachel the civil war was already underway, she added, "I was different then," and when he pressed her to explain, she ignored him.

"I'd cramp your style, Jer," was all she'd say. "You're going to want to take any drug opportunity that comes your way, and I don't want to be there stopping you."

He'd told her not to be stupid, he was researching entheogens, not indulging in them, and was choosy about how he'd go about it. He almost said, "I'm not Doherty," but stopped himself in time. She would've made assumptions that were off the mark, and he hadn't wanted to get into it with her.

She couldn't get out of her assignments on such short notice anyway, and his flight was full. They'd taken many separate vacations over the years, it was no big deal. But this one would have had sentimental value, Jerry thought, returning together to the place where "they" first began.

He lay back on his elbows, several images running behind his eyes from his mental album of their long time together. A younger Caitlin in a flowing gauze skirt and buffalo sandals. Caitlin, in the present, wearing the red high heels and tight suit that reflected her stubborn determination to move with the times. Fussing with her thick, shiny, wavy hair, gazing at him from his bathroom mirror, green eyes reflecting the light. Wearing a short apricot nightie that bared one luminous ivory shoulder.

He sat back up, grabbed a small stone, polished as a waxed chestnut, and rubbed it with his fingers. Caitlin at night, small enough to curl into a shell against him, her head nestled under his chin, the earthy smell of her hair. His large hands enclosing her small ones, clutching at them, she told him, while he slept, small spasms that reassured and comforted. In the morning, he often woke to the pleasant heaviness of her breasts resting in the cups of his palms.

Chapter Two

Caitlin's Story

Jerry died on June 29, 1983. I had a deadline that day and was writing an article for the *Star* about child poverty in Toronto when I got the news. Absorbed in my work, when the phone rang, I let the service pick it up.

Around six o'clock, too tired to concentrate, my thoughts wandered to Jerry in his big kitchen, starting supper, whistling and chopping, occasionally brushing his thick, wavy hair out of his eyes with the back of his cleavering hand, the better to peer into an open cookbook. He was as passionate about cooking as he was about everything he enjoyed. Including me.

I called him.

"Hello?" said an unfamiliar male voice after only one ring.

I hesitated on the edge of saying, "Who's that?" Instead, I asked for Jerry.

"Are you a member of his immediate family?" the voice went on with a formality that frightened me.

"Why are you asking? What's wrong?"

Silence on the other end.

"Look, who is this?"

"Officer James Royce, miz. Who am I speaking to?"

"I'm Jerry's partner."

"Is your name Caitlin Shaughnessy?" He sounded tense.

I was pressing the receiver into my ear hard enough to hurt and didn't think to ask how he knew that. "Yes," I said.

"Ms. Shaughnessy, we've been trying to reach you. I'm sorry, I have some very bad news...."

They should have sent someone.

That idea kept its teeth in my brain as everything else around me lost its grip. I ran past Rosedale's well-kept mansions with my laceless runners slapping the pavement and my unbuttoned jacket thumping against my chest like an errant sail in a high wind. My skirt was too narrow for my strides, and my shoulder bag kept slipping down to bang against my knees.

I finally looped the long straps over my head and ripped open the pleat at the back of my skirt. When I leaned over to catch my breath, my hands on my thighs, the world seemed to spiral away from me. I bit my tongue, the only way I could think to bring it back, pressing down ferociously until my surroundings zoom-lensed into focus again.

Cop cars were everywhere, their blue lights spinning so fast I was afraid they'd spin me away again too. Jerry's yard was cordoned off with rope fences and orange pylons. My breath was rattling in my chest, ragged and quick.

INCIDENT REPORT (SUMMARY)

Investigating Officer(s): Constable P. Royce,
Detective A. Lyons
Incident no.: 000142-12A-1995
Date: 29/06/1983
Incident Address: 579 Rosewood Ave., Toronto
Victim's Name: Dr. Jeremy Simpson

"Officer Royce, Ms. Shaughnessy." He was holding out a dark-skinned hand, and I raised mine as through some dense, sticky liquid. His arm did the shaking, and mine didn't resist.

"I can't tell you much, Ms. Shaughnessy," he said. "And I can't let you go inside." He looked at me only briefly before staring resolutely over my shoulder, his arms now firmly locked behind his back.

"Can you tell me who found him?" The words felt like pills I'd tried to swallow without water and had to force back up.

Officer Royce scratched his forehead near his cap like someone on a Norman Rockwell magazine cover. "Yes, miz. It was Christine DeLang."

Christine. Jerry's house cleaner for the last eight years.

DESCRIPTION

At 7:20 a.m., Dispatch received a 911 call regarding the discovery of a body in a house in the Rosedale district, 579 Rosewood Ave. The caller identified herself as Christine DeLang, employed as a housecleaner by Dr. J. Simpson, owner of the residence from which she was phoning.

"How is she?" I knew Christine was tender-hearted, and this would hit her hard. But all I could really think about was Jerry.

Royce's expression softened. "She's all right. They took her down to the station to give a statement. She was shook up, but okay." He looked me over. "Maybe you should go home. There's nothing you can do here."

FINDINGS:

Reporting Officer Sandler made the following verbal report, which is stated in summary and not verbatim. R/O Sandler stated that he was met when he arrived at end of the driveway of 579 Rosewood by an adult female, identified as Christine DeLang. The witness directed R/O Sandler to the location of the body in the study of the indicated residence. After confirming the presence of the body, R/O Sandler secured the scene, called for backup, and detained the witness.

Coroner's Inspector Mary Lou Jamieson arrived at the scene at approximately 7:15 a.m. and pronounced the victim deceased at 7:28 a.m. by visual observation that the victim was not breathing and by tactile observation that the victim did not have a palpable carotid pulse.

My thoughts were a million miles from home.

"Miz, are you okay?"

"Yes. What happened to him?"

"No comment, Ms. Shaughnessy." Though he resumed his over-my-shoulder stare, his tone was kind. "My orders are to guard the scene and not give information away. It's my first crime scene. I can't mess up again."

A light went on. "So giving me the news over the phone was messing up?"

He bobbed his head, planting his feet farther apart. "I … apologize, Ms. Shaughnessy." He looked down then up again. "I blew it."

I'll say. "What did he die of, Officer?"

His gaze shifted. "The details aren't available."

CAUSE OF DEATH

> *Inspector Jamieson stated the cause of death appears to have been blunt force trauma injuries to the head but indicated that further details would be available in the official autopsy report.*

"Where is Inez? Can you tell me that?"

I knew something was really wrong, because all he would say was "Don't worry about her" and "She's being taken care of." When I pressed him, he set his lips in a granite line.

I began to back away and stumbled. He put out a hand to steady me then led me to the grassy verge. "Sit down here, Ms. Shaughnessy, till you feel better."

I felt time loop back and swallow itself, freeze-framing Jerry's death before disappearing altogether. Another officer came up and said, "We'd like you to come to the station sometime, miss. We have some questions for you. It doesn't have to be right away."

But "right away" sounded good. Otherwise, I thought I might end up sitting on the grass for the rest of my life, vainly waiting for the nightmare to end.

———

They'd found Inez crouched beside Jerry's body, her hands and clothes brilliant with his blood.

In the four months I'd known her, I'd grown to love her. We'd spent a lot of time in each other's company right from the start. Jerry hired a live-in nurse, but she was away most weekends, and I filled in. While Jerry attended an analytic conference in Germany, I took over Inez's daily care for two straight weeks, with only the nurse for help.

Being with her could be demanding, but it was also rewarding. She was like no one I had ever met before, so soft and gentle at times, and so mysterious, her silence both a shield and portal to a different way of being. Often, I felt grateful to have met her. Now, I wished she'd never come into our lives.

I first realized when I was eleven years old that it was possible to think two ways about the same person. My best friend Ally was light and laughter and wild, springing possibilities; she was also dark needs and secret whisperings, a tangle of longings and demands that made being around her feel like jumping at a high wall from a standing start. She let boys do things to her, then wanted me to do them, too. She liked to steal from stores and shit in the woods and tell our parents lies. I disapproved of her; I adored her.

But Inez? Was it possible to keep loving someone who had destroyed my life?

Chapter Three

Jerry
Guatemala, Feb., 1983

Jerry sat in the small office on the ground floor of a two-storey building in Panajachel, watching a crowd of boys playing soccer through the open window, listening to their high, excited voices and the poff-poff of their naked feet on the dusty earth.

He'd gone there the morning after leaving the Mayan couple and battling his way back through the rainforest, racing to keep up with his memory of the route back to the bus stop.

The sign of Caduceus with its twin snakes — the international symbol of the medical profession — had drawn him.

He'd rapped on the door with his fist.

"*Hablas ingles?*"

The compact, neat man who opened up on the third knock said "Yes," his face expressionless. "What is it?" He didn't open the door any wider.

Jerry fumbled through his wallet for some ID. "I'm a doctor myself, Dr. …"

"Fernandez."

"Dr. Fernandez. I'm here from Canada." He handed the man his card. "Yesterday, I was trying to help a Mayan couple back there, in the jungle." He pointed behind him. "It's a strange story. They — please, may I come in?"

The doctor said "All right," after a pause long enough to disconcert Jerry, then opened the door further, ushering him into a tiny office.

"Please, sit down." Fernandez rummaged through his desk drawers as though he were alone. Behind him was a curtained-off area Jerry assumed was for examining patients. "I will be with you in one moment or two."

To Jerry, everything in the room looked tired, from the faded calendar on the cracked concrete wall to the worn woven mat on the floor.

His host seemed to have found what he was looking for. He shoved some papers into a file folder and shut the last drawer. "Now — what is it?" he said, placing his elbows on the desktop and steepling his fingers.

Jerry pressed a tissue to his brow. The room was very hot. "I — uh — came upon a young girl, a Mayan —" He broke off helplessly. "Her parents have ... chained her ... inside a wooden box...."

As Jerry spoke, he had to swallow again to clear his throat. The story came out in jerks and spasms, until he finally finished and said, "Can you help them?"

The doctor's face had remained impassive throughout the tale. "They didn't ask for me," he said coolly, tapping his blotter with a pen. "It's you they want."

"But why?"

"More to the point, why do you care?" Fernandez frowned and folded his arms across his chest.

"Does that matter?" Jerry snapped, too distressed for diplomacy. "I'm not heartless, that's all. I can't just ignore what I've seen. Could you?"

"No."

"Well then, surely you will do something to help."

Fernandez raised his eyebrows. "Dr. Simpson," he said in his precise, accented English, with what Jerry strongly suspected was cultivated boredom, "perhaps you don't understand the situation here in Guatemala."

Jerry sat forward in his chair. "I'm not entirely ignorant, Doctor." He ran a finger along the inside of his collar. "The civil war has been going on for many years. Marxist guerrillas and government soldiers are fighting in the hills. I've read about it in our newspapers. I was told the situation was of little danger to Canadian tourists, if we were careful. Beyond that, yes, I'm damned if I know what's going on, or what it has to do with this girl. Suppose you tell me."

"Genocide is what is going on, Dr. Simpson. Mayan genocide. And I suspect it has everything to do with this girl."

"There are no reports of it in Canada," Jerry said, then wished he hadn't.

His host's eyes flickered, and a disgusted noise rattled his lips. "Exactly how carefully do you read your papers?" Then he shook his head. "Well, it is no real surprise if our government is not advertising its savagery, I suppose. It is hardly conducive to a thriving tourist trade, and certainly our neighbours to the north do not want their complicity proclaimed to the four corners of the earth. But I invite you to think on this. How long did it take the world to discover what Hitler was doing to the Jews?"

Jerry rose in his chair. "You can't compare this to the Holocaust," he protested. He sat back again, patting a tissue along his moist upper lip. "Surely. And isn't it dangerous for you to tell me about it?"

The scowl on Fernandez's face deepened. "Do you see any soldiers here? Are you going to run off to report to them? You cannot even speak the language. The government knows that I treat Mayans. To them, that is tantamount to aiding the enemy. You can't put me in any more danger than I am already in."

Registering the man's hostility, Jerry narrowed his eyes. "Then the girl — something awful may have happened to the family ..."

"Yes. Now, tell me, Doctor, what brought you to Guatemala? The quaint Indian tribes? The beaches? The picturesque scenery? I could show you 'scenery' on which you might wish your eyes had never set."

His contempt was so forceful, it was almost a slap. Jerry made himself breathe slowly to calm his anger, a technique he sometimes resorted to during therapy sessions with difficult patients. "I'm a psychiatrist — an analyst. I was, originally, coming here as part of a special tour in ... ah ... entheogens. Drugs the shamans use. The tour fell through, but I came anyway. Why do you talk about scenery that way? It's obvious you don't mean —"

"Now you know why the tour 'fell through,' as you say. The Maya are in hiding. The military have orders to slaughter them on sight."

"Why? They aren't all Marxists."

"No, they are not. The guerrillas say they are fighting for the rights of the Maya. They hide in the countryside, and they often turn to the Indians for help —"

"What 'scenery,' Doctor?" Jerry interrupted impatiently. The word grated on him. He wasn't willing to sit through another lecture before finding out what the man in front of him meant by it.

Fernandez raised one eyebrow. "Never mind. You do not need to see it."

Jerry shifted in his chair and took another slow, deliberate breath.

"All you need to know, Dr. Simpson, is that the Maya are caught in the middle." Dr. Fernandez was again tapping his pen against the blotter on his desk. "A lot of them are not political. Many of them help the guerrillas out of simple human decency. The rebels force others into it. The government wants the insurrection stopped. The fastest way to do that is to brutalize the Maya. I tell you, the slaughter is terrible — more than a *Norte Americano* tourist can imagine." He put down his pen and sat back with an air of triumph, steepling his fingers once again.

"Don't tell me. Show me," Jerry said in anger, then wondered if he was rising to the doctor's bait or his own. "Head in the clouds Simpson" they'd called him at school. Even Caitlin remonstrated with him sometimes about his devotion to the inner life at the expense of the outer. Even Caitlin, who knew his past.

"Show you what?"

"Whatever ghastly realities you meant by 'scenery.'" Damn the man anyway. He knew what Jerry meant, he was sure of it. "Maybe I'll understand then. If it affects the girl, I should know."

When the man in front of him didn't respond, Jerry added, "Why did you mention it at all then? To emphasize my stupidity?"

"It isn't necessary for you to see these things in order to help the girl."

"It might be necessary to *understand* the girl," Jerry fired back. "I need your help, but you're not going to listen to me unless you rub my nose in what you think I'm too ignorant to comprehend."

"I do not think you are —"

"Show me anyway."

"No."

"Why not?"

"It was a figure of speech only. I have already said. It is not necessary. And I am a busy man."

"You must have had something in mind when you said it."

Fernandez's expression darkened, and it was clear to Jerry that he had in turn touched a nerve. The man sighed deeply while his eyes drifted over Jerry's head to gaze blankly at the wall behind him.

"Yes," he said. "There was something in my mind."

"So give me directions and I'll go myself. No need to take you away from your patients."

"Today is too late."

"I didn't say today."

"You will have to go back the way you came."

The thought of another sweltering trek through the rainforest was depressing. What if it meant encountering the couple again?

"All right," Jerry said.

"I do not understand why you do this."

"Because you throw my ignorance in my face, Doctor." *And because I need to,* he would have added, had he known or liked the man better.

"Pique is a strange reason to confront horror."

"Words are a poor substitute for experience."

His persistence finally wore the doctor down, and he left the office clutching a rough map, some written instructions, and an arrangement to see Fernandez after his excursion.

On the walk back to his hotel, away from the spark and thrust of their dialogue and the activation of his own demons, Jerry thought, *What the hell am I doing?*

He figured Fernandez was right. He didn't need to see any-thing. But it also didn't matter now. The expedition had acquired its own momentum. He had only to get out of its way.

After this, he thought, *I'll know in my bones what is happening in this country.*

He was so tired, he fell asleep as soon as he got back to his hotel, and he dreamed of Inez.

Chapter Four

Caitlin's Story

The first few weeks after my partner's death, I spent hours in bed sleeping or crying with the curtains drawn and balled-up tissues in soggy heaps around me. When I closed my eyes, I saw Jerry. When I opened them, he was there too. I wanted to remember him, and I wanted to forget him. When I thought of Inez, my body shook, I didn't know whether from anger, fear, misery, or pity. I wished everything would go away, I wanted to be somewhere else, even someone else, I longed with all my heart to make the anguish stop, but I was helpless and could change nothing. All my years of meditation, and I couldn't even begin to blunt the pain.

There was one small consolation, an experience I hugged to myself in the long, dark, lonely nights after his death. The night before Jerry's body was discovered, I'd woken from a restless sleep to the sound of a voice calling my name. At the foot of my bed, in the dim light I saw a shadow I knew immediately was him. It was like looking at a dream projected outwards, without benefit of a screen, a see-through vision beamed through my eyes into the air in front of me.

He was nude as a peeled grape, erection and all, gazing at me with what seemed like love and longing.

I wasn't frightened, because my rational mind was at war with my perceptions. I'd been upset the previous evening and had downed a lot of my favourite vodka, Prince Igor, before bed. One of the first things that happens when I drink too much is that my inner talk sounds like someone else asking for attention. The voice I'd heard was female, but it felt like Jerry calling.

My lips moved of their own volition, as though I were reading from a script. "Now that you have died, and your spirit is free, don't choose the first opportunity for rebirth that comes your way."

The words I spoke were a complete surprise to me. I'd seen something like them in *The Tibetan Book of the Dead*, but I wasn't sure I believed in life after death, and in the clear light of day a lot of what was written in that ancient tome sounded like fiction to me. "Try not to be frightened. The monsters you'll encounter are only products of your mind." Even as I said it, I thought it sounded dumb.

But it seemed to work. The lost look disappeared from his eyes; he smiled, blew me a kiss, pointed ahead of him, and followed his finger into oblivion.

The strangest part of this, and the most upsetting, was that it happened before I knew Jerry had been killed.

A few days after Jerry's murder, the police phoned and said I could visit Inez.

"I don't want to see her, Molly. I hate her," I said to my best friend, who had come over to comfort me.

Molly smoothed her wavy white hair away from her face before leaning forward to brush my bangs out of my eyes. "I don't think you do. Not really. Maybe it's just too soon." She sighed and shook her head. "I can't believe she meant to do this. She's been through so much ..." She opened her hands helplessly.

"It's no excuse —" I threw a balled-up tissue onto the floor.

"I don't mean it as one."

I had a mental flash of Inez darting out of sight when a loud bang from a nearby construction site had interrupted one of our walks through the Rosedale Ravine. I'd taken endless minutes to find her, crouched behind a boulder with her hands pressed over her ears.

"You have to visit her sometime," Molly said. "I think you need to for yourself, as well as her."

A light dawned. "Have *you* been, Molly?"

She nodded.

"How is she?"

"You'll have to see for yourself. I'm not like you. Words fail me."

I stroked her blue-veined hands where they rested on her lap and steeled my heart to see Inez.

She was huddled alone on a bench in a small holding cell. Her hair lay flat to her head. Even at a distance, I could see dirt stains on her bare feet.

I could feel the walls closing her in, cutting her off from the fruit of all her pent-up longing to believe in freedom, mocking my hatred and softening my heart.

They clanged the cell door open, but I didn't stir until the policewoman nudged me with the words, "You can go in now," and an inclination of her head.

I entered with a shudder and saw Inez shiver too, where she sat with her arms wrapped around her bent knees. I draped a prison blanket over her shoulders, pulling her close. It was like holding a pillar of stone until she finally relaxed into me.

Even then, she didn't look up. Tears dripped onto her knees, staining the blanket a darker grey.

She wouldn't take a tissue, so I put my hand under her chin and tilted her face to mine. Such a sad and beautiful face, I wanted to cry. Then I looked into her eyes and saw they were soft but also not soft; they held two messages. Childlike, she blew her nose when I held the tissue to it, while those twin-spirited eyes never left my face.

We sat for long minutes, and at times I spoke to her. "It's all right, Inez. Don't cry, Inez," but mostly I kept silent.

Finally, I took my leave. When I said goodbye, she dropped her eyes and turned her face away, as though even the wall offered more comfort than I did.

Back at home, the image of that awful cell haunted me, and of Inez inside it, so small and broken. Seeing her like that, it was impossible to blame anything but re-awakened trauma for the terrible thing she'd done. I thought of calling Margaret, the live-in nurse Jerry had hired. She was competent and kind and might be able to reassure me about Inez's mental and physical state, or at least make me feel a little less alone with what I had seen. But she was in France on vacation. Maybe this whole tragedy could have been avoided if she hadn't left? The thought was disturbing, and I wished with all my heart I'd moved in with Jerry while she was away.

In the end, I phoned a woman called Gretchen. We'd met in university and had barely kept in touch. I felt awkward phoning her, but she was a lawyer, and there were a lot of legal questions on my mind just then. At least we'd talked since Jerry's death, so she knew what had happened. "It's about Inez," I blurted after the preliminaries, then filled her in on the holding cell and its effect on me.

"Will you take her case?" I begged. I hadn't known I was going to ask this. Gretchen was a criminal lawyer, but I had no idea if she was any good. I just knew I didn't trust the Legal Aid nerd the court had appointed, who looked about as threatening as a piece of wet bread; also, that at university, Gretchen had the annoying habit of interrupting professors as if she knew more than they did. Which, as it turned out, she usually did.

"Whoa, Cat." I could imagine Gretchen raising the eyebrows on her impeccably made-up face, holding the phone away from her ear. "I don't know if I can help. The situation —"

"Can you get her out of that cell at least?"

She didn't answer right away. "I would like to help," she said at last, though her voice sounded clipped and on edge. "But she's accused of murder, Cat. They can't just let her go."

"And I can't just leave her locked up like that! They won't even let me pay her bail."

"Your relationship is complicated."

I knew that was fair. God knows I was still angry with Inez, even bitter towards her at times.

From the day Jerry brought her to Canada to the day of his death, she'd been an important part of my life. She was Mayan, and it was suspected that Guatemalan soldiers had massacred her tribe. She rarely spoke, and when she did, she parroted others. She screamed in the night. She was disturbed, perhaps even brain damaged.

She was also lovely to look at and often gentle. One morning, out walking in the Rosedale Ravine, she plucked wildflowers and gave me a bouquet with all the buttercups carefully arranged in the middle.

Later, she'd reached out for Jerry's hand, briefly swinging his arm before running down the path towards a stream.

Less than five months later, she killed him.

I still have that tiny bunch of flowers she gave me, her first gift. Dried, they lie on my bookshelf next to a volume of Leonard Cohen's poetry.

Chapter Five

Caitlin's Story

"This is a damn difficult case," Gretchen said about a week later from her perch amid the tissues in my bedroom, tapping her glasses against the portfolio she had propped on her knee. "I wouldn't even consider taking it if it wasn't for the fact that I know you."

I felt a stab of guilt. I'd learned since we talked on the phone that Gretchen had done quite well in her career. I wanted her to defend Inez now more than ever, so I resisted the urge to make nice and let her off the hook. Besides, I wasn't sure I believed her. A high-profile case like this was practically a gift. She was all decked out in a power suit and had the smell of ambition all over her. The fact that I couldn't afford her, a subject we had yet to broach, was another issue entirely.

"About your fee ..." I ventured.

"Oh, that," she said, flipping a stray tendril of well-polished hair off her cheek. "Don't worry about it. I take on a couple of pro bono cases a year. Sop to my conscience."

I couldn't afford to argue.

"Inez is almost a total mystery," she went on, crossing her shapely legs and surveying her surroundings with a look that made it clear she didn't approve of giving in to grief the way I so obviously had. I sat up straighter in bed and ran a hand through my straggly hair, making a mental note to at least place my next used tissue in the waste basket instead of throwing it on the floor.

Copies of the test results from Sick Kids hospital said "Possible Post-Traumatic Stress Disorder, complicated by suspected neural damage or a pre-existing mental illness possibly in the autistic spectrum." Pretty much what we already suspected. We'd written to the doctor who had examined Inez before she came to Canada. He never replied.

"I'd like to plead self-defence," said Gretchen, "but apart from the fact that I don't believe that's what happened, there's no way of proving it. I know the prosecuting lawyer. He's a clever bastard who'll do his damndest to make Inez look bad."

"Self-defence?" I said, pulling my blanket higher up my chest and clutching it tight. It had not even crossed my mind. "From what?"

Gretchen raised her eyebrows and pressed her lips together. "From who, you mean ..."

"From Jerry? No way."

"Like I said, I don't believe that's what happened." She looked down, busily snapping the clasps of her briefcase.

"And you can't possibly, no matter what, say that in court. It would make Jerry a villain, and he wasn't one. Far from it —"

"Okay, okay. I already said I wouldn't."

"But it sounded like if you thought the jury would believe it, you'd say it, even if it wasn't true."

She sighed and gave a shrug, the kind so small that even a stray fly on your shoulder wouldn't notice. "I'm sorry. I'm a lawyer, Cat. I think like one. You want Inez to be my client. I was thinking of her, only of her."

I couldn't let it go. "Jerry would never raise a hand to her, never shout at her —"

Gretchen was looking at me through narrowed eyes, one eyebrow lifted. "You're absolutely sure about that?"

"Absolutely," I said, shaken.

"Now can we move on?"

"Of course." But I missed what Gretchen said next.

She had taken off her glasses and was rubbing her eyes with the heels of both hands. I heard, "Maybe the jury will sympathize because of her past."

When I leaned eagerly forward, she held up a warning hand. "There are no guarantees though, Cat. The worst thing is we can't prove the abuse. Jerry was the only witness. He told you and Molly and some of his friends and colleagues about how he found her, but none of you actually saw her in that shed. The Canadian government believed him, sure, but the law and the government require very different burdens of proof. And nobody can find her parents."

Not even Jacinta Barrera, I thought. Jacinta owned the restaurant in Panajachel, Guatemala, where I'd first met Jerry. Because she'd introduced him to me and kept in touch with both of us, I'd written to tell her what had happened. I also asked her to find Dr. Fernandez, who'd treated Inez before she left Guatemala. After Jerry's death, we'd written to him but never heard back. Later, I asked the same about Inez's parents. Jacinta was no more successful in either venture than we had been.

"You're right," I said to Gretchen. "But Jacinta Barrera went with Jerry to collect Inez from her parents. He told me all about it, how he couldn't have done it without her. She was a witness to Inez's abuse."

Gretchen frowned and stabbed at her notebook with her pen. "Why didn't you mention this before?"

"I'm sorry. It didn't occur to me. Do you think they will need her to testify at the trial?" I thought of Jacinta in her embroidered Guatemalan clothing, her braids tied back with the traditional ribbons, her warm brown eyes and friendly smile. "She'd make a great witness."

Gretchen shook her head. "I think they will ask for letters, and as long as she sends them through the Canadian Embassy there, they'll be enough." She smiled at me briefly before her face fell again. "That will really help us, Caitlin, but you know it will not prove Inez did not kill Jerry. I'm sorry, I really am."

"It's okay. It's not exactly your fault."

She hesitated then took a big breath. "Fact is, the only choice is to plead insanity."

I gaped at her, and she dropped some of her *hauteur* and put a hand on my arm. "Cat, we have to. It's obvious she's damaged. Most people are going to believe something terrible happened to her in Guatemala just by looking at her, and now that we have evidence of the state she was in when she was rescued, no jury is going to dispute that she's mentally damaged. But if we don't plead insanity, they'll convict her of murder."

By then, we knew the results of the tests. The blood on Inez's hands and clothes was Jerry's, and her fingerprints were all over the big marble table lamp she'd brought down on his head.

The legal definition of insanity, Gretchen explained, meant mostly "cannot tell right from wrong."

That seemed to fit. I had spent so much time with her and Jerry. What kind of murderous impulse was it that didn't show in expression or tender gesture or trusting eyes? Had she really meant to kill him? Had she mistaken him for someone else?

Perhaps Inez was not guilty by virtue of anything, perhaps she didn't deserve to be in jail at all.

But self-defence? From Jerry? Even Gretchen didn't believe it.

When the story hit the newsstands — GIRL KEPT IN SHED FOR YEARS HELD HOSTAGE IN ADULT JAIL — there was a public outcry. Until then, Inez had been successfully hidden from the media, thanks to Jerry, and when they finally discovered her, it was as if they felt cheated not to have caught wind of her before. They and the public went wild. Articles in the papers, letters to the editor, petitions, news commentary that seemed to set people's hearts on fire. The extent of the furor took me by surprise. It made me even more appreciative that Jerry had so determinedly kept Inez under wraps until his death.

In the midst of the uproar, Gretchen called me. "Cat, I've got some good news. Inez's trial is booked for next month."

"What? Toronto's got a huge backlog —"

"Yes, but because of the feedback and the situation, they've made room for Inez in Newmarket."

Newmarket was a town about forty kilometres from Toronto, with a big new courthouse.

"They've brought in social workers, psychiatrists, nurses, judges — everyone's had a look at her. Nobody knows what to do, that's another reason they're rushing things forward. That part's good, but there's something not so good …"

"What's that?"

"They've decided to try her as an adult."

At first I was too shocked to speak. Finally, I managed, "Oh my god. How can they do that?"

I heard Gretchen sigh. "The doctors say she's likely around nineteen. To the law, that's an adult."

She was so slim and tiny, trusting and aggressive all at once, I thought of her as a child. Only her eyes sometimes hinted at a maturity beyond her years. "She's a child still, even if they think she's a hundred and two."

"I know. It's awful. But even if she were mentally challenged, they'd charge her as an adult. It's the law."

Then to hell with the law, I wanted to say. Sometimes Inez seemed older than any of us. It didn't make her an adult in the usual sense.

"I'm glad they're relocating," I said. "Maybe there won't be so many ghouls and gawkers up in Newmarket."

Fat chance. The first day of the trial, people were packed in so tight, even taking coats off meant an all-out wrestling match with your neighbours on the bench.

Inez, where she sat beside Gretchen at the front, looked like a sick little ghost. Listening again to the details of Jerry's death nearly knocked me down. Behind me, I heard someone say in a loud whisper, "How much you wanna bet that doctor tried to rape her? Why else would she sock him over the head with a lamp? Damn these male bastards anyway."

I was so shocked, I turned around to see who had said it. A young woman with cropped hair the colour of decayed eggplant and a button saying "A Woman Needs a Man Like a Fish Needs a Bicycle" pinned to her T-shirt stared back at me, defiant.

It was the age of rampant feminism. I thought I was a feminist myself, but after listening to this woman, I wished there was another word for what I stood for.

I couldn't go back to the courthouse after that. I dreaded being called to testify, but when I asked Gretchen about it, she said, "You won't have to go on the stand. Because the evidence against Inez is so damning, they won't question you and, lucky for you, you won't need an alibi."

"Lucky for me? An alibi?" I said, alarmed.

"Think about it. You have a key to Jerry's house. You were home alone that night, so there is no one to vouch for you. You were his partner. Trust me. Without the results of the tests, you'd be a 'person of interest' for sure. When you went in to the station that day, I'll bet they asked you a few pointed questions about where you'd been the previous night."

"You're right," I said, dumbfounded. Then I remembered. "Except that I went to the all-night grocery store around eight. That's when they think it happened, isn't it?"

"Better than nothing," Gretchen said. "But only if a cashier remembered you."

I'd narrowly escaped being a suspect in my own lover's murder? The thought was unsettling. I was more determined than ever not to go back to the courtroom. Gretchen and my friend Molly filled me in every evening I asked.

On the last day, I made sure I was there, though, and any lingering doubts about the insanity plea deserted me completely, listening to the summation of the prosecuting attorney.

"There is no hint at all of self-defence. None. Her act was one of murderous rage. A completely unprovoked attack on a defenceless man who had turned his whole life upside down to help her."

The crown attorney's voice was fat with flamboyant indignation. Through my work, I'd heard flamboyant indignation used for everyone from bicycle thieves to hardened pimps. Crown attorneys excel at it. Heaven help Inez if the jury didn't know how often and how unfairly it was used.

Gretchen's summation was excellent. She talked about

Inez's past, the horrors she'd faced, and quoted again from Jacinta's letters.

"This is what we know," Gretchen said. "Not think. Not surmise. Know. From the words of someone who saw Inez held in captivity ..." She pulled a sheet of notepaper from an envelope on the table in front of her with a flourish and read, "'*When we found her, she was on a chain, like an animal. When we left, her mother would not even say goodbye. After her father dragged her out of that tiny, dark shed, he pushed her roughly, but she didn't strike back. She smiled at Dr. Simpson. She let him hold her hand. There was not an ounce of violence in her.*'"

Gretchen invited the jury to imagine what it would be like to be closed away from the world in a windowless shed, on a chain, for what could have been years. I saw their faces soften, and a number of them glanced at Inez with what looked like a combination of shame and pity.

But what could they or Gretchen do? The evidence was all against her. The jury had already heard the experts' views of Inez's mental health, their convincing arguments that she was very likely unbalanced and had no intention to kill. It was what we wanted the jurors to think, but it wasn't going to bring Jerry back or set Inez free.

When the jury filed in with the verdict, the heat combined with the tension made me feel faint. When the spokeswoman stepped forward, I clutched the back of the bench in front of me.

"Not guilty by virtue of insanity."

A voice cried, "No, oh no." I looked around to see who it was, until I realized the sound had come from the hollow space behind my ribs.

Molly's hand was on my arm, comforting me or trying to get my attention, I wasn't sure which. The only certainty was that Inez would be sent away. "Not guilty by virtue of insanity" could be a life sentence. Shut up in a hospital somewhere, helpless, waiting for a panel of doctors to declare her sane enough to be released — she could die there.

Chapter Six

Jerry: At the Village
Guatemala, Feb., 1983

A sickly-sweet smell hung in the air long before he came upon the clearing, and a ferocious buzz of insects hovered over the silence like a hat made of bees. When Jerry walked into the open, shock made him brace his hand against the gnarled trunk of a huge mahogany and immediately take a step backwards into the jungle.

He saw the bodies through a haze of flies — in scorched piles, half-buried under adobe bricks, slumped against the walls of dwellings blackened by fire.

A child's rag doll sat propped against a tree, its stitched-on woollen smile so incongruous that for a moment Jerry didn't register what lay beside it — the swollen body of a little girl, perhaps three or four years old, her open eyes staring at the sky.

Bitter tastes flooded his mouth, and no amount of swallowing could remove them. A sudden outbreak of sweat salted his upper lip.

This terrible place wasn't far from the Mayan couple's home. Jerry made himself concentrate on whether death had been the source of the stench there, too. But that had been fetid, not sharp and rotting-sweet like this one. It had not travelled on the hot wind; the couple's hut confined its rankness, and it had seemed a by-product of emotional turmoil, not violence.

Despite his struggle for dispassion, the scene in front of Jerry began to break into fragments inside his head. The dead lying face down, hands tied behind their backs, as though executed. Bloodied stones littering the path. Bodies without heads, or hands or arms. Limbs scattered like discarded logs. Jigsaw pieces he couldn't bear to connect.

The only corpses he had encountered previously were the sanitized specimens at med school. Acid burned his insides as he made his way towards a rusted-out truck at the edge of the village.

When he reached it, he leaned heavily against it, and rubbed his forehead, hard. *I cannot bear this*, he thought. As soon as he'd collected what remained of his composure, he turned resolutely to the jungle and began the trek back the way he had come, stopping only once to rest his head on his forearms against a tree trunk, to still the spinning cone inside his skull.

He arrived in Panajachel in half the time it had taken him to reach the village.

Dr. Fernandez opened his door and scanned Jerry's ravaged face. "You saw it."

"I did."

"I warned you, Dr. Simpson."

"Actually, you didn't." Jerry swallowed bile. "You told me I didn't need to see it. That's not the same thing at all."

He clenched his fists by his sides as the two men retreated to the office. Jerry settled himself across from the doctor at his desk and waited.

Dr. Fernandez steepled his fingers, a gesture Jerry had already learned to despise. "Well, did you need to see it?"

"If you mean am I sorry I saw it, no, I'm not. Who is responsible?"

"The government is ... savage ... in its own defence, Dr. Simpson. There is no other way to put it."

"The government then. Are they so powerful they don't need to cover their tracks?"

"I'm sure for every atrocity we see there are a dozen more. In this case, a small number of soldiers came, attacked, destroyed, and were at last chased off by a large band of guerrillas. For a week, the guerrillas guarded the spot and showed it to human rights organizations. Proof of the genocide."

"Were there any survivors?"

"If so, they are still afraid to return to bury their dead. From what you have told me, I believe this couple you describe has been living where they are longer than the unfortunate tribe we are speaking of, and were able to remain hidden during this massacre. But I also believe they have lost loved ones themselves at some point and are where they are because of it. In hiding. Maya are a tribal people, Dr. Simpson. They do not live alone by choice. This family may have lost everyone they knew to soldiers, or even to the guerrillas. The girl herself may have been driven mad by what she has seen —"

"Why haven't they moved away?"

Fernandez shrugged a shoulder. "Perhaps," he said, lifting his top lip contemptuously, "they know there is nothing left for which the army need return. Perhaps this has just made them realize that nowhere at all is safer than where they already are."

Jerry flushed. "They call Inez evil. They've locked her up since she was small."

"Ah." Dr. Fernandez sighed. "Such complications. Yes, yes. If they perceive her to be mentally ill ... Sometimes the Maya see madness as a loss of vital force — life force is the closest I can come to describing it. Sometimes they think that if air charged with negative forces enters a person's body, it may cause illness, of the mind and body both. Or fright may make someone weak, because it allows vital force to escape. And the Kaqchikel interpret strange or eccentric behaviour as proof that a witch has stolen the soul." He looked closely at Jerry. "Personally, I think it is as good an explanation of insanity as any. Neurotransmitters do not address the question of the soul. I have seen much mental illness cured by the intervention of a good spiritual healer. However, it can result in tragedy —"

"I know that." Jerry leaned forward in his chair. "About the Maya and the soul. The question of the soul is why I care about this girl!" He sat back, embarrassed. He hadn't intended to say this, hadn't even known he thought it. He rubbed his moist palms together and felt heat crawl up his neck.

"I see."

"What I want to convey ..." Jerry frowned as he gathered his thoughts, "... is that I am not scornful of how the Maya define mental illness. This girl does, in fact, give the impression of being haunted in some way, of having a kind of soul-trouble. What shocked me was how her parents deal with it, not how they define it —"

"Dr. Simpson." Fernandez held up a hand. "Forgive me, but you have no idea what these people really think or feel. As I say, they are all almost certainly in danger from the military. I suspect a combination of incomprehension, fear, anger, and protectiveness is behind their actions.

"Maya, generally speaking, are good to their children, and, in any case, witches are usually thought to steal the souls of affluent or powerful adults whom they envy, not children."

"I've said nothing against the Maya, doctor. I *have* nothing against the Maya. I am trying to understand one couple. Just one couple. They could be Martians for all I care."

"Well, then, surely you know that people are people everywhere, Dr. Simpson." Fernandez looked at Jerry from under lowered brows. "There are those who can tolerate mental illness better than others. Most Mayan girls are raised to marry and serve their families. A girl like this, who snarls and spits and howls, could well, as I've already mentioned, arouse a mixture of emotions in her parents. Plus a sense of helplessness. She may be unmanageable and would run away if she wasn't chained."

"Couldn't they keep her in their house?"

"Did they even have a door?" The doctor's lips thinned and his nostrils flared. "Besides, both parents would have to be gone for long periods of time, I'm sure, to seek work or scavenge for food. Perhaps they tried chaining her in the house, and she destroyed what little they owned. A wooden box may be the only shelter they can provide for her, given that they are penniless."

"How can you be sure they aren't abusing her deliberately?"

"I can't. But I do know this. It may have taken months for them to gather enough supplies to make that box, and the chain she is tethered with, and the padlock. Weeks of sorting through garbage, scavenging for nails, tools, sheets of wood. They haven't deserted her, and they could easily have done so."

To Jerry's exhausted senses, Fernandez's voice seemed to be swelling like a boil. *Of course, he's right,* Jerry thought. *Why am I so quick to judge, even with all my training? But if he doesn't stop talking to me like he's a saint and I'm an idiot, I'm going to get up and walk out. Or punch him. Or both.*

Fernandez barrelled on. "The father, at least, seems to have enough comprehension of mental illness to have latched on to you immediately when he found you were a 'mind doctor.' He went to considerable trouble to get you to see her. That doesn't strike me as a man motivated by cruelty, no matter how rough his treatment of her. He was clutching at straws, but clutch he did. I'm sure not even they know what they expected you to do. They are desperate, it seems to me. Absolutely desperate."

"But surely there are better ways ..." Despite his best efforts, Jerry knew his exasperation was obvious.

"This child may have been raped and beaten. Her siblings may have been — no, more likely were — murdered, her parents tortured, in front of her."

"I see. I understand. But how does that justify —" Jerry broke off under Fernandez's hostile gaze.

"Whatever experiences this girl has been through," the doctor said, "may have worsened a pre-existing condition. You will never know. But are you sure the mother was not calling their tormentors crazy — those who hurt her family and reduced her child to that state? Are you sure the parents didn't deliberately try to make you feel so sorry for the girl that you would take her away from them, to safety? Maybe they counted on your outrage. You will never know." Dr. Fernandez's mouth was set in concrete, the muscles of his jaw so tense his cheeks bulged.

Jerry's stomach tightened.

"There is something you can do to help," Fernandez said at last. "If you are willing."

"I won't know if I'm willing until I hear what it is."

"What I'm going to suggest you try ..." Fernandez lowered his voice, "... could be dangerous."

"Yes?"

"You could take the girl to Guatemala City. You could go with her to the Canadian Embassy. Apply there for refugee status for her."

"But that would mean —"

"It would mean you would sponsor her. Yes."

Jerry hoped his panic did not show in his eyes. Fernandez was suggesting he do what the couple had asked, just in different terms. "I see. But why would that be dangerous?"

"Because, Doctor, the secret police swarm the hallways to, shall we say, discourage applicants. As a foreigner, however, you would have an advantage."

"Can I go there without her?"

"It would do you no good. They'll need to see her, to determine if her claim is legitimate."

"But she doesn't seem to speak ..."

"You will speak for her. But they will need to see her."

"And then, if her application is denied, the police will know who she is."

"Exactly. It is a very real risk. I would suggest you disguise her, if you go, because there is usually a delay in issuing visas, even if they grant her one. And they may not, of course."

"There's something else I don't understand. Why wouldn't the whole family seek asylum?"

Dr. Fernandez shrugged. "I'm not sure, Dr. Simpson. I suspect they know nothing of the possibilities. As I say, they perhaps have no idea what you can do, for her or for them. They are desperate."

"If I could explain the options to them — do you think there's any hope they could all come to Canada?"

"That would be far more difficult than rescuing the girl alone. Your government has a reputation for compassion. However, even they are wary. Certain strict requirements must be met.

Your officials do not always trust refugees from Guatemala, not if there is any possibility at all they are revolutionary communists, and therefore a possible danger —"

"But a mute girl who is disturbed?"

"Exactly. That is why I am suggesting it. You are a doctor, and she is obviously in need of treatment. They may allow it on compassionate grounds. Despite the risks, it might be worth trying.

"You need," said Dr. Fernandez when Jerry said nothing, "to find out more about what the parents want. You need to take someone with you who speaks Kaqchikel. Someone they would trust."

"You?"

"They would not trust me. I am of pure Spanish extraction."

"Isn't your work known in the area? The fact that you play no favourites?"

"I doubt if my fame has spread that far, Dr. Simpson," said Fernandez dryly. "I suspect they would, as you might say, *run like hell* the minute they saw me coming. They haven't arrived at my office seeking help for her, now have they?"

"Even if I tried to prepare them in advance?"

"Yes. Also, my language skills are limited. I believe it would be much easier to get them to talk to a fellow Kaqchikel. Preferably a local woman. She should come with you to the embassy as well."

"So they won't suspect me of being a white slaver?"

"It is hardly a matter for jokes. It would be wise not to excite suspicion of any kind."

"Do you know someone who could do this?"

Dr. Fernandez frowned. After a moment, he shook his head. "No. There is no one I can recommend, or even know well enough to approach with a request like this. My Kaqchikel patients come and go like ghosts, Dr. Simpson. I have no way of reaching them, and by the time they reach me, they are usually so ill, we concentrate only on health matters."

After Jerry had left, Fernandez stepped to the window, stared out briefly at the boys playing soccer in the dusty square, and closed the blinds. He rubbed his eyes then massaged the small of his back. He was the only doctor for almost a thousand people. The conflict was not one in which he could easily take sides. Nor was it one where he could ignore its casualties.

He turned no one away.

Many of his colleagues had left the countryside already. Of those who stayed, several had been "disappeared" or beaten or killed by the military for aiding the enemy. He heard that others had been murdered by guerrillas for treating wounded soldiers.

He thought about his woman friend, in jail in Guatemala City, arrested for teaching the Maya to read. It would be a betrayal to leave his practice now, or refuse to treat the Indians. But how long before he himself was arrested, or, worse, "disappeared"?

Jerry regretted ever meeting the Mayan couple, ever feeling for the girl, and, most of all, ever encountering Fernandez and being told there was something he could do "if he was willing."

Chapter Seven

Jerry/Jacinta
Guatemala, March, 1983

It was March third, Jacinta Barrera's youngest child's first birthday. Itzel had come into the world with the sound of gunfire punctuating Jacinta's labour like an ambulance siren ripping a dream wide open.

Jacinta added a tablespoon of *cacao* powder to a mixing bowl and gazed out her restaurant window. Ah, there was Jerry already, giving money to one of the shy Mayan widows who sat with downcast eyes and outstretched hand. *As if it was her fault,* Jacinta thought, *that her husband was hacked to death in front of her.*

Jerry always gave money or food to the Guatemalan widows. *Next,* thought Jacinta, *he'll chat with Maria. Then he'll come in for a* café con leche, *and maybe some* huevos, *and on his way back to his hotel, he'll feed scraps to the dogs.*

He'd been doing these things from the day he arrived in Panajachel, two weeks earlier. Then, sitting at one of her outdoor tables, he'd thrown leftovers to a cluster of spindly strays that increased in number every day so that the tourists were afraid to go past. Now, he always came early and ate his breakfast inside. Afterwards, he'd gather crusts of bread, maybe a bit of egg into a bag, and feed the dogs across the street.

She watched Jerry help Maria set up her weaving in bedraggled Widows' Row. He wasn't saying much, and he wasn't smiling. *That's not like him,* Jacinta thought.

She dusted her hands then reached for the coffee in the cupboard behind her.

When she turned back, he was coming in the door. In answer to her cheery *"Buenos Dias,"* he waved then sat down at one of her tables. *That's not like him, either,* she thought. He usually came over for a chat.

He was often her first customer, but today he was so early the sun was still rising in a pale lavender blush. Looked like he hadn't slept too well. His eyes were puffy; she could see that from where she stood at her counter. When he rested his forehead on one hand then ran his fingers through his hair, she was sure something had got to him.

Guatemala often "got" to the compassionate ones — though most who came to her homey little restaurant near the shores of Lake Atitlan were interested only in the view, the beach, the food, and the endless sun. Even now.

He was staring out the window with a weary look, and Jacinta turned to see what had brought this on.

Soldiers. Of course. Standing guard outside the bank across the street, and the boarded-up "church" from which many, Jacinta among them, swore they heard muffled screams rise at night.

She blended the *cacao* into the flour and sugar with her hands. Business had slowed during what she'd heard called "the civil war." But what kind of a war was it when soldiers killed women and children and burned down villages without so much as a scuffle taking place first? Just thinking about it made her insides hurt.

It seemed just random acts of violence to her, a dark and frightening undercurrent that had been part of her life for as long as she could remember but would never seem ordinary. But, yes, lately, every day in the papers — reports of new "disappearances," shootings, attacks. The Mayas' faces were haunted and desperately wary.

She remembered the time, not so long ago, when her heart had belonged wholly to the rebels. There were good people, people she knew, who sacrificed everything to fight a system skewed in favour of those of European blood. Now, though, she had seen and heard too much. Now the Maya were bullied into hiding the guerrillas, or feeding them, or both, and they paid a dreadful price. Even when they shared out of compassion, the repercussions were horrific. She no longer believed that the fighting was worth it, or that anything could be solved by violence. She did not know what could bring change, but surely not this terrible bloodshed. Sometimes now the rebels scared her. Their rigidity, their willingness to kill, to judge harshly those who did not agree with their "solution." She mistrusted their leftist ideology, seeing it as foreign to her country, not just imported from outside, but foreign to the nature of its people, all of them. And for what reasons was it brought in? The gaping injustices of the current regime were a hole waiting to be filled, for sure, but not with *la basura*, garbage. She did not trust governments of any kind.

Her country was in such turmoil, she was surprised sometimes that business wasn't slower. Tourists must be blind, deaf, and dumb. Just as well, or her family would starve.

She watched as Jerry rubbed his chin and frowned. Yes, something other than her *chiles rellenos* were on his mind, she was sure. She wiped her hands on her canvas apron and called out, "Jerry — you would like a cup of coffee?"

"*Muchas gracias*, Jacinta. A *café con leche, por favor.*"

She poured it for him, stirring until it took on the colour of her favourite butter *caramelos*.

Jerry was different from the other tourists. He was a serious person, a doctor, a psychoanalyst, whatever that was, from Toronto who seemed to understand how hard she and her family worked to keep food on the table. They'd become friendly on his first visit, many years ago, when she'd introduced him to her husband and their kids. There'd only been two of them back then. Now there were four.

After he'd gone home, they'd kept in touch with postcards for a year or two. Just quick notes to re-establish a connection that had dropped off after a while. When he'd reappeared a few weeks before, it had been eight years since they'd had any contact. It came as a surprise how quickly they'd picked up where they'd left off.

Most of her other customers were young North American tourists who chattered and laughed amongst themselves as if life were an endless party. She found some of them so dumb, dressing in Mayan tribal wear, with no clue of what was happening to these people they saw as "colourful" and "real." No clue even of how the Maya resented being driven out of their villages by the growth of the tourist industry around the shores of Lake Atitlan.

Even Ladino entrepreneurs were not well liked, but, until recently, Jacinta herself had enjoyed good relations with the Maya, mostly because her mother was Mayan, and her father, of British origin, had taught the Indians and helped build a school.

Learning Jerry was from Canada had first broken the ice between them. Jacinta's younger sister had emigrated and become a teacher there. She visited Guatemala every few years with her Canadian husband and had encouraged Jacinta and Diego to come to Canada too. *Algun dia*, like never, Jacinta thought. The way things were going, they'd be lucky to get enough money together to spend a weekend in Guatemala City, let alone travel to a whole new country!

When she'd mentioned the expense, her sister had said, "You'd earn more money there," but neither Jacinta nor Diego were much tempted. Jacinta believed in roots, and hers felt Mayan, despite the troubles between the guerrillas and the government, despite the distance the Indians put between themselves and half-bloods like her.

On this trip, Jerry had reminded her how she'd introduced him to a woman, Caitlin Shaughnessy, right here in her restaurant. He told her they were still a couple. Jacinta wondered why Caitlin wasn't with him now, though she didn't ask. She knew that the lives of *gringos* could be complicated and strange, but it seemed to her that a couple on good terms would travel together.

When she came back with the coffee, Jerry still looked unhappy, his mouth as soft as a tortilla, flopping down at the edges.

Maybe she'd try to find out what had got him so sad. "*Aqui esta*," she called, putting the mug near his elbow. "You a bit sad, Jerry?"

Some *Norte Americano* had once told Jacinta that she didn't "beat around the bush." It had made her smile when he'd explained what that meant.

"No," she'd agreed. "I beat the bush instead."

Jerry's eyes projected warmth, and the corners of his floppy-taco mouth drifted upwards. "Mostly worried," he responded.

"Okay if I sit down?"

She thought his "yes" sounded surprised, but she settled into the chair opposite him, smoothing her woven skirt beneath her.

"Guatemala can be hard," she said.

"Hard?"

Hearing the tightness in his voice, she put her floury hands palms-up in her lap and leaned back. Maybe she'd got him wrong, maybe he was sad because her refried beans hadn't agreed with him, something like that, but she doubted it. Smiling at her private joke, she said, "I mean, the things that happen here can be hard for an outsider to take."

"An insider, too, I imagine," he said quietly, and she smiled again, liking his understanding.

"Uh-huh. But sometimes, when you first see a bad thing, it is worse."

"True. And I have seen a very bad thing."

He spoke so softly, she had to lean forward to catch his words. "What have you seen?" she said, her head filled with images — bodies, chaos, guns.

He stared at the wall behind her head. "A child. A Mayan girl, about fifteen, maybe. She's been locked up in a shed for years. It doesn't have any windows. It looks like a big box."

Jacinta widened her eyes. "*Ay, Dios Mio!* Where? Why?"

"I don't know why, that's the trouble." Jerry brought one hand down onto the tabletop with a slap that made Jacinta jump.

He said, "It looks like child abuse," and whirled his spoon in his coffee, though she'd already stirred it for him twice. "I mean, a parent being cruel to a child. They keep her on a chain." The sad look on his face touched her. "Maybe you can figure it out, Jacinta."

She shrugged. "I don't understand children put in boxes any more than you do," she said.

"Of course. I'm sorry. Let me explain. I met her parents on a bus. They begged me to go to their home, to help their daughter, they said — or that's what it seemed they wanted. We couldn't understand one another very well because of the language. But I went with them. The woman looked ill, and both of them were terribly upset. When I got there, though, I was so shocked by what I saw that I ran right to your local doctor. He said perhaps her parents locked her up to protect her from the military?"

Jacinta pushed up her sleeves. "*Si*," she said, lowering her voice. "It could be. Things have been very bad." She glanced over one shoulder. "It could even be the guerrillas they fear. The Maya are forced sometimes to take sides."

"I'm guessing about the time, Jacinta. Her parents don't speak much English, and maybe not even much Spanish. But the man, her father, held out his hand — about this high — when I asked how long she'd been there. So I thought from maybe twelve years old."

"*Ay-yi-yi.* The girl … what's she like?"

"She makes sounds like an animal. She can't speak normally, and she looks like a hunted creature."

Jacinta, watching Jerry's face, wondered if he was trying to decide what more, if anything, to say.

"I saw a man like that once." Her eyes slid from his. "More like a boy, I guess. He was maybe eighteen, nineteen years old. Sometimes he'd growl." She lifted her hands and curled her fingers down like talons. "Like a tiger. He scared people. He'd go up to them and touch their clothes and not look at their faces. But he stared so hard at that old clock on the wall over there, I thought he was trying to make the hands move with his eyes! He got off the bus here one day. Nobody knew where he came from. Some people tried to help him. They took him to the doctor, and the *H'men*."

It was Jacinta herself who had taken him to the *H'men*, the Mayan healer, under cover of night, and scared, though the violence was less extreme then, and a mixed-blood like her could mingle with the Indians more easily.

"But he just went away one day. Someone said the doctors took him. It was sad. Maybe these parents were hiding the girl from the doctors. Maybe they didn't want anyone to take her away."

"But they've asked *me* to take her away."

"*Ai*, Jerry. Now I know why you look sad."

"Uh-huh."

She touched his forearm. "You should not be ashamed not to want her. No one else does."

A white gleam, an open smile, appeared between his upturned lips. "Jacinta, that was brilliantly put."

She wasn't sure about brilliant, but she accepted the compliment. Funny, though, that this *gringo* should be surprised to be understood.

"Not many saints in this world," she said, wishing she'd poured a coffee for herself. The smell was enticing. "This would be a big burden for anyone."

"Yes. And I'm not really settled, Jacinta." When she looked at him quizzically, he went on. "I mean, I'm not a family man. My partner and I don't live together. A child — ah, it's difficult."

"She wouldn't be *your* child." Crazy *gringo*. "Maybe you could put this girl in a hospital in Canada."

"I wish it was that easy."

A silence long enough for Jacinta to take note of the smell of coffee once again and wonder about starting another pot made her suspect Jerry wanted to talk more, but maybe not to her.

"You should tell your girlfriend about her," she suggested. Seemed pretty obvious.

"Yes, I should." But his frown deepened.

"Something got to you about this girl, huh?" There she went, beating the bush again.

"Uh-huh. You know what? I dreamt of her the other night. According to you Mayas, that means we're bound together, doesn't it?" He laughed — more of a bark, really — and looked away.

It sounded to Jacinta as if the memory had just that moment come to him, and by his sheepish expression, she guessed he was already wishing he'd kept it to himself.

It was true, she understood about dreams. She'd been dreaming now for years about a man she'd encountered when she was seven years old. He'd taken her for a ride on his donkey, down to a small, clear lake. There he'd encouraged her to go naked into the water. He'd watched her swim, then kissed her smooth, brown shoulders as she dressed, before lifting her back onto his donkey and taking her home. She'd never seen him again, but his beautiful brown eyes, so full of love for her, had haunted her for years.

"We Maya believe many different things, Jerry," she said. "One day we pray to Christ's mother, who we call the Moon Goddess, the next we are venerating Chauk, the deity of earth and water. We sing Christian hymns when we worship our sacred caves. As for dreams — it is in dreams that Mayan spirits communicate with the shamans. But for me, once I have a dream about someone, I am lost."

Again, Jerry's eyes were warm, appreciative. "Even if they have no claim on you?"

"*Si*. Even if I never see the person again. They are part of me if I dream about them."

He looked away.

"What was the dream about?"

"I don't remember the details."

Okay, so he didn't want to tell her. "You could say the main bits."

Jerry grinned. "Yes, I suppose I could."

She waited.

"She was suddenly there, dressed in a white shift. It was only a silly dream. Are you sure you want to hear it?"

"*Si*."

"Okay, then. In the dream, her face ..." When she leaned closer to hear better, he leaned towards her in turn. "In real life, it catches your attention. In the dream ... well, you know how dreams are? I knew it was Inez — that's her name, Inez — but she didn't look like herself, particularly. Except for the eyes. She has big, dark eyes. Someone was after us, I don't know who." His voice sounded tired now. "She knew where to go, but we couldn't get there. I'm not clear why. We ran a long way, I think. Anyway, next thing I remember is arriving in a house full of dead bodies." She watched his face twist. "I could tell the people had starved to death, even though the corpses were not particularly emaciated. Dream logic, again. Out in the woods, I found a wooden door that looked like someone had taken bites out of it. I know, that's weird. It was even weirder because there was food in the forest all around them, berries and shoots and leaves." He studied his coffee cup. "And that's about it, really."

"How did it make you feel?" She wondered why he smiled so broadly, then bit it back.

"Well ... mostly frustrated. Hogtied. Do you know what that means?"

"Uh-huh." She'd heard a Texan say it a few years back.

"But ..." He hesitated. "In the midst of all that horror, I looked at Inez, and I felt ... well ... I ... I don't know how else to say it — full of light." He coughed into his hand.

Jacinta had felt full of light splashing in the water with the loving eyes of the man locked on her every move, and she still felt full of light when she dreamt of him, though she knew now he was probably a pervert, and she was maybe lucky to be alive. "Some things are more about the way things should be than what they really are."

"Jacinta, you are amazing."

Again, she was baffled. Why did he say that, when she was expressing ordinary things?

"Something is pulling you towards this girl," she said.

"Yes. The last thing I need is a complication like this. But her situation, whatever the reason for it, is godawful. Is there anything I can do for her here in Guatemala, Jacinta?"

"Beats me. I know *nada* about doctors and hospitals and people like her. But she would need someone to care about her and try to understand her. Not many people like that anywhere. And she's Maya. Sometimes doctors are afraid to treat Maya."

She could tell she wasn't making him feel any better, but she couldn't take her words back. "Doesn't mean you have to rescue her," she added. "Like I said before, nobody else has. I wouldn't."

"You wouldn't?"

"No, Jerry. What could I do for her? I have my husband and kids to look after, plus this place. If she started to act funny, I'd have to lock her up, too." Maybe she shouldn't have said that. He could hire nurses, staff. Doctors, especially North American doctors, had *mucho dinero*, she knew that. "Look, Jerry. She's not your problem. But if you dream of her, you'll maybe feel worse leaving her than taking her." She shuffled her sandals against the floor. She sure wasn't making his day, she could tell from his face.

But he said "Thank you" and finished his coffee.

"Thank you? I guess I haven't made you too happy, Jerry."

"In a way you have. I don't get to speak to such a clear thinker every day." He got up and moved towards the till. "I have to be going now," he said, dropping coins on the counter. "I'll let you know what I decide."

Jacinta watched him stride purposefully away and figured she most likely already knew.

Chapter Eight

Caitlin's Story

My first day back at the *Star* after Jerry's death, I was in a complete fog. The features editor, Peter, didn't seem to notice as we chatted at the end of the day. He launched into some riff about his niece's recent graduation from a "very prestigious" law school, dropping in a comment about his son who was doing "wonderfully well" in digital media, a "terribly competitive field."

Well, of course. Nothing bad ever happened to this man or his family. He'd copped a plum job at the *Star* right after getting his journalism degree, and he was the darling of the media crowd.

My thoughts turned to Jerry, killed in his own home by someone he'd cared about and had put himself on the line for, a doubly violent death. Inez's experiences in Guatemala came back to me, too, and how she would soon be locked away forever.

"You're awfully quiet," Peter said when it dawned on him that his puff piece wasn't eliciting the expected response. He looked me over more closely. "You all right?"

"I'm thinking about how Jerry died, and about what happened to Inez."

"Um. Yeah." He coughed and shuffled papers like a hamster in a cage.

Unable to deal with either his discomfort or my memories, I gathered my things together and went home.

It got to the point where all of life was filtered through this horrible mess, as if I were looking through a sieve clogged with slime. Gazing into a mirror one morning, I couldn't find my face amongst all the dark shadows. The moment passed, and once again I was staring hollowly back at myself. Being a shadow in shadows, even for a split second, scared me. I began to carry a notepad, jotting down thoughts and memories, externalizing what happened in an attempt to gain perspective.

I had known Molly since I was a child. She was older and lived next door to my parents. After my brother Tommy died when he was four and I was nine, I would go there after school instead of home, where I sometimes felt ashamed to show my face. She would say comforting things like "Hello, little chick, I've missed you," and "Don't you worry, it wasn't your fault at all."

As a teen, I was the envy of the artsy crowd because a successful artist was my friend. We'd descend on her wearing our dreams on the sleeves of our tie-dye T-shirts, and she would say "Come in" to whoever appeared. "Come in. I need some help in the studio."

In the wake of Jerry's death, I asked her over regularly, several evenings a week, sometimes to stay the night. Disinhibited by grief, I told her things I would be too embarrassed to say in a more normal state of mind — how in Jerry I had found the one person with whom desire was a perfect conduit for love, that I hadn't known I loved him until I slept with him, how I adored him for his courage and kindness, and even for that mystery inside him which occasionally shut me out, though it frightened me now in ways it hadn't done before.

On one of those sleepovers, I let her read some of my notes.

"They were meant to help," I said over a bottle of wine.

She read standing up — all 125 pounds and five foot nine of her, wearing her old lady skin like a clever disguise — taking sips from her glass. Then she waved the pages in the air. "Write a real book. People will be fascinated. The story was all over the newspapers."

Molly's take-charge attitude had helped me in the past, but this felt like too much. "I don't want to exploit Jerry *or* Inez," I said. "I don't want to make a creative project out of a tragedy."

"That's not what I had in mind," she said dryly. "You'd be writing about things from your own point of view, that's all. How Jerry's death affected you, how you struggled to come to terms with what happened, how you felt about Inez, all the things that are bothering you right now. It would be your story, not theirs. You're entitled to that. Besides, you need to organize your thoughts. These notes are incoherent, all emotion — you need some distance." She put her hands on her slender hips and looked me up and down. If she hadn't been part of my life for years, I might have been intimidated.

Molly has black eyebrows over piercing blue eyes — and a killer look of disdain. She had played the role of hectoring angel ever since I was a miserable kid. Her nagging made me feel secure. I think she knew it.

"I'm worried about you, Cat. You've been flopping about like a flounder," she waved long fingers in the air, "a beached flounder." She sat down on my couch, running her hand distractedly over the brocade upholstery.

Like a lot of journalists, the thought of writing anything longer than four pages and not set in columns spooked me. I was afraid I couldn't do it, and I didn't want to discover I was right.

"Molly, I've been down, that's all, down. Who wouldn't be?"

"Nobody at all wouldn't be. That's the point. I know you, Caitlin, don't forget. The only way you're going to move on into the future is to bury yourself in the past.

"Cat," she added more gently, "you need to go into this business whole hog. Really look at it and wrestle with all the questions that are racing around in your head, in a systematic way. I do know you. Writing a book would be good for you." She ran feathery fingers down my arm.

I've always loved Molly's gestures. They are a counterpoint to her brusque manner. People reassess her after they've watched her for a while. Once, she plucked a blossom from an apple tree and tucked it behind my ear after I'd told her I didn't understand my life, or anyone else's.

Now, with my elbow still cupped in her palm, I said, "I'll think about it, Molly, I promise."

"Cat, if you don't do it for you, do it for me. Write it *to* me, if you think it will help."

"Why would it?"

"Because I take you seriously, and I'm not sure you take yourself seriously. If you write it to me, you'd have to."

"I don't quite get you, Molly."

"Your main line of defence has always been making light of things. That isn't going to help you now, but I'm willing to bet you'll try. I'll make sure to pull you up short.

"Arrange some time off work. You'll need to travel around, talking to people, doing research. I'll help, whenever I can."

I didn't take her advice. My excuse was that not giving one hundred percent to my journalism might lose me assignments, and maybe the freelance contacts I'd taken years to establish. I thought she was being reckless with my future until the day, a full four months after the trial, I nearly choked in an effort not to cry and ran from the room in the middle of an editorial meeting. Someone had quoted from a police report about a murder, and it made me think of the report I'd read after Jerry died. I wasn't meant to see it, but I'd picked it up from a fellow journalist's desk, knowing what it was.

Like it or not, I wasn't coping.

I would write that book, tell my employers about it, and keep my hand in by requesting short assignments for the duration. On reflection, letting them know about the book would probably up my profile considerably and help me find work after it was done.

Molly was right. It would be my story, my "take" on what had happened. How it changed me, what I did about it.

I had no idea when I started that I would have to include shameful things I did in northern Labrador, where Inez had been sent to what was called a "state of the art" psychiatric facility. I also had no idea how much I really needed to change.

There was something more immediate motivating me. Despite the support of friends and family — my father, for instance, had offered to let me stay with him and my stepmom in Nova Scotia for as long as I wanted — I'd been drinking too much and too often, missing deadlines, or hurling myself into my work so completely I'd stay up half the night, then fall asleep at meetings the next day. Perhaps I was in danger of losing assignments if I *didn't* take time away.

The next morning, I phoned in the news to the *Star*, then went to my closet and pulled out one of two boxes of Jerry's belongings that his dad had given me after he'd died. I'd never opened either of them.

Now seemed a good time to start.

Chapter Nine

Caitlin's Story

O nce I'd pulled the box onto my lap, I took a deep breath and did nothing. Shoving memories away had been my main line of defence so far. When things had been too raw for me to do it, I'd been a total mess.

Curiosity overrode my fear. What had Jerry's mean old man chosen to pass on to me? I braced myself and yanked at the tape on the box's lid.

On top were photographs and mementos — menus, tickets, programs, old guidebooks.

One bundle was wrapped in paper, secured with a rubber band.

I pulled off the elastic and discovered photographs. They were mostly of Latin America — two Ladino women carrying water jugs on their heads, one of me standing on a street corner in Panajachel, Guatemala, with my hand shading my eyes; a gorgeous shot of Lake Atitlan. And a picture of Inez, here in Canada, an arty, black-and-white close-up of her pretty face. Her eyes looked haunted, but she was smiling shyly at the camera.

I stared at that picture for a long time then placed it back with the others and pulled out the big photo of Lake Atitlan again. On the back, written in Jerry's small, cramped hand, I read:

More than 85,000 years ago, a volcano erupted and wiped out all forms of life from Mexico to Costa Rica, leaving a huge crater.

New lava enclosed the area, and over many years, life began its slow return. Intermittent bursts of green, tentacles of moss, shiny yellow-brown slivers emerged through cracks in the hardened crust. Finally, the trees stood tall, crowned with great flurries of blossoms and leaves. Hoofed and winged creatures seemed to spring forth, rather than journey there, long before the arrival of tribes who warred over access to this lush place. The crater had slowly filled with water, inch by inch, decade by decade, until it reached a depth equal to the height of the surrounding mountains.

That is Lake Atitlan, "the place of great water" in the Nahuatl Mayan language, surrounded by three active volcanoes, San Pedro, Tolima, Atitlan.

Ah, that amazing lake. Atitlan, a black stillness in the heart of primordial beauty, threatened to pull you in and hold on to you forever. It was ballast without a storm.

I read the note over again. I found it beautiful. Jerry usually wrote articles for stuffy psychoanalytic journals, in a suitably boring style, but I knew Guatemala brought out the dreamer in him. I just hadn't realized how much. I still remember the faraway look on his face when we were visiting the Mayan ruins in Tikal. He gazed off into the distance for such a long time that I asked what he was thinking about.

"Oh," he said, with boyish enthusiasm, "I'm just imagining what it would be like to be a human sacrifice."

I shuddered. "Doesn't that make you feel awful?"

"Nah." He grinned. "It's like reading *Arnie Adam's Adventure Magazine* when I was a kid. Stupid, exciting stories boys get off on," he added when I looked at him, bemused.

He was twelve years younger then. I hadn't known him all that long. We'd met in Panajachel on the shore of Lake Atitlan only a few days before. I hadn't liked him at first. But that's another story.

I put the notes and pictures down and reached into the box again. My hands touched something soft, and I pulled it out. It was a worn alpaca cardigan, a favourite of Jerry's. I pressed it to my cheek. Rummaging further, I unearthed a hairbrush, an electric razor, Jerry's navy silk housecoat.

Jerry's dad was what is known politely as "a difficult man." He didn't like me much and made his disapproval of our arrangement plain. He'd never invited me to choose anything to remember Jerry by, yet these homey items were exactly right. They brought Jerry back to me as only I'd known him — shaving in the bathroom while I brushed my teeth beside him at the double sink, slithering into the housecoat I'd bought him on mornings when it was his turn to make the coffee. The clothes even brought a smile, because I'd hated how he dressed when we first met and loved how his style had softened over the years.

He'd been wearing that comfy Guatemalan knit the day last year I'd found him at his desk with his head on his arms. I'd tapped his shoulder and asked what was wrong. When he'd sat up and said "Nothing," I wasn't sure I believed him.

Then Inez entered the room, and his face lit up as if someone had clapped their hands in front of a sound-activated lamp.

I wish every memory I had of him weren't tainted now or didn't bring up questions that weren't there before.

He used to light up like that for me.

Back then I'd found his response to Inez touching. Now I thought I should've asked more about what was troubling him.

I put everything back in the box, but on impulse I pulled out the picture of Inez again and turned it over.

Ich Liebe Dich. Written in ornate script. "I love you" in German.

Jerry did calligraphy and studied German, the first language of psychoanalysis. He often practised his fancy lettering and language skills together. It shocked me for a moment, even though it wasn't news to me that Jerry loved Inez. So did I, and Margaret, and Molly, maybe even Michael Doherty at the beginning of things. It just seemed strange to see it written out like that.

I could almost dismiss the note as idle scribbling, except you didn't need to be Freud to see the significance of where he'd scribbled it.

I looked again at Inez's lovely face. She had the most arresting eyes I had ever seen. Sorrow was written plainly in the ink of each dark pupil, but there was something else too. It was hard to define, but it looked a lot like wisdom, hand in hand with knowledge no young person should have.

Jerry, I'd discovered, was fascinated by people who had suffered, even by suffering itself.

I stuffed everything back inside the cardboard box and put the box into the closet from where I'd taken it, my head tumbling with memories and questions I both did and did not want to ask.

As soon as I felt ready to begin, I sat down at my typewriter. Writing was like pushing the hurt outside myself, so that I could at least begin to separate from it and function normally again. My journaling had been constant since the first notes I'd shown Molly.

Thinking of what I wrote as part of a book gave me further distance still. I had to admit Molly was right about that, too. I wasn't sure I could do it, and I was almost sure I would never publish it even if I could, but picturing the story of what happened contained between covers, something with a beginning, middle and, most importantly, an end, something you could close and put away on a shelf — that drew me.

I stared hard at the blank sheet in my typewriter, not sure where to begin. After a number of false starts, I thought of how Jerry and I had met way back in 1971, and then the words came quickly.

I'd never been afraid of a vegetable before, but in Guatemala, lettuce made me a nervous wreck, I typed.

It was notorious for bringing on attacks of what we tourists called "Montezuma's Revenge."

In a hotel where the shared toilet was down a steep set of outdoor stairs and across an alley, this was a more than usually horrible prospect. The vivid memory of a huge furry spider crawling across the floor as I sat enthroned one bleary-eyed morning did not help. And so I picked the shredded lettuce piece by piece out of my tacos and blew on my fingers to cool them where they'd connected with the refried beans. No matter how many times I asked, my meals always arrived like an Irishman on St. Paddy's day: "wearing of the green."

My friend Sasha and I were having dinner in our favourite restaurant in Panajachel, a homey little eatery with a spectacular view of Lake Atitlan's volcanoes. It was a gathering place for tourists, somewhere to share information, enthusiasms, and commonalities that helped re-establish who we were in the face of the alien grandeur that dwarfed us.

Sasha grimaced. "Oh, eat the stuff, for heaven's sake, Cat. I'm sick of looking at you poking around in the refried beans. They remind me of poop."

"Don't be gross, Sash."

"*Me?* You're the one being gross."

A breeze blew through the empty window frame, whirling lettuce shreds off the table in a small green blizzard.

Sasha laughed as I slapped my hand over what was left of the pile.

We had been in Latin America for about two months, on an extended vacation we'd scrimped and saved for — one last fling before going to graduate school (me) and getting married (her). The civil war had been underway for years by then. We knew there was fighting going on, but beyond that we knew very little. We were keen to see the world and, like many young people in the seventies, did not quite believe it could destroy us.

Our sympathies were with the Maya, landless and almost without rights; we liked the ones we had met on the buses and in the markets. Their men didn't chase us or try to seduce us the way the Latin men did, young lotharios who thought all North American females travelling alone were ripe for the picking. They pestered us relentlessly, especially in the cities.

"Are you gonna sing before we go home?" said Sasha, wiping salsa off her fingers. "You've only got two days to decide."

Tourists often gave impromptu musical performances in this restaurant, usually accompanying themselves on acoustic guitars while singing "Guantanamera" off-key.

"Do you think I should?" I said.

"Well, why not? You've got to be better than what we've heard so far. You should be, anyway."

"Why? Because I sang in that dumb bondage band?"

"Uh-huh."

"I only did it for the extra cash."

"So what? You were good."

"You're expecting me to pull out the leather costume and the whip? Here?" I picked up my napkin and dabbed a spot of sour cream at the corner of my mouth with what I hoped was *hauteur*. I liked talking to my best friend in a regal tone. It bolstered my confidence, which at that age still went up and down like a skateboarder on steroids.

She grinned. "Yeah, and don't forget the pink wig and stilettos, too."

I sniffed. "I don't happen to have packed them."

Sasha was enjoying herself. "I could tie you to a chair, like your bandmates did. I especially liked it when you sang tied to a chair. You really were pretty good, you know. At least until you started cracking more jokes than whips."

"*You* try to take yourself seriously in a situation like that, Sasha. I defy anyone with even a fringe claim to normalcy to —"

"Don't you miss that stuff, Cat?"

"The bondage band?" I shook my head. "I dropped it as soon as my student loan came through. The band sucked. They sounded like they were throwing pots and pans down the stairs while screaming. I was a fake S & M queen, Sash. I had to get drunk to carry it off at all. It's the folk singing I loved."

"Why'd you quit that then? You never told me."

"It was getting *passé*."

"Yeah, I suppose. Not for your parents, though."

"Oh, the Leprechauns." I shrugged. "The Lawrence Welk of folk groups. Yeah, they have a following. Very big with older people. Flower children just roll their eyes."

"All those beautiful old Irish songs," sighed Sasha. "They were good."

"They still are."

"Sorry, I haven't listened to them in a while."

"See what I mean? Nobody under forty listens to them. The Irish schtick gets to me — it's so corny. Dad never minded it, but I don't want to spend my life hanging off my parents' little green coat tails. But, yeah, I miss singing. Mostly I miss performing. Maybe I'll take up comedy next." I had a fascination with stand-up.

Sasha raised her eyebrows. "You were pretty funny in that band."

"And a bit of a ham? Come on, I'll bet you were thinking that."

"No, I wasn't. I was thinking you enjoy playing to a crowd, entertaining people. Also, you turn everything into a joke."

It was a trait I never quite grew out of, as Molly had recently reminded me, afraid I'd duck the reality of Jerry's murder by making light of my sorrows.

I think Jerry might have agreed with her. "You use humour as a defence mechanism," he'd said to me more than once. "To avoid dealing with your problems."

"Can't you ever take anything at face value?" I remember retorting. I loved Jerry with all my heart, but it was easy to get tired of shrink-speak, even from him. I hated labels. Then I laughed and hugged him. "Would it be such a bad thing if I did?"

"Only if you used it to excess."

I didn't think I did that, and I told him so. But when I finally chose to get serious about stand-up, my timing was so "off," I'm embarrassed *now* that it seemed so right *then*. The decision when it came was almost a revelation, and it took a true friend to set me straight.

But twelve years ago, in that restaurant in Panajachel, the issue wasn't pressing or important.

"I don't turn everything into a joke," I said to Sasha. "Just stuff that deserves it."

She opened her mouth to answer me, but closed it again, gazing inquisitively over my shoulder.

At Jerry.

He was tall, with a ratty beard and an aquiline nose. His

clothes, a bright Guatemalan shirt and a goofy straw sombrero, hung on his slender frame like rags on a scarecrow.

Beside him stood Jacinta, the Guatemalan woman who owned the restaurant with her husband, Diego. Jacinta was short, and next to this lanky interloper, she looked like a little girl.

"Everything okay?" Jacinta leaned over a moment later to put our *cafés con leche* on the table.

Then seeing us stare at the man beside her, she said, "This is Jerry. I thought maybe you wouldn't mind letting him sit down with you."

I'm sure the extent of our enthusiasm showed on our faces.

"Oh, come on now, *chiquitas*. He won't eat you, will you, Jerry? He likes my *huevos rancheros* much better." She beamed at him affectionately.

Jerry smiled in what I guessed he thought was a roguish sort of way and sat down.

The nerve, I thought.

"This is Caitlin —" Jacinta, who had a tendency to treat tourists as if they were children, placed a hand on my head. "And Sasha. From Canada. Jerry's from Canada too." She smiled broadly, swept the remains of my lettuce into a napkin, and left.

I stared after her, then at Jerry.

"Where in Canada?" he said to me.

I thought of ignoring him but didn't have the gall. "Richmond Hill, Ontario."

"Well, what a coincidence. I'm from Toronto, and you're from the boondocks near Toronto. Small world."

The boondocks? Another T.O. jerk. I barely suppressed a sneer and leaned away as he folded his arms on the table.

"Well," I said, "it's not that much of a coincidence. A lot of Canadians come here. And Toronto is a big place. I *used* to live there," I added pointedly. "I got fed up with it."

"Too much for you?" he said.

That immediately dropped him from "jerk" to "idiot" in my estimation. "Yeah. I don't like getting crushed in subway cars and dealing with petty bureaucrats at work. I'm funny that way."

He laughed. "Where was work?"

Nosy, I thought. "An office," I answered. "Ontario Housing on Bloor Street." I'd been clerking the previous summer, between stints at university. "And what do you do?"

"I'm in my last year of medical school. I'm studying to be a psychiatrist."

Great. Doctors of any kind were not my generation's favourite people. And unless you were R.D. Laing, being a psychiatrist was the worst.

Personally I thought Laing was an exploitative dope, and I'd learned to keep quiet about him when he was the topic of admiring conversations among my friends. That meant I was even less impressed by Jerry than they would have been. I said nothing, refusing to stroke his ego. In those days, I pigeonholed all doctors as egomaniacs.

"So where are you headed now?"

"We're not sure."

"We thought maybe we'd stay here awhile, then go back to Mexico City," Sasha said. "We wanted to go further south, but we're running out of money."

"How are you travelling?"

"By bus," I answered.

He smiled, as though the thought of buses was faintly amusing. I wondered how he'd react if he knew we travelled second class, where the Mayan women stroked our hair and marvelled at its softness, and the men smiled hesitantly at us before turning to stare resolutely out the grime-covered windows. It wasn't until years later that I realized why they liked us so much. It wasn't our hair. It was because when the soldiers stopped the buses, they were less likely to take the Maya away and kill them if white tourists were aboard.

"Why don't you come with me?" he said. "I like company when I travel. I have a van, with extra beds. There's lots of room. I could take you places you can't get to by bus. I'm heading for El Salvador tomorrow." Then, to our blank stare, "It's all on the up-and-up. I sleep in the pop-up roof; you ladies bunk on the bottom. You'll have to promise not to harass me." He smiled like he thought he was the funniest thing since Monty Python's dead parrot.

"It sounds interesting," said Sasha, and I looked at her, alarmed. "But we'd have to think about it."

"Tomorrow, at eleven. You'll have to stop thinking about it then. That's when I plan to leave."

"I can't believe he thinks we'll just up and go with him," I said later, back in our room. "We don't know him! I'm not even sure I *want* to know him."

"Yeah, but you would've said no outright, if you weren't tempted."

She was right. Both of us were keen on going further south, and we couldn't do it on our own.

"Why don't you want to know him? He's attractive," Sasha ventured.

"He's also full of himself and pushy. I could live with that if I was sure he was trustworthy. Besides," I added, remembering the hat, "attractive is in the eye of the beholder."

She looked at me sidelong and grinned. "Under that dumb hat is a good-looking man."

When I didn't say anything, Sasha shrugged. "Well, it *is* a very bad hat, but that doesn't mean he's a very bad *man*. Don't be a clothes snob, Cat."

"I'm not. His shirt wasn't much better, though."

"Oh, c'mon. The shirt looked good."

"Not on him. I grant you the cloth was nice, but all that orange and red made him look pasty."

Sasha laughed. "Oh, hell, Cat. He'll take us to El Salvador for free. I don't care if he wears polka-dotted boxers and socks on his ears. But I would like to be sure he's safe."

"He's definitely after our bodies. Both of them at once."

"Get serious."

"I can't. I haven't got a clue what his game is. I figure he put Jacinta up to introducing us, then he sat down at our table without being asked, got snotty about where I'm from, and the next minute he's asking us if we'd like to travel in his van with him. Does that sound normal to you?"

"Well, I don't think it's quite as odd as you make out. Everyone who comes to the restaurant is casual like that. There was a girl who sat with us without asking the other night, and you didn't think anything of it."

"I did, I just didn't say so. But you might be right. Maybe it's the way people act here, after a while. This *is* Panajachel, after all, Hippie Haven, Sanctuary for Lost Souls Everywhere," I said. "But what about the snottiness?"

"Cat, you can be awfully snotty yourself sometimes. He was teasing you."

"Why would he? He doesn't even know me."

"You have a kind of look about you. Like you'd be fun to tease."

I'd once had a boyfriend who said I reminded him of Woodstock, the little bird in the Peanuts comics. When I told Sasha, she said, "Yeah, Woodstock with a sharp beak. Some guys like a girl who makes them laugh before pecking them to death."

The only good I could see in Jerry then was his straightforwardness. I thought it could mean he didn't have hidden agendas.

"You're defending him now," I said, "but it was you who said you wanted to be sure he was safe. So there must be something about him you don't trust."

Sasha gave me a considering look. "He's a man, that's all. Despite what he said, men travelling alone are sometimes on the make, and that could get tedious, stuck in a van. Unless you're on the make too. I think he's basically okay, though."

"Why?" I could feel my throat go dry, the way it often did — still — when I contemplated trusting a stranger.

"He seemed normal. You can tell if someone's weird. He's just a guy who likes to travel with good company. He figures that's us. I believe him. He's taking a chance on us, too, hoping we don't turn out to be crashing bores. I vote we return the favour and go with him. There's one thing you should keep in mind, though."

"What's that?"

"He's attracted to you. He couldn't take his eyes off you, even when he was speaking to me. I'm not saying he's going to hassle you. It's just something you should know."

I hadn't noticed. I didn't even believe her. "Oh, let's go with him," I said, mostly because I hated not being able to make up my mind. "We're dying to see Central America, and it's our last chance."

"You sure?"

Whenever I felt scared about something, I did it anyway. Like I'd be a coward if I didn't. "Yeah," I said, and swallowed hard.

So we went with Jerry, and it turned out Sasha was right ...

With that line, I turned off my typewriter and started dinner.

Later, I took what I'd written over to Molly's. It was almost too easy to lean on her again, the way I had when I was a child. I knew she could be overbearing and I was a big girl now, but all the same, I had no book-writing friends, and I needed input. I was finding the process tough. Sometimes I felt like I was creating reality rather than recreating it, and I was confused.

Molly, handing my pages back to me, said she liked learning about how I met Jerry. "Of course, I knew you met him in Guatemala, but I didn't know the details." We were sitting on the elegant Art Nouveau couch in her magazine-perfect home, and she put an arm around my shoulders, pulling me towards her affectionately. "Do you know something? You were a funny sort of girl."

I shrugged. "I guess," I said.

"No wonder he liked you."

I shrugged again, touched and a little bashful, as I leaned into her bony embrace.

"Actually, I remember you back then. There was something endearing about you. Can't quite put my finger on it. You were just cute. Took yourself too seriously at times, put on airs, but anyone could see through it. That was part of your charm."

"You never said that then."

"Why would I? You were just you. You still are." She gave me a little shove with her free arm. "Cute."

"You're cute, too," I said, pushing her back, but the distance I had travelled from *cute* felt as immense as my sorrow over Jerry's death. Writing about my younger self meant rediscovering someone who had become a stranger. I'd ferreted out some of my old journals and almost didn't recognize myself. It was as though I was convinced my thought processes held the key to the universe. Talk about self-absorbed. I hadn't realized how much Guatemala and Jerry, and time itself, had changed me. I was envious of that foolish young woman who could be unashamedly *cute*.

Uncertain, I said, "I want to go over absolutely everything about *us*, me and Jerry."

"Well, that's good. You should do whatever you want with this. That's what it's for." She hesitated, bent her head, and looked up at me. "Maybe you'll end up with a clear picture of what you meant to each other?"

"Maybe," I said.

"Is that what you're after?"

"I don't know, Molly. I want to understand what happened. I *have* to. It's eating me up, not knowing. Sometimes, I think I can't stand one second more of not knowing. I don't care about anything but that. What happened? What happened? What *happened*? It's like a mantra in my head. I *loved* him, Molly, and now he's gone, and someone else I thought I loved killed him. Do you understand?"

"I think I do," she said, rubbing my shoulder. "Maybe you should do more than write."

"What else *can* I do?" I wailed.

"You can try to find out more about Inez, by going to see her."

"No," I said. "No, no, no. I can't. I simply can't. I'm not ready. There are just ... too many ... emotions involved. I'd feel sorry for her, I'd hate her, I'd want her to be my friend again, I'd want to shake her till her head popped off, I'd think I should be doing something to help her, but what, and why, really why, after what she did? And seeing her would remind me of what happened to Jerry. This is awful. I can't stand being stuck this way."

"It's so hard to get out there," said Molly almost wistfully, looking over my head into the distance, and I knew she was thinking about going to Labrador. "I wish they hadn't sent her that far north."

"There was nowhere else, from what I understand," I said. "There aren't enough places to put people they call 'criminally insane.' At least this one has a good reputation."

She nodded. "That's true. I'd feel better if someone had actually seen it, though, wouldn't you? I think the trip would involve boats and small planes, and I just don't feel up to it, at my age. But someone should go."

"I know," I said. "But I can't."

"Well, at least talk to her nurse, Margaret. She came back from holiday, didn't she? Ages ago? Or you could ask Michael about her, especially about her reaction to that Guatemalan shawl —"

"Michael? I don't want to talk to Michael. He's too horrible ..."

"What about Ravi Banerjee, then? He was around Inez and Jerry a fair bit, wasn't he? Maybe it would help to discuss her with people who knew her, even if you don't come up with any new information."

"But it might make things worse," I said. "Dragging it all out in the open again."

"Talk to Ravi for your own sake, Cat. He's a good man. Maybe even make an appointment to see him. He'd be a good therapist for you. Promise me you'll think about it?"

I did go to see Ravi, but it didn't help. I got the impression he'd never liked Inez and that he resented what she'd done to Jerry, his fellow analyst and friend, even more than I did. When I asked him whether he wondered why she'd done it, he said, "Yes, of course I do. I know she was traumatized, and I know she had her nice side, but I always thought there was something a bit cunning about her."

"Cunning doesn't make someone a killer though, Ravi, does it?"

"No. No, it doesn't. I just never thought she was as wonderful as the rest of you seem to think. She was damaged goods, and damaged goods can get vicious. It could be as simple as that, you know."

After I left him, I felt worse than before I'd gone. I didn't want to think of Inez as cunning and vicious. I didn't want to have been that wrong about her, and I didn't want to feel justified in hating her. I wanted to overcome those feelings; I wanted to believe I was *wrong* to hate her. Ravi was no help to me at all.

Chapter Ten

Caitlin's Story

The morning stretched ahead of me like a long road into nowhere. I'd woken from a dream of visiting Inez in the north. She was in a cell with echoes of Plato's cave. Icicles hung from the roof, and there was no fire, only shadows flickering like flames on the walls and over her face. Her eyelashes were white with frost.

When I went towards her, the shadows came to life and crowded her. I would get closer only to find she had moved somewhere else, surrounded once again.

I got up, thinking to shake off the cobwebs of that dream soon enough, but it didn't work that way. I felt really down, even after I'd had a cup of coffee and eaten some poached eggs on toast.

When I walked by my typewriter, I thought I might as well just keep writing from where I'd left off previously. It had to be better than brooding. The dream was like a reminder of something that had happened long ago and which still had no name; it brought deep sadness with it, but because I wasn't sure why,

I was at its mercy. So I sat down and read over what I'd written the last time. Remembering our kind of crazy innocence all those years ago in Guatemala brought tears, but it also brought a smile.

Sasha, Jerry, and I set off for El Salvador early the next morning, I began.

In Guatemala, Jerry drove an old van with "Kosmic Kartwheels" airbrushed on the side. Some former girlfriend had put it there, along with psychedelic rainbows and several idiotic smiling suns.

"What's wrong?" Sasha whispered when we encountered the artwork. "I like the rainbows."

"You would," I sniffed. "They're a perfect match for his outfit."

I glanced furtively at Jerry, who was checking the tires. He still wore the orange and red monstrosity he'd had on the day before. "I sincerely hope that's not his only shirt."

Sasha laughed, covering her mouth and nose with her hand, so all that was visible of her face were a pair of merry Asian eyes under black bangs streaked with cinnamon.

Sasha was so pretty, I couldn't figure out why Jerry was more interested in me than her. Her mother was Chinese and her dad was black. She had skin the colour of Kraft caramels, soft, full lips, and the small, neat body of a young gymnast without the excessive muscle. She also had brains and an infectious laugh.

There was never any question who had Jerry's eye, though. Sasha was right. He talked to me more than to her, and he looked for opportunities to get me away from her whenever he could. It was obvious to the point of being embarrassing, but it didn't bother Sasha. She was engaged to a handsome and successful Toronto lawyer.

Years later, when I asked, Jerry said, "You were just as pretty. Besides, you were unbelievably bold! I had never met anyone like you. You were funny, and I liked the way you talked, and having to win you over was the icing on the cake."

As we travelled farther south, Sasha and I took turns sitting in the front of the van next to Jerry. On one of my turns, he told me stories about a dog he'd once owned, a Bearded Collie named Basho.

When he described Basho peeing on someone sleeping on the beach, I laughed out loud.

"Did the guy wake up?"

"Of course."

"What did you do?"

"I pretended I'd never seen Basho before in my life."

"Did it work?"

"With a dog? I was crazy to try. Damn dog bounded over to me, tongue lolling. He even woofed 'hello.'"

"And the guy? What did he do?"

"Dunno. I was running too fast to look back."

I loved that story. It led to a conversation about animals and how much we liked them. Later, travelling through a small town, we stopped at a red light next to a mural on a factory wall.

"Do you like Hundertwasser?" Jerry said, gazing out the window at the art.

I loved Hundertwasser. I'd spent hours wandering through his exhibition at the Art Gallery of Ontario the previous summer. "Why do you ask?"

"That mural," he said and nodded towards the wall. "Something about it reminds me of Hundertwasser. I just thought you might like his work. I'm right, aren't I?"

It was my first inkling that he had the ability to look straight through me.

Later, we discovered a mutual interest in philosophy, coloratura sopranos, Bob Dylan, gross jokes, and tequila.

I began to look forward to my turns in the front seat beside him.

We drank a lot of our favourite Mexican beverage on a wonderful beach in El Salvador we found by accident on our way to the Nicaraguan border. We liked it there so much, we set up camp for a week. Even though the beach was deserted, there were outhouses, a shelter with a thatched roof, and a fire pit. We never did figure out why the place existed in such a deserted area. A failed campground? There were small houses dotted here and there in the distance, but the whole seven days we stayed, nobody came near except a local farmer who sold us eggs and, once, a chicken so tough it became an ongoing joke of many years' duration.

"How was the exam?"

"Tough."

"How tough?"

"As tough as a Salvadorian chicken."

Jerry and I often strolled beside the ocean, leaving Sasha stretched out on a towel, reading contentedly. I picked up shells and seaweed to take home for my macramé projects in various stages of incompletion while we chatted about things like meditation, which I'd just started, and why Jerry liked Ingmar Bergman films and I didn't.

"They give a ghostly rendition of reality," Jerry said.

"There's *ghostly* and there's *reality*. Why do we need both together?"

"I thought you were interested in Buddhism?"

"Yes, I am."

"Well then, one reality intermingled with another should make sense to you."

"I don't know what you mean," I said. "I don't know any Buddhists who talk that way."

"What about the Tibetans? They mix magic with their meditation, don't they? It's that simple. Magic is another reality, and they mix it up with the everyday."

"Well, maybe, but I prefer the insight schools. They concentrate on seeing things as they really are, and that is what I've always wanted to do. I think we see 'through a glass darkly.' We're all looking through a veil of our own needs and wants and fears. I want to see what's really there, without all those clouds."

Jerry smiled at me. "That's exactly what I like about psychology," he said. "It tries to get us past our hang-ups so we can see clearly. Without projection."

"What's projection?" I said.

"It's like thinking someone doesn't like you when really you don't like them. It's not owning your own feelings because you're afraid they mean something bad about you. Or you could project the opposite, that someone likes you when they don't, because they remind you of someone else who did."

"Ah," I said. "Yes, that does sound similar. Just different routes to the same end?"

"I think so."

Backlit by the sun, his head was surrounded with a halo of light, a halogen lamp with hair. *Mixed-up reality*, I thought. *Angels and men.*

I definitely prefer the insight schools. But there's no denying that when the physical and the mythical come together, chemistry occurs.

Sasha was off on a walk, and I was lying on a towel, soaking up the sun. Jerry splashed his way out of the ocean and ran towards me, water flying from his lean limbs and shining in the soft golden hairs on his chest. The less clothing he wore, the better he looked.

He shook himself like a wet dog, spraying water everywhere, rubbed himself with a towel, then stretched out beside me. It felt pleasant but strange, as though we were already intimate.

I turned over onto my back and looked at his large hands palms up on the sand, naked and vulnerable. I wanted them to touch me where I was most naked and vulnerable myself.

Just as I was allowing myself to feel connections that lay below the surface of my understanding, Jerry propped himself up on one elbow, frowned down at me and said, "I don't like psychiatry any more than you seem to, Cat."

I lifted my sunglasses to get a better look at his face. "Where'd that come from?"

"Dunno. You're always knocking my chosen profession, and I just realized I've never responded."

"Well," I said, dropping the sunglasses back onto my nose, "if it's so bad, why are you going into it?"

He had the most distracting eyes, shot through with green, rust, and gold.

"Because, my black Irish rose, the only way to become an analyst is to study psychiatry first." He gave me a long look before continuing. "It's not that I don't know the dark side. I might even know more about it than you."

I opened my mouth to say something, but he kept right on talking.

"Germany was the worst, though I expect you're familiar with that — it's the most publicized. The Nazis used shrinks to label people, then they killed them. But Canada's got its own dark history, did you know about that? The CIA did experiments in Montreal on psychiatric patients. Agreed to by

Canadians; led by a Canadian shrink, Dr. Cameron. Have you heard of him?"

I tried to listen, but the glorious sun was thrumming in my veins, and I could barely hear. I was doing much better with my eyes, watching his full lips move as he spoke. Perhaps if Jerry hadn't chosen just that moment to get serious about the ills of psychiatry ...

"That's *wild* Irish rose," I broke in, dispensing with my sunglasses entirely, having decided to go with distraction. Propping myself up, and raising my face to his, I let my gaze roam quickly over his features until it came to rest in his eyes. The tingly sensation between my legs rose and spread until even my throat softened.

Jerry touched his free hand lightly to my cheek. I took it and pressed it against the swell of one breast under the thin cover-up protecting my sun-phobic Celtic skin. He began to tease the nipple to attention with his thumb.

"I'm not *your* anything," I said, deliberately breaking the spell, even as my breath splintered and radiated inside me.

His thumb stopped moving. "I see," he said with an ironic lift of his eyebrows. "Then would you like me to remove the hand you so graciously placed upon the deliciously warm flesh of your heaving young bosom, just moments ago?"

A laugh bubbled up from somewhere deep inside. "Yes, I think so." And he did.

"Now," I continued, still smiling, "where were we?"

"Dr. Cameron. In Montreal."

He was stroking my thigh, but I pretended not to notice.

"And exactly why you want to be an analyst. Under the circumstances," I finished for him.

"I'm messed up, baby," he said with a lopsided grin, removing his hand to quaff more wine. "Aren't all shrinks messed up?"

"Maybe. I wouldn't know. What exactly are you messed up about?"

"That's my business, sweet thing," he said, his eyes now on the sea.

"Then why mention it?" I said, watching him closely. "Besides, I asked you about being an analyst, not a shrink. You're the one who made the point about the difference between them."

"True." His gaze trailed down my body then back up to my face, like a caress.

"And analysts don't hurt people?" I tipped my head back, arching my neck, shaking out my hair.

"Yes, they hurt people. Done properly, though, analysis can be healing. Did you know you have a little pulse in your throat ... right ... there?" He reached out and stroked it.

I raised my head and smiled. "Why, do you think?"

"The pulse?"

"Noooo. Why do you think analysis heals?" I sat up and curled my arms around my knees.

"Mostly, I suspect, because it gives people dignity. You listen to them, it makes them feel important. It's as simple as that. And, of course, babydoll, I have personal reasons."

"Babydoll?" I couldn't believe he'd said it. "Did you just call me babydoll? Do you always talk down to women?"

He smiled at me sideways with what I thought was a touch of perversity. "Oh, no." His voice was low and insinuating. "Most definitely not. But I confess I am prone to mistaking rude questions for signs of sexual attraction." He poured us each another paper cup of wine from the bottle sunk in the sand. "I can tell from your obnoxious tone that you want me very badly."

I laughed and downed my wine. "Oh, yes," I echoed. "Madly."

"Then will you kiss me now?"

"Shit, no. I never kiss a man I haven't fucked first."

He spat up wine. "You've got some nerve for a virgin."

"As if." I leaned back again on my elbows, keeping my knees up, knowing he'd see that, under my short gauze wrap, I was naked.

"What? Not pure as the driven snow?"

"Oh, ha ha." I poured more wine and sipped it, the air around me suddenly vibrant. "If you don't believe me, find out for yourself."

He put down his cup. "I'll tell you one thing, gorgeous," he said, shifting closer until I could feel the warmth of his thigh against mine. "That don't-kiss-till-after thing? Virgin or not, we're doing that differently."

He smiled at me like an angel, knelt in front of me on the towel, kissed me in a way that made the sun thrum louder, and slipped his hand up between my thighs.

Soon we had all our clothes off — he insisted — and I was impressed by how at home he was in his skin. He had a beautiful body, slim and fit, but I thought he would have been at ease whatever he looked like. He was the first man I'd known who seemed completely normal naked, like he could serve coffee to a room full of foreign dignitaries that way without thinking anything of it.

I pulled him and his confidence towards me hungrily, and his entry into me was like a door swinging open to a magic garden, or a lantern flaring at sea on a pitchy night; penetration as the road beyond the body, through the barrier of muscle, blood, and bone to somewhere ethereal, all feeling, the mythical homeland we recognize only when we're there.

Afterwards, I wanted him inside me forever, but he slipped out, wet and vulnerable, a newborn puppy against my thighs, and it made me want to cry.

"You weren't a virgin," he said when our breathing returned to normal.

"Told you so. Disappointed?" I said, knowing that I had never made love in quite this way before, merging with someone until for a moment the whole mystery of existence fell away.

"Are you kidding?" He was beaming like he'd discovered an unknown planet.

"Well, in case you're interested, that was the best screw I've ever had." I examined my nails with feigned indifference, basking in the way a little daring gave the world a different face.

I watched his features compose themselves into a question mark. "Actually ... ditto," he said then rolled onto his side.

We locked eyes once more. Then he kissed me, said "Thank you," and we fell asleep, though he got there ahead of me, of course.

Chapter Eleven

Jerry
Guatemala, March, 1983

*D*amn *the girl*, thought Jerry, striding along the beach towards Lake Atitlan where the vast San Pedro volcano lay trembling, enervated by moonlight and water.

At the shore, he splashed his bare feet in the shallows. The cool wetness was irrelevant, remote; when he looked out over the lake, its dark beauty reached him obliquely, like something hiding in the wings of consciousness. Even the moonlight didn't touch him. Though his thoughts oscillated more than San Pedro's watery shadow, neither the light nor the lake was to blame. This damn situation — he couldn't get a handle on it.

He wondered about last night's dream, too, the one he'd described to Jacinta. Dreams, he'd learned, were best understood in terms of the emotion they evoked in the dreamer. Jacinta's "how did that make you feel?" had amused him; it was so unexpected here and such a cliché among analysts. He said it to his patients almost reflexively.

So, how had it made him feel?

The previous night, exhausted after his trip to the village, he'd stripped off his clothes and thrown them onto a chair. His khakis felt heavier than they should. He shook them till a grubby little bag fell out of a side pocket. It was the bag the Mayan mother had pressed on him as he'd backed away from her.

He picked it up, turned it over. Though still recognizably Mayan, the cloth was filthy and the colours muted. The frayed yarn holding it closed was tightly knotted, and he swore while wrestling it undone, then turned the bag upside down over the bed.

Five tiny dolls tumbled out. *Worry dolls*, he thought, wondering why there were only five. They usually came in sixes. They were given, he knew, to Mayan children suffering from nightmares. Caitlin's friend Molly had some. Each doll was supposed to take away a fear or a worry.

These five were made from wood covered with paper and, in one case, corn husks. They were dressed in scraps of cloth tied with thread. Their woollen hair was black, their eyes and lips gaudy.

They made him think of the rag doll by the tree in the ravaged village.

He scooped them hurriedly into a dresser drawer and shoved it closed. Then he climbed under the covers and fell almost instantly into the dream he'd described to Jacinta.

As he'd told her earlier that day, the dream had floated in on happiness, but soon he felt how the dead had suffered. He felt it again now as he stood on the beach.

Rolling up the legs of his pants to his knees, he strode forward against the water's pull, dragging that suffering with him.

What he hadn't told Jacinta was that the dream had been erotic, though he and Inez had not touched. Knowing that the dead people in the dream had undergone more than was endurable had filled him with ... *yearning*. And ... a feeling he couldn't quite place … *benevolence*. Ardent benevolence? He shook his head, kicking water out in front of him in a burst of frustration.

On waking, he'd felt compassion and a wild sexual longing that puzzled him. When he thought of Inez, he felt no conscious desire to make love to her. In fact, the idea was distasteful, under the circumstances.

Usually an erotic dream about someone he knew was almost banal. They made love, or manually aroused each other, or lay close together, naked, in bed, or some such obvious thing that meant, in his estimation, that the person, awake, revived a longing to be loved and give love unconditionally.

But there was nothing to hunger for in this girl, and the whole situation around her worried him. Worry was hardly conducive to passion, and the intangible quality of that urge only increased his distress.

In general, he was not drawn to young women — they often struck him as somehow *unoccupied*, unnaturally without marks, like a ghost's fingerprints. In therapy, they could reveal interesting complexities, but even there he found these patients hard to read, their smooth faces signposting little more than their youth.

Words are inadequate, he thought. He'd been trying to put his thoughts into words for ages. *Or maybe I just don't know the right ones.* Even Caitlin, who professed to love words, was in a pitched battle with them, more often than not. No wonder *he* was struggling.

What would she make of this dream? When he'd first met her, twelve years before, she'd expressed a rich contempt for all things psychoanalytic.

"Oh, yeah, uh-huh, right," she'd said. "I'm sure that if I sat in some shrink's office, five hours a week for twenty-five years, and said every boring thing that went through my head, I'd come out of it feeling better. I mean, of course. I'd feel better because I'd *stopped*."

This dream — she wouldn't dismiss it, but erotic dreams were no big deal to either of them. He suspected that the undercurrents — his attraction to suffering, for one — would be more troubling to her.

It was odd, really, he thought, that although he'd treated a number of conventionally sexy teenage girls, he'd never once had erotic dreams about any of them. Watching them, sometimes, he'd felt desire, but it was a purely physical reaction to a flash of, say, gorgeous, smooth thigh, or the audacious height of a young bosom. He'd never felt any kind of yearning for these girls or wanted seriously to bed them. Young girls meant sloppy romantic expectations and demands, or so he thought, including pressure for marriage and children.

This girl, Inez, had a quality of youth and maturity combined. He suspected that was what had captured his sensibilities. In the dream, everything had been eroticized. Inez herself seemed sexually knowing. He *had* sensed something like that in her when he first saw her, he realized — an undercurrent of sexuality. Not directed at him, but something unvirginal.

Well, of course. It was distinctly possible she'd been sexually abused. What was the matter with him, for god's sake? She was a damaged peasant girl with no social skills, no learning, and quite possibly no potential. What was it that seemed — well, *inviolable* — about her?

The word had come suddenly, unexpectedly. Sacred? Good Lord. *Chaste?* A moment before he'd been thinking of her as sexually knowing! He stepped back from the water and ground a bare heel hard into the sand. So many years of training, reading, thought, his own analysis, and he couldn't grasp what a simple dream was about?

He'd never believed the myth, so common in the sixties, that the mentally ill were somehow superior. Too much misery all around him during his internship at Hamilton Mental Health. So why this peculiar reaction to Inez, as if she really was something special by virtue of being different?

The inpatients he remembered best — Melinda and Sam — both had minds that worked like movie projectors, throwing out scenarios from some warped internal reel. Mostly ugly stuff — paranoid delusions and wretched betrayals, scripted by a demon from hell. When medicated, both patients were less tormented, but duller. Melinda in particular.

But a *cure* wouldn't have destroyed her originality or her brilliance, or Sam's either. At least, he didn't think so.

Sam had a fine artistic gift and would've been able to paint more without debilitating depressions; Melinda, who loved physics, could've pursued her theories without mucking them up with her own personal demonology. As in, "The presence of quanta, Mr.-soon-to-be-Dr. Simpson, means that old notions of space and time no longer apply. Do you know why that's so, dear Mr.-for-now Jeremy Simpson? Let me answer that for you. No. You do not know. And that is becausebecause*because* the God of the Dynamic speaks only to me, and *that* is because He demands to be seen as independent of everyday reality, and knows that is what I-I-I-I-I-I-I *am.*"

No arguing with that last bit, Jerry had thought, hugely impressed with an intelligence that, though riddled with irrational thought, still managed to speak good physics. He'd read enough (read it, in fact, to keep up with this patient) to know that Melinda was talking about motion as a dynamic state independent of time — in effect, as she said, something that demanded "to be seen as independent of everyday reality." As she, indeed, was. Incredible.

After reeling off this remarkable treatise, she'd plopped her plump self into a chair across from him, picked an imaginary something out of her wildly disorganized hair, and examined whatever it was as though it held the secret of existence.

If only ... Jerry had thought. If only Melinda could be cured so that she could study and think clearly, without breakdowns, without a mind that turned on her and turned her ideas into something so personal, only she took them seriously.

So why this fascination with Inez's state of mind? He reminded himself to call it a condition, but it didn't help.

He ran a hand through his hair, gripping a clump for a moment before dropping his arm heavily to his side. This was utterly, crazily nuts. What did he know about her, anyway? The situation she was in was so desperate, he supposed it mobilized his rescue fantasies.

For Chrissake. That was dangerous, as well as stupid. He rubbed his forehead with the heel of his hand. "*Only I can help this patient. I must save her*"? Good Lord. Thinking that way meant you were far too personally involved to give any real help.

He knew this. It was Therapy 101 stuff.

He picked up a pebble. Balling his fist around it, he squeezed until it hurt. Then he hurled it out over the lake. He didn't hear it fall but saw it — in the distance, a sudden spray of water.

He sighed into the darkness as he lay back on the sand. An image of Caitlin came to him unbidden, leaning over him so that her luxuriant hair brushed against his belly. Sudden desire made his throat thick. No, no. He had to think. He didn't have much time to decide what to do about Inez. His return ticket was for three days hence.

He breathed in deeply, focusing on the feel of the cold sand against his back. He squirmed, the turbulence in his groin reaching all the way to the back of his mouth. He kept his eyes open, breathed slowly, waited.

The desire grew exponentially, and he decided to ride it, steering his sexual thoughts into pondering the role sexuality played in psychoanalysis.

Freud had been a radical in his day, examining sexual desire openly and unsentimentally, but by the time Jerry was in training, the discipline had been sanitized to the point where analysts were expected to be not only heterosexual but married.

Even Jerry's arrangement with Caitlin had brought him criticism from older, established analysts, criticism he was convinced had had a negative impact on his career. No wonder, he thought, that analysts could go right off the rails and start messing about with their patients. Stimulation and repression was a volatile mix.

During his training analysis, the *zeitgeist* meant he hadn't admitted to anything more than a conventional enthusiasm for the missionary position. Gossip among trainees made many of them cautious about what they revealed in these supposedly therapeutic sessions, on which their professional futures hung. Nobody wanted to be labelled "emotionally immature" or "regressed" or whatever other pejorative was reserved for those deemed "unsuitable" for the analytic profession.

There were times Jerry had amused himself by holding "inner" sessions simultaneous with his "outer" ones. As he was telling the senior analyst doing his training analysis his problems with his former girlfriend Alicia — how she wanted to get married, but he didn't — he was silently expounding on Alicia's penchant for pretending to be a cowboy riding a steer when she "mounted" him. Alicia had asked Jerry to call out "Ride 'em, cowboy!" during sex, but he had demurred until one night when he'd gotten drunk. Alicia had put on an old pair of chaps she'd acquired at a costume shop and taken off every-thing else, and he'd gotten right into the rodeo spirit, albeit laughing his head off.

He had no intention of letting old Speirs in on that one. "Free association" may have been the order of the day, but they'd have had to pay Jerry thousands to betray Alicia to that desic-cated old fart. She'd specifically asked him to tell no one of her proclivities in the bedroom. With Speirs, he wasn't even tempted.

He could imagine what would befall him if the old man had divined what he was up to. Withholding information would be labelled "adolescent rebellion"; "total, intractable resistance cou-pled with immature destructive urges." Instant dismissal from the Analytic Institute. He still laughed to himself about it and still felt the old anxiety.

All this paraded through his head as he lay on the beach, breathing in the night air. Soon, his mind folded back towards the girl, but he was again too weary to concentrate, and drift-ing towards sleep, his thoughts diffused. Several of his patients scrambled around in the ether — they were never far away. He had a couple of challenging analysands right now. How would taking the girl to Canada affect his work?

Analysis was such an intimate endeavour. A formalized, restricted, specialized intimacy, true, but that didn't mean he wasn't constantly pulled in all directions by it. Sometimes it felt like having love relationships with a number of difficult partners all at once. Exhausting. Exhilarating. Fascinating. Frustrating. Bloody awful.

His patients appeared in his dreams, his thoughts, coloured his memories. Their voices, gestures, most significant sessions interrupted the flow of the present almost constantly. It took a lot for something to break through these preoccupations, as Guatemala, and Inez, had done.

———

He fell asleep, briefly, and, waking, knew he'd dreamed of Caitlin, but could recall nothing else.

He thought again about phoning her. *But* damn *the girl. It will disrupt our life to have her in it....*

It will ... I will ...

He was asleep again before he'd remembered what "it" was, and what he'd been planning to do about it.

Chapter Twelve

Caitlin's Story

I never did get to graduate school. Back in Canada, Jerry arranged for me to write up an analysts' conference for *The Journal of Psychodynamic Self Psychology*. It was the start of my freelance career. Later, when I moved to Toronto, he and I thought about getting a place together, but it never happened.

We'd pore over the newspapers, looking for houses to rent, not see anything promising, and then not look again for ages, until finally we just stopped looking altogether.

We barely discussed it. We knew we had something special and seemed instinctively to understand that it needed to be nurtured and protected. Sometimes I thought we were simply addicted to peak experiences, and that our desire to keep our romance at fever pitch was immature.

But was immature really the right word for wanting to extend the time when every gesture, every movement, was full of meaning that did not need explanation or words? When someone's presence made everything in a room change shape and become luminous? Or was it more like striving after an impossible dream, almost admirable, but ultimately as futile as Prometheus and his boulder? And surely it was anything but immature to recognize how that wild force could take over a life in unhealthy ways, if some distance was not kept? Because that was part of it, too. This crazy ambition was something Jerry and I shared, and it bonded us even more tightly together than most lovers. Or so I believed.

We'd been back in Toronto for a couple of years when Jerry mentioned that his friend Michael Doherty had got his hands on some ayahuasca, and would I like to try it?

"What the heck is it?" I said.

"It's a mix of hallucinogenic herbs."

I felt a shiver go through me, a mix of excitement and revulsion.

Jerry was watching me closely. "Latin American shamans have used it for years," he said, "and I hear it cures depression. Most people who come for analysis are depressed, so I'm interested."

"You've already tried it?" I said.

"Yes."

"What was it like?"

"Terrifying, actually, but I woke up the next day feeling as if some load I didn't know I'd been carrying had been lifted off my shoulders."

"Why would you want to do it again?"

"It was an absolutely fascinating experience. It also wasn't complete. The experts maintain you have to use it a number of times to get the full benefit."

Extreme experiences seemed to agree with him. He had a big smile on his face. "Someday, with the guidance of a healer ..."

"So why with me?"

"For the adventure."

That drew me. Jerry was more daring than I was, and I felt restricted by my fears.

"I'm not a big fan of drugs. You know that."

"This is different," he said.

"Why?"

"This isn't about tripping. It's mainly research, plus I think it would be good for you."

"How'd you get interested in drugs like that in the first place?" I said.

"Timothy Leary."

That didn't help his cause any. "That oaf? You must be joking."

Jerry said he respected the man's courage in experimenting with LSD, which got him fired from Harvard in the sixties.

"Mr. Tune In, Turn On, and Drop Dead was a snake oil salesman, as far as I'm concerned," I said. "Anyone described as *ultra hip* has got to be ultra phoney. He spent most of his life chasing celebrity and hanging out with movie stars. I also heard the real reason he was fired from Harvard was that he didn't show up to give his lectures. What's to respect?"

"You finished? He took the rap for his daughter on a marijuana charge —"

"Did he? That's interesting. I heard he ratted out his friends to get a lower sentence when they caught him with a car full of drugs."

"The drugs were planted, and he was sentenced to ten years on a charge that usually only got six months probation. If he sang, he must've hit a wrong note. I don't believe it."

"Did he ever go to prison?"

"Couple of times. First time he was sentenced, he escaped to Algiers. Later, back in the States, he did four years, I think."

That changed my opinion, but only a little. "Did anything useful come of his drug experiments?"

"There was one where he gave magic mushrooms to prisoners. Lowest recidivist rate ever. That opened up the way to the use of drugs in therapy."

"I thought it closed it, and that the results of that study weren't accurate."

"Well, he helped change attitudes, and that opened up a lot of possibilities. He's one of a handful of professionals who had the guts to put their careers on the line by experimenting with something he thought could be useful to patients. That alone makes his contribution significant, in my opinion, anyway. We'd know a lot less about LSD without him."

"So you think drugs can help psychiatric patients?"

"I'm not sure. I'd like to find out. I've met some shrinks who've done therapy using marijuana. They say it helps their patients talk, but they usually fall in love with the world and sound like idiots."

I laughed.

I didn't agree to anything right away. I told him I'd think about it, then I did some research on shamans, to help me understand Jerry and his entheogens. Most shamans were male, and, reading between the lines, I got the impression they liked getting intoxicated and used any excuse to do it. This did nothing to convince me to try it.

Also, Michael Doherty was the only analyst amongst Jerry's friends whom I disliked. Somehow the fact that he would be supplying the drug put me off. He and Jerry were polar opposites, as far as I could tell. I never understood what Jerry saw in him. We argued about him until I gave up. How many women like all their partner's friends, after all? Seems to me most men count at least one unsavoury character among their best buddies. I decided I had to accept it, though I used to joke that Michael must be Jerry's Evil Twin.

Michael showed up at Jerry's quite a lot when I was there. He was younger than Jerry, twenty-five or so, I think, when we met, a tall, slender, loping sort of man, who looked like the models in Yves St. Laurent ads and shared their taste in clothes. His face was the kind usually described as arresting — piercing blue eyes, fine bones, a cupid's bow mouth, red against the ivory of his skin, all of it in dramatic contrast to his gorgeous jet-black hair, shiny, straight and cut in one of those expensive layered styles favoured by actors and other men accustomed to using their looks to get ahead. Despite their colour, his eyes had darkness in them, and the sharp bones of his handsome face looked like they would cut you if you touched them. He reminded me of a vampire from an Anne Rice book.

He owned a Monster Home in Toronto's expensive Forest Hill district. I wondered how he could afford it. Even a shrink's generous wages wouldn't stretch that far. Given his aura of spoiled entitlement, I suspected a rich mom and dad. He would often come over to Jerry's place in Rosedale when I was there. He liked to read the *New Yorker*, and not, so he said, for the jokes.

"The jokes are elitist," he announced one Sunday when we were both visiting Jerry, twirling the glass of amber whiskey he was so fond of until it flashed in the light. "I don't find them funny. They take cheap shots at the disadvantaged."

I gave him a long look from the elaborate Victorian day couch where I lay and held my tongue.

"What's wrong?" he said. Michael was sharp.

"Nothing." I could easily have distracted him by saying I found the jokes that way, too. It would have been the truth. It was one of those times, though, when I was torn between wanting to be blunt and wanting to avoid an issue. Saying "nothing" was almost guaranteed to tip him off that something was up, so I'd chosen the coward's way, really.

"Oh, come on now, Caitlin. I've known you long enough to tell when you're being insincere."

I could've digressed on that, too, explaining the complexities of the meaning of the word "nothing" in that context, and how insincerity was not the issue. However, nor were semantics, so I said, "Well, ever since you told me that you charged patients for their analytic hours when they were away on vacation, I've had my doubts about you and 'the disadvantaged.' To be honest."

He put his magazine down. "Why?"

"It's not exactly fair, is it, Michael?" I said, indignant. "It's also illegal."

"At least it's not highway robbery," he countered. "Like what OHIP pays us. Or doesn't, as the case may be. But leaving that aside, what's that got to do with the disadvantaged?"

Money is a big issue with Canadian analysts. They're well off, but not compared to other medical specialists, like surgeons.

In the eighties, analysts in Ontario earned about $150 an hour, paid for by the government health insurance plan, OHIP. Worked out to around $180,000 per annum, if they were in demand, as they always were.

Not bad at all, especially if you didn't have a lot of overhead. Some analysts had fancy offices, but others worked out of their fancy homes. They didn't have to worry about collecting bills. The government paid up; it had to. Analysis didn't require any machinery, unless you count a good working brain — one that could rapidly calculate income while appearing to listen intently, if you'll pardon the cynicism — and that came free of charge.

"Why should you get paid for work you don't do?"

"Never mind that right now. What's it got to do with the disadvantaged?"

Stubborn and focused, our Michael. If he went after psychological defences the way he went after a line of reasoning, I was glad I'd never been in analysis with him. The nature of a defence is to defend, after all, and I wouldn't want to be letting my guard down too soon in front of a man like Doherty.

"Your clients aren't rich. Some of them are hard up. You make them pay you anyway, even though you're much better off than they are, and you're not even doing any work."

"OHIP doesn't cover holidays."

"Oh, for crap's sake, Michael." I threw my arms up in the air. "Why should they? And if they don't, why should your patients?"

He came up with the same pathetic reasoning I've heard from analysts many times. "It makes the patient value the time; the time is set aside for them, so that even if they're not there, the analyst has made it their time, so they have to pay…."

This last was utter and complete bullshit. Almost all analysts had waiting lists; they'd pop a consultation with a potential new client into the vacant slot, or give a patient going through a crisis an extra hour or three. In effect, they got paid double.

"Michael," I said, "that sucks. It doesn't make sense."

"We aren't paid enough. It's as simple as that. OHIP pays us the same as psychiatrists, even though our training is longer."

"Oh, poor baby. Well, hell, I don't think the *Star* pays me enough, so next time I interview someone, I'm gonna make them pay me for —"

"That's different, Caitlin, and you know it. You aren't doing anything for the person you're interviewing."

"And you're doing something for the patient while they're on holiday?"

"Caitlin," he sighed, "do you know how small-time this is?" He was lolling back in Jerry's best armchair, his long legs in their expensive trousers lazily draped over one padded armrest and crossed at the ankle.

"Yes, I do."

"I don't think you do at all, actually." He curved those red lips at me in what passed for a smile. "You should concern yourself with genuine exploitation. Compared to real blackguards, analysts look like angels."

"*Blackguards?*" I croaked. "Are you reliving a former life as a pirate?"

He gave me his best death-look. Then he repeated, "Blackguards," in a self-satisfied, brook-no-argument way, staring past me into the distance.

When Jerry pressed the ayahuasca issue again a few days later, I said, "I think ayahuasca just gives shamans an excuse to behave badly."

He'd come in from a workshop about therapeutic drug use, which had prompted the discussion. "No, Cat, that's not what it's about." He sank into his favourite plush armchair, closed his eyes, and stretched his legs out in front of him. Kneading the space above his nose, he said, "They often take it along with aphrodisiacs as part of their training. It helps them understand and gain control of sexual desire."

"What if I don't want to control my sexual desire?"

He smiled and opened his eyes. "Who said anything about you?"

"Okay. Seriously, though, I think drugs just give false insight and then get you all puffed up over your incredible new —"

He frowned. "I wish you wouldn't condemn things you know nothing about."

"I do know something about it," I said, collecting myself.

"Book learning." He was smiling again, ironically now, I thought.

"Yes. Am I only allowed to comment if I've tried it?"

"In this case, I think so."

"Okay, I'll try it."

"I don't want you to do it because of me."

"Too late." I shrugged. "You said I was condemning ayahuasca without knowing anything about it. So I want to know something about it. Then I can condemn it whenever I like."

He smiled again. "Yeah, but ayahuasca's a rough ride, Cat. I don't think you should do it just to spite me."

"It wouldn't be for spite," I said. "Seriously. I think you're right. I need to know more about it before condemning it. Besides, it just occurred to me I could write about it. I'm tired of covering gardening shows and skating recitals in Richmond Hill. I want to be an investigative journalist. So I need something to investigate. I'll bet I could sell an article on an ayahuasca experience to *Discovery* magazine."

"It can be mind-boggling," he warned me. "It's a very, very powerful mix. I'm sorry I said what I did. I don't think you should try it."

Red flag to a bull. I wonder sometimes if he knew that.

We argued vigorously then planned a night for it the following week.

First, we went into his solarium to smoke a joint, and right away the evening stars zoomed close, peering in at me through the glass roof. I don't like marijuana; it makes me paranoid, and I lose track of time, which isn't high on my list of pleasant experiences, but Jerry said it would help with the nausea. Vomiting is even lower on the list.

"You're supposed to throw up, though," he said. "It's part of it."

"What's that mean?"

"You're supposed to barf up your demons."

"Charming. Maybe I'll skip the dope, then."

"Oh, you'll throw up, anyway, don't worry. Just not so much. For a first time, I'd highly recommend Ms. Mary Jane."

He waited for me to mellow out then led me outside and handed me a cup of dark, sticky-looking liquid. I took a small, hesitant sip, gagged, spat, and choked. It tasted the way rank garbage smells, and my throat clamped around it like a stuck disposal unit. I clutched at Jerry's arm, gasping. He patted my hand then shook me loose to run for ice water. I managed to take a few sips of water and hand the glass back to him before dropping on all fours and retching like a dog.

Between bouts of nausea, I was confronted by tigers the size of killer whales, panthers with an anger management problem, and the occasional enormously upset lion. Later, a leopard dragged me by the hair to the edge of a cliff, and when I looked down there were animals suffering in ways so terrible I'm not going to describe them, and a voice commanded me to keep looking, a voice of such authority that I thought it must be the voice of God.

Then I turned towards Jerry. It seemed my hand was in his. We were joined together by a ribbon of light that simultaneously connected us and snaked all around us in constant motion.

Suddenly, he disappeared, and the ribbon of light went with him. I was lost in a vast darkness. I called his name for what felt like an eternity, until I must have finally fallen asleep. When I woke up, Jerry was lying next to me in his big bed, holding me close.

Jerry was right that ayahuasca was a powerful mix. The experience affected me the way a bad nightmare can colour a whole day, but for much longer. I was acutely aware for at least a week of pain and suffering everywhere I looked, and I think there was a small but permanent shift in my outlook, so that I no longer thought of happiness as a right, but a gift, like grace. I also clung to Jerry in unattractive ways. I'm lucky he didn't dump me before I got over it.

One thing, though. I didn't sell an article to *Discovery,* but I did to the *Star.* I was sure they'd prefer an exotic locale, so I set the piece on the beach in El Salvador, which was dishonest, but excusable, I thought then. I couldn't take writing for the Richmond Hill *Liberal* much longer. I'd been to El Salvador and I'd taken ayahuasca, just not at the same time, so I put the two together. I didn't invent a shaman, or a religious experience, I told it as it happened, only on a beach, not in a backyard.

I've never combined locales like that again. When stories invented by journalists became big news, they get carefully examined. I felt lucky I wasn't good enough to win a Pulitzer, then get exposed. And I figured I'd paid my dues by taking the damn drug at all.

I talked to several people who'd tried it and found it life-changing, and I included their stories. Not everyone gets the *Giant Jaguars on a Rampage* experience. Some get the *Soul Without a Body* adventure, or the *Love is All There Is* trip. When I heard those, I felt hard done by and wondered irrationally if there was a reason I'd been treated to a psychic horror show instead.

I worked hard on that article, and it was the start of a long, profitable association with the *Star.*

I never told anyone how I broke in. I didn't think about it for years at a time. Jerry was the only one who knew. I think Doherty read the article, so he must have suspected, at the very least, but we never talked about it.

No one on the paper could figure out for the longest time why I always volunteered to do the most gut-wrenching articles without a by-line. No one does that if they don't have to. I did it to make myself feel better. I'm not cut out to fight my way to the top. I was lucky to find that out early. And, to be honest, after my foot was already firmly in the door.

Eight years later, Jerry returned to Guatemala, hoping to find a shaman skilled at working with ayahuasca, as he'd said he'd wanted to all those years ago. He never did. He met Inez instead.

Chapter Thirteen

Jerry
Guatemala, March, 1983

Jerry woke from a deep sleep, knowing he didn't really have a choice. He would try to take Inez to Canada. He'd ask Jacinta, who was fluent in Kaqchikel, to accompany him to the couple's hut.

On second thought, it occurred to him that it might be dangerous for Jacinta, and he didn't want to put her in danger. Perhaps she could recommend someone to him, someone he would pay to come along.

He sat up. *Phone Caitlin.* There where times she could shake the beauty out of suffering, like dust out of a rug, and that would free him from Inez.

He headed for his hotel.

He pictured it before he reached it — his room, with its heavy colonial furniture, the latticed bay window overlooking the courtyard where the hibiscus bloomed in profusions of scarlet, and the hyperactive parrot shrieked *Buenos Dias, Buenos Dias, Buenos Dias,* loud enough to conjure fantasies of wringing its feathery neck. There also was the large burbling fountain that soothed him to sleep. What did they do with that parrot at night, tape its beak shut? He never heard it after dark.

He entered the courtyard, went straight up the marble stairway to his room and picked up the telephone. He'd stayed here with Caitlin, in this same suite, years ago, on his first trip south.

Now he could call her.

Caitlin was ensconced in her favourite armchair, engrossed in a novel. She got up on the third ring.

"Hello?" she said, one hand still clutching the book. "I hope this isn't one of those telemarketing things, because I'm reading this great book —" She was heading back to her chair, trailing the long phone cord.

"Caitlin?" she heard in response, and immediately, "Hey, Jerry!" she answered. Jerry's voice, all warmth and gravel, was one of her favourite things. She slapped the book on an end table and sat down hard in the overstuffed chair. "How's it going!" Excitement gave way to concern … "But why are you calling? Are you okay?"

All the way from Central America, he came through muted. "Yeah. Uh-huh. I'm fine! It's good to hear you."

She leaned back, curling her feet under her. "Uh-huh, ditto. I miss you. What else is new? What's up?"

"Well, it's a long story …"

"Go on. Your *peso*." She pulled her knees up and rested the point of her chin on the tent of her skirt, hugging her legs with her free arm.

"There's a girl here …"

She swallowed away a sudden rush of saliva and closed her

eyes. Her skin prickled all over in a way that made her think of the pet hedgehog she'd had when she was a girl.

"I think she's somewhere around fifteen. She's been terribly treated, Caitlin ..."

All the tension left her in a soft whooshing outbreath she hoped he didn't hear. *Oh, thank god, he hasn't found someone else!* "That's awful. How?"

As Jerry told her the story of the couple, the bus, the box, and Inez, her grip on her knees loosened, and she sank deeper into her chair. When he fell silent, she said nothing. The receiver seemed an extension of her hand, which had gone numb, *like my brain,* she thought.

"Caitlin?" Jerry's voice crackled. "Are you still there?"

"Yes," she answered slowly. "Yes, I'm here. My god, I had no idea how terrible things were there."

"I know. It's ... horrifying."

"I'll say! I just — it's hard to take in."

"I know," he repeated.

"You're bringing her to Canada, Jerry?"

"I'm going to try."

She tightened her grip on the receiver. At last, "She sounds fascinating," she managed. Another, shorter pause. "It's not the tragedy of this that's compelling, though, is it?" The question came out like an accusation.

He didn't respond.

"It's the triumph of it, isn't it? Her triumph, I mean. She sounds like a survivor ..."

"Well, yes. Yes. But she's not undamaged, Caitlin. Another kid might have survived better. She's damaged, all right. She doesn't speak, and she's angry —"

"Of course. But there's something about her, isn't there? From what you've said. She's special."

"Yes." She heard him swallow. "Yes."

"But, Jerry, why do you have to bring her here?"

He explained the danger Inez was in.

"I'm not thinking straight. I'm sorry. It's — what will you do with her once she gets here?"

"She'll have to be assessed, first, and then found a place in some suitable treatment centre. It's hard to tell what's wrong with her exactly. The first step will be trying to figure that out. Tests. She'll have tests done, and —"

"Where will she stay while this is happening?"

There was a pause. "With me."

"But —"

"I know. It will be difficult. But there's nothing else that can be done. I can't find her a placement until I get home, and there's no way to get proper testing done here, either."

"How will you cope?"

"I'll hire a nurse." And when she said nothing, "There's no other way, Cat."

"You're right. There isn't. What an amazing story! It'll take me awhile to get used to it, you know? Let me think. Clothes — she'll need clothes, I guess, when she gets here, and toiletries. To start. I can help with that."

She settled in for a long discussion, and his sudden, "I have to go, Caitlin," caught her by surprise.

"Just one more thing," he said. "Please keep this to herself. You of all people know what therapists can be like. And the media, too," he added almost as an afterthought. "I don't want this child exploited. And if the media gets hold of it, I dread to think what could happen. Okay?"

"Okay, but —"

"Sweet dreams. I'll see you soon. And thanks, thanks so much, I love you."

"You too, Jerry," she said, before it hit that he really was signing off. When he hung up, she kept the receiver at her ear for a long moment.

After placing it back into its cradle, she went into her kitchen, where she reached for a plate of date squares and ate them. All. Food could be comforting, and Jerry's story troubled her. Why had he hung up so soon? They needed — *she* needed — to talk this over. She'd been stunned to learn of the genocide. As for Inez …

She imagined being shut up in her tiny kitchen — much bigger, though, than the box Jerry had described — and shuddered. How had the girl stood it? She herself could never bear being enclosed anywhere, let alone in something the size of a closet. Since her brother's death, even being in an elevator for too long made her feel smothered, as though a giant paw had descended over her face, and was pushing down, down, so that no air —

The nightmares that had haunted her then were all of being choked or stuffed with cotton batting. Dry, made heavy by guilt, it scratched at her insides and clogged every orifice, and in those dreams she would come close to death herself, then wake up, gasping.

She turned her thoughts deliberately to Jerry. What he was doing was admirable, even rather wonderful. The girl's predicament was horribly fascinating. The journalist in her was intrigued, though this was one story she could never write up for the newspapers.

She was glad once again that she and Jerry had never moved in together. It would have complicated things even more.

Jerry lay on his hotel bed. It was early morning. The lace curtains blew in and out of the open window, softly, like a bellows fanning contentment.

He stared at the particles shimmying in a beam of white light shafting through the open window. A parallel universe of dust motes. He'd been intrigued off and on by the concept of hidden worlds since he'd been given his first microscope at age six. It was one of the reasons he'd decided on medical school. Access to the unseen. Microbes, germs, cells. The interest in psychiatry had come later.

Today he was going back to Inez's parents, to take the girl away with him, if they still wanted him to. He planned to head with her directly to the Canadian Embassy in Guatemala City. He'd made initial inquiries. The embassy staff had been sympathetic. They had told him they would prepare the official papers ahead of time, though of course nothing was guaranteed, and they would need to interview him, and see the girl. They'd even warned him, as had Dr. Fernandez, to disguise Inez, for her own protection.

He'd spoken with Jacinta, who'd insisted on going with him. "Nobody else I can think of," she'd said when he'd asked why. He was pleased but told her of the dangers — well, she knew them already, but he had to make sure — even said, on second thought, that he might do better on his own, at which she'd scoffed.

He stretched and tipped his head backwards on his pillow, until he was looking straight up at the high, white ceiling, crisscrossed by tarry beams. Today he welcomed going into the Guatemalan countryside — all heat and blowsy beauty — despite the trek though the jungle that would follow, and the uncertainties of what lay ahead.

He showered then took a pair of cargo pants out of the big wooden armoire, pulling them over the lean, strong legs that, along with his muscular arms, were his reward for the bicycling and weight-lifting he did to offset the time spent sitting in a chair, listening, hour after hour, day after day.

When he pushed his feet into his Mexican sandals, made of new leather and old tires, the soles curled up like a pair of disdainful lips, pinching his toes. He yanked them off and searched for a pair of socks. He'd wear Nikes instead. Damn. It felt too hot already for socks.

Heading out the door at last, he was happy to discover the sun tap-dancing in the palms and spinning webs in the hibiscus bushes. The sky was a burnished blue, a giant, unblinking, mesmerizing eye. Days like this electrified Jerry. Glazed by light, his own eyes dancing, he almost floated towards Jacinta's.

Days like this, he loved Guatemala nearly as hard as he'd fallen for Caitlin all those years ago. They also pricked him with the same kind of pain. Was it longing for the beauty never to end, or fear that it would, he wondered? He decided on longing, because those states were not the final destination. He wanted something more.

On days like this, he wished he could live in Panajachel forever, but there was no way. Too many ties, too many responsibilities back home. He wasn't prepared to give up the satisfactions of his career in Canada. There were difficulties, but he'd carved a niche for himself in the analytic community and was just beginning to feel confident in his work. He wouldn't want to start from scratch in a new country, where people's problems and their context were so different from what he dealt with in Toronto. The prospect of learning a new language was daunting in itself. Plus his work would feel like elitism here, where only the rich could afford him, and the poor were constant in their presence.

The houses lining the street he walked along were not elaborate, just chunk after chunk of square stone block, but they were vibrant, a jumble of blues, whites, pinks, reds. Canadian houses, by comparison, he thought, all looked the same — at least those outside the more exclusive neighbourhoods such as his own.

Remembering that he was affluent, even in his own country, further took the edge off Jerry's enjoyment. He began to think about affluence. An abundance of riches. The poor. Poverty. Inequality. Injustice. Luck. Fate? War. Even the flagrantly exuberant hibiscus blooms didn't distract him.

He arrived at Jacinta's. She looked up from her large, rusty till into a pair of melancholy eyes.

"Yes, Jerry," she stated. "It is a serious day."

He agreed, though it wasn't Inez who was making him gloomy just then.

Jacinta was wearing a white puffed-sleeve blouse embroidered with purple roses and green leaves, tucked into a knee length skirt of brilliant turquoise. It pleased Jerry that traditional Guatemalan clothing was rarely obviously utilitarian. She would trek through the jungle in this beautiful outfit, unconcerned about snags, tears, or dirt. Her only concession to the expedition ahead seemed to be looping her long, dark hair out of the way at the nape of her neck, but even so, she'd interwoven it with ribbons. Her face was "lived in," weathered. He liked the contrast between her straightforward manner and her exotic style. She had a womanliness he found attractive, her stocky build offset by rounded hips and a soft mouth.

He nodded as he smiled. "Yes, it certainly is. I'm glad you're coming with me."

She smiled back. "*Si*. Let's go then." Gathering up a small bundle in a plain red shawl, she came out from behind the till. "Diego," she called, "we're going now." She tied the sides of the shawl together and slipped it over one smooth brown arm. "I'll be back by afternoon."

Her husband emerged from the curtained doorway and said good-naturedly, "*Ciao*, Jacinta. *Ciao*, Jerry. Good luck."

They left just as the sun rose and set the San Pedro volcano on fire.

Chapter Fourteen

Caitlin's Story

When Inez came into our lives, I was unprepared for all the changes she brought with her. For one thing, we had to be so careful. Jerry was adamant that no one should know the real circumstances surrounding her, because he thought they were sensational enough to excite interest. "Psychiatrists have a thing about feral children," he told me. "They use them for their own ends." He told me stories of children subjected to tests and scrutiny, then unceremoniously dumped.

So he told his housekeeper that Inez was a relative he was taking care of for a little while. That was to be the cover story, if we needed one. That she had been orphaned and Jerry was an interim stop along the way to finding her a permanent home.

Only a few people knew the truth: Molly was one of them, and Ravi Banerjee, a colleague and friend of Jerry's. Michael Doherty was another. He was the last person I would have trusted. I was suspicious when he seemed to find her fascinating.

He came over a lot just to see her. But when Jerry told me he wanted to work with her, I was more suspicious still.

"Work with her how?" I said.

"He wants to hold sessions on a regular basis."

"Why?"

"He likes her, and she interests him."

I had to remind myself that most people who met Inez were drawn to her, each for their own reason. We all seemed to see something in her that we not only liked, but thought we needed.

"Why him?"

"He offered. He's a brilliant analyst, and he expressed an interest. Also, I trust him not to run off at the mouth about her. He knows how to play things close to his chest. It's just till we find her a placement, unless he decides to continue seeing her after that. I don't see how it can hurt. I certainly can't treat her, not while she's my ward."

"Why does she have to see anyone? She's got Margaret. How can an analyst treat someone mute?"

"He won't be *analyzing* her, Cat," he said, puffing his cheeks in exasperation. "For god's sake. He was a shrink first, like all of us. A psychiatrist who specialized in traumatized children, actually. He knows what he's doing."

"How do you know he won't try to use her to further his career?"

"Because I know him better than you do, Cat. I know he isn't willing to put in the time to take her on permanently, for one thing. He's got too many other things going. He'd have to fight to get her away from me, and he wouldn't do that, either. It wouldn't be worth his while."

"He's not going to drug her, is he?"

"Oh, come on, Cat. No. Of course not. The best role for drugs in therapy is with neurotics. He knows that. Neurotics can give informed consent. They generally excel at denial, and they block a lot, so the drugs help them get at issues they couldn't get at otherwise."

When I complained about Michael's free and easy way with the government health plan, Jerry said, "What Michael does is as common among analysts as cheating on your income tax is among the general population. I may not like it, but it's not enough to spoil a friendship. He's treating Inez for free. Does that make you feel any better?"

It didn't. Michael did not project kindliness, and I wondered if, despite Jerry's protests, his willingness to see Inez without payment meant she was some kind of specimen to him. The few times I saw them together, though, Inez seemed happy enough in his company.

The truth is, over time, Michael did seem to be helping Inez. He certainly wasn't doing her noticeable harm. I remember admonishing myself that my dislike of him, though not necessarily misguided, was irrelevant. Jerry respected him, and I had to wonder if I was prejudiced against him for no reason other than his personal style.

Something I'd been prejudiced against in Jerry, too, when we'd first met, I reminded myself. My judgement of people was hardly infallible.

Michael spoke to Inez sometimes in Kaqchikel. That did impress me. Jerry also had been trying to learn the language by writing back and forth to Jacinta Barrera in Guatemala. But the post was intermittent and unreliable, and weeks went by without hearing from her.

I was surprised Michael had taken the time to research the language here in Canada. It could not have been easy to find information about it. He'd say a Kaqchikel word then translate it into English for Inez.

Her face would light up when she heard her own language. She picked up on English quite quickly. She didn't speak it, of course, unless she was imitating, but the combined efforts of Margaret and Michael meant that over time she seemed to understand more of what was said to her.

Once I saw this, I relaxed. Michael was obviously a professional who was reaching Inez in ways no one else could.

Then came the day he delivered her back to us in a near-catatonic state.

"My god, what happened?" I said as he shepherded a cowering Inez into Jerry's living room.

She was leaning into his side, her head almost buried under his arm. Michael looked pale. He was gripping her tightly, and a sheen of sweat took the edge off his blade-like face. "She saw something that reminded her of Guatemala. At least, I think that was it."

Inez peeked at me out of wild and frightened eyes.

"What did she see?"

"A shawl, a *rebozo*. Look, I'm terribly sorry ..."

"Did you show it to her purposely?"

Jerry, who had taken Inez to the couch and sat down with his arm around her trembling shoulders, looked up at me sharply.

"No, no." Michael shook his head vehemently. "One of my girlfriends came in wearing it —"

Jerry shifted his gaze to Michael. "In the middle of a therapy session?"

"I don't give Inez *sessions*, in the usual sense, Jerry. I do a kind of play therapy. You know that. I give her things then let her act out scenes with them."

"Things like *rebozos*?"

"Cat ..." Jerry warned.

"No, of course not. I give her dolls, usually. My point was, we aren't secluded. We were in my living room. She seems most relaxed there. Alita came to my door, and Inez followed me when I went to open it —"

"Is Alita Latin? Perhaps it was her, not her clothes that frightened Inez," I said, before realizing Michael would have thought of this himself.

He shook his head. Inez whimpered, and Jerry stroked her hair.

"She didn't react until Alita took off her jacket," he said. "She was wearing the *rebozo* wrapped across her chest, like a scarf. Inez took one look at it and screamed. Alita said, 'What is it, Inez?' took off the shawl and held it out to her. That really set her off ..."

I looked over to the couch, where Jerry was sheltering Inez against his side, and felt a stab of unexpected envy. He was a big man, and my head barely reached his heart. Being clasped to his manly chest was delicious, and the way I fitted into him in bed, as though I was the centre of a whorled shell, gave me feelings of safety I couldn't admit I wanted in the bright light of day. Now Jerry was being protective towards another small person; one, even I could see, who deserved it more than me. How could I resent that this fragile young woman was the recipient of his kindness? I told myself not to be small-minded and went to sit beside them on the couch.

After the incident with Michael, it took Inez weeks to find her way back to a good place. A sure sign she was feeling better came the day she picked up her paintbrushes again.

We'd discovered she liked to paint, usually patterns in electric blues and greens and yellows. Molly said Inez's sense of shade and shape were strong and that the shiny accents reminded her of the work of Gustav Klimt. It was she who had introduced Inez to painting. She came over regularly, at least once a week, to work with the girl.

Once I interrupted a session to find them both with paint on their faces. Inez was plopping a dab of colour on Molly's already decorated nose.

It was amazing to see them having fun together. Inez could be joyful, but "fun" is not a word I ever associated with her. It was obvious Molly was good for her. She'd been good for me, too, when I was a kid.

I liked watching Inez paint. Some of her pictures looked like Mayan deities, and that fascinated me. Surveying her canvas with a considering eye, she seemed the young woman she was, not the child-self I felt oddly maternal towards. Oddly, because I got stuck looking after my little brother a lot when I was a kid, and I'd neither enjoyed it, nor done a good job of it. Also, because of my own mom, I was plagued by a suspicion I'd inherited her total lack of maternal instinct.

"Do you suppose they let her paint in that hospital?" Molly had just finished reading my latest book pages.

I felt myself shut down. "I don't know."

"Sorry."

"No need." I tucked my legs up under me on the couch. "Molly ..."

"Yes?"

"When Inez and I took all those long walks, I started confiding in her."

"Did you?"

"Yes. Maybe I shouldn't have."

"Why do you say that?"

"I got tired of pointing things out to her and saying what they were in English. I didn't think she needed to be taught all the time. And I got tired of the silence, too. So I started talking about my life."

"What about your life?"

"First, it was just stuff about my work. Then I got into other things."

"Such as?"

I dodged the question. "She never responded. I thought she was safe. But maybe she understood more than I thought."

Neither of us said anything for a while.

"I can't explain why I did it. Told her my troubles, I mean. I felt comfortable with her. It just happened."

I was remembering the day I told her about my brother's death, and how Inez patted my cheek and stroked my arm. It was a hugely tender and comforting moment. I pulled her close and kissed the top of her head, right where the hair parted. But when we unclenched, her remarkable eyes were full of fear, and she briefly narrowed them at me before her velvety lashes swept down and hid them away.

"Sometimes I think she did understand," I said. "I shouldn't have mentioned Tommy, and I wish I'd never said anything to her about Jerry and me."

"What did you say?"

I was reluctant to admit anything further, it sounded so bad. But Molly was looking at me expectantly, and I needed to talk.

"I said I wanted to protect what Jerry and I had, that I thought it was special, that love that had any depth at all was rare. That Jerry and I loved each other that way, but I knew it couldn't survive the wear-and-tear of daily life, not at that pitch, that's why we didn't live together, but that didn't make the love any less special. It was like having an orchid and giving it what it needed to survive. If you plant an orchid in earth, it'll die." I stopped, embarrassed, when I noticed Molly's raised eyebrows.

"You said all that to Inez? You never said it to me until a few days ago."

"I was just babbling, really. I never thought anything reached her; she could be so distant. But maybe I always knew some of it did."

"What if she did understand? Although I think that's highly unlikely. What harm could it do?"

"I don't know. Except that she killed him. There had to be a reason. What if it was something I said?"

There were times I was with Inez when I spoke about wanting life to keep its mysteries, wanting to taste danger enough to know I was alive, but not enough that it poisoned me. I couldn't think of one specific thing I'd said that might have damaged or enraged her. At least I'd had the sense not to mention Tommy again, given what might have happened to her own family.

But I'd been careless. I'd treated her at times as if she existed for my benefit alone. No good could come of that, I knew it.

I loved to watch her when she thought she was unwatched. When we trusted she wouldn't run away or get lost, we sometimes let her go for walks in the ravine by herself. She needed to do things on her own, to be free. I was nervous enough to keep my eye on her, and once she went straight to a beautiful clear pond at the bottom of a secluded gulley, slowly took off all her clothes, and walked into the water until it absorbed the globes of her breasts. With only her shoulders, head, and neck free, she raised her arms, and a watery cascade glistened down from her fingers back into the pond. I had never seen such a radiant expression on anyone's face before. She had an otherworldly aura, a pure, almost angelic beauty, and though sensual, she was completely devoid of sexual guile. But it was frightening to see that she did not understand the need to protect herself, even after all she'd been through.

I laid my head on my folded hands while Molly murmured reassuring words and proffered tea.

Chapter Fifteen

Caitlin's Story

Admitting to Molly that I'd used Inez as a personal sounding board was a relief. But still, that night in bed, I lay awake worrying about it. Rollercoasting between empathy and anger, I stopped the ride the only way I knew. I got out of bed and went to the kitchen to find food and drink vodka.

It was the third night in a row I'd got up to stuff my face and numb my soul.

Deliberately focusing on the darkness every day, as writers tend to do, was getting to be too much. My love of words was threatening to engulf me. If they did their job well, they grew away from me and hinted at complexities I, or least that part of me that was not a word-lover but a normal human being with limitations and fears, would rather not contemplate. I longed for a light without shadows. I decided that I had to visit Molly, to tell her I needed a break from the book project.

I found her in her studio the next morning, a gazebo in her backyard. Light checkered her long-fingered aristocrat's hands as she wiped them with a rag ripe with turpentine. She'd bought the gazebo after her doctor told her that working with paints in a closed environment was damaging her lungs.

"It's no good, Molly," I said. "Trying to write about what happened is making me a nervous wreck."

I waited for her to put down her rag and talk to me, but she said, "Writing's probably a bit like painting. You only think you're in control," while staring fixedly at her canvas. After she stopped rubbing her fingers with the smelly rag, she tossed it through one of the holes in the latticework onto the lawn.

Picking up a brush and pointing with its handle to a broken doll amongst the larger mannequins in her painting, she said, "I mean, look here … I had to put that doll in. I hadn't planned it that way, but I needed it to balance the design. I can't explain exactly why it had to be there, but it did."

Molly collected and made dolls, so I wasn't surprised she felt compelled to put one in this painting. I did wonder, though, that she wasn't aware of how often she did it. Dolls were one of the few consistencies in her work.

"This painting," she said, as if reaching a decision, "was inspired by Inez."

Then why did the broken doll strike her as a mysterious addition? Surely it was Inez, fractured and alone amidst faceless giants.

"In what way?" I ventured.

"Not sure. I was just thinking about it when the image came. I was also thinking of you."

"Me?"

"Mmm."

I peered at the painting again. The mannequins were all facing in different directions, frozen in place.

"It's not a bad thing, really," Molly went on, "being taken over by art. Especially for you now. You'll probably end up discovering things you never would otherwise."

"You aren't listening, Molly," I said. "Writing the book is a problem, not a solution. A big problem. I'm not strong enough."

I watched her deliberate over where to put some russet red on her black and white creation. "Yes, you are." Plop. The russet ended up on the edge of one of the mannequin's heads, like a gash. "If you stumble up against something uncomfortable, that's all to the good. You started this project because of unanswered questions, no?"

"I started it because I didn't know what else to do, and you made up my mind for me."

"Oh, certainly, that was the surface reason." Molly sounded so blithe, I wanted to hit her. She narrowed her eyes before taking another swipe at her canvas with her brush. "But I know you too well. You've got the soul of an investigative journalist, and you want to know exactly what happened, and why."

"I do," I cried. "I want to know the truth, with all my heart, but I don't want it to destroy me. What good would that do? Can't I proceed with caution —"

"Listen, Cat. Sometimes you don't know what's best for you. You've always been like that. You should trust me more. Have I ever led you astray?"

I had to admit she hadn't. When I was desperately distressed as a child, she didn't push me or say idiotic things like "pull yourself together." She'd waited a good long time before encouraging me to put the past behind me, and she'd done that mostly indirectly, by — well, now that I thought of it — supporting my love of reading, and writing, too.

"You were a lot gentler back then," I said.

"You were a lot younger back then," she countered. "You had more time. Look, Cat, all I have to say is that you need to write that book. You *have* to write that book. It's essential you write that book. Do you get it yet?" Her hands were on her hips, brush and palette sticking out at awkward angles on either side of her like car race flags. "I understand it brings you up against things you'd rather not deal with —"

"Yes, it does," I broke in, "and I wish you'd take me seriously when I tell you they hurt. They hurt, Molly! Last night they hurt so much, I ate an entire family bag of ripple chips and drank about a litre of vodka and Diet Sprite —"

"Yuck." She made a face. "Diet Sprite? Really? You're more desperate than I thought."

"Stop it," I said. "Please. I'm serious. I can't."

She dropped her hands to her sides. "I know it hurts, Cat. I do. I'm sorry to be a harridan, but I honestly think you have no choice but to carry on. Hurt is part of it, and you're way stronger than you think."

I wiped my eyes and blew my nose. "I don't know if I believe you. As a matter of fact, what you're asking me to do verges on trite. 'Write a book.' Why do people think that's a cure-all? This damn book means I have to look at things really closely. Not just what happened with Inez, but everything —"

"You'd be doing that anyway."

I stared at her. She was right.

"And you'd be writing it down in a notebook, wouldn't you?"

"But I'm scared!" I wailed. "I've started drinking to numb myself."

"Well, yeah, that would be scary." She reached out and stroked the back of my hand with one slim finger. "But you're not going under."

"I'm not?"

"No, you're not."

"How do you know?"

"I just do. You've never had a problem with alcohol before, so this is just a temporary coping mechanism. Or at least I think so, and if I change my mind, you'll be the first to know. I'll haul you down to AA so fast, you won't know what hit you. So be warned."

"AA? AA would drive me to drink."

"Oh, very funny. Why?"

"All that bad theology."

"Okay. So be warned, because I'll take you there anyway if you need it."

"Why would I need bad theology?"

"To scare you sober."

I rolled my eyes.

"In the meantime, drinking is probably helping you survive. A lot of creative people drink —"

"— themselves to death," I finished for her.

"Oh, come on, Caitlin. Ever the dramatist." She gave me an appraising glance. "Tell me what in particular brought this on."

When I didn't answer she said, in a gentler tone, "I suspect part of what's bothering you is that neither of us know if Jerry was actually who he seemed to be."

I felt heat rise into my cheeks. "That's not it. We've been over that a hundred times already."

"Actually, we haven't. It was in the air all through the trial, but we've never sat down and talked it through."

"I …" I rubbed one eye and then the other. "I don't want to —"

"You have to. There's nothing to be afraid of. Jerry seemed to me a very nice man. Even a good man."

"Yes?"

"Yes." With a comforting nod. "And I don't believe anyone could seem that nice without being nice, because what I'm talking about isn't just charm or politesse — it's the things he did."

"Okay," I said, not sure where this was going.

148

"He was good — very good — to his patients, wasn't he? With them, too."

It was true. He was known for it. His patients adored him. Loads of them — mostly female — had shown up at his funeral, weeping copiously.

The unhealthy hero worship analysands have for their analysts can be annoying for their nearest and dearest. In Jerry's case, at least it wasn't sought after. When he talked to me about his patients, he often commented on how important it was for them to become independent of him.

"Personally, I always admired him." Molly smudged a charcoal line on the canvas with a cloth. "He was smart and dedicated. He wasn't even remotely snobbish, and he never put anyone down. I know others may think he hurt Inez …" She seemed suddenly very interested in a top corner of her painting. "But I don't. She was one of his more spectacular good deeds." She swirled her brush on her palette. "I don't *know*, any more than you do." Poke, poke at the canvas. "I'm convinced he was a good man, though. I don't need outside proof. You might need —"

"I do not need proof!" I balled my hands into fists at my sides. "I don't. It's just — it's just — why did she kill him?"

Molly put down her brush and reached out to touch my cheek. "Cat," she said, "Jerry didn't have to have done anything at all to make Inez hurt him. She was in many ways an unknown quantity. So different that we can't ever know for sure what motivated her, not just about this, but about everything." She tucked a loose strand of hair behind my ear, like a mother comforting a child. "I think it most likely she had a reaction she couldn't control to something Jerry said or did in all innocence."

"Maybe," I said, swallowing, "but the worst thing she'd ever done before was throw plates. At least, that's the worst I ever saw." I thought for a moment. "Okay. Maybe I never really knew Inez, and maybe —" I swallowed again. "I never really knew Jerry either."

"There. That's good. You've said it. You've always maintained that you couldn't believe Jerry would hurt Inez in any way, but you're still suspicious. We need to know why, exactly."

I closed my eyes. I figured she already thought she knew why, despite the question in her voice, but she was wrong.

To many, women especially, the simple facts that a) Jerry was a man and b) he was white and middle-aged, and Inez was brown and young and c) that Jerry had paternalistically "rescued" her from her roots and dragged her away from the Third World to ours — those facts made him the worst kind of exploiter.

I found this ludicrous. Was it better for Inez to be locked inside a box in Guatemala, brutalized and in fear for her life, than to be championed by a white doctor and brought to Canada? Of course not. Especially when the doctor was protective of her to the extent Jerry was.

She should have been adopted by some Latin Americans, I read in a letter to the editor of my local paper. *He stole her from her culture. No wonder she attacked him.*

The worst accusations were the sexual ones. The first I'd heard was at the trial, when the woman behind me made her horrible assumption about Jerry. Since then, I'd seen opinion pieces in a couple of feminist journals that expressed similar sentiments a lot more politely, letters to the editor of my paper, and comments like this: *Of* course *he had sex with her. And even if he didn't, he got his rocks off playing Great White Saviour.*

"I don't think Jerry had sex with Inez," I said to Molly.

She stared at me, wide-eyed.

I rushed on. "He just wasn't the type. I know what people say — especially the feminists — but that's ridiculous. It bugs me that they assume it without knowing either of them. I —"

"Caitlin, I certainly never thought Jerry took advantage of Inez that way. There'd have to have been some sign, wouldn't there? If he'd slept with her, I think you'd have been able to tell. You're sharp and a bloodhound by nature. You would have smelled a rat and run it to ground, if there was any rat to smell.

"Besides, you two were the envy of me and all my women friends. You seemed to have an incredible ... well, it was obvious you were wildly attracted to each other. I don't think Jerry would have had enough energy for anyone else, to be honest." She was looking down, but with a grin on her face.

I hesitated before saying, "Things changed when Inez came on the scene."

Molly looked up, then leaned in, her hands on the table. "What happened when Inez came? What changed?"

I should have known she'd make too much of it. "Dunno."

Molly didn't drop her eyes this time, she narrowed them. "You can't tell the whole story till you know what it is, is that it? About Inez changing things between you ..."

"Something like that," I said, afraid she'd get more persistent if I refused to answer. Molly, like a cat, sees a closed door as a personal affront. "But maybe not in the way you think. If you want to know more, you'll have to wait."

"Good god," she said. "I do believe you have the instincts of a storyteller after all."

I also had an instinct for self-protection. I had always avoided thinking about whether the addition of Inez into our lives and the lessening of desire for me in Jerry were more than coincidence. At least mentioning it to Molly meant I had to face how far I'd fallen away from my goal of seeing life as it really was.

I tried to sidestep my growing confusion, tried to fill my head with a memory of Jerry reaching for me as if I were salvation, begging me to let him lose himself in me, "Let myself loose, too," he'd said. But it didn't work. I stood helplessly in front of Molly, waiting for her to clear the fog in my brain with something I feared might be as corrosive as acid.

"Maybe you're the one who's worried," she continued after a moment, "despite what you say. But don't be. If he was going to fool around, he would have done it years ago, with one of the Wilting Violets. From what I saw at the funeral, he could've had his pick of the lot of them."

Not acid, but something that further clouded my mind, like milk in water. "I just told you I wasn't worried about it! I mentioned it because it's what I heard other people say, not me. But I don't understand. They were in his study. What — *what* — threatened her? I can't imagine what Jerry could have said or done that would scare her badly enough to hurt him."

I noticed I was wringing my hands, and stopped. "Of course, I know that Inez is disturbed, and an enigma — I still can't believe she's capable of cold-bloodedly murdering someone she seemed fond of. Something big had to have happened to make her do what she did. I can't let it go. I've tried. You know how I always want to understand things ..."

"Yes I do, Cat." She gave a crisp nod.

"Well, I can't understand this."

Molly backed away from me.

"I'm sorry ..." I said, bewildered. "I didn't mean to shock you ..."

"You didn't." She was smiling. "I have to leave, that's all. I'm already late to meet someone. Why don't you go do some writing, and we'll talk when I get back? This kind of question is what it's all about."

"Haven't you been listening?" I snapped. "I can't."

"And haven't you been listening? You have to." She was cleaning her brushes, screwing lids on tubes of paint.

"Where are you off to?" I twisted one of my shirt buttons as if it were a pressure valve that could ease the tightness in my chest.

"Just to meet a friend."

"What's up?" I could hear the plaintiveness in my voice, despite my best efforts to disguise it.

"Ah, Cat, you don't really want to talk about that right now, do you?"

"Yeah, I do."

The twin caterpillars over Molly's eyes rose so high, I thought they might butt heads. "Well, if you're sure… Okay. Just a quick word, then I'm off. My friend Gail is adopting a child. A black child. She's been getting flak about it from black people in her therapy group. She needs a friend right now, that's all."

I felt cold and pulled my sweater tighter round me.

Molly was watching me closely. "You're thinking about Jerry again, aren't you? That's good." She shook out her brushes. "You need to write about it. When are you going to start?"

"Soon," I said. "Most likely."

"Today," she said. "For sure. Now scoot. I need to get ready, and you need to get going."

"Gosh, I love the way you suggest things in that subtle way that makes me feel like I reached the decision all by myself."

She was too busy doing up her coat to pay me any mind.

The next time I visited Molly, she looked a little the worse for wear. She was rarely anything less than well turned out, and that day she was rumpled.

"Hi, Molly." I peered at her from her front doorway. "What happened to you?"

"Stayed too late at a party. Come on in."

"What kind of party?" I said, following her into her living room, which reminded me of a checkerboard. It was black and white, from the huge tile fireplace to the Oriental rug that she'd hooked herself. A black and white Oriental rug is a sight to behold.

"It was one of those ghastly fundraising things, actually. The kind where people exchange business cards and network."

"What the heck were you doing there?"

"I do have one or two friends in the professions, you know, who actually encourage me to socialize with them. Despite my being an artist. And it was a worthy cause. Oh, and, by the way, someone you know was there. Michael Doherty."

"That supercilious boy toy," I scoffed. "No wonder you had a lousy time. Do you know he had the nerve to come on to me once? Right in Jerry's house? The man is a total sleaze."

I hadn't seen Michael for ages. He went twice to testify at Inez's trial, but I wasn't there. He didn't show up for the verdict, or afterwards, or even call to offer condolences. He'd attended Jerry's funeral, though. I guess he thought it politic to do so.

"I didn't speak to him," she said.

"Well, if you had, it wouldn't have helped. What were they raising money for, more perks for analysts?"

"Naughty, naughty Cat. It was a film show and a fundraiser for a new therapy centre for children in Toronto."

"Why didn't anyone invite me?" Suddenly, without Jerry, I was no longer a part of the therapeutic community?

"I don't know."

Perhaps my criticisms of analysts were better known and more resented than I'd realized. "Why didn't *you* invite me?"

"Because my friend Jean phoned me at the last minute, last night, and begged me to go with her. I was hoping to see you there."

"I suspect Michael was there for the networking, not the cause."

"He may have been there for the women. The young and the beautiful were out in full force. I've never much liked him, same as you. Though, I must say, from the bevy of beauties surrounding him, we are definitely in the minority."

"An *elite* minority," I said.

She laughed, running her hands through her wavy mane, but I thought the laugh was sad.

"Is something bothering you? Apart from being hungover, I mean?

"I'm not hungover. I'm just tired. I stayed up way past my bedtime."

·"So you must have been having a good time."

"Well, no. That's the thing. I couldn't bring myself to leave and yet there was no one there I really wanted to talk to. I've never done something like that before. I thought I liked being alone."

"Something must have changed?" I said.

She looked up at me, an unreadable smile on her face. "Who knows? It might be that I lack human connection, and I'm finally noticing it."

"You've always been connected to me," I said, meaning it.

"You're all grown up now."

"I still need you, and you still help me."

"Maybe I need to help someone else as well."

"You helped Inez," I said. "With her art." I had a sudden intuition. "Do you miss her?"

She sighed. "I miss what I thought she was."

We looked at each other in silence. The conversation was making me feel strange. I wanted to defend Inez, say who were we to assume we knew what or who she was, even now, and not to give up on her, but my feelings were too conflicted.

"About Michael …" I said.

"Like I say, we didn't speak, but I did hear him talking about you," she said.

"What did he say?"

"He was asking someone if you were there."

"Who?"

"I don't know."

"Male or female?"

"Male. Gruff-looking old guy."

"Probably one of the senior analysts who used to make Jerry's life miserable."

I was thinking it might be Dr. Whitfield, the head of the Analytic Society. A few months before Jerry died, he had told me he suspected the man of abusing his patients. I'd supported his urge to blow the whistle, though we both knew how risky it would be. He hadn't been sure where to start, and now it was too late. Unless I did something about it myself, but how?

"Might be," Molly said. "But Michael wasn't treating him like that —"

"You mean, he wasn't acting obsequious, the way he would if the man were his professional superior?"

Molly shrugged. "Maybe so. They seemed more like cronies, really."

"What did the older guy look like?"

"Lots of whiskers," said Molly. "Like a psychiatric Andrew Weil, but outdoing him in the eyebrow department. They were amazing eyebrows — grey with streaks of white, thick and smooth as otter fur. Astonishing."

Whitfield, for sure. Hobnobbing with that evil old fart had to be a new low, even for Michael.

"I wonder why they were talking about me?"

"Beats me. The older one said he didn't think you were there, and then Michael said, 'I wonder how she's doing?' or something like —"

"Not enough to call me."

"True. The old man glared at him for some reason. I was going to intervene and tell them about you —"

"What? You didn't!"

"Well, no. Suddenly the hostess was there, introducing me to some more people I didn't want to talk to."

"Oh dear," I said, still thinking about Michael. Somehow, it didn't warm my heart to know he'd asked after me.

"He was probably relieved I wasn't there," I said.

Molly laughed. "Actually, he sounded sad."

That baffled me. What had Michael Doherty got to be sad about, when it came to me?

Chapter Sixteen

Jerry
Guatemala, March, 1983

The trek to Inez's parents' place seemed shorter this time. The dust, the clack-clack of the insects, the sun like a drill were unthreatening, because even his bones and muscles knew they wouldn't last. He was free to notice the stones on the paths, the mist that lingered still, in places, dulling the sharp green of the foliage, though they were well into morning now. The redness of the earth. The leaves brushing his sweating face.

He thought about how to handle Inez, if they did take her away that day.

He'd been told the Canadian Embassy occupied the upper storeys of an office building in Guatemala City's fashionable Zone 9. You had to walk past a security guard and board an elevator that didn't stop till it got there. At the top would be guards — Guatemalan police — and a heavy steel door, locked and unlocked from within. You had to shout your business through an intercom.

Now the forest began to seem oppressive, the mist's distortions alarming. He ran his sleeve along his dripping brow.

Jacinta was more surefooted than he. She was getting too far in front, he thought, and he searched for the flash of her hair-ribbon between the trees. "Slow down a little, please, Jacinta," he called, flushing from more than just the heat. "I can't keep up with you, and if you lose me, you'll lose the way, too."

"Maybe not," she countered cheerfully, stopping anyway. "You see, whatever way I go, I will come to the top of this hill and, from there, I should be able to look around and see your little house."

She was right, of course, but she wasn't sparing his ego any. "Okay, Jacinta, you win," he said. "I need you to go slower so *I* don't get lost."

He saw her grin, looking down at him from her place slightly higher up the hill. "Eh, Jerry. What are you *gringo*s made of? Banana mush?"

He laughed. "Some nerve, Jacinta. Try surviving the Toronto subway during rush hour before you decide I'm a total wimp."

"Why? They have cobras there, too?"

"Cobras?" he said in alarm before noticing the sly smile. "Jacinta …" He rolled his eyes and gave an exaggerated sigh, noting that though she was shiny with perspiration, she was also full of energy. "But you're right. I'm a mess." He leaned against the trunk of a towering tree. "Phew. Let's rest a minute."

She shrugged. "If you need to." And they sat down together at the base of the mahogany.

"You worried, huh?" she said, opening a small leaf-wrapped bundle she'd taken out of her shawl. "Here. Have some tomato sauce," she offered. And when he hesitated, "Like *gringo* ketchup. Only better."

Still, he shook his head. "No, thanks. I'm not hungry. Too worried, as you said."

"What exactly about?"

"I'm not sure." He licked the salt sweat off his upper lip and gave her an appraising look. "What if I don't like her this time?" he said. "And I'm afraid of what will happen at the embassy, and after."

"But right now, it's mostly her, huh? I mean, how you'll feel about her."

"Uh-huh. I'm stuck with her now."

Jacinta re-tied her bundle and got to her feet. "Only one way to find out," she said, heading off into the jungle.

Behind her, Jerry picked himself up off the ground. Whoever had said it was right. Jacinta was not one to beat around the bush. He followed her through the trees.

The house was as dilapidated as he remembered, the sagging roof full of holes, the lace around the wooden cross ragged and torn. Bits and scraps, tag ends and loose ends, a visual cacophony even as it formed a whole in his mind. Just as he thought this, the lace on the cross snapped outwards, caught in a passing breeze so hot, it felt like fevered breath against his head and neck. He turned to Jacinta, put an arm around her shoulders and brought her to his side.

"There it is."

Jacinta did not seem shocked or horrified. She did look sad. *I guess you never really get used to human misery,* he thought, simultaneously aware that some did, all too easily.

But Jacinta, he knew, belonged to the ranks of the tender-hearted. She was pressing her lips tightly together as she surveyed first the shack, then Jerry. "Well," she said at last. "You first!"

When Jerry reached the doorway, he called softly through the cloth curtain, "*Buenos tardes.* Anybody home?"

The Mayan woman appeared, holding the filthy blanket across the doorway away from her head with one hand. She answered with something that sounded like "*Quien es?*" to Jerry, then, seeing who it was, stepped forward.

"Doctor," she said flatly, no hint of greeting in her voice, the pleading in her eyes as evident as on his previous visit.

She looked healthier, though. Her hair was smooth, almost sleek, pulled away from her face and braided, the pigtails tied together behind her head to prevent them falling forward when she worked. She was wearing a *huipil* of woven cotton, striped red, yellow, and green, gathered comfortably at the waist with a wide belt, embroidered in vibrant colours. Her tubular skirt, deep blue with a sewn stripe of watery mauve and yellow cutting it in half, stopped stiffly just above her dusty ankles.

"*Kirik a,*" he said impulsively, the only words he knew in Kaqchikel, "*I'll see you again.*" He hoped she'd know he meant "I'm back" or "I've decided to come here again."

However, the woman looked puzzled before stepping back into the shack, letting the greasy curtain fall behind her. He felt like an idiot. She returned in a few moments with her husband.

"*Buenos tardes,*" he said flatly, as if by rote, and avoiding Jerry's eyes. He was wearing, as before, a check western shirt and polyester slacks.

Jerry turned to Jacinta, struggling for the words to introduce her, finding them unnecessary as she stepped forward and launched a volley of friendly speech at the man in what Jerry assumed was the Kaqchikel language.

Suspicion, sadness, something close to pleasure, gratitude, and worry raced close on each other's heels over the man's face. He did not look like a man who would purposely abuse his daughter.

But how am I to know? Jerry thought. He'd met "nice" abusers before. He had also treated an unusually empathetic boy who had tortured his sister because his schizophrenic mother told him she was evil, and that by torturing her they were cleansing her of sin.

The man was talking to his wife, gesturing occasionally towards Jacinta and Jerry. The woman nodded eagerly, though her eyes were still wounded.

Jerry wished they'd hurry. The heat was unbearable. There was no shade. The impossibility of deciphering the couple's motives was making him irritable. He was just about to call something to Jacinta when the three stepped towards him, with Jacinta translating as she walked. "They are very happy that you will take Inez to Canada. They are grateful and would like you to know that though they have nothing to give you, you will always be in their thoughts and prayers, along with Inez. Now we're going to get her. You coming?"

She knew the answer and walked past him, the Kaqchikel couple trailing along behind. She stopped to let them catch up. Saying something to them questioningly, she pointed in front of her. When the man nodded, she set off again.

Jerry followed them all silently then caught up to Jacinta. "Did they tell you," he said, pulling up alongside her, "what happened here?"

Jacinta shook her head in a way that said both "No" and "I can't discuss that now" and kept walking.

Jerry shrugged and fell back. It seemed the couple hadn't opened up, even in their own language, to a fellow Guatemalan. They must have said *something*, but Jacinta was right. It would have to wait.

He picked up his pace as they entered the trees, approaching the girl in her box.

There were no noises this time. *Thank god,* he thought. Inez, when she was led out, looked as he remembered her — big slanted eyes, wild hair, fine bones. That awful chain. When she turned, he noticed the full roundness of breasts beneath her torn shift. *Most likely older than fifteen,* he noted automatically.

Pity trapped his breath in his throat, but he also felt distant, as though these people on a fundamental level did not concern him.

He'd been afraid of that but still moved without hesitation towards Inez, already planning the trip to the embassy in Guatemala City.

Getting her to go with him might prove to be the most hazardous step of all. He approached the girl slowly, saying her name.

She stood taller when she saw him coming, tilting her head up towards his. She met his eyes directly then searched the area around him, as though seeking an escape. *Speak to her gently*, Jerry reminded himself. *Tone is everything with autistics.* Though she might be emotionally disturbed, and disturbed children responded better to reason, tone was all he had.

"Inez," he said again. And kept speaking to her softly, in English mostly, with as much Spanish as he could muster thrown in. "We've come to take you with us on a trip. In a car *(had she ever even seen a car?)* to Guatemala City ..."

Inez's face looked open, as if she might be enjoying the sound of his voice.

Then her father undid her chain and pushed her forward.

She stumbled, regained her balance, and ran.

"Idiot, idiot!" Jerry growled under his breath as he sprinted after her. There was no time for technique or finesse. He grabbed her from behind, wrapping his arms tightly around her.

She surprised him by not struggling. After they'd stood together for several seconds, he loosened his grip until she could, if she wanted, wriggle free. He held his breath. When she pulled away, he brought his arms slowly to his sides and took a step backwards. Would she run again?

No, thank god. She faced him.

Jerry kept his eyes on her while talking to Jacinta, who was close behind. "Speak to her for me, Jacinta. Tell her we want her to come with us, that we are going to set her free."

Jacinta said something gently in Kaqchikel. Then, "No more box."

The girl frowned. Jacinta said more.

While she talked, Jerry examined Inez's face. When she stared, even her bone structure appeared to shift, and when she pulled her upper lip inward, under her teeth, the planes in her face seemed to reorganize. The reformation was subtle; her eyes changed shape, her cheekbones became more prominent.

He had a fleeting thought that she might not photograph well. Without the faint alterations that took place when her feelings changed, it was possible her features would appear rather ordinary. Bewilderment, suspicion, anger, and finally a tentative joy transformed her in quick succession, as if light flickered over her countenance, or small luminous winged creatures fluttered there.

Suddenly she covered her eyes with her hands.

Jacinta talked to her softly, holding out the parcel of clothing they had brought with them. Jerry tensed, readying for another chase.

But Inez dropped her hands and stood tall. When she took the clothes, her expression was one of complete trust. Looking at the bundle in her outstretched arms, she smiled.

Jerry hid his astonishment and made quick mental notes. You never saw this kind of trust in an autistic child. You did see it occasionally in abused children. They reached out to strangers in a kind of crazy hope that here, at last, were their true parents.

A set of abused twins he'd treated during his training had placed so much faith and hope and confidence in him that he'd been incredibly touched. But if Inez ever turned that gaze to him — and he strongly suspected she would — he would be looking for something a lot more than good therapy. How could he let her down? More to the point, how could he *not* let her down? She would expect more of him than he could possibly give. She would anticipate nurturing and protection twenty-four hours a day. She would expect perfect love from a perfect love object. And then, when it wasn't forthcoming … Jerry felt sick.

Jacinta helped Inez into the new clothes, first pulling her tattered shift over her head, exposing a sleek, strong body, developed enough to confirm Jerry's suspicion about her age. He turned hastily away. *So they fed her as well as they could,* he thought. *And they must have allowed her some freedom to move about, or she would not look like that.*

She was malleable in Jacinta's hands, allowing herself to be dressed in the white T-shirt and loose cotton pants they had chosen for her. She seemed pleased by the trousers, admiring her clad legs from different angles, smiling.

When Jacinta slid Inez's feet inside a pair of canvas slip-ons, the girl stared at them with a puzzled frown. Then she banged her heels on the earth, reached down, tore off the shoes and flung them away.

Jacinta retrieved the sandals. She said something in Kaqchikel. Then, "The shoes can wait, Inez. The shoes can wait.

"I think she is ready, now, Jerry. And also that she has never worn shoes. I have told her that you will be taking care of her from now on."

Jerry closed his eyes briefly as he nodded. When he opened them, Inez turned her head slowly his way and looked up at him with just the combination of sweetness, hope, and trust that he'd been dreading.

The force of her gaze was almost physical, and he felt as if he swayed under its influence. He swallowed away a lump in his throat. "Her parents, Jacinta," he said gruffly. "They should say goodbye."

Jacinta turned to the couple. The father's expression was sad. The mother, as usual, had her face partly hidden behind her shawl, and her eyes looked frightened.

Jacinta drew Inez towards them, speaking all the while. Inez looked into her parents' eyes, from one to the other, as if a direct exchange of thoughts was taking place. She looked at peace. Her father reached a hand towards her, but she stepped back, and he made no further approach. He spoke to her softly in Kaqchikel then lowered his head. The woman said something to Jacinta and ignored her daughter completely. Inez kept her eyes on the mother, and her expression seemed graver than it had been when she was surveying both her parents at once.

"We're ready to go now," Jacinta said to Jerry, linking her arm with Inez's and turning the girl around. They began the long journey back to the roadway. Watching Inez, Jerry found her unusually graceful as she pushed through the underbrush when she had to, but more often dodged branches, parted ferns with her hands, found a way around tangled vines. Sometimes she even led the way, with a boldness and physical optimism that startled him. Had she travelled this route before, stealthily, so she wouldn't be detected?

They walked in silence. Something in the girl's manner dictated it. The sounds in the jungle became clearer by contrast, sharper and more beautiful.

It wasn't long before the intense heat stifled him. He was dreading having to restrain Inez, overpower her, drag her along with them, but she kept moving steadily down the hillside, sure-footed and serene.

That worried him. Where did she think she was going? Not only had they taken her from chained darkness, they were walking her away from her past, her family, everything that was familiar to her. How much did she understand of that?

She never looked at either one of them. She walked faster than he did. He couldn't see her face. What was she feeling?

Jacinta reached the roadside first and beckoned them forward.

At the edge of the forest, it seemed Inez reached some inner limit. She stopped and stared through the opening in the trees then covered her face with her hands as she'd done when Jacinta held out the new clothes. She was trembling.

Jerry and Jacinta moved closer, flanking her, exchanging worried looks.

What source of strength has she suddenly lost, Jerry thought, fighting panic. Had she never seen a road before? Or, worse, had she been taken along one to some unspeakable horror?

He held out his hands, palms upward. "What is it, Inez?" he said, keeping his tone level and warm. "Why are you frightened?"

He was glad they hadn't brought the car this far. To put Inez inside a small, enclosed space now — almost surely a strange, new one — would have been disastrous.

As it was, the girl was clawing at her T-shirt, panting.

"Sit down," said Jerry firmly, gesturing.

To his relief, she did, and he moved slowly until he was sitting at her side.

She looked at him. He recognized longing, as well as fear. She trembled as her breathing quickened. Tentatively, he stroked her hair. It felt prickly against his palm.

Jacinta was soon beside them, rubbing the girl's back. It was she who broke the silence. "She could walk now, I think."

Each put a hand under one of Inez's elbows and raised her to her feet.

To Jerry's relief, she now seemed calm and still. But it was as if she had never been afraid, and that puzzled him. She could have numbed herself deliberately, because whatever she was terrified of was too much for her. He'd seen that in patients. He'd even seen it in Caitlin.

They began walking down the dirt road. Inez's steps were faltering, not at all the bold stride she'd displayed in the forest, but she moved forward of her own volition, until they were standing by the car. He'd parked it near the bus stop, just a few yards down the road from where they'd exited the jungle.

What would she do now? Jerry worried as he opened the door to the back seat.

"I will get in first," said Jacinta. "To show her it is safe." She clambered to the far side, leaving room for Inez.

She patted the seat beside her. "See, Inez. Nice, very nice," and then some reassuring Kaqchikel. "Come, come," she finished. "Sit here with me."

Jerry didn't breathe as Inez stepped forward, bent her head awkwardly, then plumped down noisily onto the seat beside Jacinta. She didn't smile, but her eyes shone.

Jacinta grinned at Jerry in triumph. "Phew!" she mouthed, wiping her forehead and rolling her eyes.

Jerry grinned back.

He got in, went to turn the key in the ignition, and stopped. Looking over his shoulder at Jacinta in the back seat, he said, "Warn her. Tell her there's going to be a big noise, and that we will begin to move forward. Tell her it's a bit like riding a horse. Though she may never have seen a horse — get her to imagine one — like a ... uh ... a giant, featherless, four-legged chicken."

Jacinta stared at him then burst into laughter. "Leave it to me, Jerry. I think I can handle it, without bringing in any four-legged chickens. Lots of mules in my country, you know. Even horses." She turned to Inez and spoke.

"Okay," she said at last. "Step on the gas!"

Jerry held his breath and turned the key.

Inez jumped. The car slid forward. She smiled. And stayed smiling for many miles, before the wailing began.

Chapter Seventeen

Jerry
Guatemala, March, 1983

After mopping his brow with his sleeve, Jerry took note of the sweat mark and shrugged. In this blistering heat, even bureaucrats should expect a little perspiration.

The silence Inez had sealed herself in since their arrival in Guatemala City was a blessing after the hours of unearthly wailing in the car. Jerry was pleased that he hadn't resorted to the tranquillizers Fernandez had supplied. Would it have been wrong, though, to use them to ease her suffering? The question was hopelessly muddled by his anguish at listening to her.

As the three began the long walk to the Embassy, Jerry thought about how Inez's silence was a wall against overstimulation, but also a magnet that drew you in. *She knows enough to use silence as a tool, and in more than one way.*

A few blocks from their destination, Jacinta said, "The government soldiers will be suspicious if they see a Mayan woman with a man and child go into the embassy, Jerry. Even if the child is wearing an American baseball hat." She tugged on the peak of the Blue Jays cap that hid the girl's black hair.

"It's Canadian," Jerry said reflexively then felt like an idiot.

Jacinta shrugged. *Big deal.* "Okay, Jerry. Good luck."

"Good luck? You're not coming any farther?"

"No."

"But that was part of the plan. Dr. Fernandez thought we'd look less shady if you came with me to the embassy."

"Dr. Fernandez was wrong. That is what I think. He can't be right about everything, and I look Mayan. If the secret police see me going there, I could be in big trouble myself."

"Why did you come all this way then?"

"In case you needed help with the girl on the journey, of course. And now she seems okay." She smiled at Inez.

"Wait for us," Jerry said. "We can drive you home when we're through."

"No need. It will upset the girl and waste time. There are buses. You should stay in the city until you get your visa, buy plane tickets, and leave. But I will wait for you at the bench across the *plazuela* from the embassy until I see you come out. Do not wave. If you need me, if something has gone wrong, scratch your head — like this — twice, and I will meet you at the car, and we will go back where we came from together, but I will walk to the car on my own, okay?

Jerry nodded, and Jacinta wished him luck once more. "I will get to the *plazuela* in a little while."

Inez stared after Jacinta with a quizzical look as she crossed the road and disappeared down a side street.

Jerry took her hand and said, "We will miss her, no?" and saw a depth of pain and confusion in the girl's eyes, and such a conspicuous absence of anger that he was moved beyond measure, reaching out to touch her cheek in a helpless gesture of commiseration.

In a moment, she was scanning the city centre, and she struck out one step ahead of him in the direction of its tall buildings, palm trees, and paved boulevards. He was still holding her hand, and though he expected she had no use for it, he didn't let go.

As they walked, he felt the sureness of her stride. She seemed suffused with a softer version of the pride she had shown in their trek through the jungle. He wondered at it, at her dignity, and also at her certainty. Without his guidance, she was heading forward determinedly, as if there were something she was resolved to meet, or try, or do. He was humbled by that, and his attempts at detachment disappeared into the girl's commanding silence.

The embassy was in a tall building, large but unimposing. Only the heavily armed military men outside the walls and flanking the entrance indicated it was a place of importance.

As Jerry and Inez walked up the stone steps to the bulky wooden door, Jerry leading now, Guatemalan soldiers stared at them, some laughing, even while gesturing with their rifles.

Jerry was reminded of a particularly jolly little dog he had once owned that killed chipmunks with the most innocent joy imaginable. The memory did nothing to relax him. He was exceedingly glad that Inez looked more like a boy than a girl and was therefore unlikely to be recognized if the military were to see her again, undisguised.

The Refugee Claimants office was on the sixth floor. The elevator, as Jerry had been informed, had only one button, *Six* written on it in large, plain letters.

As the doors slid shut, he held Inez's hand tightly. She breathed more quickly for a moment and her eyes flickered. Then she steadied herself. As the elevator shuddered slowly upwards, she startled him by laughing. It was a short, sharp sound, almost without humour, like the bark of a hungry seal, and the moment after she had uttered it, any vestige of a smile left her face.

The hallway on the sixth floor was dimly-lit and deserted.

In front of the locked steel door he'd been told to expect, Jerry announced who he was through the intercom. No answer. He spoke louder. Still no response. Only when he shouted "Dr. Simpson from Canada here to ask about refugee status," did an answer come back, just as loud, "One minute ..." and then the lock opened with a *thunk*.

Inside was a long, glassed-off reception desk. A lone uniformed clerk sat behind the glass, and on inquiry, directed them to another, smaller room, where three refugee officers sat at a table, sorting papers.

Greetings and introductions were exchanged. Jerry and Inez were invited to take seats, and the door was closed behind them.

With Inez sitting ramrod-straight on her wooden chair beside him, Jerry answered their rapid-fire questions as well as he could.

"Where did you find her?"

"She is a Kaqchikel? How do you know?"

"What kind of condition was she in?"

"Who are her parents? Why are they not with her now?"

The questioning went on for some time. The officers were concerned and efficient as they examined the papers they had him fill out. They saw the danger in the situation. They conferred behind the scenes. They came back with a visa. It was signed. It was stamped. It was miraculous.

It was over. Jerry and Inez stood on the embassy steps, gazing out over the sun-drunk *plazuela*. Inez's stance was that of a warrior on a hilltop, proud and straight. Not sure what to make of it, he was warily grateful that she seemed in no mind to run away. He badly wanted to hug her, lift her off the dusty earth, defy the languorous air, but he didn't dare. Instead, he placed a hand carefully on her shoulder, and when she didn't flinch, he steered her down the steps and past the soldiers. Soon they would go to the airport, and, if she made a scene, he need do no more than explain she was a psychiatric patient of his, and they would be left alone. Now, if she just didn't bolt ...

Down the steps they went without incident and started back the way they'd come. Soon, Jerry stopped and looked towards the Plazuela Espana, seeking out Jacinta. He spotted her amid the couples strolling hand-in-hand around the beautiful fountain with its fiery horses shooting water through their nostrils, the balloon-sellers with their multicoloured, wind-boxed wares, and the cyclists wobbling by on ancient machines. She was leaning casually against the fountain's bowl, looking in his direction, getting drenched, he was sure, one hand shading her eyes.

He didn't wave. His scalp itched, and he had to remind himself not to scratch it. But how was he to be sure she'd seen him? They'd forgotten to work that out.

Jacinta stood on tiptoes and waved off to his left, in the general direction of a large department store. "Manuelo!" she called in clear, carrying tones. "Manuelo! *Hola!* Good work!"

Marvelous, he thought. It figured Jacinta would know exactly what to do.

Later, when Jacinta learned of Jerry's death in a letter from Caitlin, the first image that came into her head was that of Inez smiling broadly in her direction across from the *plazuela*.

Later, responding to Caitlin's request to seek out Dr. Fernandez, Jacinta learned from the locals that he had moved on. "The soldiers were showing too much interest in his practice," they said.

"I do not think he will return here," said a shopkeeper who had taken her child to him when the boy had a fever. "Not safe for a good man like him any more."

Not safe for good men anywhere, thought Jacinta, swallowing away tears.

Chapter Eighteen

Jerry
Guatemala, March, 1983

Inez stared with vibrant eyes at the activity in the *plazuela* and smiled broadly at the balloon-seller, reaching a hand out towards him.

Jerry wanted to buy her a balloon, to buy her all the balloons. Instead, he placed a tentative hand under her chin and turned her face gently towards his, praying that her expression would not change from wonder to terror. When she looked straight into his eyes with the same enchanted glance she'd been bestowing on the *plazuela*, he was momentarily enchanted himself.

Then he took a step backward.

He'd been taught that healing came through simulated situations, not real ones. *It isn't healthy for her to see me as her rescuer,* he was thinking nervously yet again. *I'll have to get her seen by someone ASAP when we get to Canada. I'll have to let someone else take her into treatment.*

He squared his shoulders and put his arm around hers, steering her back towards his car.

Jerry began to sweat when they got there. The trip to Guatemala City had been awful for her.

When she climbed in front without hesitation, he breathed easier. As he fastened her seatbelt, he noticed that her eyes were locked on the dashboard, or, more precisely, the small figurine perched there. Smiling, he detached it and handed it to her. It was a cheap metal statue of a Scottie dog, shorter but wider than a cigar, something a child patient had given him years ago.

Inez turned it over and over in her hands, stroked it, sniffed it. She began to make excited animal noises, the first sounds apart from the brief laugh in the elevator she'd made since they'd arrived in the city. Then she put the statue in her mouth.

"No, don't," said Jerry, reaching between her teeth.

She threw her head back onto the headrest and bit down.

Jerry cursed, loudly, and clamping his free hand around her jaw, forced her teeth open. Blood ran down his hand — from his fingers, and from her mouth, which she had closed so forcefully over the metal Scottie, with its sharp whiskers and pointed tail.

"Damn," he muttered. "Damn and double damn." He kept Inez's mouth squeezed open as he extracted the little dog. Despite his best efforts, he felt the figurine scrape against the inside of one of her cheeks. He slipped the statue into his pocket, curbing a desire to hurl it into the street, relieved that she didn't seem to notice that he'd hidden it away.

Inez's mouth hung open, obviously sore, as tears slid down her cheeks.

"Inez, I am so sorry." Jerry wiped her tears with a tissue. "How stupid of me to frighten you like that. I'm so sorry." He dabbed gently at her lips, cursing himself, silently now, for his foolishness, for treating her like a two-year-old.

His fingers still hurt, but he scarcely noticed them, he was so upset at what he'd done. What a damn fool move! He knew he was lucky the girl hadn't gone completely catatonic, or violent. There was nothing but dumb pain on her face now. She stayed deep within herself while he closed her door and got back in the driver's seat.

She sat quietly beside him for the trip to the other side of town, where he'd made reservations in a large hotel. Occasionally, he glanced her way. Her expression was unreadable, but she seemed absorbed in the passing scene.

At the hotel, the desk clerk looked at Inez with disdain, and at Jerry with contempt. Jerry was indignant. What did the man think — that she was a child prostitute, and he her client? He'd had to book a room for two. She couldn't be left alone. Possibly the inelegance of her dress was an affront in this plush place with its chandeliers and gilded mirrors. Even after he'd explained the situation, the clerk's attitude remained dismissive. *Because she is Mayan? Poor?* he thought.

A mistake, then, to bring her to this grand European chain instead of to a small place that catered to locals.

As soon as they reached their suite, his stomach growled, and he remembered they hadn't eaten since morning. He opened the mini-fridge and pulled out a sandwich.

He hesitated before handing one to Inez, afraid that it might be food she wasn't used to. But she reached out and snatched the cellophane package from him before he could stop her. As she unwrapped it with frantic speed, he noticed that her right cheek was swollen, as well as her top lip. Looked like the metal Scottie had done more damage than he'd thought.

Inez bit eagerly into the sandwich then whimpered and let the pieces of bread and cheese drop to the floor. She clamped her hands over her mouth, her eyes above them wide with pain.

"Inez," he said in alarm, touching her cheek. "Let me see. Inside your mouth — let me see. Please." If she couldn't eat something as soft as a sandwich, what was going on inside her mouth?

She backed away.

Jerry backed off, too, his hands signalling surrender. "It's okay, Inez. Let's go get back in the car, okay? Okay, Inez?" He was walking towards the hotel room door, keeping his eyes on her. When she looked quizzically at him, he said, "It's all right. I'm going to take you to see Dr. Fernandez. He'll fix you up, you'll see."

The tiny waiting room was full. All five mismatched wooden chairs were occupied. All eight people — Jerry counted — including the mothers cradling sick children, looked tired and ill. A man with a bloody bandage over one eye slumped against the shoulder of the woman beside him.

Two people sat on a worn serape on the floor. A man with an open sore on his leg gestured to Jerry, then spread the serape out further, inviting — with gestures — Inez and Jerry to sit down. Inez did so and immediately reached out to touch the man's sore. Jerry crouched down beside her and gently, very gently, drew her hand away.

It was crowded even on the serape, the air thick with illness and heat.

Jerry had driven here at a speed that demanded all his concentration, scarcely caring that he had set off on a three-hour journey when he could have found a doctor in Guatemala City.

That city had become sinister to him, despite his success in obtaining a visa. He wanted out of the hotel where staff and guests had looked down their noses at Inez. He wanted her seen by someone sympathetic. She wouldn't die of her wounds on the way, of that he was sure.

When Fernandez came out of his office, Jerry jumped to his feet, pocketing the tissue he'd been using to wipe Inez's flushed face.

The doctor, bearing down on a young man with a bandaged face, stopped. "Dr. Simpson," he said. "You have the girl with you?"

Jerry drew Inez to her feet. "Yes. She's hurt."

"Bring her in." Fernandez called out something in an apologetic voice to his waiting patients before leading the way to his office.

Despite his guilt at jumping the line, Jerry didn't hesitate. "This shouldn't take long, Doctor. She bit down on a little metal dog and tore her mouth. I've even got the dog, if you need to see it."

Fernandez shook his head. He said something softly to Inez in Spanish. Then, to Jerry, "She looks frightened and tired. Have you had much difficulty? Did you get a visa?"

"Surprisingly little. And yes, we got the visa."

"Excellent. Will she balk if I touch her?"

"I don't think so. Just don't make any sudden moves — like I did." He waved his sore fingers in the air.

"She bit you?"

"It was my fault. She put the dog in her mouth, and I jumped to take it out. It scared the hell out of her. Really a stupid move on my part."

Fernandez nodded, which made Jerry feel worse. "While she is here," he said, "I would like to give her a full physical examination."

"That would be great, but what about —"

"My other patients? It should not take long, and it needs to be done. That is why I suggest it."

"Well, yes, then, and thank you."

Fernandez led Inez over to his examining table, pulled the curtain closed around it, and lifted her gently to sit on the edge, facing him. Her pupils were dilated, and she shied from his touch. Lightly, he pressed one corner of her mouth, then the other.

"Does this hurt?" he said, using one of the few Kaqchikel phrases he knew.

Her eyes filled up with tears, and he wiped them gently away.

"Can you open your mouth, Inez?" he said in Spanish.

Her mouth fell open, and he carefully inserted a finger partway inside. When he saw the fear in her eyes, he quickly pulled away. "It's all right, Inez," he said softly. "Lie down now."

Inez, her eyes fixed on his face, leaned hesitantly back onto her elbows and stopped.

"You don't want to lie down?"

She closed her eyes. When she opened them again, he was looking into them.

"Are you all right?"

Inez blinked then smiled radiantly, as if a wonderful event had taken place, such as hearing two hearts beat as one, or having a *quetzal* alight on her hand.

Watching her, Dr. Fernandez was baffled. Still, he thought he understood what Jerry meant, why he cared for her. Her mix of trust and fear touched his heart.

Inez's body became fluid under his touch. Sometimes she tensed, but as soon as he re-established eye contact and asked how she was doing, she flowed again. He was able to feel all along each limb, shine a light in her eyes, and peer into each ear. But when, at last, he dared to bring the metal speculum towards her, her expression turned to one of horror, she braced her elbows against the table and struggled to sit up. When he continued to speak to her in a soft, low voice, stroked her hair, and smiled at her, she calmed down enough not to bolt from the table. It took many minutes and many words and much tenderness, but eventually, he was able to examine her. He was grateful but also troubled that she allowed it. He examined her closely and was more troubled still.

"Dr. Simpson, I believe someone has·had intercourse with this child. There is scar tissue in the vagina, and ..."

Confirmation of what he had suspected hit Jerry hard. Looking at Inez's sweet face, he felt like crying.

"... just from feeling her limbs, I suspect she has had breaks in both arms, perhaps one leg. You should have her X-rayed in Canada. Her parents seem to have fed her adequately. She is slight but muscular. Her overall health is surprisingly good. She is probably older than you thought. The Kaqchikel are a small people, but her development is such that she is possibly seventeen or eighteen. As for her mouth ..." He handed Jerry a small bottle of what looked like purple mouthwash. "... if you can, get her to rinse with this. I'd suggest miming it for her first. Feed her only nourishing liquids for the next day or two. From what I can tell, the tail of the figurine may have dug deeply into the roof of her mouth, but it should heal without trouble if she uses the rinse regularly." He looked down. "She responds well to good treatment. It is amazing, given what· she seems to have been through." He seemed unsure what to make of her receptivity, given that all signs pointed to a brutal rape in her past. "But, you know, Dr. Simpson, her response may indicate brain damage." A fly buzzed near his face, and he brushed it away.

"I know. I am aware of that. It can also indicate severe split-ting of the personality. Inez could be autistic, retarded, and emo-tionally disturbed. In which case, she would not necessarily learn from past experiences. Which may be the reason she is still able to trust."

Dr. Fernandez nodded and brushed the persistent fly away again, more vigorously. "Still, she *has* learned from past experiences, has she not?"

"Yes, that's true. She bit me," Jerry smiled ruefully, "because she thought I was going to hurt her, as she has been hurt before. But it's obvious she can recognize good intentions."

The doctor frowned. "Or the semblance of them," he said, avoiding Jerry's eyes. The fly, which had landed in his coffee cup, struggled wetly upwards from the dark lake inside, lost the battle, slid down, thrashed briefly, and drowned.

After they left Fernandez's office and were on their way to the airport, Jerry stopped at a McDonald's and bought Inez a milk shake, which she drank eagerly after he mimed sucking it through a straw. He couldn't think of anything else to get her for the time being. Her eyes grew round and bright when she tasted it, as though she could not quite believe how delicious it was. She slurped it down with such obvious delight that he was simultaneously touched and appalled. Junk food. It was irresistible. He made a mental note not to resort to it again. As they continued on, Inez played quietly with her fingers or gazed out the window. Jerry thought he heard her humming, but whenever he listened closely, there was only silence.

He turned on the radio, cautiously, fiddling with the dial until he came to a *folklorico* music station. He watched Inez's face from time to time in the mirror as he drove. At the sound of the marimba band, her eyes widened. Then she tipped her head to one side and frowned. The furrowed brow and turned-down mouth were soon replaced by a smile as wide as her eyes as she bounced in her seat and clapped along to the music.

Like a toddler, thought Jerry. *Rather disturbingly so.* Still, from a clinical perspective, and despite the discussion with Fernandez, he was inclined to think her responsiveness was a good sign. It could mean she had not shut herself off from experience. It could mean she still had hope. And, therefore, so could he.

After a long wait at the airport, most of which Inez spent huddled against his side, they boarded the plane and were soon flying over Central America. Inez was asleep, her swollen lips parted. Jerry was relieved that, so far, her moods had fluctuated between joy and withdrawal. She amazed him with her ability to cope with all this change. What in heaven's name must an airplane look like to her?

The only bad moment had come when the engines roared awake. He saw panic in her eyes, and she began to wail. Was he going to have to use the tranquillizers? She'd wailed for three hours straight in the car, and here there were other people to consider. He spoke to her soothingly, using all the Spanish he could muster, and soon, thank god, the keening stopped. She shut her eyes, and her breathing stayed ragged, but she put one small hand trustingly on his arm and leaned her head against his shoulder. In no time at all, she was asleep.

He looked at that fine-boned hand, still resting on his jacket sleeve, and at her broad but delicate head. Her neck looked thin and fragile, as if it could snap at the slightest pressure. He had to remind himself that Fernandez had pronounced her physically strong.

The stewardess stopped by and said quietly, nodding towards Inez, "How is she doing?"

He'd given the airline some background, to enlist their cooperation if anything should go wrong.

"She seems fine," he said. "She must be dead tired."

"Yes." Still looking at Inez. "She's lovely, isn't she, poor thing?"

"She is."

"And how are you, Dr. Simpson?"

"I'm dead tired, too, now that you mention it."

"Would you like a pillow?"

"Yes, please, I would." She brought him one.

Leaning his head on the pillow and gazing wearily out the small window into the early morning sky, Jerry felt as if he were floating on a sea of impressions, some of which created echoes inside him he could not trace to their source.

As the hum of the engine began to act on him like a lullaby, one of his patients wafted into his head, a heavyset young woman with a fear of falling. *Perhaps that's why she's heavy*, he thought idiotically, as his mind drifted down like sand on a dune. *Cushion the fall.*

The last image he saw before dropping off to sleep, Inez's head still nestled on his shoulder, was Caitlin's smiling face.

Chapter Nineteen

Jerry/Caitlin
Toronto, March, 1983

C aitlin was waiting for them at the airport, her arms full of flowers.

As they approached, she arched up onto the balls of her feet. As her high heels lifted off the floor, she freed one hand and waved. "Jerry! Jerry! Over here!"

She craned her neck for a better look at Inez as Jerry returned her wave. The girl was tiny. Her clothes, a T-shirt and jeans, engulfed her. Her face looked delicate but blank.

Disappointed, Caitlin sat down, newly conscious of her aching feet.

It seemed to take forever for the pair to come through customs. She was about to go in search of a coffee when the two of them finally re-appeared. She ran to Jerry and hugged him, the several bouquets commingling behind his head, enfolding them both in a haze of scent.

"*Ooof.* Caitlin."

She closed her eyes and pressed her face into his shoulder, breathing in the smell that meant more to her than flowers, the intimate smell of his clothes and skin, then pulled away, anxious not to exclude the girl. "And this must be Inez."

"That it is," said Jerry. "Don't overwhelm her, Caitlin. It's best to approach carefully."

Caitlin opened her mouth to protest but stopped short of speaking. Knowing Jerry, he'd made some blunder like that himself.

At closer quarters, Caitlin saw how arresting Inez's eyes were, golden and dark at the same time, and how luminous her skin.

"Hello," she said gently. "You must be tired."

Inez met her gaze then dropped her eyes, still clutching Jerry's hand, moving closer to his side.

"Actually, she's been asleep for the whole journey. Me, too," Jerry was saying as Inez raised her head and looked everywhere but at Caitlin.

Caitlin reluctantly turned her attention to Jerry. "Really? But you feel okay now?"

Jerry frowned.

Anticipating criticism, Caitlin made her face expressionless. *Okay,* she thought, *he's fixated on being reflected accurately by me, especially when stressed, but god in heaven —*

"I'm okay," said Jerry, and she relaxed. "But this is complicated, Caitlin."

"I know."

Inez was looking her way.

"I brought these snapdragons for you," Caitlin said, holding the bouquet out to the girl. "See what they do?" She pinched a flower, and when its powdery mouth popped open, she was gratified by the smile that lit up Inez's face. "The roses are for you, Jer, lilies for me —"

"Thank you," said Jerry. "They're lovely. I'm not sure now is the time to show Inez —"

"I know you can't carry them now, but —"

They were talking over each other, and Jerry laughed, taking the sting out of his remark. "It's wonderful to see you."

"Me too you."

Their eyes travelled over one another's in that quick way that re-establishes intimacy between lovers.

Inez was standing a little apart from Jerry now. She'd dropped his hand and was looking at Caitlin with frank interest.

Caitlin smiled at her. "What a proud look you have," she said approvingly and watched as the girl's gaze slid off to one side with a dreamy languor.

"Well now, I suppose we should all go home." Jerry placed a hand on each of Caitlin's arms above the elbow and stepped back to look at her, as though holding an admired artwork at perfect viewing distance.

"Was there any problem in arranging that?" Caitlin said as Inez once again leaned into Jerry, her head at a slight angle against his arm. *She has a soft, girlish beauty, almost baby-faced,* she thought. Big eyes, sweeping lashes, a small but full-lipped mouth. There was nothing noticeably Mayan about her features. The slant of her eyes gave her a Eurasian look. "Getting permission for her to stay with you, I mean?"

"Not really. Not once I've been appointed her legal guardian."

He'd told her he'd have to do that. It seemed a big step, but he'd explained it meant only that he would be free to arrange treatment for her.

Inez blinked slowly once, like a cat, before looking away from Caitlin.

Caitlin said, "If she slept all the way here, she must be hungry. What do you think she'd like to eat?"

188

"She can only have liquids for the next few days. She hurt the inside of her mouth."

Caitlin spoke to Jerry but kept her eyes on Inez. "After that? Tortillas? Refried beans?"

A light flickered briefly in the girl's eyes at the word tortilla.

"Beans and corn, definitely." Jerry shifted his gaze to follow Caitlin's. "Rice might be good, too." He smiled at Inez. "A doctor in Guatemala said she's been reasonably well fed, so we don't have to worry about shocking her system with too much food." He gently tucked a wayward strand of hair behind Inez's ear.

"Okay. Then I guess I should go do some shopping."

"You don't mind?"

"Of course not."

"Okay then."

"Okay then," she echoed adding, "I'll take these ..." she inclined her head to the bouquets still bundled in her arms, "... to your place, and meet you there after I go for groceries."

Caitlin was still shopping when Jerry and Inez arrived at his front door — the side door was for patients. As Jerry turned the key, Inez banged the polished brass knocker, a whimsical replica of the head of Sigmund Freud. When you knocked, you struck the great man on the chin, just below his cigar. "Isn't that a bit sadistic?" a colleague once asked Jerry. "Hitting the old man on his cancerous jaw?"

"It's before he got cancer," Jerry countered. "That's a young Freud you're pummelling, my friend."

Now Jerry smiled as Inez banged the knocker again. When he opened the door, she shuddered. Given her calm acceptance of elevators, planes, and a thousand other newnesses far more bizarre than his house, he hoped, this caught him unawares.

Once inside, he took off the down jacket she was wearing and hung it in his hall closet. He'd taken the coat from his luggage before leaving the airport, to keep her warm. Even so, he'd noticed how the cold had surprised her when they stepped outside. Perhaps it was the first time she'd ever felt cold during the daytime, he thought, as she shivered and blinked her eyes, staring around her, bewildered, as if looking for the source of this strange new sensation.

He steered her gently now through his sunken living room, allowing her to stop when she wanted, to look around or pick things up (a wooden ox, a small Greek jug). She pinched one of the snapdragons Caitlin had brought where they sat in a vase on a side table, along with the roses and lilies, and was rewarded with the sudden opening of a flowery mouth and a soft drift of pollen.

Jerry was thinking how different having Inez in his house was from being with her in Guatemala. Here she seemed alien, not only to her surroundings, but to his life. It helped a little that she was still dressed in standard teen wear — the pants and T-shirt she'd worn to the embassy. He touched her shoulder, more to reassure himself than her, then led her to the staircase.

On the way up, they passed masks he'd brought back from Africa, East Asian wall hangings, Chagall and Dali prints as well as posters for art exhibitions, and a couple of original works by talented friends. Inez ignored all of these but stopped in front of a portrait of Jerry, painted for him by a patient.

It was a good likeness, and Jerry assumed she recognized him, but she didn't look from it to him. She just stared, until at last Jerry led her towards what was to be her room.

She balked in the doorway, and he didn't force the issue. Had she even seen a bed before? "Bed," he said to her, moving into the room, patting the patchwork coverlet. "For sleeping." He made the conventional gesture, resting his head sideways on his praying hands. Inez looked puzzled and a little frightened, he thought.

God, she had so much to deal with. Even someone from an untroubled background would feel overwhelmed. He felt a little overwhelmed himself just thinking about what lay ahead.

He reached for her hand and led her into the room.

Sitting at Jerry's kitchen table, Dr. Ravi Banerjee was watching Inez eat.

Opening her mouth wide, she bit into a banana, chewed noisily, swallowed, then spat out the peel.

She was looking at him with what he interpreted as an expression of triumph — because she'd fought the peel and won, or because she knew what she was doing was disgusting to him? Unsure, Banerjee raised his eyebrows and managed a smile. "Why didn't she peel it, Jer? She must have eaten bananas before."

"I don't know. It's odd. I gave her one yesterday and she did peel it." Jerry popped a grape in his mouth as Inez spat out another wad of fruit.

Ravi leaned forward to pick the last piece of intact banana off the table.

Inez snatched it out of his reach like a starving animal and growled.

"Inez," said Jerry reprovingly, "Please. It's okay. Let me peel that for you."

He reached out a tentative hand and Inez spat at him then picked up her plate and threw it. It shattered into pieces on the tiles.

"Wow." Banerjee sat back in his chair. "Good luck teaching her table manners! Does she always do that when you try to show her how to eat?"

Jerry, down amongst the china, said, "That's the first time she's ever reacted like that. But then I never tried to take food away from her before."

"Do you think you'll keep her here much longer?"

"Not if I can help it." Jerry said it lightly but lowered his voice, just in case Inez understood. He stopped picking up broken crockery and sat back on his haunches. "She must be close to sensory overload as it is. Day after tomorrow, we have an appointment at Sick Kids for a complete examination. I'll also want at least one other psychiatrist to evaluate her. Then I'll see about a group home. She's doing remarkably well, considering that she's probably seen more of the world in the last day than she's seen in her whole life up to now. But she's already broken two of my best Oriental figurines. I've had to put away almost everything that isn't nailed down." He sighed. "She was so docile on the way to Canada, I really hoped this wouldn't be a problem."

The whole time he was speaking, he was aware of Inez scrutinizing him, even as she stuffed the last piece of banana into her mouth. Her gaze was more exploratory than bold, and Jerry wondered if she was feeling contrite.

"You should have known better than that, Jerry." Ravi laughed under the thin line of his moustache. "If you had kids …"

"I know." She'd had her moments, after all, in Guatemala. "I keep expecting too much of her. I don't know why." Jerry got up, threw the pieces of plate into the garbage, and sat down at the table.

"Uh-oh," said Ravi. "Not a good sign, Jer."

Jerry sat straighter in his chair. "Well, she *is* an adolescent, not a child, and clinically speaking, she exhibits some very promising traits." He said this in a clipped tone, crossed his legs, leaned forward, and put one forearm on the table.

"Indeed, Dr. Simpson." Ravi raised an eyebrow as Inez began picking at her teeth with her finger.

"Considering what she's been through, I think she's doing really well. Once you've been around her for a while, you begin to notice. She's full of enthusiasm sometimes. And, even more surprisingly, to me, at any rate, joy. She glows with it. Most abused children, and I've never seen one as severely traumatized as Inez, don't show half her resilience."

"Yes."

Inez continued to play with her food, smiling broadly, her eyes travelling from Jerry to Ravi.

"She does seem to have quite a capacity for enjoyment."

Inez smeared her face with banana and laughed.

Ravi laughed too, along with Jerry, who was reaching for a paper towel.

"You're an interesting young lady," Ravi said, wondering if he was right about the trace of mockery he saw in her actions.

It was the first time he had addressed her directly. She dropped her eyes. When she looked back up, her expression was solemn, incongruous above the mess on her cheeks.

"You're quite grown up, in your own way, aren't you?" said Ravi.

A smile spread across Inez's face. Still looking at her, Ravi addressed Jerry. "I don't know how much she understands, but that looks like a knowing smile to me."

Jerry nodded as Inez grabbed playfully for the hands wiping her cheeks. "I'm going to hire a live-in nurse next week," he said. "I have to get back to my practice."

"Good idea." Ravi took a sip of his coffee. "Quite a change for you, though, Jer. Where are you going to put the nurse? The servant's quarters?"

Jerry flushed. "Very funny, Ravi. The spare bedroom on the third floor. It's big and right next to Inez's. There's a window overlooking the back garden. It's private up there. They can work together uninterrupted in one of the other empty rooms. I'm hiring a psychiatric nurse."

"You're developing a program for her to follow with Inez?"

"I'm expecting the nurse to do that. I'm no expert on either autistic or feral children. They're a far cry from your usual analytic patient."

"True. So you'd better get someone good. Maybe ask Joseph Smythe at the hospital. He's been head of the psych department there for a long time. He knows the best nurses. And I've known him for years. He'll be discreet if you ask him to be. Solid as a rock, that man."

"I'll do that. It'll be a while before I can get her into a residential program. I understand there's a good one at Merryvale."

"It's excellent, that program. She'd probably do well there."

The next morning, Jerry woke up sad. He could recall only fragments from a dream — a deer running ahead of him through a forest, then showing up in a zoo. *Some regret about handing Inez over to other professionals, I'll wager*, he thought, bored by the mundane imagery. He got up, while Caitlin, who had spent the night beside him, slept on.

Staring out through the French doors opening onto his second floor balcony, Jerry's view of a lemony dawn was clouded by an onslaught of misery, much stronger than the residual sorrow of his dream. He thought again of Inez, how troubling she had been these last few days. How difficult. But sometimes, how touching.

Just the other day, he had been trying once again to slow her eating, when she'd put down her spoon, *beamed* at him, then touched his cheek. She held soft fingers there, shyly lowering her gaze, then picked up a slice of apple and held it out towards him almost reverently, as though it were a gift from the gods. Or *to* the gods, he thought uneasily.

He'd taken that somewhat brown and tired offering and eaten it while watching her watching him with the most intense and benevolent interest. The proffering of the food was something an infant would do; the look was that of a grateful adult.

Suddenly a picture of her face contorted with rage came to him and made him want to weep.

It seemed that every time he connected to her, Inez would become wild with anger, screaming and wailing, throwing everything she could get her hands on. It was the most disconcerting experience, even though it made complete sense. When, after all, had human contact brought her anything but pain? He remembered her trust in him on the plane, and the affection she had shown. The fact that she cared for him must be terrifying to her.

When she looked at him that certain way, it hooked into something deep inside and dragged it upwards, reminding him of the first time he'd seen her, of the impression she had made. He wasn't sure if it was a Grendel or a Neptune she snagged, but it tugged at his entrails, and it hurt.

Jerry climbed back into bed, curving himself around Caitlin, who snuggled her bottom into the bowl of his stomach, making him think of happier connections, of home.

"For you, Jer. It's your father." Caitlin held the phone out between two fingers. She'd been mixing muffins and was trying not to get flour on the receiver.

When he grimaced, she held her hand over the mouthpiece and whispered, grinning, "At least it's not Agnes."

Agnes was his most difficult patient. Her real name was Teresa. It was against medical ethics for him to discuss his clients, but he'd let it slip to Caitlin just how often this woman phoned. He'd called her Agnes to disguise her identity. She left messages on his office machine at all hours of the day or night. He allowed it because she was so troubled.

He smiled. "If I ever give her this number, shoot me, okay?" He took the receiver from her. "Hello, Dad, what's up?"

"What's up? Is that any way to greet your father?" The bantering tone held a threatening undercurrent.

"Uh-huh." Jerry said this in a small, bored voice. He felt drained of energy, as he often did around his father. "So, what's new?"

"You've got a pretty limited vocabulary for someone so overeducated, my boy. What's new is that I was thinking about you."

What's not new, thought Jerry, *is that you're trying to show me how truly great you are to care about me despite my many failings.* He picked at one of his shirt buttons.

"Just wanted to see how you were getting on in the head shrinking business. 'Course you're not really a shrink any more, are you? What's that you call yourself now? A psycho?"

Oh, Lord spare me. "A psychoanalyst, Dad." Jerry clenched his jaw. "Look, it's nice of you to call ..." *Good thing I'm not Pinocchio, I'd be breaking my nose on the opposite wall.* "Things are going pretty well here." There'd be time enough later to tell him about Inez. "How about you?"

"Oh, they're okay, I guess. Not much doing since your mother died."

No one handy to pick on, thought Jerry.

"But I'm doing okay. I watched the baseball last night, and tonight there's that TVO thing, *Mystery*. You watching that?"

Jerry warmed a little, glad of a connecting thread. "Sometimes. I saw the one about the alcoholic nurse who got murdered, last week. It was pretty good."

"Yes, not too bad. Glad you're keeping well. Regards to the ... almost said wife. Regards to Caitlin. And, Jerry, don't forget you're both welcome here any time."

"Thanks, Dad. We'd like to come, but you know how busy we get. I'll call you in a couple of weeks."

"Good enough. Goodbye, then."

"Bye, Dad."

Jerry hung up.

Caitlin shot him a sympathetic glance. "How's he doing?"

"Oh, same as ever. He's lonely, so he phones me up and insults me. It's a form of communication, I suppose."

Caitlin nodded. "No wonder he gets on your wick."

"Yup." Jerry hacked into an onion, sending a slice flying off the cutting board onto the floor.

Chapter Twenty

Caitlin's Story

Sadness was a genuine emotion, and I wasn't sure Doherty had any, so it gave me pause to think about him being down in the mouth at the fundraiser. But sad about me? I couldn't come up with any reason why he would be, except that I'd rebuffed him when he came on to me. But that didn't make a whole lot of sense. His ego might have taken a hit, but I doubted that would result in a fit of melancholy at the mention of my name.

In the end, I decided he might actually be sad about Jerry. Whatever I might think about Michael, he and Jerry had been friends. So maybe he was sad by association. Thinking about me made him think about Jerry. Ergo, sadness.

It was late in the evening, and I tuned my radio to the classical music station at very low volume, hoping to soothe my overheated brain before bed. They were playing Mahler.

Jerry and I had once gone to a Mahler concert at the O'Keefe Centre in Toronto. Coming out, he'd picked me up and twirled me in the air until I was dizzy. Hours later in his living room, he was still humming snatches of Mahler and interrupting conversations to conduct an invisible orchestra.

After Inez and Margaret moved in, Jerry and I went to see *Jules et Jim* at the local art cinema retrospective. Back at his place, Inez threw herself into Jerry's arms. He picked her up and twirled her in the air.

Afterwards, he took my face in his hands and said so seriously I had to stifle a laugh, "I'll always love you, Caitlin. No matter what."

"You mean I can take another lover and still keep you?" I said, pulling away and settling myself into an armchair. "Like the woman in the movie?"

He said, looking anywhere but at me, "Yes. Yes. No matter what."

Getting carried away was one of Jerry's more endearing qualities, but I thought it made him vulnerable. Everything touched him and left an impression. I knew he idolized Inez from the way he spoke to me about her right from the beginning. What if she had disappointed him and he hadn't been able to handle it, frightening her into defending herself? What if it really was a case of self-defence?

But what exactly would he have done? I couldn't picture it. Shouted at her, raised his hand, to keep the pain of disillusionment at bay? In the small hours of the morning, after yet another sleepless night, it just didn't ring true.

Later, when I tried to discuss this with Molly, she looked thoughtful and said, "Did you feel safe with Jerry?"

"Most of the time." I was thinking back to the night I'd spent at his place, early in our relationship, when I'd woken from a nightmare with my heart beating so hard, it hurt.

Jerry was humming "Plaisir d'Amour," a song we liked to sing together.

I rocked him gently back and forth, thinking the humming meant he was awake. One of my favourite memories of our trip through Central America was being comforted by Jerry after a bad dream, and I was looking forward to a repeat experience.

"Jerry, Jerry …" I whimpered.

"What?" he said, turning a puffy, irritable face towards me.

"I'm sorry. I had this really awful dream —"

"Oh, Christ!" he snarled. "Spare me. I'm tired." He turned his back and yanked the covers over to his side.

I yanked back. "Who do you think you are?"

He flopped around to face me. "I am," he said deliberately, as if talking to a very dim child, "an exhausted med student. I do not wish to interpret dreams in the middle of my own. Go to sleep, Caitlin."

"Jerry, I —"

He sat up abruptly. "Shut up, Caitlin," he said and pulled the sheet from under me, rolling me off the bed. "If you won't let me sleep in peace, go sleep on the couch."

I can laugh sometimes at the memory of myself, flat on my naked ass on the floor, but mostly I remember how scared I felt, and angry.

I did not move to the couch. I went back to my apartment, humiliated and confused.

He told me later that he didn't remember the details, only that he was desperate to go back to sleep. "Besides," he added, infuriatingly, "you were overdramatizing."

I supposed I had only half-woken him from a deep slumber, and he'd acted from instinct. Still, it bothered me.

After that, I steered clear of emotional appeals, and the incident receded in importance. There were so many other moments, close and warm and thrilling.

"Not always?" said Molly.

"Does anyone always make a person feel safe?" I retorted. "Think how boring they'd be if they did."

Molly'd had several love affairs. She said she didn't pine for them. "I always like the memories best," she'd confided to me. "I guess I'm a natural solitary. I'm glad I had those men in my life, though. It's just I prefer them in retrospect."

I wished I could be more like that. I don't think Molly was ever afraid the way I was that her lovers would leave her, or stop loving her, take up with other women, or even trade her in for a man. With Jerry, I'd felt safer than I'd ever thought possible.

I'd thought he did, too, until the day Molly said, almost in passing, "Did I ever tell you about the time Jerry cried because you were mad at him about something? I don't remember what it was, but I do remember he called me, and he had tears in his voice."

"He was really crying?"

"Yes," she replied. "His voice had a distinctly wet sound. He'd had a few drinks, I think. He was slurring his words. It was so unlike him. He said he wasn't sure you loved him any more."

"He said that?"

"Uh-huh."

"Did he say why he thought it?"

"No."

"Did you ask him?"

"No."

"Why not?"

"It wasn't about that."

"What was it about, then?"

"How he felt."

"Were you able to reassure him?"

"I think so, Cat. I told him you did love him, that I knew it. He seemed to be consoled by that. When he rang off, he sounded more cheerful."

That conversation made me wonder about the secret places — some possibly immense, even the smaller ones important — inside this man I thought I knew so well. And though I felt hugely grateful to Molly for reassuring Jerry that I loved him, it did nothing to help me believe that the feeling had been mutual at the time of his death.

I'd been struggling, ever since it happened, to come to terms with the terrible argument I'd had with Jerry on the day he was killed. I'd never confided in anyone about it, because my heart broke every time I thought of it. I loved him so much. I couldn't bear the thought that he might have died despising me.

And how might our argument have affected his dealings with Inez? I would never know. It may not have affected them at all, but I would never know, and that in itself nearly drove me mad.

The morning of the day he'd died, I'd interviewed a woman for an article on psychiatric survivors for *Mental Health News*. Her name was Marla.

She and I sat across from each other at a card table in her dreary rented room, drinking watery coffee. I wished I'd thought to bring some buns or muffins. She had a lean and hungry — and impoverished — look. When I asked what she'd been through, she leaned forward and slid her low-cut blouse off one shoulder. It could have been a seductive gesture. I pulled back, perplexed.

But she had other things in mind. "Look," she said. "See these scars?" She touched her thumb to an arc of thick white cicatrices near the top of her arm. "I got them from a shrink who admitted me at Scarborough Lakes."

"What happened?"

"I bit him."

That didn't explain *her* scars. My next thought was that he'd bitten her back, but he'd have to have had a mouth the size of a deep sea bass to leave an arc that big.

"Yeah, when no one was looking, he dug his fingernails into my shoulder, holding me down until the orderlies came. Big, hulking guy he was."

For some reason unknown to me, I responded to this with a flip, "Maybe he wasn't too thrilled about being bitten."

"*I* was delusional," she said, covering her scars as she leaned back and crossed her arms. "*He* wasn't." Then I couldn't get anything more out of her.

I regretted that. I wanted to know more about this willowy six-footer with a fighting spirit, gouges on her shoulder, and the mind of a wild animal, at whose power and dark corners I could only guess. I wasn't surprised she'd clashed with a discipline that professed to understand but could also misunderstand so profoundly, it made common sense look brilliant. The excesses of almost anything interest me. But the excesses of psychiatry, partly because of Jerry, interest me the most.

I had gone home angry.

When Jerry came over to share tea and scones, I was still angry. We were on my balcony. Watering my plants usually had a calming effect, but not that day.

"Don't you think there's something odd about offering love in psychotherapy?" I said, sloshing too much water into a potted begonia. "You know if a patient was in need outside the hour, you'd put them off."

"I don't always put them off, Caitlin." He slapped his magazine down and pinched his lips together in a way that gave new meaning to anal retentive. "But who says I offer them love?"

"It's implied." I straightened, holding my watering can tight to my chest. "Isn't it?" I pinched off a dead pansy blossom as though it were the head of an enemy. "You re-create the parent-child relationship, with you as the parent," I said. "The loving, caring parent. But you know you're not going to bail your patients out if they lose their jobs and can't pay the rent, or even want to call you at midnight because they're really scared. I know you can care about them, but not in the sense of taking responsibility for them."

I bent to the plants again. "Aren't you setting them up for the same traumas they went through growing up?" I said into the fronds of a deck tomato.

"In a sense, yes, I suppose. But there's a false premise behind what you're saying."

"And that is ..." I twisted my head to look at him.

"That love can be given in only one way." He shifted in his chair to get a better look at me. "I do care about my patients' development, even the ones I'm not all that fond of. But I'm not about to have them move in with me, or go for walks with them when they feel bad. They know that, and it does cause problems for them. But what do you suggest? That I don't offer them even the limited caring I can? What good is that? I've seen lots of patients get better just because I wish them well, and really listen to them for a couple of hours a week. It may upset them that I don't love them above all others, that I'm not married to them, or really their father, whatever — but that's part of the process. They can work things out with me they couldn't with a lover or a parent —"

As I listened, I watched his eyes. I found his gaze behind the words seductive, and my throat began to morph into that strange state that is both thick and fragile, the state that can precede either desire or tears. I wasn't sure which one I was headed for, but neither was welcome. We hadn't made love in weeks. "There's a lie at the heart of psychotherapy," I said to stop the melting.

"Yes, there is." The heat in his eyes didn't diminish. "And it drives patients crazy. But I recognize that, Caitlin, and, believe me, it makes a difference. Perhaps ..." he watched me pull weeds, "... it's a bit like growing a garden. A good gardener tends her plants with a loving hand but wouldn't give her life for them."

He's talking about people as if they don't have any feelings at all, I thought with a sudden surge of anger. *Like you can pick them up and put them down at will.* "It's not the same at all. What I'm talking about is a form of treachery. You want your patients to believe you care for them, and yet they know that you wouldn't lift a finger if they got in trouble outside the hour. So how is that true caring, and how are they not supposed to feel betrayed?"

The warmth left his eyes. "You're being a little insulting, Cat. Watching you garden is distracting, by the way. You're very nurturing. I try to be the same with clients." He snapped his magazine open and pretended to read.

He didn't even think I was worth talking to? "Stop being an asshole," I said.

He looked up, his eyes wide. "What's this really about, Cat?" he said. "The way I am in therapy, or the fact that your mother didn't want you?"

I gasped. "You bastard," I said.

"I'm not being a bastard. I just think you're old enough to understand where you're coming from without taking it out on me."

I wanted to scream, "She *did* want me! She just wanted Ireland more!" but instead I felt tears clog my throat and fill my eyes. "You are a bastard," I said, "or you wouldn't have said it that way. What's the matter with you anyway?"

"Nothing is the matter with me." Jerry's snapped his magazine again. "Except that I don't like being blamed for something somebody else did."

"That's ridiculous," I said. "I didn't even know until I was eighteen that she'd handed me off to my dad. By the time I found out about her, it was too late to have much effect."

My dad had met my mom when they'd worked side by side as letter sorters at the Irish Post Office. They were both nineteen, and Catholic. My dad wanted to be a musician and spent his off-hours in the clubs, playing Irish folk music with his mates. Apparently, according to him, anyway, my mum didn't show much of an ambition for anything. They became friends mostly because of proximity; she followed him along to the clubs, talked vaguely of becoming a nun "to do some good in the world" while simultaneously mocking his heartfelt, unexamined faith, and making a case for "free love" whenever the mood took her. She slept with him, he swears, less out of love than curiosity.

"You know I thought my mom was dead until I was practically an adult," I said. "By the time I learned differently, it was too late to feel anything but surprised."

Jerry was looking at me with a superior little smile on his face.

"What are you smirking about?" I said.

"'Anything but surprised'?" he said, his tone scathing. "Sometimes, Caitlin, you can be so dishonest with yourself, it's shocking. Especially with your much-repeated ambition to 'see life as it is.'"

"I am seeing life as it is. You're the one putting a funny twist on it, not me."

My dad told me, when he finally had to, that my mum had never said she was pregnant — or maybe she didn't know. His family decided to emigrate to Canada, and they wanted him to go with them. She said it was all right by her, but to be sure to write.

They parted with kisses but without tears. My father kept writing, and she wrote back for a while, with never a word about me. Then she stopped writing altogether. My father was busy with his new band, an Irish Rovers-type outfit that was already doing well because of the Irish thing. There was no shortage of young ladies interested in him, he told me. Life moves on, as they say.

When I told Jerry about it, he'd actually laughed, saying it was an incredible story that made me more interesting. Now he was looking at me with raised eyebrows and an expression of disbelief.

"Well, *okay*," I said. "Maybe it did mess me up a bit, but that's not what I was talking about today. I was talking about your peculiar profession."

"Oh, yes," said Jerry. "And attacking my ethics for no good reason that I can see. Other than that you kept mentioning 'parents' and 'responsibility' and unkept promises. I think you're lucky I saw through you, to be honest."

Damn. He had a point. "But my dad loved me a lot," I said. "Suzie was my mother in all the ways that count, and she loved me too. So why the heck would I care what Erin O'Grady did a hundred years ago?"

I could tell by the set of his mouth that Jerry was really angry. I wasn't sure why. I'd been on the brink of an apology.

"Your father is a saint," he said tersely.

He was right about that. No one knew he was the father, and never would have, if he hadn't come forward of his own volition. That's why he's my hero. He was only nineteen, a continent away, and had no deep love for my mother. He only found out about me because the mothers kept in touch. He was a Catholic lad with strict Catholic parents, but when he heard my mum was planning to put me up for adoption, he told his mother that he was that baby's father, and he wanted his child. He didn't particularly want to marry its mother, mind you, but if that was part of the deal, he'd take that on, too. He admitted he was greatly relieved to hear my mother would have none of him, but she was glad he wanted the baby, a little girl, Caitlin — me. It was a long and complicated procedure, but because my paternal grandparents offered to be my legal guardians, the papers went through, and Baby Girl Caitlin arrived in Toronto about three months later.

"You know what he did for me," I said to Jerry. "You don't need to imply he'd have to be saint to love me."

That really set him off. "Oh, for god's sake, Caitlin, drop it, would you? Just grow up. If you can't see that what happened with your mom hurt you, then I give up."

In her revelatory letter, my mother had told me her story, said she was now an MP in Ireland, and invited me over to meet her. She offered to pay my fare.

Of course, I went. After I got over the shock.

I found a smart, driven woman who had never married and never had another child. She told me she hadn't wanted to interfere with my life, though she'd kept in touch with my dad and helped out financially, as soon as she could. He didn't really need her money. It was a matter of honour, she said. Which made me wince, I'm not sure why.

She claimed she'd wanted to be more involved with my upbringing earlier on but didn't think it was fair to me. My dad had agreed, apparently asking her to keep her distance.

"I know she cares more about Ireland than about being my mother," I said. "But that makes sense to me. She's a rare breed, and Ireland deserves her more than I do."

Jerry's eyes narrowed, and he gave a derisive little snort. "That is just so ridiculous, Cat. You expect me to believe that you think a country deserves your mother's love more than you, her only child? Give me a break."

He's right, I thought. Now pride got in the way. I felt really stupid but didn't want him to know. "That's not the issue here," I said. "I was talking about something else entirely, and you decided to dodge the whole topic with some free psychoanalysis which I did not ask for and don't want."

He didn't say a word, but his eyes were shooting flames and his mouth was set in a line so tight, I thought his lips might disappear.

His coldness shook me, and I could feel my anger rising again to dangerous levels. "You're jealous," I said, blinking back tears. "Because your father is an abusive, insulting asshole, and my father loves me, he *loves* me —" My eyes spilled over, and I crossed my palms over my mouth to hide my trembling lips.

"I'm sorry, Cat," Jerry said, and by the sea change in his eyes, I knew he meant it. "Of course your father loves you. I'm under a lot of stress, and you sounded so accusing. I'm not the only one who gets nasty under pressure."

I knew he was right, but my heart felt like a stone in my chest. When he reached out a hand to me and I took it, the hurt was still keen, and tears still blurred my vision.

"I didn't mean it," he said. "About your mother not wanting you."

"But she didn't want me. So you were being cruel."

"I was. And I'm sorry."

"You wouldn't do that to a patient," I cried. "Can't you treat me at least as well as you treat them? You wouldn't talk to Inez like that."

"Inez," he said in measured tones, "isn't a patient. Besides, she would not insult me the way you did, implying that I don't really care about my analysands. About whom, by the way, if it's any consolation, I am not always as forbearing as I should be. Despite the fact that I *do care* about them."

"You care about *her*," I said. "Sometimes lately I think that's *all* you care about. How do you know that deep down she doesn't think you're as much of a jerk as I do?"

"Is that was this is about? Not your mother, after all, but a defenceless, traumatized, wounded innocent? I'm disappointed in you, Cat, I can't begin to tell you how much." He closed his magazine and got up from his chair.

"I didn't mean it, Jerry. I'm sorry."

"You can be as sorry as you like for as long as you like. Maybe it will do you some good. I'll leave you alone to wallow in it."

Chapter Twenty-One

Jerry/Margaret
Toronto, April, 1983

Margaret Richards put the last touches of makeup on her pale, freckled face, squiggled skinny fingers through her shoulder-length red curls, and headed for the door.

She was on her way to an interview with Dr. Jerry Simpson about his troubled charge.

The previous week, Dr. Smythe had made an announcement during one of their floor meetings. He said Dr. Simpson needed help with an abused Guatemalan girl who showed signs of possible autism. He said he couldn't go into more detail at that time.

Margaret found this intriguing. She went up to him after the meeting to get more information. He repeated that he couldn't say much, which was also enticing.

"Not until I'm sure you're serious about this," he said. "And even then, you're sworn to secrecy."

"I'm serious," said Margaret, because now she was.

Autistics were Margaret's specialty; travel was her passion. She'd spent a year nursing in Africa and had travelled to India and Nepal. Canada sometimes seemed barren and materialistic to her now, its people bland, even smug. She'd never been to Central America, but she'd read about it. The Mayans appealed to her, and when Joseph Smythe described the political situation in Guatemala, and the condition in which Inez had been found, she knew she wanted the job.

When Dr. Simpson opened the door to her knock on Freud's chin, she was glad she'd come, for a far more visceral reason. As she looked him over, she mused, *Good genes. Rich, too.*

She held out her hand, and Jerry shook it. *Oh, shit. So what if I'm twenty-nine and unattached? Am I going to start slavering every time I see an eligible male?*

Behind the smile plastered on her face ran a stream of familiar thoughts. She wasn't even sure she *wanted* a partner, for god's sake, not when she'd seen what happened to her formerly interesting friends, who now discussed mortgages and income tax with the fervour formerly reserved for good books and foreign countries. It was children she craved, not husbands, she reminded herself. Some day. *All that takes is a sperm donor, or the right adoption agency, so there's no need to ogle every available man, is there?*

Jerry's casually elegant clothing — a V-neck mohair sweater over a white shirt, and slacks — said to her that he was likely easy to get along with. *Though the look is maybe a little too studied, a little too artfully laid back…. Could be the hand of a woman behind it, could be he's dressed by a girlfriend….*

"Dr. Simpson? I'm Margaret Richards. I'm here for my interview."

"Ah, yes. Pleased to meet you, Ms. Richards."

Most people, thought Margaret approvingly, asked what

title you preferred, instead of using Ms. as it was intended, a replacement for Miss or Mrs. rather than a brand name for feminism. "You can call me Margaret. I'd prefer it."

She followed him into his office, where everything looked expensive — tasteful, too. She'd have liked to run her hand over the rich ebony and mahogany of his desk.

This office — and that desk — they're a lot more formal than he is. It's nice in here, though, she thought. *He's chosen warm woods. The whole place seems warm. It almost smells warm.*

There weren't any windows. The fireplace, though unlit, created a peaceful cosiness in the midst of the showy decor.

"Your desk is lovely," Margaret said, touching it lightly. "Mahogany is such a gorgeous wood." She noted Jerry's smile.

"Thank you," he said. "Have a seat."

Margaret did, in the white leather chair Jerry indicated. It was tall-backed, straight, and armless, with a seat as soft as butter. Its padded back pressed against hers like a steadying hand.

"Did Dr. Smythe fill you in on the details of this position?"

"Yes, he did, Dr. Simpson." She crossed her legs and straightened the skirt of her denim dress. "I understand you have brought back a girl from Guatemala who was horribly mistreated and could be both autistic and emotionally disturbed, and that you are looking for a psychiatric nurse who can live in. Also, that it is necessary to be discreet."

"Yes," he said. "I don't want a media circus. There have been too many cases of feral children exploited by doctors, as I'm sure you know."

"I'm interested in the position because I'm interested in autistics, not ferals so much, though of course that is fascinating," Margaret said. "But I'm not at all into publicity or experiments of any kind. I'm a nurse, not a scientist or novelty-seeker. I think I have a special feeling for autistics, that's all." Margaret was surprised to feel warmth rise into her face and quickly looked down at her thin, freckled hands.

"Go on."

"I had an autistic friend when I was a girl." She frowned, debating how much to reveal. "He was a little older than me. I — uh — I loved him." *Damn, she hadn't meant to say that.*

"You loved him?" echoed Jerry, and Margaret recognized the psychiatric technique, the implicit encouragement to go on. She smiled at that rather than at his question.

"Yes. He was ... um ... mysterious to me. At that time. I was only a child myself. He seemed to be in touch with another reality, in a way." She stopped. How was Jerry taking this? If he was as cut and dried as most medical men, despite the artistic desk, she could be talking herself out of a job.

"That's a very romantic attitude to autism," he said.

Just what she'd expected, but she hadn't expected the lack of criticism in his tone.

"Yes, I know. I was only a little girl." A glancing pause. "Tell me about Inez."

"Inez is mysterious, too, Margaret. But she is also, at times, angry and destructive."

"I can imagine. I worked with autistic children, even before I became a nurse."

"Your work experience ...?"

"I worked for three years at the Muki Baum Centre for Disturbed and Autistic Children, here in Toronto. I've also worked with Vanier homes where, as you know, most of the residents are mentally challenged, but some are autistic, also, or emotionally troubled. As a psychiatric nurse, I've handled many hospitalized disturbed children, both at Mt. Sinai and Lakeshore Psychiatric."

"How about young adults? Inez is possibly in her late teens."

Margaret shook her head. "Not a lot. The Vanier autistics

were mostly adult, but I didn't work specifically with them."

"And currently?" Jerry flipped a page on her resume.

"Currently, I'm working at Prince William." *And hating it, but I'd better not say so.*

"Why would you like to switch from hospital work to caring for Inez?"

That one was easy. "I prefer to work one on one, Dr. Simpson. In a hospital setting, there are so many patients, you can't really get to know them. It's not a residential hospital, so they come and go quite quickly, too. I like to develop relationships with the people I work with, and there's not much opportunity to do that." *And there's always the damn hierarchy to deal with,* she added to herself. *The "drug these patients and keep them out of my hair" doctors, among others. And the sense of futility. How can you hope to change someone's psychology, if you can't even change the rules in your department?*

Jerry looked up from her resume. "What if Inez is not autistic? We have no firm diagnosis, and many of her characteristics don't fit the usual description of autism. If she is mentally challenged, or emotionally disturbed, or both, would you be able to deal with that? Would you want to?"

Margaret nodded. "Yes, I would. As I mentioned, at Vanier and Muki Baum, I met and worked with my share of children like that. Whatever is troubling Inez would interest me. If she's traumatized, I would love to help her. If she is slow, I think I have the skills to work with her." She smiled. "I'm quite fascinated by her story. And I welcome the chance to help her in any way I can."

"Would you like to meet her?"

"Yes, of course."

"Just a minute, and I'll get her."

While Jerry was gone, Margaret stared round the office, noting the shelves of books, the small Chinese statues behind the glass doors of an exotic ebony cabinet, the long-necked lamps protruding like tentacles from the walls, the framed Chagalls. She was confident of her skills with troubled children, but not sure how to demonstrate them in this setting, or quite what to do with an adolescent. *I hope I like Inez*, she thought, twining her fingers together in her lap and double-wrapping one long, thin leg around the other.

Inez came in on Jerry's arm. In her gauzy Indian cotton dress, she looked frail, and her arresting eyes had a haunted look. Margaret was intrigued to see in them the same luminosity she remembered from her friend Anthony. Inez wasn't as beautiful as Anthony had been, with his lustrous dark hair, pale skin, and classic Greek features; still, she was lovely, and the spirit was similar. It was the spirit that had so entranced Margaret in her youth. She could think of no other words for it but purity of heart.

"This must be Inez."

"Yes. Inez, this is Margaret. She may work with us."

Inez sat down in the white chair. Margaret dropped to one knee in front of her.

"Hello, Inez," she said, and held a hand in front of her face, peeking through the fingers.

Inez flashed a smile and fanned her own hand open.

"Hand," said Margaret, surprised by the simple pleasure on the girl's face.

And when Inez held the nurse's hand to her cheek, Margaret hoped Jerry thought she, Margaret, was absolutely brilliant. If she had knowingly elicited Inez's reaction, she would have thought so herself, but all she'd been going on was how Anthony used to love watching hands move, and how an autistic adult at Vanier Homes enjoyed playing peek-a-boo.

Jerry beamed. "She seems to like you," he said.

"For now." He must know how mercurial these people were. "She might hate me in a second. But her responsiveness is encouraging."

"Watch her now, though," said Jerry.

Margaret saw Inez's eyes turn vacant. Her mouth slackened, though she still sat as straight as the high-backed chair.

"That's not unusual, if she's autistic. They're more often like that than the way she was a few moments ago." Though she was speaking to Jerry, her eyes were on Inez. The girl came awake and returned her gaze. Margaret had the sense of being looked into, as though her most secret parts were seen and assessed. Yet the girl radiated benevolence.

Margaret was moved and intrigued and wanted to touch Inez but stopped herself.

She felt Jerry's eyes on her and said, "It's rare to see the amount of connection she's displaying now." Was she pontificating? He worked as an analyst, not a psychiatrist, but she thought he probably knew the symptoms of autism well enough.

"She's often like that." Margaret heard excitement in Jerry's voice. "It's more natural for her than the tempers and the withdrawals, I'm sure of it."

"You believe in this girl, don't you?" she said, looking directly at him. "You really want to help her. So do I."

After Jerry offered her the job, Margaret walked home so fast, she figured an onlooker might think she was in urgent need of a bathroom. As soon as she got in the door, she made herself macaroni and cheese out of a box — a dish she loved but rarely admitted to eating, especially to other nurses. Plunking her bowl down on the kitchen table, she pulled her notebook out of the skinny black tote she took with her everywhere and started writing.

Behaviour Mod works best with autistic children under age four. That's not Inez, but her mental age may be young enough to make it worth considering as an approach. BUT Behaviour Mod is tough love, in some ways. Inez too damaged? Too hurt? Might interpret therapist as cruel — THE OPPRESSOR.

Is Inez truly autistic? Not with that eye contact! But may be in the autistic spectrum.

At the interview, she'd asked Jerry, "Why are you waiting so long to have her tested?"

"Because," he'd said, "I want her to be at her best. Just think how disoriented you'd be if you'd been spirited away by a stranger to a strange land, after living for years in what amounted to a damn box, let alone whatever other horrors she's had to face. It will take her at least a few weeks to find her feet."

He has empathy, she thought. *Ah, hell. Probably has a dozen girlfriends.*

She knew he wasn't married, because she'd asked around about him. And at somewhere near forty, which she guessed him to be, that was not a particularly good sign, as far as she was concerned. Maybe he was gay. Maybe he was impossible.

Oh, stop it, she admonished herself. *The longest relationship you've ever had lasted two years, and even that was too long. Give it up. You have no luck with men at all. Why would he be any different? Damn, where was I? Inez looks like she could learn from behaviour mod, but I'm afraid it's not supportive enough for her. So … modified behaviour mod.* She smiled. *Modification modified. I'm not so sure that can be done.*

She got up, suddenly restless.

What Inez needs is love.

Love from her nurse? Well, now, that's a slippery slope. Working with autistic kids usually meant you had to be made of steel, strong enough to listen to a child's panicked shrieking without backing down. Or getting angry. Strong enough to insist that the child enter the therapist's world.

But an abused teen was different. Surely you could afford to indulge your softer side, and you probably needed to.

Oh, Lord, I don't know. Margaret paced the room, barely hearing the mournful hoot of the six p.m. commuter train in the distance. *I'll have to spend a lot of time just getting her to feel safe with me,* she thought. *Though if, as Dr. Simpson says, she's trusting already, I'm not even sure about that.* She continued to pace, almost bumping into a patchwork beanbag chair, brushing past a Starhawk poster on the door. *Well, I'll play that part by ear.*

She sat down. *Establish trust as necessary,* she jotted in her notes. *Then begin gentle behaviour mod.*

She went to the Old Ontario box cupboard in her bedroom and drew out the toys she used to coax her young patients into the everyday world — wind-up toys, clockwork soldiers, hopping frogs, balls like jelly candies.

Was it fair, she sometimes mused, to entice a child into consensual reality using such fanciful things?

A week later, she was standing in the room Jerry had assigned her. It was up inside the roof. The steep slant of the lemon yellow walls made her think of rays of sunshine. The four poster bed was both grand and cozy, with its curtained canopy and elaborate brass headboard, enamelled white.

She slowly unpacked the first of her suitcases, wondering how long she'd actually be in this place. Jerry had forewarned her of his plan to send Inez to a residential facility, perhaps within a few months. She was disappointed but determined to take the job anyway, though at the interview she'd been afraid it would make her seem unstable, throwing over a well-paid position for something that might not last past summer. But Dr. Simpson hadn't said so, and he'd hired her after all.

The insecurity of the position had its advantages, from her point of view. She'd already decided she wanted to be footloose for the next few years, staying on a job if she was needed, and she liked it, moving on if neither was the case; probably travelling to other countries again; taking courses; exploring all possibilities; finding out, before it was too late, if she was already where she wanted to be — and figuring out how to change direction if she wasn't. She thought of the next few years almost as a last fling before settling down, in whatever form that might take for her.

She tossed the last of her long gauze skirts onto a hanger, unfurled her Chinese paper parasol and placed it in front of the bedside lamp to cast a turquoise glow. Then she unpacked her books, a tumble of craft manuals, nursing texts, New Age philosophy, psychology. She put them in thematic piles on the built-in bookcase, as white as the enamelled bedposts.

There. I've done enough for one night.

She lay back on the bed, her arms behind her head. *It's a pretty room*, she thought. She liked the olive green love seat near the window and the small writing table with its matching chair.

She'd look in on Inez in the morning. She'd suggested to Jerry, who had rejected the idea, that she and the girl sleep in the same room. "Though it depends on the degree of her autism," she'd explained. "If it's severe enough, it might be good for her to be around someone as close to twenty-four hours a day as possible."

"You're sure of that?" he'd said.

"I've heard it can help."

Two weeks had passed since that conversation. She wondered how long it would take her to feel at home. *Probably till just before I have to leave!*

———

The room Jerry had set aside for their work was almost exactly as Margaret had hoped, big but homey, with dusky pink walls, soft carpeting, loads of colourful cushions, and a picture window overlooking a large elm in the backyard.

"Come and let me hold you, Inez," said Margaret, her arms wide.

With a joyful leap, the girl was beside her amongst the cushions. She burrowed her face into Margaret's chest and laughed.

Wow. Guess I don't need to spend time teaching Inez about touch, Margaret thought as she stroked the girl's head. *But she's very puzzling. She simply does not show many of the common autistic symptoms.* She took Inez's face in her hands and looked into the translucent, soft gaze of her charge. Most autistic patients had to be taught to relate to others, carefully acclimatized to physical caresses.

Behaviour mod often worked well with these patients, if you could harden yourself to their initial screams. But Margaret thought of high functioning autistic adults she knew, who could graphically describe the horror they still felt at physical closeness, and she wondered what really went on inside these kids as they were "cured." Was human touch ever truly welcome to them?

Margaret kissed the top of Inez's head. It couldn't hurt, could it, to give comfort to someone who had been so badly treated, autistic or not? *What I really need to work out,* she decided, *are Inez's "triggers," what makes her scream, or cry, or become destructive.*

"Now it's learning time, Inez," she said, extricating herself from the girl's embrace. She took Inez's hand. "Come with me."

Inez stayed as close to Margaret as a hungry puppy before sitting in the chair the nurse pulled out. Margaret sat across from her at the table, placing a rag doll and some chocolate chip cookies from her bag in the lap of her filmy skirt.

She held up the small stuffed doll. "See this, Inez? It's called a *doll*," she said, but Inez continued to stare at the opposite wall.

"Look at me," Margaret began gently. No response. "Look at me," she repeated more firmly, and louder, touching Inez lightly on the chin and drawing her head downwards.

Inez stared straight into her nurse's eyes with a look so loving, Margaret caught her breath. *I don't deserve such love*, she thought. She had to struggle not to turn away.

"Good girl, Inez. Good looking!" She offered her charge a small piece of chewy cookie — a treat she knew Inez adored, one of the few Western foods she was allowed.

Inez smiled and reached for the cookie. "*Good girl, Inez. Good looking!*" she said.

Margaret sat bolt upright in surprise. Not only had the girl spoken, she had spoken in Margaret's voice, exactly, as though she were a human tape recorder.

"Inez?" she said. "Do that again."

"Inez? Do that again."

Same tone, same inflection, Margaret's voice came back at her clearer than an echo.

She held the doll out again. "This is a doll."

Inez sat still and said nothing.

"D-oll," Margaret enunciated slowly. "Can you say d-oll?" Then she released Inez. "If you say it, I will give you the doll."

Inez looked away.

I wonder if she's frightened to do anything more than imitate. "Look at me, Inez," she said again, turning the girl's face back towards her and rewarding her with a piece of cookie. "Doll," she said again. "Say doll."

Inez screamed.

Margaret jumped in her seat. Was it the demand to speak, the doll, too much stress? The screams grew wilder, and Inez began pulling her hair. She screamed until her face turned crimson. Margaret swallowed panic and continued with the lesson, as she'd been trained to do.

"Look at me," she repeated, over and over. "Look at me!"

Finally, Inez turned her terror-stricken gaze to Margaret and slapped the young woman's outstretched hand so hard that the proffered cookie flew high into the air.

"Good looking, Inez," said Margaret calmly. "I like that good looking."

Inez continued to scream.

"Is that really helping her?" queried Jerry after the session. They were sitting in the solarium. Margaret had sheets of notes spread on her lap. "She screamed for ten minutes straight, Margaret. If you hadn't made me promise not to interfere, I'd have been in there like a shot."

"I *want* you to come in later." Margaret leaned back in the green wicker chair, making it squeak, and twitched her arm away from a loose bit of raffia. "But the first sessions are usually the hardest. It's tough to watch if you're not used to the approach. Besides, you're a psychoanalyst."

Jerry smiled. "True. I am. I'd rather know the source of Inez's terror than force her to suppress it."

"So would I, Dr. Simpson," said Margaret wearily.

Perhaps she'd been foolish to think that her pragmatic approach would be acceptable to a psychoanalyst. Their worldviews were completely different. She looked down at her patterned skirt and fiddled with the material. The heavy scent of the pink and blue hyacinths scattered throughout the room felt oppressive. *Maybe if he only had one plant …*

"I should tell you," she said, "that Inez spoke today."

Jerry raised his eyebrows then lowered them into a frown. "She spoke? What did she say?"

"She repeated something I'd said. 'Good looking,' or something. Her voice sounded exactly like mine."

"That's amazing."

"I know. At least we know she's capable of speech, but she was imitating me. She's a brilliant mimic, by the way."

"Have you ever run across anything similar in other patients?"

Margaret nodded. "Yes. Twice. Both boys. They parroted what other people said to them. Sometimes they did it almost simultaneously with the person who was speaking."

"Immediate Echolalia," said Jerry, rubbing his chin and frowning. "A symptom of, among other things, autism. Mimicry is sometimes seen in behaviour disorders."

"It can also result from a head trauma."

"Or it can be a talent." Jerry was smiling now, and Margaret smiled back.

"True. It's so easy to over-pathologize, isn't it?"

"Uh-huh. But, sad to say, I'm not sure that's the case here, only that she may be talented in addition to whatever else is going on with her. Did the boys you were talking about ever speak as themselves?"

"No. They were diagnosed as severely autistic, but neither of them really fit any clinical condition. A lot of kids who are different are like that. I guess you know what an inexact science diagnosis is, especially when it comes to mental health."

Jerry did know. The terms and definitions in *The Diagnostic and Statistical Manual of Mental Disorders*, the bible of clinical psychiatry, changed constantly. "I think it's a good sign that she spoke in your presence, even if it was just mimicry. She's never done that with me or anyone else here."

Margaret nodded. "But," she said, "and it's a big but — kids who only mimic and don't speak as themselves sometimes do it because they don't know who they are."

"I understand." All vestiges of a smile left Jerry's face. "They can't do anything but copy because they are not in touch with their own feelings —"

"Or opinions. Or thoughts. Or anything. If that's the case with Inez, it could take years to reach her ..."

"And we have only months, at the most." He looked at her with regret. "It's best not to expect too much. The waiting list at Merryvale is long, but I should think they will have a place for her within a year. It's a shame to send her away, really, but I think I have no choice. It's a good program there, and she'd benefit from it."

"Does Inez know of your plans?"

Jerry shook his head and said gently, "How could she, really?"

"She could sense it. Perhaps not now, but as the time comes closer. You realize, of course, it will be very upsetting to her to be moved?"

"I do. If there was anything else I could do, I would do it."

"You have me now, and there are others who would help her, I'm sure, once she's been here a little longer ..."

Jerry's brow creased. "I just ... don't know. About her living here, I mean ... but I'll think about it. In the meantime, I know you will do your best with her. I should tell you that I'm not as opposed to what you're doing as you might think. I know understanding has its limits. Actually ..." She noticed a distant look in his eyes even as his voice became friendlier. "I was very sad when I found that out was the case."

"Why?" She had a mental flash of herself at the Muki Baum home, crying to one of her supervisors, "I've given her everything

I've got. I've listened to her, and loved her, and tried so hard to enter her world, day after day, for months. She doesn't respond to me at all. There's nothing I can do to help her!" And her supervisor, answering, "Perhaps there is" ... marking the start of her education in Behaviour Mod.

Jerry addressed her question. "Because both my training and my nature tend towards understanding and empathy. It's hard to explain, but when I run across cases where the psychodynamic approach really isn't what's called for, it upsets my worldview."

She had to clench her teeth to stop her mouth from falling open. Jerry pushed his hands into the pockets of his khaki pants and tightened his lips. *Does that mean he's closing off?*

"I suppose I need to believe in a world where love matters," he said.

Guess not! Margaret wasn't sure what to make of this degree of openness between employee and employer, but she smiled at him encouragingly. "Me too, Dr. Simpson."

"Jerry," he invited.

She drew her head back involuntarily. "Maybe this will surprise you, but I feel much the same way," she said. "Especially about autistic children. There's often something touching, almost angelic about them. When you start to train them as I do, you lose touch with that. You have to. You have to reject their autism — all of it — in order to bring them into our reality. But it's a real loss, all the same."

"How so?"

"I'm sure you can imagine," she countered, afraid to lose his attention by stating the obvious.

"Not really. I know how *I* feel about it, but I'd like to find out what it means to you."

How very psychoanalytic, she thought but heard enough interest in his tone to encourage a genuine answer. "I ... uh ..."

She twirled one hand in the air in front of her mouth, as though trying to put a spin on her words. "Because," she began again, "because there *is* something beautiful about autism. I don't know how else to say it. Because some autistic people — and Inez is like this, I think — really do live in a different world from ours, and in many ways it's an interesting, unique, and valid world. A world we're missing out on. When I focus on training Inez to live in our world, I'm afraid I'm doing violence to that part of her.

"But, Dr. Simpson — I mean, Jerry — most autistics are *not* happy. And though they do lose something when they return to us —" *When we force them to return*, she thought sadly "— I hope I'm never guilty of underestimating their difficulties if they stay as they are. Can you imagine having people stare at you wherever you go? You can't get work, people make fun of you. Autistics may not be the most social of people, but, especially if they're high-functioning, they feel this, it gets to them. They gain so much from treatment that it seems selfish not to use my skills with them."

"Even with Inez?"

"Of course, with Inez. She is wonderful, touching, magical, but that sadness, that pain inside — that's real, too." She was punching one knee lightly as she spoke. "I've seen a lot of autistic adults. Many seem unhappy. Some are mentally challenged. They simply cannot take care of themselves. Inez shows strong signs of what we consider normal emotions. If she is not autistic, they must still be worked with, to bring out —"

"I don't think she's slow-witted, do you?"

"No, I don't." She was surprised by the question. "I was speaking very generally. She actually seems highly intelligent to me. But I could be wrong. Her intelligence may be limited, or restricted to specific areas — it's too early to say — but truly slow? No."

"Surely for someone like her there is a middle ground —"

Margaret shot upright. "I am *on* the middle ground," she said with some passion. "I plan to give her lots of love and attention and caring and empathy. But I'm a teacher, not an analyst, and you hired me to do a job.

"I'm sorry if I sounded angry." She was thinking that she hadn't meant it personally and was disappointed that, judging by his expression, he seemed to have taken it that way; afraid also that their differences would bring the job to an end before it had begun.

"You must understand that I won't have Inez treated too harshly, even if it's for her own good. It's my belief she has had enough bad treatment to last her a lifetime. She may not even be autistic ... just damaged."

"I do understand. What I was doing was not overly harsh. She began screaming, and I continued to try and re-focus her. If I had given in, and comforted her, the screaming would have continued just the same."

Jerry flushed. "That's very true, Margaret. I apologize. When I was driving her to Guatemala City, she howled the whole trip. I — and the other person with us — treated her with every kindness. And the howling went on."

"When did it stop?"

"When the car did."

Margaret made mental notes. "Does she always scream in cars?"

"No. She was fine on the trip we took to the airport. There was no trouble driving her to my home."

Margaret deliberated over this. "It will take me some time to understand what triggers her upsets," she said. "My experience is mostly with autistic, not emotionally disturbed children, and that may be part of the problem. Inez may be both."

"You don't think of autism as an emotional disturbance?"

"I think of it more as an organic disease. Brain damage." Was he going to see this as the last straw?

But Jerry nodded. Margaret wondered if he was tiring of the conversation, as she was. She smoothed the lap of her skirt. The sun felt reassuring on her head and the back of her neck, transporting her to a pleasant month she had spent in Morocco. She surveyed the sunroom's botanical array, spider plants, English ivy, an elegant jade tree in a big stone pot, a giant peony in full, riotous bloom, and plants she didn't recognize with striped leaves and huge yellow blossoms.

"I really should write up my notes soon before I forget the details." She watched Jerry's face for signs of disapproval or impatience.

"That's fine, Margaret," he said without expression, leaving her in the dark as to his emotional state. "When do you plan to hold your next intensive session?"

"They'll be the same time every day. Early morning. Most clients respond best then." She paused. "Uh ... Jerry. I'm worried about the weekends."

"You mean because Inez won't be on a program then?"

"Mm-hmm." His question was astute. He looked so authoritative with his intense gaze and strong features. She glanced down at his smooth, tanned hand, emerging from the white shirt edging the expensive cloth of his jacket sleeve.

"Yes. That's it exactly. I don't know how she's going to do without being in almost constant contact with me ..."

"Perhaps she'll need the time to relax. You'll be around occasionally, anyway, and it might be good for her to see you in a different role. And I'll be with her," he added. "I'll have to be. And my partner, Caitlin. She'll be here a lot too. She's been a tremendous help already, these past few weeks. Inez seems to like her."

Margaret suppressed a sigh. A partner. She might have known.

Chapter Twenty-Two

Caitlin's Story

In the morning I woke up with a hangover so bad, I thought my eyeballs might shoot out and hit the wall in front of me, so I decided to open the last box of Jerry's things.

I had cried myself to sleep the previous night, the words of our last argument haunting me like hungry ghosts. Demons had been awakened that could only be knocked out by vodka. Now I was paying the price, which included a shakiness that was more than just physical.

I was desperate to bring the memory of Jerry's love to life again. If he had only lived longer, I told myself, he would have forgiven me and loved me as he had before. I cringed my way to the kitchen and brewed some spiced tea. Then I swallowed three extra-strength Aspirin and stumbled back to my hall closet. When I leaned down to pick up the box, I saw a colourful piece of cloth sticking out the top.

The pattern was distinctive, with far more purple than was usual in Guatemalan weaving. I knew what it was right away

— the bag Inez's mother had pressed into Jerry's hand before he took Inez away, the bag containing five Guatemalan dream dolls.

The last time I'd seen the dolls was in Jerry's study, scattered across his desk like tiny corpses.

After the police had finished combing through the house, they'd cordoned off the study for some weeks before letting anyone in. By the time they'd taken down the tape around the house and from the inside doors, I'd worked up the nerve to go in. I figured Jerry's dad would demand return of my key soon enough, and I wanted one last visit.

In the study, I'd stood frozen in place for a long time, overcome by what had happened there. Then, when I focused more on my surroundings, I wasn't sure what I was looking at. The study as Jerry and Inez had left it, or the results of police work? I couldn't bear the thought of either. I began madly cleaning things up, putting papers away, straightening pens and pencils and figurines. When I came across the dolls strewn across the desk, they made me shudder, and I swept them into the bag that lay beside them and threw them into a drawer.

Then I sat in Jerry's office chair, put my head down on his desk, and wept until my ribs ached. The calendar beneath my folded arms was as soaked with tears as my sleeves.

Thinking about the dolls now, I guessed his father had packed them up later, though why he saw fit to give them to me was a mystery.

I lugged the box to the couch, still squinting with pain from my headache.

When I pulled out the bag and shook it over my lap, out they tumbled, like a gaggle of toothpick Inukshuks.

A jagged sliver stuck out the side of one. I picked the doll up then examined the other four. All were snapped in two at the waist, something I hadn't noticed before, the torsos held to the legs by the scraps of cloth they were dressed in. I wondered if they were like that the last time I'd seen them, and I'd been too anxious to get them out of my sight for it to register. But if they weren't broken then, why were they broken now?

My head still hurt. I needed more tea. I went to brew some, found there wasn't any. Tempted to drink Prince Igor instead, a very bad idea so early in the day, I decided a trip to my favourite health food store, the Big Carrot, was in order, and the box would have to wait.

A walk would clear my head, I thought. As it happened, the trip did more than that. It was a turning point that jolted me out of inertia.

The names of the teas the Big Carrot carried were an adventure in themselves — Rooibos Mango, White Peony, Chocolate Christmas, Golden Monkey ... I also got a kick out of what was written on the boxes. Without making any actual health claims, the blurbs managed to promise immortality, or at least a pinnacle of health so high you'd require supplemental oxygen to survive it. Such verbal dexterity renewed my faith in the written word.

I needed a tea that would cure hangovers, promote peace of mind, sharpen the intellect, and help formulate action plans. I settled instead for Caramel Maca Surprise.

Standing in line at the cashier's desk, I leafed through the brochures. They were even more high-toned than the tea boxes.

There was one that made me laugh out loud. It felt so good to laugh that I stuffed it into one of my shopping bags to share with Molly later.

It was from some oddball outfit called Vision Quest International, and it began like this:

Tired of the same humdrum round? Come on one of Vision Quest International's four-day spiritual journeys and become one with the stars! Find out who you REALLY ARE. Get in touch with your inner child, past lives, and a future limited only by the limitless reach of the cosmos!

All tours led by Certified Vision Quest Inner Professionals. Only $1,000. Sleeping bag not provided.

Spiritual tourism, Jerry would have said disparagingly, despite his penchant for ayahuasca tours, but back at home, I kept picking up the brochure in spite of myself.

Feeling the need to get away from everything for a while, I'd already considered going on a silent meditation retreat. However, I knew bad memories could rise up and overwhelm me there.

This Quest felt much less serious and could be a real time-out. Also, I'd be doing something besides spinning my wheels at home. I was at a point where even the illusion of purposeful activity would be welcome. I decided to look into going.

When Molly wanted to come with me, I couldn't believe it. I'd expected her to snarl "escapism" when I told her my plan and to give me hell. But she said it would be fun, and we could both use some of that. It was only later I learned she saw it as a way to get me out of the hole I'd dug myself into.

She insisted I send off the hundred dollar deposit immediately, for her as well, and she'd reimburse me.

The woman had no faith at all in my ability to stick to a decision.

"It says here," I said, waving the Vision Quest flyer in the air when Molly opened her door to me later that day, "that they'll send us out to the wilderness, then leave us there for four days. No food. Sleeping bag not provided."

"Those things are expensive," she said, ushering me into her living room.

"Sleeping bags? I know."

"And we're going to need good ones, given the weather."

"Molly, don't you think it might be a mistake to go on this thing?"

"Not at all," she responded, chipper as a woodchuck in a pile of kindling. "A week in the wilderness might be very enlightening. What have we got to lose?"

"A thousand bucks. Each. We could probably get to Morocco and back on that."

Her mouth drooped. "Well, okay. It *is* a lot of money just to get dumped somewhere with no mod cons. Still, they're supposed to stick around and watch over us, aren't they?"

"Well, yes. They stay in vans at the edge of the wilds, where we can reach them if we freak out, or get chased by bears, or —"

"Bears? I never thought of bears, Caitlin. I'm a little old to outrun one, van or no van."

I laughed. "My point exactly. Right now, we're only a hundred in the hole. What say we pull out before either the bears or debt collectors get us?"

Molly shook her head. "No, Caitlin. I really want to go. It's something different, and I want to do as many different things as I can, while I can. And I really want *you* to go. You're the one who suggested it, so you can't back out now."

Two weeks later, we were packing for takeoff. I felt silly and giddy and awash with relief — I was giving myself permission to leave my troubles behind.

After a brief moment of indecision, I'd stuffed a bottle of vodka inside a T-shirt in my bag "just in case." The bottle was plastic so it wouldn't rattle and give me away, but Molly spotted it.

"You won't need *this*," she said, snatching Prince Igor out of his cotton cocoon.

"Yes, I will," I said, snatching him back. "I might get bogged down in memories without it. That's why I'm bringing it."

Molly gave me a look that threatened to congeal my blood.

I handed her the vodka. "*Okay*," I said. "Stop looking at me like that. Store this for me until we get back. If you throw it away, I'll sulk and make your life miserable for months."

"Deal," said Molly, heading off to put the vodka somewhere out of my line of vision.

I watched her — and it — go with mixed feelings, but I was mostly relieved to have the problem taken out of my hands, along with the booze.

Chapter Twenty-Three

Caitlin's Story

It was already evening when we arrived at the designated meeting spot near Bancroft. There was no time for us Questers to get to know one another. Talk was discouraged, and we were split up, sent off at five minute intervals from each other, so we would find a home base alone. When Molly set out ahead of me, I watched her disappear into the woods with more than a little trepidation. Then it was my turn. By the time I reached a small clearing on a knoll overlooking a wide swatch of grassland dotted with trees, it was almost nightfall. I rolled my sleeping bag out near a boulder that felt like a shield. Behind me the dark forest pressed close. I lit my kerosene lamp, strung my tarp, and sat down in the pool of flickering light it created.

Against all the rules, I took out my notebook and pen.

Writing in the mottled light of a lamp that threw shadows like rolling dice over the page took concentration. It was a few minutes before a strange noise registered, a sound like the chirping of a million giant crickets.

Tempted to crouch down and pull my sleeping bag over my head, I forced myself to get up, lamp in hand, and investigate.

At the edge of the knoll, I looked down. In the meadowland below were dozens of deer. As I swung the lamp, they raised their heads and stared in my direction. The silence was so deep, you could fall into it as easily as you could fall into the meadow if you took one misstep in the dark. The strange sound had been the noise of their grazing.

When they lowered their heads to graze again, I crawled into my sleeping bag and fell asleep to the click-click of deer teeth and the image of many gentle faces, looking up.

In the morning, after boiling water on my camping stove to make tea, I snuggled my feet back into my sleeping bag and clasped my mug contentedly to my chest.

Fresh air, sun, silence, trees, tea, and dozens of deer in the night. I didn't care about a vision.

Soon I went walking, a soft blanket of pine needles under the trees making a springy carpet for my feet. The pines were packed so close that almost nothing grew on the forest floor. The lower branches of the trees were brown and dead, and the light filtering through was dim enough in places that even though it was daytime, I was glad of my flashlight. In amongst the biggest evergreens were smaller trees that smelled like cedars, and it was the scent of cedar and pine together that kept me taking long, deep breaths for the sheer pleasure of filling my lungs.

I walked all morning through the forest, down the tunnels of diffuse light on the well-trodden paths between the trees, returning to my camp at intervals to remind myself where it was. I even forgot to be nervous about bears. I thought there was no room for them in this tight, entangled place. The silence was deep, the warmth and the play of sunlight calming, almost numinous.

More tea around lunchtime. Afterwards, thinking the cushiony needles beneath an enormous pine would make a perfect zafu, I sat down to meditate.

There are many ways to begin. One is to count breaths to calm the mind. I'd learned that if I sat quietly, my mind would quieten down on its own in time, but I always began with breath counting. There is something about following the breath from the nose to the belly and back again, over and over, which automatically alters perception. If nothing else, it brings into high relief how connected we are to the air, that we cannot live without it.

I was hoping for a "good" experience, one that would take me to a state of deep peace. I had reached such a state many times on retreat, even if I'd been itching with boredom half the time leading up to it, and my knees or feet were screaming for mercy.

What I didn't want was for slow stirrings to begin under what had become stagnant repose, then grow rapidly until they towered over me without showing their faces. I had reached this state, too, many times during meditation. Old traumas, suppressed emotions — all the things that horrified and tormented me. All the reasons I'd decided against a traditional retreat, where avenues of escape were inaccessible by design.

Even as I counted my breaths, many of the old questions arose. *What happened? Why? Did he suffer? How much? Was there a reason he had to die as he did? Was Inez sent to kill him? Did any of us deserve what happened?*

But these posed no threat. I knew if I did not pursue answers, the questions would float away and disperse on their own.

My fears centred on how meditation plays with memory in unpredictable ways. Sometimes when I relaxed deeply, painful recollections winged through my mind without alighting. Other times, a bad memory would emerge with startling immediacy, no longer softened by the passage of time. I once spent a weekend retreat mourning Tommy, dead for thirty years, as if he had died the day before I'd come.

Perhaps Jerry surprised Inez as she was picking up the lamp, and he shouted at her without thinking, like the metal Scottie dog incident he'd told me about, and she'd panicked and hit him with it — really hard, because for a minute she thought he was a Guatemalan soldier. Maybe Jerry told her to pick up the lamp and look at it, then she tripped and brought it down on his head as she fell. When she saw his blood, it brought back nightmarish memories. Or she woke up from a dream that morning, a dream of the family she left behind, and some voice in her head told her Jerry was the cause of all that had gone wrong, and so she wanted to kill him for doing this awful thing, for exiling her from everything that seemed real to her. Or maybe he did something that made her think he was going to send her back, or shut her up somewhere and keep her captive forever — or she understood that he planned to send her away, and she could not bear it....

Here, I shuddered, then had to struggle to regain my composure, returning my attention over and over again to the now faster pace of my breathing. I was almost glad when the throbbing in my knees distracted me.

I broke the pain up into little pieces in my mind and watched how it was affecting my body, but it still hurt. Because here I was not at the mercy of bells and gongs and "Senior Meditators" who insisted on the value of a complete experience of pain, I gave myself permission to stop meditating and go for a walk.

For the next two days, I settled into a routine of alternating walking and meditating throughout the day, punctuated by cups of tea and light snacks, always breaking my concentration if my thoughts took too nasty a turn.

By the third day, I felt stronger. Midway through that evening, I began to feel transparent, as though the world flowed through me. Time began to weave in and out, spiralling back on itself, bending me out of shape, simultaneously weak enough not to matter and powerful enough to annihilate the world.

Until a wave of gut-wrenching terror engulfed me.

I had learned to ride strong emotion, not block it, and I decided to try that before giving up and getting up. *Psychological Surfing*, I called it. But this fear had been lurking in the wings ever since Jerry had died. Allowing myself to experience it wasn't going to be enough.

I told myself to stop immediately, but the need to know what was behind this was stronger even than the fear, and I stayed where I was.

Okay then. Think of it as a Zen koan. Contemplate it.

What are you afraid of?

I waited, but nothing came.

Ages later, I was still sitting, and the fear left as mysteriously as it had arrived.

While my mind was still blessedly clear, I went to bed and fell asleep as though riding a wave into oblivion. I woke with the sun. Whatever dreams I'd had left a lingering sadness. I shook myself but couldn't shake the sorrow.

Wrapping a blanket around my shoulders, I stood at the edge of the knoll and looked down over the grassy stretch where the deer had grazed.

Once again, I recalled Jerry at his desk with his head down on his arms, lighting up like a Roman candle when Inez came into the room.

I was suddenly exhausted and longed to shove the scene somewhere far away, such as off the cliff I stood on. But meditative recall knows no mercy and wouldn't let Jerry belong to the broken landscape of the past. I thought about the times he'd said he was too busy to see me after Inez had come, how sometimes he didn't want to make love, when he'd always been so eager in the past.

When I asked, he told me about problems at the Analytical Institute, troubles over his article, concern over a high-ranking analyst who was mistreating his patients. Later there were major problems with his clients. So, he said, he felt too sad and worried sometimes to be sexual. It was as if he'd forgotten how much we could do for each other that way. As if he had deserted me, taking with him something vitally important to both of us.

His behaviour changed subtly in many other ways. He stayed up late, coming to bed after I was asleep (after I'd lain awake waiting for him, puzzled and concerned, then finally dropped off), he was restless, he spoke angrily against his profession in ways he'd never done before. He said he was angry at how hidebound it was, how hard it was to get his colleagues to see that Freud was in many ways a product of his time, accurate then, less so now, when different neuroses and afflictions beset modern humanity. And yet I heard that self-psychology was gaining ground, and that he was seen as instrumental in this change. When I told him I thought he was at the centre of a rising group, and considered to be its leader, he scoffed and wouldn't discuss it.

I gripped the blanket tighter round my neck, guarding my throat against a chill breeze.

The night I'd found some of Inez's clothes — her *under-wear* — in his bed, he'd explained it as a mix-up in laundry. He'd picked the cotton panties off the sheet, laughing as they crackled with static and sent off sparks. It made sense that they'd stuck there after washing and not been noticed till we climbed into bed together that night.

It made sense. But good sense wasn't what this was about.

And there was our awful argument the day before he died. Had it pushed him towards her, made him do something he might never otherwise have done?

Had he taken advantage of Inez, or tried to? I'd denied the possibility so fiercely, I hadn't even known I was afraid of it. Until now.

I dropped to my knees as the world blurred around me.

Throughout the rest of the day, I tried my hardest to picture Jerry and Inez in a passionate embrace.

Given the girl's past, it was hard to imagine her wanting to make love to any man. Yet sensuality radiated from her. And she seemed to have a deep, unfathomable intelligence that could allow her to understand the difference between love and lust, and know that the former involved sex of a totally different kind from what she had experienced so far. But now that I had at last confronted my fears enough to picture the dreaded possibility, I knew it was no real possibility at all.

Why? Because I hadn't forgotten *Ich Liebe Dich*, nor how Jerry looked at Inez sometimes, or stroked her cheek, or held her hand. He loved her, and I was sure that meant he would be saddened by any advances she might have made. Because Jerry was a good man, and a smart one, and he would also know that any sexual move towards her on his part would destroy her.

And should she be terrified by the very thought of sex, he would never have forced it on her. The thought was beyond ludicrous.

I wanted to shout with joy. I had faced up to my biggest fear and found it baseless, discovering in the process that I did know Jerry, and, more importantly, trusted in what I knew.

It wasn't until much later, when the sun fell into starlit darkness backed by the eerie hoot of owls, that another burning question made its presence felt.

Had Jerry been in love with Inez?

"In love" was threatening in ways that "loving" was not. "In love" could mean anguish and violence and fear. And it was more plausible than sexual abuse.

I had no proof, just hints so delicate they were almost imperceptible, such as the time Margaret had shown Inez how to write the word *love*, and the tender look Jerry gave Inez while she wrote it.

Perhaps the impression of music surrounding them when I'd come upon them alone together was less fanciful than I'd supposed. Did the flash of light that sometimes passed between them illuminate more than I thought?

I knew I should go slowly, but my head was racing as fast as my heart. The love I felt for Jerry had seemed to take me through a door to a new level of existence. I told myself it shouldn't matter if for him there was another entry to what most of us glimpse only through a mist. But I felt sick.

Struggling with my emotions, it took a while for me to realize I was walking blind.

Where was I? Where was my home base?

I shouted aloud, hoping a fellow Quester would hear and come to my aid.

But all that came was a huge black crow, ugly, arrogant, and oblivious, flapping into the arms of a nearby pine, where it settled and stared down at me.

I laughed.

Was this my power animal?

That crow was so radically confident, so blithe in its crassness, so unapologetically itself that it made me smile. I greeted it cheerily. It tipped its head to one side, as if listening, before launching itself into the air.

I followed it, for want of anything better to do. Through the woods I went, looking up now and then to see it just ahead of me in the trees. Suddenly the terrain looked familiar, and there was my tarp, a big green signpost hanging from the branches.

The crow took a nosedive. It had probably found food in my camp before and was looking for some now.

So the crow led me home.

Some time later, I sat recuperating with a cup of tea, still smiling. I hadn't stopped smiling from the moment I saw it.

It was the second-last day of the Quest. On the last day, I made a decision that would royally piss Molly off.

Chapter Twenty-Four

Jerry
Toronto, May, 1983

Jerry liked to take walks down by the waterfront late at night, especially when he was troubled. Just exactly how *were* weekends going to go? In three days he'd be starting up his practice again. One of his current patients was difficult enough to be exhausting. He knew he'd need a break on the weekends, not another responsibility.

As he walked, he thought about that patient, the woman named Teresa Priolo. She was enraged with him almost constantly these days, and he was wrestling with whether his approach was helping or hindering.

Though the Freudian style required the doctor to remain a blank slate, hardly ever speaking, never becoming emotionally engaged, Jerry had grown to believe such "analytic neutrality" was a minefield, where the perceived coldness of the doctor could create huge anxiety in a vulnerable patient. He and many of his colleagues were now heavily influenced by a branch of psychoanalysis called self-psychology. It emphasized the interaction of the analyst with the analysand and allowed for much closer involvement between patient and doctor.

He'd decided that the self-psychological approach was the right one with Teresa. She had been badly neglected as a child, with a distant, withdrawn mother and a self-obsessed father who seemed to treat her as an extension of himself. But things were not going at all well with this patient.

"You're such a phony!" She had spat this out early in the hour. Teresa, who had once adored him, seemed always angry with him now. "You want me to love you. It really turns you on to be worshipped! But you give nothing, *nothing* back. You can't give. You can't give anything."

Was he deliberately withholding from Teresa? If so, why? It was totally contrary to the new approach and something he'd never believed in. *Something* was hurting her; that much was not in question. But was it him? He recognized Teresa's transference, that analytical case of mistaken identity that mobilized change but was not at all the same as a relationship in the everyday world. The kind of rage she expressed usually meant he'd turned from idealized to demonized parent in his patient's eyes. But had he really gloried in her idealization of him, as she claimed? Gloried in the fact that it wasn't returned?

When he was in Grade Ten, he'd taken a girl named Erika down to a secluded copse of trees, the intention being to show her his erect penis, because — being a young woman of small inhibition and large curiosity — she'd asked to see it.

He'd found the request strange, something you'd expect from kids playing doctor, age eight or thereabouts, or, alternately, from some whacked-out girl from a bad home.

Erika was middle class, with loving parents, artists with day jobs. Well, come to think of it, they did encourage her to be a free spirit.

He and Erika had been pals since they'd caught frogs together in the stream below her house, when they were ten. She'd been cute and daring then. At fifteen, he found her *hot* and daring.

On hearing her request, a slow grin had stretched across his face. "Weell," he drawled, raising an eyebrow, "I dunno ..." His fingers tilted her chin upwards so their eyes met. "Why *erect*, E.?"

"I have brothers, Dumbo. I've seen the regular kind."

Well, yeah. He pushed a strand of her dark, wavy hair gently off her neck and moved a little closer. Isn't that what the hero in the movies would do? At that age, he had no experiences of his own to build on. "It's a possibility," he said. "A distinct possibility." He took her hand and angled it towards his crotch.

She pulled away. "Not here, Romeo. And I said *see*, not *touch*."

Down in the trees, well-hidden from the road, with Erika looking at him teasingly then pressing herself against him, he was hard in a moment.

Erika, who doubtless felt the time was ripe, pulled herself out of his embrace. She eyed the bulging crotch of his jeans and said, theatrically, "I esteem your manhood," bowing and grinning.

"You sure you want me to unveil it, my lady?" He liked the way his cock looked, erect — smooth and veined and brown, like his hands after a few hours in the sun. It felt silky to his touch, almost like he'd put baby powder on it, for Pete's sake — but he wasn't sure how Erika would react.

"Not if I have to show you my Valley of Unearthly Delights in return, your lordship."

"I'll let you off this time, Lady Erika," he said.

She unzipped him and reached in.

He jumped back, excited enough to fear he might come if he let her hand stay where it was. "Whoa, milady! I thought you said *see*, not *touch*. You sure aren't shy any more, are you?"

"EEW!" was her response, snatching her hand away, leaving him exposed and vulnerable.

"Eww? That's all you have to say about my manly Sword of Love, Greensleeves?" He was putting himself away and zipping up.

"Well, it's *slimy*," she said. "And it looked sore or something, all swollen up like that. Like you could poke it and horrible gunk would come out. Like a bloated slug. They look nicer when they're soft."

"You never minded slimy with the frogs." He struggled to keep his voice light.

"Frogs are different. Frogs have nothing to do with me. I mean... eww!"

Mortified behind his devil-may-care manner, Jerry grabbed her and kissed her roughly. She pulled back, mumbling something against his lips, then turned her head to free her mouth.

"Stop it, Jerry!"

He didn't stop. He'd rather do something he shouldn't, something strong, than stay in the vulnerable state she'd put him in. He grabbed her roughly by the arm and pulled her to him.

"Jerry!" The chocolate of her eyes was pure black now, and she kneed him in the groin. "I hate you! I hate you so much!"

He doubled over as she broke free and ran. The whoosh of her legs against the long grass blurred into the pain, and the snap of breaking branches made him think of fires burning out of control.

It was far-fetched to think that Teresa was paying for Erika's rebuff, but all the same, it was telling, he thought, that he should remember that incident now. Perhaps it came to mind not because of what Erika had done, but because of how aggressive he'd been, how determined to assert himself at her expense.

What he'd thought he'd wanted with Teresa was to show her he was different from her other therapists. She'd been hurt before. Badly. She kept accusing him of covering up for his colleagues, for not caring about the injustices of his profession. That rankled, given the situation with Whitfield.

"You're all phonies," she'd shrieked at that awful session. "You all love power. You've got this game set up so I'm bound to fall in love with you, just so you can control me."

He was worried that her hatred of him was intense enough to make her terminate the therapy. In his opinion, it was way too soon. She had to work through her hostility, not run from it.

He was concerned, too, about recent sessions when he'd felt unable to work with her because her criticisms were so endless — and accurate. With the uncanny instincts of the enraged analysand, she had found his sorest spots and poked at them.

The worst had been when she'd accused him of not caring about her, something his father had tormented him with for many years with reference to his mother, who was often ill. As a boy, he'd been less than loyal, getting out of the house whenever he could, mainly because his dad was an unpleasant, bad-tempered dictator. But the old man wasn't even there the day she had a heart attack and had to crawl to the phone because Jerry had snuck out with friends. He hated the sick room, the atmosphere of illness, gloom, and cloying demands. His dad never let up on him for that one. His mom, either. "If you'd cared about me at all, you'd have been here! I could have died!" After one too many tirades, he'd shouted, "I wish you had!"

The beating he got was severe, but it wasn't what upset him most. It was the suspicion that he truly didn't care, and that it was only because she provided a buffer zone, albeit a feeble one, between him and his father that he wanted his mother around at all. He thought he loved her; he knew she wasn't perfect but, up till then, he'd thought he loved her.

And now this patient.... When, after a full onslaught of hatred, she'd told him, sobbing, she still loved him, and could he at least say he *liked* her now, he couldn't bring himself to say it, let alone feel it. The ensuing silence — he wished he could forget it — had an ominous feel.

Jerry started. A sudden loud cry, somewhere between a howl and a plea, was shipwrecking the darkness. He looked all around the dark waterfront but saw nothing. He waited but heard nothing more. Frowning, he pushed his hands into his pockets and kept walking. Must have been an animal, he thought. But what kind?

When the silence grew, he shrugged and let his thoughts travel to his troubles with the Analytic Society. The infighting and the turf wars. Lavalle accusing him of plagiarizing an article. An essay he'd read in *Psychoanalytic Inquiry*, years before, had heavily influenced him. He thought he'd built on it, not sto-len it. Perhaps he hadn't built on it *enough*. Shit. The accusation stemmed from professional jealousy and was infuriating, but that didn't stop it from making him sweat.

There were definitely some shadows in his life now, cou-pled with a sense of futility. He'd been passed over as a Training Analyst once again, and that troubled him.

They'd told him it was because they didn't feel he was ready yet, that he didn't have enough faith in his own abilities. Well, how could he, when they didn't have any faith in them either? He suspected it had more to do with the fact that one of the more powerful members, a pompous ass called Coxwell, disliked him. "Your humour is extremely defensive," Coxwell had said at an analytic meeting, when Jerry had responded to some criti-cism from the head duty nurse with an off-colour joke. "It shows a lack of maturity, to say the least."

It amused Jerry, when it wasn't threatening to him, the way analysts used analytic theory against each other. "He obviously had an unsuccessful training analysis" was a common insult, as was "It goes without saying he wasn't fully analyzed."

His moral dilemma with Whitfield was never amusing. He didn't like the man, never had. They'd clashed a few times at conferences, which was nerve-wracking enough, given Whitfield's position and power in the profession. Jerry suspected Whitfield disliked him as much as he disliked Whitfield, and now Jerry was sure he was hurting patients, treating them as if they were his *subjects*, from what he'd heard. The man was a die-hard Freudian, dead set against the "new" self-psychology, but now he seemed to have forgotten what analytic neutrality was all about. There were a lot of nasty rumours. One patient of Whitfield's Jerry was sure about. The man was unlikeable, true, but there was no question he'd been damaged further by his treatment. Jerry knew through a mutual acquaintance that the man had begun to suffer anxiety attacks at work after his analysis had been terminated abruptly and, it seemed, cruelly, by Whitfield. Eventually, the ex-analysand was demoted at work because of acute anxiety and depression.

Whitfield's style, from all Jerry had heard, was verging on insane. He insulted patients routinely — at least, the ones he deemed "arrogant" — and often didn't show up for appointments, offering no explanation. He'd even heard that Whitfield provoked arguments in session then blamed the patient for being "aggressive." *Damn*, thought Jerry. He shoved his hands deeper into his pockets and stared out over the lake. *Is anyone going to pay the slightest attention if I blow the whistle? Whitfield is powerful. Head of the Analytic Society, for god's sake. No one will want to deal with it if he's gone off the rails.* Jerry ran a hand through his unruly hair. *Last time I tried to tell Doherty about it, he shut me up before I even got to the point.*

"Don't talk about Whitfield," he'd said. "I can't handle it."

Well, nor can I, thought Jerry. *What a mess. The man's harmful to his patients, and nobody wants to know.* Then he thought of Teresa. Damn her anyway.

The strange cry rocked the darkness again, and Jerry strained to see. Mist sprawled over the black lake, and it took him some time to realize the small pinpricks of light were coming from a boat far out on the horizon, the long moooo of its horn carrying balefully over the water. It didn't sound at all like the keening he'd heard just moments before.

Closer to shore, something bobbed on the waves. The cry came again.

Jerry narrowed his eyes and stepped closer to the shoreline. The cry again, desperate and plaintive. It was one of the strangest sounds he'd ever heard, as eerie as a loon's call, but sharper, like a stab of pain. He stared harder, grateful that the moonlight had grown brighter.

There it was again, something bobbing on the water and splashing about. Whatever it was kept disappearing then resurfacing. Coupled with the cry, he felt sure it must be something in distress. But what? He didn't think it could be human. Then again, he knew that people *in extremis* — the dying, women in labour, patients reliving terrible traumas — could make strange sounds.

There was nothing he wanted to do less than dive into Lake Ontario, numbing even in the dog days of summer, let alone in spring. He wasn't a strong swimmer. It might just be some large fish cavorting in the waves. The cry? Fish were not exactly vocal. Anyway, he probably wouldn't make it out there in time, no matter what was going on.

But, if someone *were* in distress, their only hope would be if he acted — now.

He thought of Teresa as he plunged into the lake. He didn't know why but was in no position to dwell on it. He churned his arms and legs with all his strength. He couldn't even see the bobbing thing now. The mist was a tangle of cobwebby shrouds and the water, ice-cold. Soon, his legs were anchors rather than propellers thrusting him forward. He gasped and floundered on, craning his head, searching in vain for another glimpse of whatever creature was thrashing, along with him, in the frigid lake.

Faltering at last, treading water, he heard the silence as acutely as the earlier, eerie cry. His aloneness was palpable. He was certain there was nothing out here but himself.

He was lost. The shoreline had disappeared.

The darkness was streaked by light from a cloud-encumbered moon, a dull grey light that danced incongruously when it hit the water, but offered very little illumination.

Panic made him paddle in circles in the desperate hope of sighting land, of locating himself *somewhere*. He could not let disorientation overwhelm him, knew he must ground himself at least in his own mind. He took several deep breaths until his heart stopped its attempt to strangle him. He looked up at the moon.

Yes, clouds were obscuring it. But they were moving, oh so slowly. The light was bound to get better. And he couldn't have swum *that* far. He remembered he was still wearing his watch and remembered also that it was waterproof. He lifted his left hand out of the lake, continuing the swirling, froglike movements of treading water with his legs and other arm. Fourteen minutes past eleven. He'd come down to the lakefront about ten forty five and probably walked for fifteen minutes or so before being seduced by that crazy siren song he no longer cared about or heard. So he *must* be closer to shore than he thought.

He was exhausted by the time the clouds scudded away from the moon's pale disk, and, almost unbelieving, he saw land.

He struck out for it immediately, before the light could

disappear again, taking his bearings with it.

It was much farther away than it had first seemed through the spoors of moonlight. *Just swim through that veil, and you'll be there,* he'd thought. But it kept moving ahead of him, until it became the veil of his own blurred vision.

His chest and throat ached equally, not that he could pinpoint any feeling with accuracy but weariness by then. He understood how people could let themselves drown, just give themselves up to the water. Jerry was falling into a dream state, a lassitude so great, even awareness could not dispel it. How wonderful it would be to stop trying, to stop straining for the shoreline which he was sure, by now, was mythic. He did not particularly want to die; he simply didn't care about anything but rest. Perhaps he'd fall asleep and go under, snoring.

Then he hit a rock. He grabbed at it with one hand, but it was too large, too slippery for his grip to hold. It rose above the surface in a great, black mound.

It took a moment for this to register. Then Jerry's mind snapped into focus, and he realized, *I must be close to shore.*

With a burst of energy he knew must be short-lived, he convulsed the water with arms and legs that, moments before, had been flailing about uselessly, disconnected from central command.

He reached the shallows and scraped his toes badly before standing up, half unbelieving, the water streaming from his sodden shirt, his hands still trailing in the lake. Stumbling forward, he felt the pull of the undertow against his legs like the dead weight of the corpse he had almost become. The weeds were spirit hands trying to drag him down.

Dry land, too, was a shock. He sat on the gravelly sand, aware of the absence of water more than the presence of earth. He pulled himself further onto shore then lay back, panting. He didn't feel the clammy weight of his clothes for several minutes.

When he did, he became aware also that he was shuddering and that his head was reeling as though under a rain of blows.

He pulled himself to his feet and stumbled for his car.

Inside the vehicle, he shuddered still, waiting for the engine to warm up the heater, which was turned on full blast. He drew his knees up and clasped his arms around them. Thank god his keys were still attached to his belt loop. And thank god too that he'd resurfaced near the spot where he'd first entered the water.

After several minutes, Jerry leaned back in his car seat, basking in the now warm air from the vents. He closed his eyes and breathed deeply, shivering still when he thought how close to death he'd been, and all for a cry that turned out to be nothing more than a noise over the water.

What in hell, he thought, *was all* that *about?* Just how much had his state of mind influenced his perceptions and everything that followed?

Back at his house, he let himself in the patients' door, carefully, so as not to waken Margaret or Inez.

He headed upstairs, still dripping, unbuttoning his pants as he went. He'd already removed his jacket and shirt in the car and thrown them down the basement stairs, in the general direction of the laundry room.

He went into his bedroom and turned on his bedside lamp.

It wasn't until he'd removed his jeans and boxers that he turned and saw Inez.

In the lamp's peach glow, her skin looked as warm as fresh tea, and as milky brown, her body a shadow through her cotton nightgown. Jerry nearly jumped out of his naked skin then grabbed his coverlet, wrapping it swiftly around his waist.

"Inez," he said, with outward calm, grateful that something he felt was beyond his control had prevented him from shouting her name, either in anger or in shock. "What are you doing here?"

"*Cogeme,*" she said. "*Cogeme.*"

Her voice was rough and deep and … masculine. It took Jerry several fraught seconds to recognize what she'd said — "Fuck me," in Spanish — and several more to realize that she was of course parroting someone else.

He could not imagine what she wanted. It made him sad to think the word or something very much like it had most likely come from her attackers. She could not possibly mean what she said, yet her gaze on him was unafraid, though sad and full of yearning. He thought he saw tears in her eyes.

She moved slowly towards him. The moisture in her eyes glistened in the light. Jerry moved forward, too, entranced — by her, his strange near drowning, the eerie cry over the water, which echoed again in his ears now, this whole crazy, inexplicable night. A night full of dark magic, where anything seemed possible.

He tripped on the hem of his bedspread toga and stumbled.

"Inez," he said again, righting himself, "you must go back to your own room now." Perhaps he should lock her in. No, he couldn't, not after what she'd been through. She'd be leaving soon anyway; she'd have to.

Inez sat on the far side of his bed and pulled her nightgown over her head.

No, no. Her body was truly lovely; brown, compact, faintly muscular, her full breasts tip-tilted, the nipples small, dark, and erect. Her pubic hair, unlike the hair on her head, was curly and light. It made him think of duckling down.

"*Cogeme,*" she said again in the same harsh tones. She curled her legs beneath her and looked up at him. She was crying openly now, her eyes full of confusion as well as melancholy. Such large, arresting eyes.

"Inez," he said more sharply, still keeping his voice low, "you must get dressed and go."

She continued to look up at him, and he felt himself responding sexually, sweating, too, from nerves. He had to stop this somehow, without threatening or frightening her.

His desire, he thought later, was the result of the atmosphere. If she had done something like this during the day in his living room, he knew his response would have been purely shock and concern. But here, nearly naked, still raw from the importunate waters, in his bedroom lit by an erotic glow ...

He knew what to do. He grabbed some pajama pants from his dresser drawer as Inez lay against his pillows and closed her eyes. He drew the flannel trousers on under the coverlet, keeping his movements slow and smooth, and headed for the door.

"Margaret," he called, "I need your help. I'm sorry to disturb you, but I need help with Inez."

Chapter Twenty-Five

Jerry/Margaret
Toronto, May, 1983

Margaret watched Inez, backlit by a yolk-yellow sun, spin slowly round the room with her arms extended. *Good thing Jerry has a cool head — and integrity.* She'd noticed his eyes following the girl with a particular light more than once.

The session had gone well, and she was pleased that the night before she had not reacted with alarm or censure. It was sometimes still a challenge to deal with the sexuality of some of her clients. The issue was even more complicated with Inez. Considering that Inez had been violently raped, Margaret couldn't believe the overtures she had made to Jerry were sexual. But what then had she been doing? Perhaps it was a test, to see if Jerry would take advantage of her. She'd seen the way the girl looked at him sometimes — with love, but not with lust. *Perhaps she responds to compassion in a man*, she thought. *That would be a sign of strength, not confusion.* But it was just one possibility among a bewildering list of possibilities.

She had stroked the girl's head after dressing her in her nightgown and tucked her in between the sheets. "Go to sleep now, Inez," she'd said and kissed the top of her head.

"Go to sleep now, Inez," said the girl in a perfect imitation of her nurse's voice.

Now Inez picked up her favourite toy — a tiny merry-go-round with wooden animals in frilly costumes all around the bottom. When you wound it up, it made pretty music and sparks shone, and the little animals moved round and round in a circle.

"Thank you, Inez," said Margaret when the girl handed the carousel to her. She put it in the toy box, closed the lid, and snapped the metal clasp shut. "Well, that's it for today."

A terrible look clouded Inez's face.

"Are you all right?" Margaret leaned close.

Inez ran and hunched over in the far corner of the room, banging her head on the floor.

"Inez."

Very gently, Margaret slipped both her hands beneath Inez's forehead. Margaret's knuckles banged against the floor, once, twice, three times.

Inez sat up and looked at Margaret, plainly bewildered. Then her lips curved slowly upward. She was still smiling as tears fell and wetted her blouse. She closed her eyes, leaned back against the wall, the smile like an etching on her face.

Margaret wiped the moisture from Inez's cheeks. She'd never seen an episode of head banging so easily resolved. *She's starved for affection*, she thought. *Show her any kind of care and she responds.*

The little carousel ... Did she get upset because I put it away? Perhaps when she gave it to me, she was entrusting me with the most delicate part of herself. And what did I do? I shut it in a box.

Later, in her room, she thought, *Who is this Caitlin, anyway? He says she comes over a lot, and I haven't seen her yet. I wonder how old she is? If she's as old as him, maybe he'll prefer me.*

Wincing at the uncharitable thought, *You don't even want him*, she reminded herself. *Just his genes.*

In the shower, Jerry concentrated on washing his belly. He liked the feel of the bar of soap against the whorls of hair around his navel.

This brought a smile, but remembering how he'd woken gripped by an indeterminate longing, just as he had after his dream of Inez in Guatemala, sobered him.

No one had ever made him feel as she did — that they were offering something mysterious he hadn't known he craved. "Airy-fairy stuff," his father would call it, and for once he might be right.

Jerry shivered, though the water was hot, and abruptly turned off the shower. He knew better. Inez represented unmet needs he didn't recognize, something he should work on, nothing more. He grabbed a towel off the rack and began rubbing himself down, hard.

Still, he couldn't help but wonder at the beauty of the emotions she evoked and feel grateful for them.

He dressed and headed for the kitchen.

Margaret was already there. She looked away when she saw him. "I feel a bit funny sometimes, rambling around in your space."

"It's quite all right." Jerry thought it was surprisingly uncomfortable for him, too, but he might as well get used to it. "It's your space now as well as mine. I hope the cupboard I emptied for you is big enough."

Margaret, who wasn't sure that it was, hesitated. "It'll probably be okay," she said. "I'll more than likely eat out a fair bit anyway."

"Don't feel you have to. I can make more room, if you like."
Damn. This sharing was not going to be easy. All the more reason
to arrange for in-patient treatment for Inez as soon as he could.

"I have to tell you something, Jerry."

He looked up at her from his seat at the table. "Yes?"

"I admire how you handled Inez last night."

He stopped buttering his toast.

"I think it will help her immensely that you did not take
advantage of her."

"Of course I didn't," he said brusquely, not willing to admit
to his momentary flash of desire. "I'm glad you think it will help."

"Don't you?"

"I do." He was about to expand on that when the phone rang.

He picked it up.

"Dr. Simpson?" The voice was unfamiliar and frantic. "One of
your patients, Teresa Prialo — I'm sorry, Doctor. She's attempted
suicide. We've got her here in St. Mike's. She's asking for you."

Jerry broke into a sweat. "How is she?"

"Her condition is critical."

"What did she do?"

"Jumped from her tenth-floor apartment balcony."

Christ.

"She's pretty banged up," the voice on the other end was saying. "In fact …"

"In fact?" he prompted, though he knew what was coming next.

"She might not make it."

Shit. Oh, shit.

"I'll be right over," said Jerry and hung up.

A jumper or a sleeper? Margaret wondered as he threw his
half-eaten toast on his plate and left.

Chapter Twenty-Six

Jerry
Toronto, May, 1983

Her eyes were bottomless, blank, all pupil. Jerry had seen eyes like that only once before — his mother's, the day she died.

He sat down at Teresa's bedside. Though she was facing him, he knew he wasn't seen. It was a strange feeling, as though he were made of cellophane, or smoke.

The room was cold. A breathing machine whooshed noisily beside Teresa's head. Tubes and wires projected from her body. What he could see of her face was a mess of cuts and bruises. Red stains marked the bandages around her mouth.

Ought he to have come? As her doctor, he felt obliged, especially as he'd been told she'd asked for him. And he couldn't *not* come, not after the way he'd held back from her in her therapy sessions. Had he done that out fear? *Cruelty?* He put his head in his hands.

"It wasn't you."

His whole body twitched. Had she really said it? There was no light in her eyes, and her face still had the eerily uninhabited look that had spooked him when he'd first come in.

"Teresa?" he said, leaning forward.

Her mouth was slack.

"Teresa?"

He pulled his chair closer. Ignoring the medley of machines, he touched the hand that protruded from the covers. White, cold, strangely thick, it reminded him of lard.

Where did people go when they got that hollow, empty look? It made him think of despair, not simply death or the absence of life.

"I'm sorry. You deserved better from me." He took a deep breath.

She showed no sign she'd heard. Probably nothing could reach her now.

"I care for you, Teresa. I do." He was horrified that even now, the words were stiff. But how could they not be? It was a stupid, unnatural thing to say. All the same, he had to say it. "I don't want you to die." Too late to matter.

He stood beside her, his hand on her arm. He picked up his coat. Giving the ravaged face on the pillow one last look, he bent down, kissed her forehead, and left the room.

At the nurses' station, he told them he thought Teresa might be failing.

"Her family is on the way," one of the nurses said. "I hope they're not too late."

She died a few hours later. The hospital called to let Jerry know.

Caitlin was sitting with him in his living room when the news came.

"I hurt her, Caitlin. I really hurt her."

"How?"

"She fell in love with me."

Caitlin pulled a face. "What else is new?"

"Sorry if I can't share the joke right now. I think I was cruel to her."

"Why?"

"I don't *know*. It was pretty terrible, Cat. Analysts are supposed to understand their motives."

"Analysts aren't perfect, Jerry." Caitlin came over to stroke his hair. "Not expecting yourself to make mistakes is just pride."

He pressed his head to her belly for comfort and to dislodge the irritation he felt. Even if she were right, the picture of Teresa's ravaged face was too fresh in his mind to make much difference. "I owe it to my patients not to hurt them," he said.

Caitlin kept stroking his hair. "Yes, but how cruel were you? Did you out and out reject her?"

"I might as well have, I think." He turned his face to one side so he could speak more clearly, still taking refuge in the warmth of her stomach. "I just *froze*. I couldn't find a damn thing to say to her. I think maybe I got sucked into her depression. She kept downgrading herself, and I never said anything to contradict her. That's how we're trained, but I almost colluded with her negativity. She figured it out before I did. She kept accusing me of being unable to give. I was just beginning to see it for myself, and now …" It was after the strange incident at the lake that he'd finally felt he understood Teresa's disappointment in him, her *hope* in him.

"What kind of person was she, Jer?"

He pulled away and looked at her. "Fragile. Elements of borderline personality disorder. Deeply unhappy."

"Do you think she killed herself over you?"

"I hope to hell not. But that's what I suspect. Because I *hurt* her. I don't think she could cope with the fact that I actively hurt her. Oh, damn it, Caitlin, what was the matter with me?"

264

Caitlin looked pensive. "Not much, Jerry. That's the truth."

This small sweetness disarmed him. "You're biased," he said.

"No. I think it's terrible what happened with Agnes, but I've heard you talk about borderlines before."

"Her real name was Teresa," he interrupted. "I can tell you now. Teresa Prialo."

"Well, whatever her name is, borderlines are impossible. Most analysts won't even take them on. Remember the one who threw a book at you because you moved something in your office? She was phoning here, screaming because you put the tissues on a different table, for Pete's sake ..."

Jerry gave a short laugh. "Yeah, I remember. Funny thing is, I liked her."

Caitlin rolled her eyes. "See what I mean? You're practically a saint with these people."

"I'm not. Not at all," he said. "I felt I understood that patient. And also —" there was a smile on his pale face, "— she was completely upfront, completely oblivious to how whacko she was."

"So that made it okay?" Caitlin, who'd been gently kneading his shoulders, dug in with her thumbs.

"Ow. In a way." Caitlin could be so *sympatico* and then — WHAM — it was as if she lived in a different world. Well, she did. She lived in the world of news facts, not lost souls. "Sometimes she was so outrageous, she made me laugh. Also, she was reliving her childhood ..."

"Oh." Caitlin shook her head impatiently. "I can't believe you're trotting out that old, tired excuse."

Jerry leaned further back into the couch, away from her massaging hands. "It's not an old, tired *excuse*, Caitlin. It may be the behavioural equivalent of a cliché, but it's not an *excuse*. That's what happens in therapy. People replay their childhoods. I'm the miscreant parent and they're the hurt child. It just happens."

He stopped, given that there wasn't much point in continuing.

He was thinking how hard it was to make outsiders, even intimates like Caitlin, understand what happened in the course of an analysis. He was also pondering for the thousandth time why therapy had the effect it did. He'd heard at least a half-dozen good explanations for it, but it was still a source of amazement to him, watching his patients become children, and feeling them relate to him as other than he was. He understood transference intellectually, but no theory fully captured it, as far as he was concerned. "Caitlin —"

"What?"

"The worst of it ..."

"Go on."

"... the worst it is that I didn't suspect she was suicidal. She hadn't displayed any of the classic signs. She was angry. Anger usually means that someone is not depressed enough to hurt themselves —"

"... no, they hurt *you* instead."

"Ah, Cat. As well they should." Then, in response to her furrowed brow, he added, "She had things to work out in therapy. That means, with me — I'm *it*. That's what I'm paid for, Cat."

She sat down in the armchair across from him. "Anyway, it isn't your fault. How are you supposed to tell someone is suicidal if all the signs point to their being anything but? Be kind to yourself for once, Jerry. I know it's horrible, and I know it's hard for you not to feel responsible. I would too, in your shoes. But it really wasn't your fault, not in any way. You did more than anyone else would have, I'm sure. Developing an antipathy towards a patient is fairly standard, too, isn't it?"

"Well, yes. But the idea is not to show it."

"Oh, dear Jerry ..." Caitlin reached out a hand to rest it on his knee. "Even if you hadn't felt it, she would have assumed it at that point, wouldn't she? As part of the transference?"

"You know something?" he said after a moment. "That's true, Caitlin. That really is true. Thank you."

"Not at all, my dear. I require nothing in return but your unflagging devotion and a promise to clean my cat's litter twice a day for a year."

"No way." He managed a wan smile. "That's too high a price to pay even for a clearer conscience."

"In that case," said Caitlin, snatching her hand from his knee, "next time you're down, you can give *yourself* a peptalk, you ungrateful wretch."

He laughed then pulled her to him and kissed her deeply, with love, in a way that made her sigh and rest her head against his chest. He held her there, one hand on her head, the other against her back. When they parted, they smiled at one another, and Cat stood on her tiptoes to kiss his nose.

She was kind. She was perfect. He felt lighter and freer than he had since he'd returned from Guatemala.

But still, after she left, he wanted to be with Inez.

That night, tired of questioning himself every time he thought of the girl, he sought her out and took her on a walk round the neighbourhood. The soft glow of the streetlights was full of unreadable messages, and the mist from the ravines hung sorrowfully over the clipped green lawns. Jerry thought how Inez fitted seamlessly into this landscape of mystery and sadness. He found her company soothing and put a comradely arm around her thin shoulders.

Inez stepped out of his embrace and let her hands dance over his body, fluttering like butterflies or the beautiful *quetzal* of her homeland, her fingers tracing melodies in feathers all around him.

Jerry was stunned by this strange and lovely display. The play of Inez's fingers felt like the caress of wings passing in a soft breeze. After she had finished, he grasped her hands in his own and raised her fingers to his lips.

"What a dear, lovely creature you are, Inez," he said, letting go of her hands.

And immediately, his voice came back to him. "What a dear, lovely creature you are, Inez."

He stared at her. It was eerie. She had spoken exactly like him. Her face was expressionless, serene. She tipped her head a little to one side when he continued to stare.

Later, in bed, he found no solace between the covers. Images of Teresa twisted in the deepening fog of his mind. Only the memory of Inez's dancing hands let him fall finally into a restless sleep.

A bloody sun was sliding down the sky, enflaming the land and the body of a young girl, so that the streaks painting her naked chest and thighs became part of a pattern. Blood and the sun were the pattern of her days and nights; pain and despair, interrupted by beauty — the soft spill of the scarlet sun; islands of cloud punctuating the run-on blue of the sky; huge scarlet blooms gashing the old wooden fences, brick walls mad with colour, and shadows like black hands, moving.

She used to run away regularly, for some hope was in her then, some idea of freedom.

She used to look for love in their eyes, at first. Because it seemed that they must be breaking her open for a reason. Where they touched her, sometimes there was tenderness. And afterwards, there were walks among the flowers.

Sometimes she is happy. Sometimes she cuts herself, like tonight. She finds small, sharp rocks and slices at her arms, or the inside of her thighs. Sometimes she pushes round stones into the space between her legs.

In the house where she lives are other girls. Often, there is much laughter and talk. Life here has a strange, bloody hum.

A breeze rises; petals from a nearby hibiscus drift downward and across. A bird, bright-hued and full-feathered, swoops down at her from a tall tree, blinding her with its wings.

In that other land, a child stands facing a soldier. The hatred in the soldier's eyes is a mystery to her. So much so that, in the moment when he raises his rifle, she neglects to be afraid. It is dusk, and her family stands behind her.

It is only for that one eternal second that she is without fear. She ran in terror when a brace of soldiers stormed her family's one-room shack. She would run again in terror now, were it not for the fact that she can't move her legs; were it not for the fire that has become her body; were it not for the numbness at the edge of the fire, which deadens the scream before it bursts from her throat, and snuffs out the fire which is her body, and the horror inside her mind.

Behind her, the cut fields of maize blaze and crackle, and on the hills yet further back, the hand of night bleeds black.

Jerry, in the midst of these violent dreams, twisted in the sheets. Awake, he remembered only feelings of danger, of being female and alone, until the memory of one harrowing nightmare snapped clearly into focus. He was running towards Caitlin where she stood on a bridge with a man leaning over her, pulling his fist back and pounding it into her, again and again.

Jerry raced forward but got no closer. He grew increasingly desperate as it sank in that he wouldn't be able to save her.

He could still hear the voice from the dream: "Keep active! Keep active!" it said again and again, in mocking tones.

Why? thought Jerry. *Why keep active, when in the dream it did no good?*

Weariness suffused his body like damp infiltrating an old, crumbling castle. He realized he had felt worn out for quite some time. Lovemaking with Caitlin used to be the centre of his existence, a fire on a desert night, yet lately he was too tired even to think of it, and his feelings were chaotic. He couldn't understand himself, and that exhausted him. And now the awful tragedy of Teresa's death.

Analyzing the feelings Inez aroused in him was not working, and he had fallen miserably short with Teresa.

Perhaps that was what the voice had meant. "Keep active" because he was a failure at analysis?

Chapter Twenty-Seven

Caitlin's Story

Molly and I were almost home, the Quest behind us. We'd been silent for most of the ride. Part of my head was still back in the woods; another part was mulling over how to spring my next plan on my friend.

It wasn't unusual for Molly to be quiet when she was a passenger in a car. She said it put her in a trance-like state that reminded her of pleasant family trips when she was a girl.

On the outskirts of Toronto, I could feel us both gearing up for our return to regular life.

Molly spoke first. "So, Cat, you haven't told me much about your quest. Why's that?"

"You haven't been exactly forthcoming about yours."

Her expression in the rear-view mirror was sheepish. "That's because I spent most of it making designs out of sticks and drawings in the earth."

"Molly!"

"I know. But I got lots of ideas for paintings. Now what about you?"

Here we go, I thought. *Brace yourself.* "I've decided to do stand-up comedy."

"*What?*"

Luckily, we were going forty on a side street, so when I jumped in my seat, it didn't cause an accident.

"That's ridiculous. For god's sake, Caitlin, why?"

I told her about the crow. "Imagine that ugly, cocky thing being my power animal! He made me laugh and chased all my fears away. I was lost, remember? And scared. It felt so good to laugh, it got me thinking about how serious I've become. Obsessed and serious. I need something to take me out of myself. And I've often thought about doing stand up, you know. I miss performing."

Molly's eyebrows dove into a V. "That was supposed to be what the Quest was for. That, and making a decision about what to do next."

"It worked. I decided I need to laugh."

"So go to some funny movies."

"Not good enough. They'll just remind me of how Jerry and I went to the movies almost every week. I have to do something daring."

"Pull over. Stop the car."

"What?" I swerved and slammed my foot on the brake and pulled over. "Why?"

Before I got the car in park, she said, "If you want to do something daring, visit Inez. Stop trying to dodge the obvious, Caitlin." Her face looked dark but her eyes were on fire.

I stared. After the agony I'd been through facing up to my fears, she was accusing me of *avoidance?*

I did a stunned but rapid reappraisal. "I don't know, Molly, I ... it seems better than wallowing. I had to face up to a lot out there." I indicated the Bancroft woods with a backward inclination of my head. "Maybe I'm ready to move on."

"Or maybe you're looking for a way out."

I was shocked by the anger in her voice. I'd been prepared for some heavy-duty nagging, but not this. "Of what?"

"That's so obvious, I'm worried about you. You didn't even react to my suggestion about visiting Inez."

"Why are you so angry?"

"Because you keep doing this." Her hands were knotting imaginary ropes in her lap. "I think I've shown the utmost patience, waiting for you to get your act together. But this is the last straw. You're going to stop writing. Aren't you?"

"There's no point writing about something impossible to figure out. What I realized out there was that I needed to accept that some questions are unanswerable."

"I see," said Molly pinching her lips together.

"I'm not really sure you do." I twisted the key in the ignition so hard, I was grateful it didn't break, and steered the car back onto the road.

We stayed silent all the way to my apartment. I brought the car to an abrupt halt in my parking space, yanked up the emergency brake, and leapt out.

I flipped the trunk open and hurled a bag onto the driveway. "I wasn't even thinking about the book until you mentioned it." *Thump.* "I'm not trying to avoid writing it, but I do know —" *Flump, thump.* Sleeping bag followed by suitcase, "— after the quest *you* insisted we go on — that it may be best to move on, not pore over things I can never know." *Slam.*

Molly picked up my sleeping bag and crushed it to her side. "Such as?"

I stood straight. "Such as whether Jerry was in love with Inez."

I thought she'd drop the sleeping bag. "In *love* with her?" She almost shouted it. "She was sixteen going on four going on a hundred!"

I opened my mouth to say something, picked up my stuff instead and headed for the back entrance.

"Look, Cat," Molly growled, huffing along beside me, "how could he be in love with someone who can't communicate?"

"Spoken like a true woman. To a lot of men that would be an asset." I twisted my key in the lock.

"It wouldn't to Jerry."

I didn't answer until we were in the elevator. "I know." I took a deep breath to calm myself. "But some love is chemical, not rational — you might not want to be in love with that particular person, you just are, and besides, I think silent people encourage projection." I was thinking about how I'd confided in Inez partly because she was a blank slate on which I could write my own truth without fear. "I think Jerry thought he saw something in Inez he wanted." I could feel my lips tremble, so I pressed them together hard.

Molly stared at me. I stared at the elevator doors.

"Okay, okay, Caitlin. But what did he see?"

"I don't know."

She scowled. "We'll have to talk about this —"

"*Floor three,*" said the electronic voice. We struggled out with my belongings.

"Caitlin," Molly said in her most take-charge tone as we lumbered into my apartment, "you are possibly having a MAC attack — you know, Middle Aged Crisis. It would explain why you've suddenly started to worry about Jerry being in love with a teenage girl. A *mute* teenage girl with mental problems."

"That's possible. It's not a real worry. Let's forget it." I hurled myself onto the sofa then immediately got up to grab my cat Hannibal, who, in true feline fashion, was pointedly ignoring me because I'd gone away and left him to the mercies of a kindly neighbour.

"All the more reason you need to deal with it."

"That's where we disagree." I put Hannibal on my lap and scratched his ears. He stared off into the distance and refused to purr. "What I learned out there was that life's too short to spend feeling wretched. It sounds trite, but that doesn't matter. I avoid trite because I think I'm too good for it. It was a genuine break-through, Molly, to allow myself to be ordinary. I just need to do something fun. You know how I can't let things go."

She collapsed into an armchair across from me. "I never saw that as a fault, Cat. I admire your tenacity. I'm convinced it's good for you to keep investigating what happened and your feelings about it. And I'm really, really tired of your stupid eva-sion tactics."

That hurt. I stroked Hannibal vigorously. He was coming round. I watched his huge furry feet making dents in my cush-ions and listened to the rusty rev of a purr warming up.

"It's typical, really, that you're thinking about doing comedy. You want to laugh it off. And sometimes, Cat ..." her eyes bored into me, "making light of something is the worst possible road to take."

"You mean I'm not funny?"

"Damn you, woman, you know I don't mean that." She sprang up from her chair and strode around the room. "Stop it! Just stop it! I thought you were committed to the truth. I respected that. I knew you needed time to deal with this, but I never thought you were a coward. Ever."

"What's coward got to do with it? I'm a former rock singer. I miss being on stage. I miss, goddamn it, doing something I don't have to analyze." My throat constricted, and I coughed to clear it.

Molly's face twisted scornfully. "How the heck would you even get started?"

"By going to Yuk-Yuks Comedy Club and by watching comedy videos. It's not brain surgery. I've had a hankering to do stand-up for years. Yuk-Yuks has comedy workshops, too, you know, and —"

"This is crazy. This is just plain nuts. It won't help you. You'll push what happened out of your mind and then it will come crashing back all at once. You know this, Caitlin. What's happened to your brain? I wish you'd never gone on that quest. It's turned you into an idiot. Have you given up entirely on the book?"

"I'm not sure," I said flatly.

What I thought was: DAMN THAT BOOK.

"Caitlin, you might think you've given up on finding out what happened —"

"I have."

"No, you haven't. You've added a new wrinkle, Jerry being in love with Inez, and it's scared you into full retreat. *Again.* Are you going to forget all about Inez, locked away in Labrador for the rest of her life?"

I thumped my balled fist on the arm of the couch. "I *want* to forget her. She killed my life partner, the man I loved and needed and wanted. How can I deal with that if I don't put it behind me?" I glared at her then put my face in my hands and sobbed.

I felt Molly's hand stroking my back. "What's troubling you, Cat? This is something more than what happened between Jerry and Inez, isn't it? Tell me."

I felt so wretched, I couldn't contain myself. I raised my face, still soppy with tears, and clutched my friend's arm. "Oh, Molly." And I told her about the argument we'd had on the day Jerry'd died, how Jerry had stormed out saying he was disappointed in me, and how we never spoke again. "He died despising me, Molly."

I could barely choke the words out. "I know it was only a temporary feeling, but at the time of his death, he did not love me."

"But, Cat," she said, lifting my chin and smiling into my eyes. "The time he phoned me with tears in his voice, wondering if you loved him? That was the same night. He loved you, Cat, he told me so."

Chapter Twenty-Eight

Caitlin's Story

After I learned that Jerry still loved me, despite our terrible fight, I fell into a deep sleep and awoke feeling as if a dark spacecraft had taken flight from my body, carrying off some heinous cargo and leaving a trail of light. Knowing that Jerry loved me, even after our fight, was the most wonderful feeling I'd had for a long, long time.

Even reading over the Victim Impact Statement I'd prepared before Inez's sentencing didn't spoil my mood. I'd never had to use it because of the verdict, and I hadn't been able to look at it since I wrote it. Now I wanted to remember, to ready myself to see Inez.

Sometimes, when I think of Dr. Simpson dying — the pain and the fear — at the hand of someone he cared for and sacrificed for and even loved, I wish he'd left Inez in Guatemala where he found her. I know Inez can't control her rages, but I loved him, and it's so hard for me to think about how he died. I wish I'd been with him, so that he would have felt less abandoned and betrayed.

Jerry Simpson was a good man who worked selflessly for those in need. He did therapy free of charge with people who could not afford it. He played baseball with the mentally challenged adults at White Acres Community Living. He sat on the volunteer board of the Toronto Committee for the Prevention of Child Abuse.

He made time for me too, though I'm not sure how, and I treasure the hours as well as the years we spent together. I've lost my best friend, my life companion, and I know my life will never be the same again.

But punishing Inez will not help. She is no more capable of malice than I am of not wishing at times that she had never come into our lives. I do not know why she did what she did, but I am sure that locking her away will do no good. It will certainly not bring Jerry back.

I'd written that, striving to be my best self. Now I could stand behind it wholeheartedly. *I love you, Jerry. Oh, I love you, and you loved me, right up to the end.*

Even if he had been in love with Inez, that would change nothing.

I spun around the room like a schoolgirl, clutching the statement to my chest. *And you did not die unsure of me.* The thought was light as air, but sobering. I kissed the sheet in gratitude and set it down.

I'd always known I would visit Inez one day, when I was ready. For the first time since she was sent away, I could imagine being with her. I could see her distinctive features clearly in my mind when I closed my eyes, even the sweep of her lashes.

I was still visiting her in my mind when the phone rang. It was Gretchen, my lawyer friend.

"How is Inez?" she said as I wondered what had prompted the call. I hadn't heard from her in ages.

I was ashamed to tell her I didn't know any more about Inez than she did.

"Well, I have to let you know that Jerry's dad wants to have her declared a dangerous offender."

My hand stopped mid-reach for my coffee mug. "What? Are you serious?"

"Yes. He came to see Larry about it." Larry was Gretchen's partner in crime — prosecuting, that is. "That's how I know. Larry told me."

Jerry's dad was a bitter man and could be vindictive. But this was ridiculous. "Why would he do that?"

"I'm not sure. Larry says he was all worked up because of this news article he'd read about a psychiatric patient who escaped and killed his doctor. And he'd heard rumours that Inez had attacked an orderly in that hospital ..."

"For god's sake! Who does he think she'd go after, him? They never even met."

"He's a troublemaker, that's all," Gretchen said. "Or at least Larry thinks so. When Larry wouldn't take him on, he called him an idiot and a crook."

"Maybe it's *him* who should be declared dangerous."

"Yeah, I know, but that's not going to happen. Have you got any idea why he's doing this?"

"Probably just venting spleen. He was a lousy father but very proud of Jerry. It's got to hurt that his son is dead, and the girl who killed him isn't. He's also racist. But doesn't he know he's wasting his time? An 'insanity' judgment is more a life sentence than a regular life sentence! There's no parole. They'll never declare her 'cured.' Someone ought to tell him."

Pregnant pause.

"Oh no. Uh-uh. Not me, Gretchen. No way."

"Don't you talk to the old man anyway, Cat?"

"I do not. I don't like him. We never saw much of him, Jerry and I. He doesn't — thank god — think of me as either friend or family, but I know that with any encouragement, he'd be phoning me all the time, anyway, like he did Jerry, and I'm sure the calls would be unpleasant —"

We'd hardly talked since Jerry had died. At Jerry's funeral, I'd avoided him. The shock of the coffin was quite enough to deal with. I didn't trust myself near an abusive jerk who'd demanded we hold a service in a church, never mind that Jerry was completely against organized religion. Jerry had died young enough to not leave instructions for a funeral, and because he and I weren't "legal," Senior Simpson had *carte blanche* to create a fiasco, which I believe he did.

Sit next to him? Talk to him? I'd sooner have made nice to Vlad the Impaler.

"Well, okay," Gretchen said. "Then I'll ask Larry to give him more detail. That'll probably be the end of it."

For me, it was more like the beginning. My heart went out to Inez. Later that afternoon, I looked up her hospital at the library, read its history, located it on a map. I knew I should have done it ages before, but at least I was doing it now.

Great Northern Psychiatric had been built for two reasons, apparently: a new facility for the criminally insane was desperately needed, and it would help to develop the North and create work for the Inuit.

The government chose to locate the hospital on the coast, near the mountains north of Nain, the most northerly coastal town in Labrador. Nothing had ever been built there before. The Inuit set up camp in the area in the summer, to hunt and fish, but even they travelled south in the winter.

The site's isolation was one reason it was chosen — psychiatric facilities for the criminally insane are not welcome in most neighbourhoods.

The hospital had its own landing strip. That far north, almost everything had to be flown in. The project cost billions, but to Northern Development, it was worth it.

The government hired hundreds of Inuit to help build the facility. Then when the patients and medicos came, a grocery store and gym opened in the complex. It wasn't long before several other small businesses sprang up to serve the patients and staff, and a permanent settlement grew up around the hospital, where both visitors and employees could live or be housed.

At first medical personnel had been hard to find, but because it was a teaching hospital that developed a good reputation for innovation and research, some of the best medical school graduates began their psychiatric careers there. Some stayed on because they loved the work; those who left were quickly replaced with other fresh, young minds. Or so the books said.

But to Inez, it was a prison.

About a month after her arrival in Canada, I'd taken her to the Toronto Zoo. On the streetcar, she stood up from her seat and tried to push her way into the crush in the aisle. I pulled her back, afraid she'd run away. She fought me, and in the struggle ended up in the window seat. It was the best thing that could have happened. Looking out into open spaces rather than a press of hot bodies, she quickly lost her "horse in a barn fire" eyes.

But I was nervous after that. I remembered her tentatively stroking my cat as if she couldn't quite believe this soft, fluffy creature was hers to enjoy, while I prayed that Hannibal would not make any of his sudden moves and sighed with relief when he purred and went belly-up. She loved animals. How would she react to a place where they were caged?

I needn't have worried. The zoo animals were behind glass or barriers, not bars, and the only time I saw Inez look even slightly troubled was when a gorilla threw up into one giant paw. You could tell the animal was embarrassed, and both Inez and I looked away. I felt awful, like a voyeur, and I think Inez did too.

Now she was caged herself, treated like the specimen Jerry had fought so hard to prevent her from becoming

The next day, I called Molly. "I want to see Inez," I said.

She didn't answer right away. Then, "Good. But why now?"

"Jerry's dad wants her declared a dangerous offender."

"What? That's one of the stupidest things I've heard in this lifetime. She can't be declared an offender anything because she was found *not guilty* by virtue of insanity. That means she's not legally an *offender* at all."

"I know that, Molly."

"Then why?"

"I thought you *wanted* me to go —"

"I do! But this is so sudden."

I was surprised she didn't get it. "It's partly because of what you told me yesterday, because I know Jerry didn't die despising me, or thinking I didn't love him." I had to swallow. "I feel stronger now. I can face her, and I've neglected her."

"That's understandable."

"You were right to say I should visit. I can't let go until I do."

"I know that. I'm glad you feel better about you and Jerry, but are you sure that means you're ready to deal with Inez?"

"Not totally, but I never will be. You were right to yell at me, you know."

"I felt bad about it afterwards. I don't want to push you into something you really can't handle."

"I think I can. I have to try."

"Well, if you're sure, Cat …"

"I am."

"Just be careful, then. And call me. I'll call you too, if you give me a number as soon as you get there."

I promised I would and signed off.

The next week, as Molly helped me pack to go north, she said in a meaningful tone, "Be sure to take your notebooks. You're not through with that book yet. There's a lot more to what you're doing than you think, my dear, and you'll need to write it down."

On the plane, a couple of glasses of wine led to a pleasant wooziness followed by a long nap. I was woken by the lights and the seatbelt announcement indicating our imminent landing in Newfoundland. I don't remember much about the airport, except that it was small. I was too busy finding a cab to take me to the ferry docks, and thus to Labrador.

As the taxi approached our destination, the landscape got whiter and more barren, and the East Indian cabbie got chattier.

"Lady," he said as we pulled into the parking lot by the ticket office, "you could be in very much trouble if you are not remembering to look out for moose."

He was watching me in the rear-view mirror — I could tell by the upward tilt of his head and the reflected image of his right eye.

"I do not want to be frightening you, but it is something you must watch out for. Many tourists act very crazy around moose, stopping and giving them food, what have you. Very foolish. I would advise you not to drive at night, lady. Very dangerous. Moose are not understanding cars. They are so big, they are hurting you more than you are hurting them."

Drive? Did I look like I was hiding a car in my suitcase?

"Also, if you are visiting Viking ruins, be most careful. They are not open now, but you tourists often go in, anyway. Hopping the fence, as you would have it. Moose are out there, feeling very hungry, I wager."

"Surely it isn't mating season?" It was the middle of October. "I've heard they can be aggressive in the mating season."

"Oh, no, lady, not the season for mating, haha, no no. They are hungry for *food*, that is all."

"But they aren't meat eaters, are they?"

"Oh, they will not be eating you, lady." He seemed to find this amusing. "They are just in bad moods and they will chase you and run you down, just because. They have very big feet, very, and heads like mountains."

"Just because?"

"Just because they are not liking you in their places, I suppose. Very hungry. Very angry. I have seen tigers like that. They are much worse, because they are man-eaters, some of them."

I would have liked to have heard more about the tigers, and about life in India, where I supposed it was he had encountered them, but I was aware of the huge ferry boat churning its way across the Strait of Belle Isle to the dock.

"I have to dash," I said. "Thank you for the advice."

"Most welcome. Don't be forgetting it, okay?"

"Okay!" I said, fumbling for cash then running for the ticket booth, just in time.

I loved the ferry ride, even though I shuddered with cold through most of it, standing on the boat's vast deck, watching the sea froth and melt and froth again. When my hair started to freeze solid and the wind felt like a flame of ice on my face, I took refuge below deck.

At the Labrador dock, I had to charter a small plane to take me to the hospital. There was no other way out there. It was

October, and already the supply boats, the sealifts, they called them, couldn't navigate the ice in the Labrador Sea.

"It's a long way," said the pilot. "You sure? It'll cost you two hundred bucks. Mind if I ask why you're going?"

I did mind, but I said, "I'm visiting someone," and was glad when he didn't ask who.

On the way to the plane, I walked backwards into the wind to save my freezing face. I could see out over the water, and, in the distance, seals lolling on the ice floes. Close behind them, on a bigger floe, a huge polar bear crouched, covering its black nose with its white paws.

"Oh, look!" I said. "Why is it doing that?"

The pilot laughed. "That bear? It's stalking the seals. Polar bears cover their noses when they hunt. Guess it makes them blend in with the snow, so if the seals turn around, they maybe won't notice them."

I didn't know whether he was joking or not. "How do they know their noses are black? Does it work?"

"Beats me. But he doesn't look like he's starving, does he? It's strange, though, when you think about it, huh?"

I had to agree. I couldn't imagine anything, even a seal with an advanced case of myopia, turning around and not recognizing a polar bear on the hunt, covered nose or not.

"Maybe they think the bear has a cold and isn't up to chasing them," I said, running to catch up to him where he was hoisting himself into the plane.

It was a long flight, and a noisy one, but there is something simultaneously soothing and exciting about the noise of an airplane's engine. You had to shout to be heard, and that cut the small talk to zero.

From the air, the hospital's vast grounds and many buildings looked like a spread of glaciers.

Great Northern Psychiatric was supposed to be a place where they mended souls, but there wasn't an ounce of warmth anywhere, not in the climate, the architecture, or the setting. The complex consisted of small, squat buildings with complicated antennae and metal satellite dishes rearing up from their rooftops, and needle-nosed towers poking holes in the glowering sky. The main building was huge and white, like an outcrop of ice.

I found it scary. I could only imagine how Inez had felt when she first set eyes on it, especially if she understood she could be locked in there forever. But did she? It was always hard to tell how much Inez understood of almost anything.

Tall metal poles topped with flags marked the boundaries of the institute's grounds. Later, I discovered they delivered a nasty electric shock to anyone who ventured between them.

To the east was the Labrador Sea. You could see the roiling waters and, when the plane's propellers stopped whirling, you could hear them, too, as awe-inspiring as an overture by a thousand Kodo drummers.

We landed inside a blinding flurry. The runway was well-lit but deserted, nobody guided us in, and we had quite a trek ahead of us to the iron gates of the hospital grounds. There was no one there to meet me. I hadn't expected anyone, though I'd written to say I was coming. I'd received a very terse response, but I was surprised how suddenly small and lonely I felt here in this isolated white expanse.

The pilot helped me down from his plane, and I was grateful now for his interest and his company.

"You visiting a patient or a staff member?" he asked as he trekked with me to the big iron gate and pushed a button on what must've been an intercom.

"Patient," I said. "Named Inez," I added when I realized he'd asked not out of curiosity, but so he could announce my intention to whoever was on the receiving end of the intercom.

"Someone here to see a patient named Inez," he shouted against a howling wind into the device.

"My name's Caitlin Shaughnessy," I added hurriedly.

"Caitlin Shaughnessy," he yelled. "They say they aren't expecting you." He turned to me.

"Let me talk to them." I moved closer to the speaker as the wind whipped my scarf around my face and whirled snow into my eyes.

"I'm a journalist," I shouted to the stonewaller on the other end, clutching my arms round my body against the bitterness of the cold, "and very close to the — Inez. I'm like family. You can't refuse to let me in. She's allowed visitors, and I have nowhere else to go."

"Okay, Ms. Shaughnessy," the woman's voice crackled on the line. "But it's not visiting hours, and we're not a hotel."

"Fine," I said. "I'll work something out if you let me in."

She did, and I began the long trek, alone, to the main building.

Chapter Twenty-Nine

Caitlin's Story

There is something about the North that makes your soul want to leave your frozen body and go adventuring without you. You can't see the end of anything, sky or sea or snow. The katabatic winds roar down the mountainsides and blow the edges off the icecaps, and could probably blow your head off too, if you were ignorant enough to venture out. There are dangers all around, from sudden blizzards to avalanches, frostbite, falling ice. There also are the Northern Lights, hanging in the sky in wispy curtains, shooting out coloured rays, and polar bears that dive from fifty-foot icebergs into the sea.

A thousand miles from nowhere and a million miles from home. It was easier to be brave there — and I needed to be brave.

It was also easier to get reckless. There wasn't enough ballast. Dreams could take you over, and pride could get the upper hand. I noticed that first in the people who worked with Inez. It took me longer to notice it in myself.

Beyond the gates, small buildings squatted like albino frogs. Others were so tall they merged with the blank white sky. There were no trees.

The guards in black stood out as starkly as cavities in a hundred watt smile. I shuddered inside my big down coat as I approached the first building.

Inside it was all white, too. As I dusted myself off, nurses and doctors in white coats scurried past, carrying clipboards. There was an icy purity in the atmosphere, incongruous here, where most of the patients had committed crimes of passion. Even the desks were white.

I spoke to the first white-coat who approached me. "I'm here to see one of your patients, a woman named Inez." The cold still encased me, and I shivered as I spoke.

"Are you a relative?" he said.

"I was the partner of the man she killed."

"She's only allowed to see relatives."

"She has none, unless you've been more successful than we were at contacting the people in Guatemala who kept her chained in a shed."

I angled past him, almost pushing him out of my way, and strode towards one of the sterile desks. It was then I noticed the other distinguishing features of the room — metal and glass. There was a typewriter at every station. Fingers clicked on keyboards with a "pick-pock" surround-sound that grated on my nerves. Behind a glass partition I saw people moving — patients, I was sure — dressed in white slacks, T-shirts, and shifts. To match the decor? It struck me then that I thought I could see lips moving, no sound penetrated the stillness or the clack-clack of the typewriter keys.

The whole place was sound-proofed, I later learned. Each of its rooms, visiting, private, ward, office, was sealed within its own silence. The place was huge, with guards at every door who could look in and check on inmate patients, or inmates and visitors. Offices and visiting rooms were equipped with panic buttons or intercoms. Patients' rooms had none, which explained the eerie silence that permeated my skin every time I was there, punctuated only by the occasional shrill buzz or disembodied voice or, even more frightening, a steady, loud pounding, as of a fist on a locked door.

The white-coat I'd spoken to came up behind me. "I know about the box," he said. "And the other terrible things." He eyed me with a look that conjured up memories of arrogant teen athletes casing out the chicks at a high-school dance. "She's out on the grounds."

"By herself?" I didn't try to keep the disapproval out of my voice.

"Yes. There are surveillance cameras everywhere. She wears — they all do — electronic anklets — and there are barriers all around."

"I wasn't worried she'd escape," I said shortly. "Where is there to go? Look, I've got to see her."

"Well, who are you?"

I took out photos, ID, a letter from her lawyer.

Eventually, he said, "Just for a few minutes. There are regular visiting hours, you know."

The outside stretched endlessly. My breath plumed in front of me then rose like steam from a dozen hot springs.

The light reflecting off the snow meant that at first I couldn't distinguish Inez from her surroundings. Then I picked out her quilted coat with its fur-trimmed hood big enough to swallow her. She was staring at the sky, rapt.

Her eyes grew wider when she saw me, and her mouth opened then regrouped into a smile of almost impossible sweetness. Running towards me, she churned up the snow that dusted the top of the ice. She stretched her arms out, but I didn't hug her. I held that radiant face between my mittened hands and ran my eyes over it.

There was no shame, or fear, or uncertainty in her expression, only love. I clasped her to me as sudden tears fell onto the hood of her coat and instantly froze.

Then that damn image came. The one the housekeeper described. Inez crouched beside Jerry, drenched in his blood.

All the good intentions in the world, all the Vision Quests, all the comedy routines, all the meditative revelations, all the coping skills of all eternity could not wipe that picture from my imagination. Inez, cowering against the wall of Jerry's study, T-shirt clinging to her, her hair matted and slick, as though she'd used too much gel, but it was blood, more blood, Jerry's blood.

I pulled away, breathed deeply again and again.

When I opened my eyes, she was staring at me, bewildered.

"Inez ..." I put an arm around her small shoulders. "Let's go inside." My voice felt weak.

She let me lead her back in, all docility and gentleness. I took her to one of the designated visiting rooms, where the door locked behind us with a domineering clang. She smiled at me trustingly while the white-coats hovered and swooped outside the confines of our enclosure — the room we were in, with its huge glass window, and the encounter itself, which sealed us from everything around us, except, of course, our shared past.

I returned Inez's smile reflexively. When I asked what she saw, I knew there'd be no answer.

We sat down side by side on the soft white couch. I held both her hands in mine and said, more to myself than her, "Inez, you

looked as if you were listening to the voices of angels out there."
Her cheek, still rosy from the cold, felt like ice to my touch.

I still couldn't quite believe I was there, that *she* was there.

"If only you could tell me what happened. I could help you
then. Please can't you tell me?" I knew it was hopeless.

I stared into those fine brown eyes, now dreamy and faraway.
"Look *at* me, Inez, please."

She dropped her gaze.

"Inez, don't turn from me, please don't." I stopped myself from
lifting her chin with my hand, but I couldn't help but wonder —
in avoiding my eyes, was she avoiding all that had happened?

"Oh, Inez. If only you would talk … I know you can. You can."
The frustrations of the past few months crowded my head
until they became concentrated into one word, one question.
"Why?" I almost groaned it. "Why, Inez?"

She looked at me for a frozen moment, eyes suddenly clear.
Her mouth fell open. Then she parroted, in my voice, "Why?
Why, Inez?"

Oh, oh. It was all I could do not to shake her. It mocked me,
that response. I had to let her hands go in case I crushed her
fingers. What was I hoping to do? Squeeze the truth out of her?
Shake her till the words fell off her lips?

The futility was awful.

And then she parroted me again. "Listening to the voices
of angels."

Oh god. I grabbed her hands a second time. "Inez," I began. It
took a moment to remember that she had no sense of who she
was. How could she answer from her perspective, when she might
have none? I didn't even know if she understood anything I was
saying, at least in our terms. I dropped her hands and stood up.

She started as if I'd struck her and raised her arms over her
head. There was a warning light in her eyes.

"Inez, I'm not going to hurt you." I was surprised at the hardness in my voice.

She lowered her arms, watching me warily.

"You killed him."

When she parroted my words, "You killed him," words I never should have voiced, I couldn't bear it. "No — *you*," I burst out. "You killed Jerry. Not *me*, Inez. *You* killed him."

Again, she repeated everything I said, exactly as I said it, while a thoughtful look crept into her eyes, one I'd never seen there, as though an inner light were dawning, and though bewildered, I pressed my advantage.

"You did, Inez. All I want is to find out why."

Grey shadows dulled her bronze skin. Her eyes never left my face. "I ..." she said, in a tortured voice, "I ... can ..." and fell silent, her face contorted.

Shock froze me in place. *I?*

Inez had never said *I* before. She had never said anything personal at all. All she had ever done was mimic and repeat.

And she had said it with emotion.

"You can what, Inez? What is it you can do?"

Then she said something I couldn't catch, but which sounded like "new buy."

"What does that mean, Inez? What is 'new buy'?"

But her eyes glazed over, and she curled up on the white sofa like a prodded squid. The "I" stayed between us, both the word and the self it represented, and I knew Inez was in there, that there must be a torrent of feeling she'd like to start with "I," if only she dared.

I waited and waited, but nothing more came.

"There is a meaning to what happened that only Inez knows," I said at last, reckless, lightheaded. "Inez is sad it happened."

Her face remained blank as she repeated my words. But when

I said, "Inez is sorry she killed Jerry," a silence heavy as tar fell before she broke into a wail that brought the white-coats running.

I desperately wanted to run myself, but I was afraid the guards might drug her or hurt her if I didn't stay and keep an eye on them. Inez was remarkably compliant as they led her away, though she kept crying out wordlessly in a high, strained voice. She did not look back.

As soon as she was out of sight, I went straight to a desk, struggling for composure, and asked for help finding accommodations. I knew about the settlement that had sprung up around the hospital, where people rented out houses and rooms to visitors.

The nurse gave me a number and directed me to a public phone.

"Just for the night," I said to the lady on the other end of the line.

I planned to leave Labrador as soon as I could book a flight out. I was afraid to see Inez again, afraid I'd do real damage.

As soon as I arrived back in Toronto, I phoned Inez's nurse, Margaret. I hadn't seen her for months, but I needed to tell her about my visit to Inez in the white citadel, including my reckless stupidity.

We were in my living room. I told Margaret I wanted to go back, but that with no therapeutic background, I might do more harm than good. I said, "If only Inez would talk about what happened ..."

Margaret responded, "That could take years, Caitlin. It may *never* happen."

"I know."

"We know she can speak, of course. But she never speaks as herself. There are two major problems, and both could be insurmountable ... now. The first is that she may be afraid to talk, for some reason we don't know."

I swallowed. "The other?"

"The other is that she probably doesn't know who she is," Margaret said in a low voice. "She can't talk about herself or her feelings until she's aware she has them, if you follow me. I think she's afraid to recognize them because of what may have happened to her in Guatemala."

"I understand," I said. "Jerry told me about this. But Margaret, she said 'I' to me ..." I watched the nurse's eyes grow round. "She said 'I can' as if she were starting to tell me something about herself ... she said it with feeling, and in a young woman's voice, and she was not parroting anything I'd said. And then she added something I couldn't understand, but I think may have been in her language — which means she was talking as herself."

"Really?" Margaret's eyes grew rounder still.

I told her the details, about how I'd upset Inez. "I need you, Margaret. Inez needs you. Look, I'll pay your plane fare, and you can share my digs for free ..."

I told her I could do little in the way of wages. I was worried about how I would afford this. Not only did it cost to get out to the hospital, but the whole time I was gone, I wouldn't be earning a thing. There were no paid vacations in freelancing.

After talking to Margaret, I thought about how kind people had been to Inez during the trial. It had been all over the papers. On TV too. Her past was so terrible that, despite the murder, the media had made her something of a heroine. Some journalists suspected that Jerry was the villain of this piece, taking her away from her tribe and her country, and they had supporters.

Inez was fortunate in her beauty, and all through the ordeal she'd projected an innocence I found either moving or outrageous, depending on my perspective. Her expression was often sweet, her big eyes wide.

That innocence, I believed, was real, no matter what she'd done. Her aggression, her triumph, her rage — things a more "normal" person would try to hide — were right up front. She was without guile or subterfuge and no more able to hold a grudge than a puppy.

If circumstantial evidence had been less incriminating, I suspect the jurors would have felt compelled to set her free.

Perhaps that public sympathy could help me now. Perhaps if Margaret co-operated, we could make an appeal for money. Then she could stay with Inez for a while, be her personal therapist.

I suggested this to her, and she agreed it was worth a try.

"Let me know what happens next," she said. "I'm willing to go out there for a couple of days at my own expense. But if it's possible and helpful for me to stay longer, let me know. Then we can team up on the fundraising."

"It's a kind of frozen hell out there," I warned her. "The landscape is awesome, the Inuit are kind, but the hospital, it's like something out of a high-tech horror film. Utterly sterile."

She wasn't to be put off, not after she'd learned about that incredible "I ... can."

As for me, I'd started to have doubts. Had Inez actually said "I"? Perhaps she was beginning to parrot "Inez" or some other word I'd spoken, and what she said afterwards was not in her language at all, just nonsense words. I didn't tell Margaret this. Too much was at stake.

Soon after I'd talked to Margaret, I contacted all my friends in the media and began a campaign to solicit funds that would allow me to hire a special nurse for Inez and go up north to be with her. An editor at the *Star* allowed me to write a piece in which I mentioned the threat of having her declared a dangerous offender, even though I knew this couldn't amount to anything, and how, if she was ever to recover, or at least achieve a measure of happiness, she needed better help than she was getting.

On ice in her crystal palace, I wrote in my best journal-ese, *Inez is destined to remain as frozen as she was the evening she was found, covered in the blood of a man she attacked out of fear and uncontrollable dread. We don't know why Inez did what she did. We do know enough of her past to understand its horror, and to wonder how we would respond to a perceived threat, or even to proffered friendship if we had been through what she has been through. Regardless of her "crime," Inez deserves the best treatment our society can offer. It is my belief that, at the present time, she is not receiving it.*

And so on. Contacts are a wonderful thing, and so is the media, used in the right way for the right reasons. In a matter of weeks, I had amassed several thousand dollars.

I phoned Margaret to give her the good news.

A week later, I flew back to Great Northern on my own. I'd offered Margaret a three month contract, and she'd readily agreed, but when she told me she had a few loose ends to tie up before she was free to travel, I was relieved. I wanted to be alone again with Inez — in the sense of, alone with the thought of Inez, as well as in her presence. I felt strong enough to handle both now, especially knowing that help was on its way.

I knew my next step was to go and talk to a Dr. Peterson, the man who ran the white citadel. I'd heard about Peterson. He was supposed to be good, a rare mix of compassion and competence. I doubted I'd like him. Kindness coupled with power has a way of making my skin crawl. I decided it might be to my advantage to mistrust him. I'd have to wait and see.

A few days after my return, I was at last ushered into Peterson's office, after a great deal of initial resistance from the staff. I told them of my relationship to Inez, I told them I was a journalist working on a story, and finally I told them that if they did not let me see him, I would contact a lawyer. It worked. Perhaps it was the threat of bad publicity, coupled with the stirring of doubt about whether they could legally refuse me access that propelled them into action.

First, they had to persuade the great man himself. I wasn't privy to their efforts, but I was, eventually, escorted into his domain.

It was like being ushered into the presence of a heathen god. Huge double doors swung open on my approach. This was enough to make me expect a raised throne and a cloud of smoke. What I really saw should have paled by comparison. Far from it. You could have skated across his desk, it was that wide and shiny. It was dead centre in the room, atop a creamy, deep-pile carpet with as much give as a waterbed. On the wall behind him loomed an immense painting, twice the size of anything I'd seen in the Art Gallery of Ontario, of two swans rising off a lake. Even at a distance, the picture dwarfed that excessive desk and its distinguished owner. All that was missing was full orchestral accompaniment.

The handsome gent with silver hair stood up. "Miss Shaughnessy," he said, "please sit down." He gestured to a plush armchair in front of the monument to his own importance.

"I prefer Ms.," I said, sinking so low into the cushioned seat, I thought my knees might connect with my nostrils.

"Miz?" He crinkled his forehead. "Oh. Of course. Excuse me."

Good recovery, you supercilious bastard, I thought, taking in the well-tended hair and the rich wool of his suit. What caught my eye, too, even at a distance, were the frames of his glasses. They were a mottled tortoiseshell mélange, flecked with gold, and it was obvious they were as expensive as everything else about him, right down to his manicured nails.

His kind face made me think of the puzzle of Inez. I understood his type of contradiction more readily than hers, though; genuine kindness bolstered by privilege, a privilege that was deeply important to him. His geniality was in my eyes conditional, and thus unreliable.

"What can I do for you, Ms. Shaughnessy?" he went on, smooth as butter in a warming pan, and I outlined what I wanted.

"I don't think that will be possible. Inez is already receiving treatment from our staff. I can see you're worried, but we have an excellent program here. Her main therapist is a Dr. Maxim, a man of compassion and ability ..."

His tone, concerned as it was, was beginning to make me gag. Good intentions have that effect on me when they seem as misguided as his. "Have you ever dealt with an autistic before?" I knew he would not be expecting me to quiz him.

He frowned. "Yes, of course. But her condition points to much more than autism, if she is autistic at all. Dr. Maxim —"

"They may have decided Inez had a mental illness at her trial, but she could be emotionally disturbed. Or traumatized. Do you have a trauma expert on staff?"

"There are other factors involved here, Ms. Shaughnessy."

Ah, the professional dodge so soon. I was disappointed in him.

"I can assure you, Dr. Peterson, they would not be beyond my powers of comprehension."

He looked at me with frank disapproval, and I thought I'd sussed him right. But his next comment surprised me.

"You are putting me a little on the defensive, Ms. Shaughnessy. It matters to me to be helpful, and I fear you do not see me that way."

This last was worthy of a psychoanalyst.

"Are you trained in analysis, Dr. Peterson?"

"Thank you for the compliment." He smiled, surprising me again. "But no. I am a psychiatrist only, by training and inclination. Which does not mean, I hasten to add, that this Institute does not employ the very latest in psychodynamic techniques. Where warranted."

"Are they warranted for Inez?"

He leaned back in his magnificent leather chair. "Yes, they are. Very much so."

"First you must reach her," I smiled back. "You must get her to speak to you. In order to do that, she must first recognize herself."

He tipped his chair forward so that his mohair elbows rested on his personal stretch of tundra. "What do you mean by that?"

"It is my belief, as it was Dr. Simpson's, and that of her live-in nurse, Margaret Richards, that Inez does not experience herself as an independent being. Even in moments of love and anger, she does not recognize those emotions as belonging to her. She has never used the word 'I' in relation to herself. Except once. The first time I visited her here, a few weeks ago."

Both silver eyebrows rose a perceptible degree. "She said 'I'? About herself?"

I explained what had happened. It was the second time I'd used this piece of information to get what I wanted.

"Then it is you I think she needs to see. Not this Margaret Richards. And not, of course, in therapy." This last was pointed. He narrowed his eyes and leaned even further forward as he said it. "If you visit her as a friend, perhaps once a week, it could be that she would open up to you further. It would be best ..." he gave the

301

word *best* an unnatural emphasis, "if her therapist was also present when you were with her. I cannot insist on it, and I wouldn't deny you access, given your connection to her, and your place in her life. But I must advise you that my staff think it would be unwise for you to see her alone. Under the circumstances." Another pointed remark. "And I must also caution you — in the opinion of this institute, amateur therapy could result in disaster."

Heat rose up my neck, and I had to look away. Obviously, the staff had drawn some conclusions about Inez's distress at the end of my visit. I almost forgave him his horrible office, including the triumphant swans, but a little voice told me not to let up. "I agree." I forced my eyes up to his face. "That is why I wish to see her with Margaret Richards, who is also her friend, though in a different way. Margaret knows what she is doing. Even if Inez does not need to see her every day, I need Margaret to accompany me here, at least. I need her advice."

He drew his head back. "Nobody can stop her accompanying you, Ms. Shaughnessy, but I will not allow her access to Inez."

I wanted Margaret to be granted access, but I knew I'd wrung a lot of concessions already from Mr. Proud-and-Kind, and I didn't want to push my luck.

"Okay, Dr. Peterson," I said, gathering my things and getting up. "And thank you."

Chapter Thirty

Caitlin's Story

I'd decided to try reading to Inez. Truth to tell, I couldn't think of anything else to do. Perhaps my reluctance to bring Margaret with me right away had to do with her reaction when I mentioned this. I was actually hoping for some advice on the kind of material to take.

"You plan to read to her?"

"Yeah. I thought I'd give it a try. It means I can communicate with her without needing a response." Books, I'd decided, would keep me away from the tragedy that bound us together; would keep me from doing further harm.

"Kind of like she's in a coma?" Margaret raised her eyebrows before scrunching them into a disapproving V.

"I didn't think of it like that. But maybe you're right. It just seems non-invasive."

"Sometimes it's necessary to be invasive to be helpful."

I knew about Margaret's training and her "style" with autistics. I didn't object to them, but I wasn't a therapist, and Dr.

Peterson's words were still echoing in my ears.

"I'm not her therapist, Margaret. I'm going up there as someone who cares about her. I can't sit back and expect her to converse with me. So I've decided to act like a mother with an infant. Except I'm perverse; I'm going to take some hard stuff with me."

The idea of including challenging selections had come to me while Margaret was talking, so I suppose she did help out with the reading material, in a way.

Her point was well-taken. Inez wasn't in a coma, or mentally slow, or a baby, and she sometimes gave the impression of knowing a lot more than any of us. After all, she'd had experiences in her short life that most of us would never have no matter how long we lived. Who was to say that she hadn't thought things over and decided the world wasn't worth her time?

Maybe if I showed her the beauty of words, she'd want to use some of her own. Or maybe she'd just soak them in, and grow inside, and never let us know. I figured that was up to her. Besides, if she was autistic as well as all the other things that could be wrong with her, weren't autistics sometimes fascinated by abstractions? And mechanical things? It was people they didn't seem to care much for. Maybe Inez would like it if I read her a book of mechanics, or something about how clocks worked, or even the nature of time.

I ended up taking the *Tao of Physics*, David Macauley's *The Way Things Work*, and an anthology of twentieth-century poetry.

Chapter Thirty-One

Caitlin's Story

He wasn't bad-looking. There was just something about the eyes. He had dark, bushy eyebrows over small eyes. I didn't like his mouth, either. It looked like it was pulled together with basting stitches.

I was back inside Great Northern, checking out Inez's main therapist, Dr. Maxim.

"Aren't there any women doctors in this hospital?" I grumbled.

Dr. Peterson, who was doing the introductions, said, "Not many. Perhaps women don't like the north."

Or the psychopaths.

"Or the pay," quipped young Dr. Maxim.

How stupid was this man? Everyone knew working in the north came with a high salary. Unless you were Inuit.

"How often do you see Inez?" I said.

"As often as I can, given my schedule." His tone was far from genial.

"How often's that?"

"Once a week."

We watched each other.

"Look, Ms. Shaughnessy. We are very, very busy. The government does not provide us with enough money to give individual, in-depth therapy to each inmate. They are here for their crimes, after all, not solely for treatment. But there are nurses who —"

"They were all found not guilty of a crime, Doctor. I have enough money to provide Inez with a personal therapist. A Ms. Margaret Richards, a nurse who has worked successfully with her —"

"Excuse me," Dr. Peterson intervened, as smooth as his silky hair. "That really is beyond Dr. Maxim's scope. As you well know, Ms. Shaughnessy."

He addressed the young doctor, whose furry eyebrows were threatening to merge into a pelt over his little mouse eyes. "Ms. Shaughnessy and I had agreed that this Ms. Richards would not see Inez personally. If the matter comes up again, please refer it to me."

He turned his unctuous face my way. "Inez is with helpers nine hours out of every ten. She is almost never alone —"

"I suppose helpers include guards?" I said.

"Of course," said Maxim.

"Is that why I found her wandering on the grounds by herself when I first arrived?"

I heard Peterson swallow. "Ms. Shaughnessy," he said wearily, "even on the grounds, our patients are monitored. They wear electronic monitoring bracelets. It was felt that for her, for *brief periods* occasionally, Inez needed to be alone —"

"A girl who was shut up in a box for god knows how many years needs to be alone?" I said. And when he scowled at me, I added, "Just asking."

"Sometimes people who are used to solitude need time away from others. You are not a professional therapist. Her caregivers are. She has been here for two months now, without your kind assistance, and, in the opinion of the staff, has come a long way. As for your relationship with her, it has, if I may be so bold, its complicating elements, does it not? In all fairness, can you be sure you always have her best interests at heart?"

I was impressed. He was perceptive, as were at least some of his staff. If I was going to get what I wanted from him, I would have to be careful.

"I can be sure," I said. "But it's not a simple issue. I'd be happy to discuss it further with you, if you'd like — at another time."

I did respect the question. I did think he deserved as full an answer as I could give him, in confidence. But I also saw an opening. I wanted to keep him interested in this case. This place was vast, and it would be so easy for one small person to be swallowed whole here and forgotten. If that meant showing Peterson a bit of my inner life, it was a small price to pay. No price at all, really, as I didn't intend to reveal anything I didn't want to.

Until my first meeting with Inez at the hospital, I *had* been sure I had her best interests at heart. What happened that day had changed everything.

It was that, and my journalistic curiosity, I intended to conceal from Peterson. The need to know, just to know. It is not my most attractive quality. It was complicated in this case by an ambiguity I found painful.

I could tell that I'd piqued Peterson's interest, which was exactly what I'd intended. The curiosity of shrinks is almost as predictable as that of writers.

"That might be profitable," he said, drawing me away from Maxim, "but there is much we can discuss now, today. Such as the effect of your last visit with Inez."

He really was a clever bastard. I swallowed and stood straighter. "That's why I need Margaret," I said. "Please tell me how Inez is now."

He scrutinized me over the top of his fancy glasses. "Much better than just after you left," he said smoothly. "Much better."

I struggled to keep tears out of my eyes — and my voice. "How ... how did you manage to console her?"

He smiled a tight little smile. "I am gratified you admit she needed consoling, Ms. Shaughnessy. It just took time and patience on the part of her caregivers for her to recover. I imagine she buried deeply once again whatever trauma may have been reawakened in her by you."

I struggled to keep my head high. "Will you allow me to see her?"

"As I said before, I can't forbid it. But I promise you that if you upset her again, I will do all in my power to ensure you never see her again without a doctor present."

That afternoon, I met with Inez in one of the hospital's civilized little visiting rooms. I approached her cautiously, calling her name.

She looked at me warily.

I had long ago got into the habit of speaking to her as if she could understand. "Inez, you look beautiful today. Don't be afraid. I'm going to read to you, that's all, and I will not hurt you." I smiled at her and touched her arm. "I won't, Inez. I promise. Remember I sometimes read to you at night ... before?"

She blinked, and I was sure she'd understood. Margaret's work with her, and, I had to admit, Michael's, meant she had a much larger command of English than when she'd first come to us.

When her eyes almost immediately clouded over and her mouth trembled, I imagined dark images forming inside her head, like black ink spilled over a photograph. I hoped with all my heart I had not brought them on.

"Here we go, Inez," I said, to distract her. I pulled out *The Anthology of Twentieth Century Verse*. I'd already chosen the poems I wanted to start with that day. I led off with Gerard Manley Hopkins. If she understood the words, the images might be too discordant for her; on the other hand, they could be similar to how she experienced life. The joy this poet took in what he saw and how he saw it might have relevance for her.

I planned to read first, then go through each poem word by word, using pictures I had gleaned earlier from magazines to show what they meant.

On the first read-through, I was hoping the rhythm would reach her, the musicality of the language. Hopkins can be hard to understand even for English Literature students. I chose him because of the images. Someone like Inez might respond to poetic meaning more readily than facts.

True, my big dream was for her to fall in love with words, so that she longed to speak them herself, but I didn't expect this. What I needed most was to re-establish a connection. There were limited possibilities to do this in the context of a structured visit. Before, outings with Inez were the main way I spent time with her.

> As kingfishers catch fire, dragonflies draw flame;
> As tumbled over rim in roundy wells
> Stones ring; like each tucked ring tells, each hung bell's
> Bow swung finds tongue to fling out broad its name

I read a few more Hopkins poems, watching her face. From her bright, intense eyes and the way she leaned forward, I was sure she was listening. Then I started on some e.e. cummings:

> *Anyone lived in a pretty how town*
> *(with up so floating many bells down)*
> *spring summer autumn winter*
> *he sang his didn't he danced his did*

Inez, sitting on the couch with the light from the window streaming over her face, closed her eyes and sat back, her mouth slightly open. I saw her lips quiver. I wished I could read something in her native tongue, but as far as I could discover, the Kaqchikel have no written literature.

As I continued to read, sometimes she frowned or shifted in her seat, but I thought it had more to do with me than with what I was reading. I could almost hear questions percolating under the surface of her skin — *Why are you here? How long will you stay? Will you hurt me? Will you ever come back?* — but I could also sense them flow together into something tranquil and whole, something that had to do with a vision I couldn't see.

When I was done, I longed to touch Inez, as if that would allow all that she was thinking and unable to say to travel along my arm, straight into my mind.

But I didn't touch her. Perhaps I was afraid I was right.

Chapter Thirty-Two

Caitlin's Story

Early that same evening, with the mouth-watering smell of lasagne wafting round me from the woodstove in my kitchen, I gazed out the window at the Kaumajet Mountains rising like snaggle-toothed dinosaurs from the Labrador Sea. Behind them, the sky brooded in tones of mottled grey.

At the grocery store that served the hospital (and where anything even remotely green, no matter how tired and wilted, cost three times what it did at home), the Inuit owner warned me a blizzard was on its way.

"Worse one this year, looks like," he said. "New to the north?" He peered at me out of a pair of perfect dewdrop eyes.

When I answered in the affirmative, he added, "Best go inside and stay there, then, till the winds die down. Blows like a hurricane. Even the caribou hide."

On his advice, I stocked up on food and fuel. He said the snow got high as a mountain in the drifts and could trap me inside my house for days, so I bought an emergency radio as well. He showed me how to crank it up if the batteries died.

At home, grateful for the firewood chopped and ready by the outside wall, I hauled some logs indoors and crumpled paper to stuff under them in the concrete fireplace.

Once prepared, I relished the coming of the storm. As the sky became a blotchy mix of dark grey and white, like some stagey cauldron full of dry ice, and the wind rattled the windows, I pulled my feet up under me and leaned back into the softness of the armchair near the grate. How snug and cozy and safe I'd be when the wind began its tantrum! I'd have the fire lit by then and a cup of steaming hot chocolate in my hands.

I put on Jerry's big alpaca sweater, made myself that cocoa and, cradling it, stood by the window, looking out over the sea.

Because the blizzard still only threatened, I could see the closest icebergs clearly. They were streaked with bands of sediment that made me think of huge mounds of chocolate ripple ice cream, mainly because I was hungry. I checked my watch — only ten minutes till my lasagne was done.

When Inez first saw snow, a March storm in Toronto the first month she was with us, her eyes widened, and she rushed to the door. It was all I could do to wrestle her into a coat and boots and mitts before we went outside, with Jerry laughing over his coffee in the background.

Outside, Inez kicked up clouds of powdery whiteness then fell to her knees. Grabbing snow in both hands, she threw it into the air, where it turned into a crystal waterfall that shimmered down, covering her face with a veil of tiny sequins.

How rich her experiences seemed, even without words, perhaps because she had no words to separate herself from the world.

My father tells me I spoke my first words very early. "Onut," I said, watching him eat a cruller, and, a little while later, "Og," meaning dog. The first sentence followed soon after: "Og want og food."

Seems I had a little trouble with the letter "d," so my dad coached me. Pointing to himself, he said, "Dad," emphasizing the d's. After a while, I laughed and said, "Og Dada."

"And Og Dada I stayed for years," he told me. He made a little sound with his tongue against his teeth. "Ztt. Never mind, you were a right little chatterbox after that. Couldn't keep quiet for a second."

Truth be told, I still call him Og Dada at times, just for fun.

Remembering this, I was struck by the thought that Inez lived in the primordial silence that Buddhists say is the source of all creation, the silence that is always there behind the noise, the wordless world, unnamed, undefined, vast, timeless, bursting forth into thought, image, noise, things, us.

In the beginning was the Word, the Christians say, and perhaps words did begin it, changing the all-in-all to the one who is part of nothing until it remembers its source.

Inez understood much of what was said to her, I was sure. That meant her world had to be somewhat conceptualized and restricted. Still, I couldn't remember a time even far back in my childhood when I'd experienced the world with anywhere near the immediacy she seemed to.

I'd used words in my childhood fantasies to make them come alive. If I was pretending to be a horse, snorting while pawing the ground, I described what I was doing to myself, in my head. For a bookish child, words were thrilling.

But Inez? As far as I could tell, Inez lived as we imagine animals do, in the everlasting present.

How could I, of all people, entranced by words since childhood, reach her?

———

The first time I took Inez to Centre Island, she'd headed for the top deck of the ferry with what Jerry called her "animal stride," loping like a puma. Dressed in a pair of terrycloth short-shorts and a tank top that showed off her lithe brown limbs, she stood by the rail, her hair blowing behind her, her arms stretched over her head in a kind of greeting to the elements, I thought. She was catching some people's attention, and a funny little boy with a serious blue gaze came up beside her.

"Why you standing dere with your arms up?"

Inez looked straight into his bright wide-open eyes and picked him up. When she lifted him like an offering to the sun, I panicked and ran towards them. They were so close to the rail …

By the time I reached her, she was putting the little fellow down, and he was smiling.

"Whee!" he said. It was his turn to have his arms in the air. "More! More!"

But Inez was busy bending backwards into the shape yogis call The Bow and crab-walking the deck.

The boy ran after her. "Girl, girl," he called out, "how do dat, girl?"

Down on his chubby knees, he tried bending backward then fell over onto his side, laughing. Inez ignored him.

I wondered whether the reason she didn't show him how to do a backbend had less to do with not understanding what he wanted and more because, in the absence of speech, connections were not assumed by her, or natural. In other words, she would not assume a response was needed. They say autistics lack the ability to relate to other people, but Inez connected often with those she knew well. It wasn't a consistent thread, though. It could be broken and often was. There was no conversation to glue it together.

If this was the case, what I was hoping for seemed impossible.

At last, the little boy's mother — and I must say I admired the *sang froid* she had shown up till then — scooped him up and away. "That's enough of that, Brian," she said. "Let's go downstairs now. It's cold up here."

The oven timer rang, interrupting my reverie, and I headed for the kitchen. Reaching into the oven, I thought, *Maybe I should try to reach her visually.* It seemed a good idea and came so suddenly that I almost dropped the pan.

I put some lasagne into a bowl and carried it to the table. As I ate, I thought about the time Inez had seen a photo of Jerry standing in his backyard.

She went to sit next to him on the sofa in his living room, clutching the picture. She wouldn't let us take it from her, carried it around for days. It was a talisman, I think, a security-blanket, what analysts call a transitional object — something to connect her to Jerry when he wasn't there.

On another occasion I showed her a shot of the rainforest. She began touching the trees in the picture then stared at the landscape close-up. She seemed puzzled.

"Guatemala," I interjected, touching the photo. "Where you came from."

Her eyes narrowed while her breath came and went as fast as a panting dog's. When I tried to take the photograph from her, she pulled away, clutching it tightly to her chest. Crushing it, she stuffed it into one of her pockets.

None of us ever saw it again. I suspect it was so creased and torn that over time it disintegrated. It may even have been thrown into the wash at some point, still inside her pocket.

———

I decided to phone Molly. I wasn't sure how long the storm would last, and when it came it could cut off communication.

"I've been thinking about artists," I said to her over crackling static.

"Oh yes," she responded.

"And that means you."

"I suppose so." She waited.

"You're different," I said, "from writers."

"That's rather self-evident, isn't it, Caitlin? Ah well, it's your dime."

I laughed. "It's just that in working with Inez, I've had these thoughts about understanding things visually rather than verbally, and I figure that's what artists do. Do they?"

"I'd have to draw you an answer."

"Gee, *thanks*, Molly."

"Tell me about Inez. What's this got to do with her?"

"It's just that I feel as though reaching her on a non-verbal level might be better than reading to her, even with pictures for back-up." I didn't go into detail. The communication between Inez and me was delicate enough to be threatened by too much dissection.

"Could you send me one of your pictures, Molly?"

"To show Inez?"

"Yeah. Uh-huh."

"You want a picture of any particular thing?"

"I want you to send me a drawing of her."

"From the trial?"

"No. One where she looks happy. Okay?"

"I'll have to draw it from memory. Or a photograph. Do you have any?"

"Of Inez? Only one, and she looks lovely, but sad. Jerry took lots, but his dad grabbed the photo albums after the funeral. I hope to get some back someday, but now's not the time to ask. If you draw Inez from memory, will it look like her?"

"Yes. I remember her face well. But why d'you want it? Inez has seen pictures of herself before. You said Jerry took lots of photos."

"She never showed any recognition of herself."

"Why should it be any different now?"

"I'm not sure it will be, but the difference is I plan to work with it. We never pursued this with her. We'd point her out in the photos and say 'Inez,' but when she looked bewildered, we just let it drop. I'm ready to push further now."

"Why?"

"Because I think I understand better how to communicate with her. She doesn't relate to words the way we do. But nonverbally, I may be able to reach her."

"How?"

"I'm not sure, Molly. It's only a hunch, or a lead, I'm not sure which. Just send me the drawing, okay? I'll let you know what I decide to do with it."

"Why don't you or Margaret take a photo of her?"

"Because I think if she recognizes herself in a photograph, it might seem like she's been captured by the camera somehow ..."

"You don't mean to say you think she's primitive, so she'll assume the camera has stolen her soul?"

"No, Molly, I don't mean that. The Maya were far from primitive, even before the Spanish came, and Inez is a complex young woman. As we both know. It's just that a photo is such an exact replica of a person it could confuse her."

"Doesn't sound like she was confused over the photo of Jerry."

"That's different. She's all mixed up about who she is. She'll understand that a picture has been drawn by someone, that it isn't *her*. She draws and paints. She knows how it's done."

"Okay, I'll do what I can," she said, "but don't ring off just yet. I was going to call you myself. I have something to tell you. I was at the university library the other day, doing research for a painting I'm working on. On an impulse, I went to the languages department and looked up Kaqchikel. I couldn't find much, but when I played around with different spellings of that 'new buy' you thought she said, I found something very much like it. *Nu bi*." She spelled it out over the phone.

"Yes?" I said, eagerly.

"Caitlin, it means *I am*."

The storm came in with a banshee shriek and riffed on my walls like a drummer gone mad. I was glad of my radio and my torch. The electricity failed, and the world outside was so black, I felt like I could scratch lines in it. I kept my fire lit, but the cosiness I'd hoped to feel was eclipsed by howling fury. I shuddered and wrapped myself in several blankets. For a while, I held my hands over my ears. Finally, the wind subsided from a yell to a moan, and I fell asleep, huddled in my chair.

I dreamt that Inez was in the wind along with Jerry, and that they smashed through the windows of my little house and whirled me up with them in a spiral. We spun outside and were dancing in the air, holding hands in a circle, a tornado of mixed feelings.

I woke to find snow pressed high against my windows, flattened into huge wet snails against the glass. I had to dig my way out the back door, but at least the snow there came only to my knees. I looked up to the sky. It was a mix of blue and rose and grey and white, as if it had stolen colours from the ground

and freed them like a helium balloon that slips from a child's
inconstant grasp.

The next day, it was a struggle to get to the hospital, because
of the snow piled in high drifts and the still-strong winds, but
I was determined to once again seek out Inez's "main man," Dr.
Maxim. I hadn't liked the way he'd spoken about "crimes" and
"guards" the first time I'd met him. Then Peterson had distracted
me with his comments on my own bad behaviour, and I hadn't
had a chance to talk with Maxim again.

I went to one of the blindingly white desks perched everywhere on the vast ground floor of Great Northern.

"Dr. Maxim is very busy, Ms. Shaughnessy," said the nurse-
receptionist. "Do you have an appointment with him?"

"No, but I could make one."

My easygoing response seemed to work. I made a mental
note, thinking I might adopt the same approach with Maxim.

"I'll see if he can spare a minute now," said the weary-looking
young woman. "But I just don't know, okay?"

Five minutes later the good doctor himself was flapping
through the glass portals towards me, a great white heron
with attitude.

"Yes, Ms. Shaughnessy?" this big, important bird addressed
me through his pinched beak. And waited.

His manner bugged me, but there was something I wanted
to know, so, flush with the success of my laid-back approach
with the nurse, I said sweetly, "I'm seeing Inez again today,
Doctor, and I wanted to ask you something before I do." I drew
the line at batting my eyelashes and telling him what a wonderful job he was doing, but I made sure to smile, rather pleasantly,
too, at least for me at that hour of the morning.

"And what would that be?"

I found his eyebrows antagonizing. I wanted to peel them off and paste them over his paltry upper lip.

"How are Inez's therapy sessions conducted?" It was a whopper of a question, and not one he was likely to answer, but I figured he'd think he had to give me something — and, at that point, anything would help.

"Are you referring to her sessions with me, or with her nurse counsellors?"

"Both. She's such a mystery to me, doctor." I prayed I wasn't laying it on too thick. "I've been reading to her because I can't think of anything else to do. I mean, she doesn't exactly communicate, does she? So I was wondering how you — you and your staff — deal with her."

I had a pretty good idea already of how Dr. Eyebrows dealt with her, but I was curious to hear how he'd describe his once-weekly once-over. "*Good morning, Inez,*" clipboard in hand at her bedside, no doubt, eyes on some chart rather than her, "*And how has she been doing, nurse? Good, good. Any changes? No? So, Inez, you've settled in, have you? Good, good.*"

"The nurses do a kind of group therapy with her, hoping she feels included, even though she doesn't connect well. Her nurse counsellor, I believe, takes her for walks on the grounds and speaks to her as if she is capable of response. It's felt that if she is treated as normal, she will eventually behave that way."

Great goddesses. In the real world, this approach had gone the way of shock treatments. I'd done similar things myself, but I wasn't a doctor, and I did them out of ignorance or desperation. I never thought they were good ways to deal with Inez. The "I believe" killed me. It was like he had to take it on faith, never having bothered to check it out. I lowered my eyes, for I suddenly realized I was staring at him. Who was he? What motivated him? How could he be the way he was? This was not the time for such questions, and I tried to dismiss them from my mind as I dropped my gaze.

I was still waiting to hear how the great man described his role.

"I oversee the therapy, of course, and talk with Inez once a week."

That was it. "You talk with her?" I said, then took time to think it over, figuring he wouldn't be able to stop himself filling the silence with some carefully chosen words of great wisdom.

His eyes narrowed, and I worried he'd caught on.

"Yes. It seems she has no recollection of what happened," he said. "At least she gives every appearance of not knowing what she's done."

I cringed at the memory of my own clumsy and hostile efforts to elicit a response from Inez. But this was her therapist. Did he really talk to her about her "crime"? How else would he know that she seemed unaware of killing Jerry? Such brilliant psychodynamic technique. I could barely control my scorn, especially now that I'd got my information.

"Thank you, Doctor. That helps a great deal. I'll continue to read to her. It seems to be quite as effective as anything anyone else is doing." I was still smiling.

He looked at me quizzically from under those brows. I'd been so sickeningly sweet up till then, I suspect he couldn't quite believe I was being as sarcastic as I sounded. He nodded abruptly and turned to go.

I shook my head at his retreating back. Seemed all this high-tech razzle dazzle was window dressing for some pretty primitive thinking.

Chapter Thirty-Three

Caitlin's Story

Inez was already in the visiting room when I arrived, curled up on the corduroy couch.

I sat down beside her and she unfurled. I stroked her head before opening one of the books I'd brought with me. I still had no picture of Inez to work with, so I'd decided to continue reading to her. It was a way of filling the time, and she seemed to relax when I did it.

I started with Hopkins and cummings again, threw in some Dylan Thomas — "oh, as I was young and easy under the apple boughs" — for good measure. The rhythm of "Fern Hill" was so much more lilting than either of the other poets, whose worldviews, though, I'd been guessing, might better reflect hers.

Inez had the peaceful look I remembered from our picnics on the Island, our walks, our quiet moments alone together in Jerry's beautiful garden — times when I had imagined Inez spoke to me.

The words I put in her mouth then were always gentle, slightly elevated in tone, sometimes mysterious. When I was a kid,

I spent time in my imagination with noble and wise figures of my own devising. As an adult, I'd been turning Inez into one of them.

"I come from darkness," I had her say once. And "What's past remains with me. I cannot share it in a way you could understand. But I will tell you this — they shot my brothers. It was as if the world exploded. When I tried to put it back together, nothing fit."

"Autistics inspire fantasizing," Jerry said when I told him.

"Do they?" I responded. "Generally speaking?"

He nodded. "A lot of them are beautiful, and their dreaminess can be taken for spirituality."

"Is that all there is to it?"

"Yes. They're neurologically damaged. They have this mystique. People project all kinds of things on to them. It's bad for them, treatment-wise."

I didn't ask any more questions, because I could easily imagine the problems he was referring to. I suspected, as was usual with him when he was critical of something I'd said or done, that he had been dealing with these things himself.

Why did I pretend Inez had lost brothers? Because my own brother Tommy was murdered when I was nine.

I kept reading to Inez, though that day she showed no sign of listening. She seemed calm, as though the words were soothing, functioning like music for her, which was great, but I knew we'd never progress to meaning that way.

So I reached for David Macauley's *The Way Things Work*, nudging her gently to get her to open her eyes, as I showed her the picture of the clock tower.

She was instantly alert. I pointed out the various working parts. "Look, there's the pendulum," I said and had her rapt attention.

For a few minutes she was right with me, and I was sure she understood what I was saying. It didn't take long, however, for her attention to drift, but it was a different kind of falling away. She moved with what looked like purpose to the window and gazed out over the ice.

I didn't call her back. I glanced at my watch.

"Time to go," I said, closing the book carefully so as not to alarm her. "I'll have to say goodbye for now, Inez."

She didn't turn from the window, even when a guard knocked on the door to tell us our time was up.

At our next meeting in the little room, she was examining her fingers as if they belonged to someone else.

Fixing those gold-splashed eyes on me, she swayed her hands in the air in gestures that were eerily similar to those a geisha makes when dancing. I almost expected her to move across the floor with the soft toeing motions geishas make, like little horses pawing the ground.

Instead, she began to cry.

She wouldn't let me hold her, but I did manage to mop her face and hands with tissue. For a full half-hour she cried. She was still crying when they led her away.

I went out for a walk. I hated the cold, but I needed to think. I didn't "get" what had set Inez off, and it troubled me. I was glad Margaret was due in soon. I would talk it over with her.

Nearby was a small cluster of dwellings where overhanging wires cut the sky into squares, rectangles, tilted triangles. The squat buildings of corrugated tin had rows of little windows that tipped open from the bottom like fish scales. Why anyone would have those windows open on a day like today was beyond me. Even my teeth ached with the cold. Perhaps it was just a style, and behind each raised scale was a pane of triple-glazed glass.

I headed towards a small stone church, surrounded by snow so pristine, it was clear no one had preceded me.

The church was roughly put together and looked as though it had sprung straight up out of the ground, an eruption of earth into architecture, led by a tiny jagged spire that made me think of Lego.

The door was locked and the place seemed deserted. I couldn't see much through the ice-encrusted windows, but I was surprised by golden light, dim and warm, embossing the wooden benches in their soldier-like rows, and the outline of an altar. I thought of Jerry's funeral, how the ambience of the old United Church building had imbued the ceremony with meaning, despite the unpleasant connotations organized religion held for me and the irritations of the service itself.

I shuddered and rubbed my mittened paws together then tried the door one more time. That golden glow looked so enticing.

Neither Jerry nor I cared for winter. We hated the cold, plus Christmas was not our season. It brought duties and family obligations we — especially Jerry — would rather avoid, and along with them, vague feelings of loss about choosing not to become parents.

I admired my father and stepmother Suzie for combining parenting and careers the way they had, but our life was a mess for a long time after Tommy was killed.

My dad didn't turn to drink, as I might have, or go seriously gaga with grief, but sadness hung over our house and pressed downwards sometimes, like the ceiling in Poe's "Pit and the Pendulum." Suzie became a *space*, where there had been a definite and helpful something. Had it not been for Molly, I would have had no mothering at all for a long, long time.

No one blamed me, but at Tommy's funeral, I overheard a woman say, "Just think, if little Cat had come home on time, maybe the burglars would have run off, and no one would've been hurt." That kind of comment seemed ubiquitous at times, and I was consumed by guilt.

The day it happened, I had come home from school to find a strange man in our house. "Your mom's gone to the store with your brother. I'm her cousin Ian. Did she tell you I was coming?"

I stared at him, unsure, but he was incredibly lucky. Suzie had mentioned something earlier that week about a relative from Nova Scotia coming to visit. Maybe. Sometime. Also, I was late. I was supposed to arrive home fifteen minutes earlier than I did, but I'd dawdled, played hopscotch with friends. So it made sense to me that Suzie had got tired of waiting and left for the store with Tommy.

"Would you like a piece of chocolate? Would you like to go outside? What did you do at school today?"

The questions were rapid-fire. Bewildered, I said, "Yes. I'd like to go outside, please," because I didn't know what else to say.

I ran to my swing set, and he came and pushed me on the swings, chattering at me the whole time. Anyone with any sense would have realized he was talking much too fast, that his voice was too rough and strained to be friendly, and that a lot of what he said was nonsense, but all I thought was that although I didn't understand everything he said, sometimes he was funny.

He'd already killed Tommy by the time I'd arrived home. He swore later that he hadn't meant to. He'd bound and gagged both Suzie and Tommy. He didn't know my brother wasn't feeling well. He and his buddy were too preoccupied grabbing our worldly goods to notice the little fellow choking on his own vomit. They panicked when they saw me coming. The man I was with knocked Suzie on the head with the butt of a gun before coming out to the foyer to talk to me. He must've figured he'd better get me out of the house, fast. Meanwhile, his partner ran away.

I was lucky that he was incapable of thinking on his feet. He said later that he took me outside to give himself time to figure out what to do next. He didn't want to kill me if he didn't have to. Was the mother dead? If not, he could let me live, but if he'd killed her, I was the only witness and would need to be disposed of. He didn't know yet that Tommy was dead, too. As he was deliberating, one of our neighbours came by. She said later that she didn't trust the man was who he said he was. When she kept asking questions, he ran, too.

It bothered me that I'd felt no intimations of danger, nor horror, or even mistrust. Even as he was likely going over in his head the best way to get rid of me, I liked that man. I never forgot that I'd liked someone who'd murdered my little brother, that I'd had no fear of him at all.

I've talked about what happened that day with only two people in my adult life, Molly and Jerry. Both thought I was making too much of it. Rationally, I agree with them. But I am still cautious about men. Jerry understood because he knew how the mind worked. "It was such a big shock to you," he told me, "that it registered with your nervous system permanently. That can happen after a traumatic event like the murder of someone close to you, especially if you're a child. It's like your mind knows you aren't to blame, but your body doesn't. Bodies can be slow learners."

I'm an adult now, but what happened between Jerry and Inez affected me, too, in ways more subtle than guilt or a fear of strangers. I can never forget now that we die, or that our lives can change overnight. Everything is shadowed by that knowledge. I can't see any point to knowing this; it means I understand far more clearly the need for the "eternal Now," but am also far less likely to experience it.

In my calmer moments, I knew that must apply to Inez too. Her terrible experiences in Guatemala — how could she not be affected by them? It tempered any anger I still had towards her to think about her this way.

After Tommy's death, my dad seemed mostly bewildered. His music suffered. If he'd been a classical pianist, he might have used his despair to enhance his art, but you can't use tragedy when playing an Irish jig. Luckily, he was so well-established — and his fans were so sympathetic — he could coast for a while. I found out later he'd wanted to give it all up.

He doesn't have that baffled look any more. It's like he's understood what happened to him, in that wordless place I'm rediscovering.

I jangled the handle of the church door one last time, almost angrily, still enticed by the warm glow inside. It did not give, so I turned my back on the false oasis of the little Arctic church and made straight for the warm confines of my small cedar house.

That night, I looked out the window to see a spider's drop rope of silvery moonlight slicing the mountain range in two, and I wished Molly was there to translate the scene into something I could hold in my hand.

Chapter Thirty-Four

Caitlin's Story

The following day, I went to see Peterson.

I wondered if he knew how silly his office looked the second time you saw it, especially the swans, rising up in back of him as though he were a marsh they were leaving behind.

I planted myself in front of the ice rink he called a desk. "There is something I wish to discuss."

He rose and offered his hand. I was surprised we could reach each other across the frozen wastes.

"Sit down, Ms. Shaughnessy." He gestured to the pneumatic armchair.

I tried to settle in without losing all sense of a separate identity.

"First," he said, "I would like to follow up on our conversation of a few days ago." He smoothed one side of his silvery locks with the flat of his hand. "You invited me to. Remember?"

I did, but I couldn't conjure up Peterson's exact words, and I needed to, because I did not want to cut him any slack.

I took a stab at it. "You said, I believe, that you weren't sure if I had Inez's best interests at heart. Why —"

"I asked you," he leaned forward over the ice floe, "whether *you* thought you had her best interests at heart. An important distinction."

True. Damn. "You asked me that after you referred to ... certain complications in my relationship with her." I blessed the return of my powers of recall. "Could you elaborate?"

Bullseye. He sat back in his throne and twitched. But only for a second. "You agreed with me," he said, in what I interpreted as a deceptively gentle tone. "Perhaps *you'd* like to elaborate."

Touché.

"Not really." It was a graceless move, but I was almost sure it would get me what I wanted.

I was right. Peterson was far too classy to indulge in childish wordplay for long. "I suggest," he intoned, leaning forward once again, "that we drop this silly hedging, Ms. Shaughnessy. The complication I was referring to, of which you are well aware, is the fact that Inez killed your partner of many years."

The unctuous expression on Peterson's round, pink face made me long to slap him.

"Why is that a problem?"

He tapped his gilt pen on the desktop. I thought of a remark that would take the edge off his annoyance but stopped myself in time. It would be better to make him angry.

"Do stop playing games," he said smoothly.

Ah, the urge to win had triumphed. He was good at this.

His expression changed from annoyance to compassion. "I know how hard this must be for you. I truly sympathize."

That caught me off guard, because it sounded genuine. There's nothing more daunting than an opponent with heart.

"Oh, do you?" I said lamely.

"I do."

The ensuing silence felt dangerous. If he'd kept talking, I'm sure smarminess would have sashayed back into his tone, and I'd have gone automatically on the offensive, which is where I wanted to be. I'm not bad at withstanding silence, but I have my limits; and I was talking to a psychiatrist. They are skilled in the listener's art. I had a feeling I would break first, and I was right.

"I *don't* take it personally, Dr. Peterson, and I hold no grudge against Inez."

"I would not expect a person such as you to hold a grudge, Ms. Shaughnessy. But I would expect a certain turbulence."

He used the strangest words. "Like a bumpy flight?"

"A moral turbulence."

I'd known he meant that. I'd been trying to delay the moment when our eyes met, and he saw he'd gotten to me.

At least he thought me incapable of petty jealousy, but what he thought me capable of instead — what I *was* capable of — was nothing to be proud of.

"I see." My voice came out softer than I'd intended. I lowered my eyes, immediately wishing I hadn't.

"And such turbulence, I've found," the great man went on, "can lead to a different kind of resentment. Nothing so unforgiving — and uncomplicated — as a grudge, but ambivalence towards the cause of the suffering. Ambivalence that if not closely monitored, can result in prejudicial behaviour." There was another pause, less fraught this time. "Ms. Shaughnessy, in your position, I would doubt my own motives."

He meant well, he truly did, but that did it. "What about the position you're in yourself?"

He didn't blink. "And what position is that?"

"A position of power. Power corrupts."

He sighed. "Only if you let it."

"And you haven't?"

"I've tried very hard not to. Very hard indeed. I do not believe in undemocratic attitudes to the mentally ill, and I've done my best to diminish the barriers between patient and doctor here in the hospital."

I was sure he'd made a lot of patients happy with his gravelly "good mornings" and kindly questions, but I couldn't help thinking that any man who inhabited an office the size of New York, furnished in Late White Male Dominance, was somehow missing the boat when it came to equitable doctor-patient relationships.

"What *are* your motives, Dr. Peterson? With Inez, I mean?"

"I haven't any, other than to run the medical side of this facility efficiently enough that she gets the best care possible. That is how I see my function as an administrator, to ensure good care for all those incarcerated here."

"So you have no particular interest in Inez's case?"

"I find her interesting, as you do, but no more than many others here. Their stories are all fascinating, if somewhat macabre."

"Are you convinced she killed Jerry?"

"Yes. The evidence was incontrovertible."

"Do you have any theories as to why she did it?"

"Yes. I suspect it was in retaliation for something he did to her."

I winced. He was voicing fears I thought I'd conquered, and he had no right. "Why do you think that? You're accusing someone I love of something you —"

"*Accusing*, Ms. Shaughnessy?"

I froze.

"I'm accusing Dr. Simpson of nothing," he went on, smooth as cold cream. "Why would you think I was? From past experience, I suspect Inez reacted to something that he did or said that reminded her of past abuses, and she struck back. It's a common enough response in cases of PTSD."

"You think Inez is suffering from Post-Traumatic Stress Disorder?"

"It would be something of a miracle if she wasn't."

"Does that justify what she did?"

"Not at all. But I don't hold her responsible for it. And neither did the jury. She lashed out. She does it here, too."

"But don't you think that the facts we don't know behind the act should have affected the verdict?"

"She was found *not guilty. Not guilty* by reason of insanity. That is the best that could be done. It isn't possible for the law to take unknowns into consideration. She is happy enough here, and well taken care of. What is it that you want for her? That is what I mean by ambivalence. Do you even know?"

Again, he had made a direct hit. I didn't understand what I was after, beyond the truth, and wasn't sure why I wanted it. It would be wonderful to clear Jerry's name, if I could prove he had never touched Inez, but I had to admit that was neither the initial nor the main impetus for my quest.

"It's just …" I was fumbling, and Peterson caught on. I could tell by the way he sat back triumphantly in his chair. "It's something to do with justice," I blurted, "and the truth."

"How do you know that the truth, as you call it, will do her any good whatsoever?" He was leaning forward again, his eyes looking straight into mine. "Can you be sure your fondness for this truth is not more a product of curiosity than compassion? Some of us are driven by such a passion to know that we forget to ask whom we might hurt in the process of finding out."

Damn him, damn him, damn him.

"Why," I burst out, "do my motives matter to you? Why have they even come into question? I came here to give Inez some company, some contact — why is this a concern of yours?"

"All my patients are a concern of mine. Inez is a fragile young woman who has experienced more horror in her short years than most of us go through in a lifetime. If nothing else is possible for her, I would like her to achieve a measure of peace."

"But I want her to get better! I want her to grow into the woman I believe she can be." Before I said this, it was only one among many possibilities, buried in a chattering crowd.

"Beliefs like that are often the products of rescue fantasies. Rescue fantasies, as any psychiatrist will tell you, are dangerous. For a layperson, they are even more treacherous."

I could feel tears welling in my eyes. He was right, and besides, he'd made me think of Jerry and how a rescue fantasy may have planted the seed for this tragedy.

"Ms. Shaughnessy ..." His voice was soft. "I am aware that certain parties are endeavouring to have Inez classed a dangerous offender. It is a frivolous charge — true, she attacked an orderly here. So do most of our patients at one time or another. Some over-eager member of the media got hold of it and blew it out of proportion, but it does reinforce my opinion that Inez is safer here than anywhere else."

I clutched the arm of the Incredible Devouring Chair and dragged myself upwards, cursing my tears in my heart. "I can't help what I want for Inez," I managed to say, though it came out in a waterlogged snarl. "I can't help hoping she'll at least get a chance to recover. And to go free. What if she is innocent, Dr. Peterson? Not 'not guilty.' If she killed Jerry by accident, she should not be here. Period. Do you know what her treatment consists of? *That's* what I came here to discuss with you, not me and my so-called motives. Do you know your Dr. Maxim seems to want to confront her with Jerry's murder? Is that going to help her, Dr. Peterson? I'm sure that you don't think so, and that's why I'm here. Someone should call that man off. At least if I read to her, talk to her, spend time with her — at least then she knows she is cared for — she is —"

"You are free to do so, but there is something I want you to remember. You are not responsible — for her, for her actions, for the tragedy of Dr. Simpson."

I glared at him out of eyes gone suddenly dry. For one blinding second, I hated him. Then I went numb.

"Thank you, Dr. Peterson." I began the long walk to his door, calling back over my shoulder, "Perhaps sometime we will speak together again."

"I will look forward to that, Ms. Shaughnessy."

Back in my temporary home, I sank down on my bed. I had lost all focus. Inez wasn't going to get any better. The good doctor was right. All I really wanted was to know, for myself, what had happened between her and Jerry.

Then I remembered Molly, who found my curiosity natural and had always encouraged me to follow my instincts; in fact, she had insisted on it. I'd already done my worst on my first trip, hadn't I, hounding and harassing Inez? I wasn't about to make the same mistake twice. Besides, Margaret was due in soon. Her input would not be complicated by mixed motives. She was a professional with a definable, clear-cut role. I was sure she'd help me stay on track with Inez. It was why I'd invited her.

Take *that*, Peterson! I felt better already.

The morning of Margaret's arrival, a letter came from Molly. I was rushing out the door when it slid through my letter-box, so I pulled the lovely drawing of a smiling Inez from the envelope and put in my tote.

On the way to the hospital, I thought about Margaret. I didn't know her well, but I liked her. When she'd moved to Jerry's, I was surprised that some of my friends expected me to worry. Carrying on with the live-in nurse, I'd told them, was not his style. Shared experiences were what mattered. He valued the longevity of our relationship for its own sake and wouldn't jeopardize it for a fling.

We arrived at the front doors of Great Northern within minutes of each other. Margaret was wearing an Inuit parka, and I wondered when she'd found time to acquire it. She looked like one of those northern nurses you see on TV shows, alighting from helicopters, the fur on their parka hoods blown fetchingly back from their shining, earnest faces.

When we went inside, she whispered, "My god, it's like something out of a sci-fi movie."

"Isn't it?" I'd already described the hospital to her, but I didn't blame her for being surprised. Such high-tech sterility is hard to visualize. Besides, maybe Margaret had me pegged as prone to exaggeration.

We'd decided to go together to my regular appointment with Inez. I planned to slip past the staff with Margaret in tow, acting like nothing untoward was happening and hoping nobody called my bluff.

We approached a desk together.

The nurse looked up briefly before returning to her paperwork. "Ms. Shaughnessy to see Inez," she said, saving me the trouble.

"Yes. And a friend."

Her head immediately rose. "Do you have clearance?"

"This is Margaret Richards," I said confidently. "The speech therapist I spoke to Dr. Peterson about. Remember?"

"No, I'm sorry, I don't remember." She seemed to think it was her power of recall that left something to be desired, not my truthfulness. "All right then, go ahead."

Inez was curled on the couch near the window. With her cheek resting on her arm and soft strands of hair falling over her face, she radiated tranquillity. When Margaret came in, she looked up and smiled like a buddha then got to her feet, walked over and stroked her nurse's cheek.

Margaret stroked her cheek in turn. "Good, good, Inez. Hello. It's been a long time."

Inez went back to the couch, gazing over the tundra with a faraway, contented look.

"Inez," Margaret went on, "I've brought some of your favourite things." She laid out shiny tops and balls on the couch.

Next she pulled a small photo album out of her bag and took it to Inez.

"Here's me," she said, as I peered over their shoulders. She was pointing to a picture of herself outside a brick split-level — her parents' house?

Inez looked from the picture to Margaret and back again, then patted Margaret's cheek. This was a first.

I was humbled. Margaret already knew to use pictures with Inez.

Encouraged, I pulled Molly's drawing of a smiling Inez out of my bag, and handed it to her.

She looked at it only briefly.

"That's you, Inez," I prompted. No response, except a faint suggestion of boredom.

That in itself was intriguing. I realized I had never seen Inez bored before. Dreamy, distant, angry, neutral, loving. But not bored.

It made me suspect she could be faking it. Also a first. "Inez," I began, my voice a little harsher than I intended, "you know that's you, don't you? Don't you?"

Behind the girl, Margaret shook her head and raised a warning hand.

She took Inez by the arm and led her towards the door.

There was a one-way mirror in that door, masquerading as a window. Inez had never shown any interest in it.

Good luck, I thought to myself. Inez had looked in mirrors before. They had no effect on her.

But Margaret stood behind her so that both of their reflections were visible. She touched her own cheek. "Margaret," she said. Then she reached round and touched Inez's cheek. "Inez," and turned the girl towards her. "Inez," she said again, directing the girl's gaze to Molly's drawing.

Damn it, but the woman knew what she was doing. At least I could congratulate myself for bringing her here.

Inez's gaze was that of an infant, alert and curious, but unsurprised. It was we who were startled, not by the sound of her voice, which by then we'd become used to, but by its tone. She didn't sound like Margaret. She didn't sound like me. She didn't sound like a man.

She sounded like someone young and female and innocent. "Inez." She'd said it softly, reaching out to touch the mirror. Then she went back once again to the seat by the window, to gaze out over the grounds.

Tears pricked my eyes. I said, "Inez is happy," and waited for her to repeat it.

She did, and smiled, turning to look at me. Perhaps she was only parroting, but I leaned down, placed my fingers gently on her lips, and said, "*Happy* is a word for how *you* feel right now. *You* are happy."

She brushed my hand away gently, staring at the picture I was holding out.

"Pic-ture," she said haltingly. "Not me." All the joy fell from her face, and her eyes filled with tears.

It was all happening too fast.

"It's okay, Inez," I soothed, stroking her head. "It's okay."

She pulled away from me and went straight to the mirrored door. There she began touching herself all over. "Me," she said, patting her face. "Me." Patting her chest. "Me." Touching her legs. "Me, me, me!" Her face blossomed into a smile. She reached out to the mirror, placing one finger on the image of her upturned lips.

It was like nothing I'd ever seen before, this traumatized young woman discovering who she was.

I was moved beyond words. Would it keep making her happy, this sense of a separate self? It was exactly what Buddhism had led me to see as the source of all suffering. Already, realizing the picture was *of* her, not part of all she was, had made her sad. And yet for Inez, for me, for Margaret, it was the happiest moment we'd ever shared.

"Yes," I said to her, "that is you, my sweet, precious girl. You."

We beamed at each other in the mirror, tears reflecting off all our faces.

Margaret and I were outside with Inez. It was one of our new privileges.

Snow fell in a dance of light. The watchtowers were heaped with it, transformed into the trees that wouldn't grow here. Often, it was too cold even for snow. The Inuit storekeeper told me that this was the mildest autumn they'd had in years, blizzard and all.

Inez was especially playful, her best self. She ran through the floodlit evening, catching flakes between her mittens.

Then Margaret and I made snow angels, spreadeagling on the ground and sliding our arms up and down to create the wings.

"Come on, Inez," I called out. "You make one too."

But she wouldn't.

When we got up, Margaret said to her, "Look, there are angels in the snow now."

Inez gravely assessed our winged depressions rapidly filling up with new snow. "There ... are ... angels," she said. Then, to me, eyes alight, "There are angels."

I hugged her close.

She was making such good progress that I was almost willing to believe there were angels myself. Peterson now allowed Margaret and me to work together with her. Sometimes we showed her pictures, sometimes we read to her. She looked at us, not through us, but the best times were when she expressed her feelings.

"I ..." This word was always said with wonder and puzzlement followed by a big smile. "I ... am ... happy."

The most thrilling news in the world could not eclipse my excitement when she said that. "I ... am ... sad" was equally a breakthrough, but it made me nervous. How much sorrow could she bear, after all? I was relieved she still didn't seem to remember too much, or connect Jerry's death to herself. Thinking that way was quite a change for me.

We were outside again on another snowy evening. Margaret chased Inez playfully around rocks and drifts. I squatted on my haunches and sorted through my tote bag, searching for my camera. Frustrated when I couldn't find it, I pulled out a handful of items and dropped them in the snow.

Inez looked down and pounced.

At first, I couldn't see what she'd snatched from the pile. When I did, I was shocked. I hadn't packed the bag of Guatemalan dream dolls. Why would I, after Inez's reaction to the *rebozo* she saw at Michael's? I must have stuffed them in with a load of other things at the last minute, by mistake.

While Inez stared at the bag, I tried to think how best to get it away from her.

"Inez ..." I reached out my hand. "Please give me that ... please."

A ridge formed between her brows.

Glaring at the bag with what looked like hatred, her golden irises almost giving off sparks, she tore it open and shook the tiny dolls into the snow. Before we could stop her, she was picking them up one by one and snapping them into pieces. She sobbed as she tore off their cloth heads, their woven clothes, their hair, and threw the shreds around her in a wild confetti blizzard.

Finally, she was done. I approached her cautiously. She was breathing hard, clutching the little bag to her chest. Just as I reached her, she turned wild eyes on me and raised her arm as if to ward off blows. When she shrank down into the snow, she clasped her elbows over her head.

I bent towards her. Her eyes were wide with terror, and she shuddered. Then something else caught her attention, and she scooped it out of the snow. My wallet.

She stood up. I looked over her shoulder. She was holding the wallet in the flat of her hand with the credit card sleeves fluttering like butterfly wings. She smoothed them open to a photo of Jerry.

Was it good for her to be looking at him just as she was beginning to understand who she was? It could be dangerous to alarm her, and I held my breath.

She bent her head to look closer, then said, "Inez," with a question in her voice, placing one palm flat on her chest.

I came up behind her and put my hand over hers. "Yes.

That's right. You are Inez." I wrapped my arms around her shoulders.

"Je ... ree," came a tentative voice.

"Yes." My eyes clouded over. "Jerry." I gently stroked the top of her bent head as she touched his photograph.

She sighed deeply. I continued to hold her.

"May I have my wallet now?" I moved around to face her and held out my hand. "My wallet ..."

Her face was a question mark. "Inez," she said again.

I nodded, waiting.

"Inez." Hand to her chest as before. "Jerry." Holding the wallet out to me, still clutching the bag that had held the dolls, now buried under the snow.

"Yes." I took the wallet from her.

"Inez." This time her voice was deep, her tone commanding, her expression determined.

Startled, I said nothing.

"*Inez, here are the little dolls from your mother.*" She was still speaking in that loud, insistent voice. "*From Guatemala —*"

I froze.

"*Guatemala, Inez. Where you come from. Where the bad things happened. What did you do, Inez? What did you do?*"

Then she howled like a wolf in the night and tried to rip the little bag. When she couldn't, she began tearing at it with her teeth.

Between us, Margaret and I got it away from her. Then she fell into Margaret's arms, sobbing, and we took her back inside.

The whole time she'd been talking, I'd been seeing Michael Doherty.

Because Inez had been speaking in his voice.

———

342

Inez stopped eating. She stopped smiling, too. She did not say one more word, in her own or anyone else's voice, the next day, or the next, or the next, after she'd smashed the little dolls and left them buried in the snow.

Chapter Thirty-Five

Caitlin's Story

"It was the dolls. As soon as she saw the dolls, she fell apart —"

Dr. Peterson had sent for us. We were standing away from his hideous desk, in a huddle near the devouring armchair.

"Where did these dolls come from?" he said to me, his voice unusually low. "What are they?"

"I'm not sure." I looked at the plush carpet, experiencing its many subtle shades as echoes from another time. "The police found them on Jerry's desk, in his study." Even then, I'd wondered about them being out in the open. "Jerry's father sent them in a box of Jerry's things." I stopped and took a breath. "I brought them here by accident."

"But Jerry loaned them to Michael Doherty," Margaret said. "Weeks before he died."

This came as a surprise. "He did?"

"Yes. Michael asked to borrow them. Jerry told him he'd shown them to Dr. Fernandez, and Dr. Fernandez commented on how they were all broken in the same place. Michael wondered why. Jerry never showed them to Inez, because he wasn't sure what their being broken meant —"

"But why have them out in the open, where she could see them?"

"Perhaps he was looking at them and Inez surprised him. It's odd. I didn't know they'd been returned."

My head felt a little loose on my shoulders. Jerry hadn't mentioned loaning the dolls to Michael.

"What did this Dr. Fernandez say about them?" Peterson's silvery voice matched his hair, with darker undertones.

Margaret was frowning. "Because they were all snapped at the waist, he wondered if someone had done it purposely. He said that if a dream doll was broken deliberately, it should not be used to chase away nightmares. And because the dolls were given to Jerry by Inez's own mother, he wasn't sure what that signified. He warned Jerry to be careful, just in case there was something sinister about them. There were only five. Usually there are six."

"But from what Inez said yesterday," I said, "Michael practically forced her to look at them ... Did he say why he wanted them, Margaret?"

"He said he was doing research and needed to check them against other dream dolls."

That made sense, up to a point.

What didn't make sense was forcing them on Inez.

Margaret and I flew back to Toronto a few days after this conversation. We could do nothing more to help Inez at Great Northern. If we came near her, she shuddered and hid her face in her hands, and I had a pressing need to visit Michael Doherty.

———

"What the hell were you thinking, Michael?" I almost yelled it. "Why did you show those dolls to Inez?"

He'd only just answered his door to my knock. "Whoa, Caitlin. Hello to you too."

I weighed him up, from his feathered hair to his Cardin loafers.

"Do come in." He led me into his chrome-and-leather living room, where our reflections repeated endlessly in mirrors, silver statues, tables of pink-tinted glass. "Have a seat."

I chose the least sterile chair I could find, black leather on a steel pole.

"Now, if you'll excuse me, what in god's name were you talking about?" His voice, despite the expletive, was as neutral as a hospital wall, his eyes blank.

"The dolls, Michael. The dream dolls. Why did you force them on Inez?"

"I don't know what you're talking about, Cat." The blank stare again. He smoothed the layers of his expensive hair.

"Are you saying you don't know what dolls I'm talking about?"

He waved a hand, brushing away my words. "No, of course not. But I didn't show them to Inez."

"Michael —"

"Look, whatever you think of me, Cat, there is no way I would show those dolls to Inez. Wait here. There's something you should see."

He swept out of the room, returning a few minutes later with an envelope he thrust towards me. "Read that." His eyes looked darker in the shadows of the room.

I pulled out a letter. Scanning quickly to the bottom, I saw "*Sincerely yours, Dr. Enrico Fernandez.*"

I started at the beginning.

Dear Dr. Doherty,

I received your letter yesterday. What I have to say has to do with the dolls you mention, and is a matter of some urgency. I have been in touch with the Mayan woman who is Inez's mother. As circumstances would have it, she was in fact ill when Dr. Simpson saw her. She had cancer. Her husband brought her to me because she was failing, and in pain. She died yesterday.

Before she died, through translators, she told me something of what happened to her family, and to Inez.

Government soldiers killed all her children save Inez. The soldiers had come to the village once before. At that time, they had killed only a handful of men, as a warning. They also raped some of the young girls, Inez among them. They believed the village had been collaborating with the guerrillas. In fact, at one point, the Mayas had allowed the guerrillas to harvest corn to feed themselves — at gunpoint. This time, they had some warning, and the whole family was hidden away in the forest, as were most of the other villagers.

They were not found until Inez began wailing. The mother maintains they could not quiet her once she had seen the soldiers again. She also said that Inez had always been strange, difficult. She believed her to be possessed by evil spirits.

The wailing of Inez drew the soldiers, and they murdered the five brothers and sisters in front of the family. The mother suspects they would all have been killed, but the soldiers were called away by their commander.

Inez never spoke again after what had happened, except to echo others. The mother never forgave her. She did not seem to like her daughter very much even before the tragedy, but I believe the death of her children unsettled her mind.

She wanted to be rid of Inez. Dr. Simpson was an opportunity. The father was more forgiving and hoped your friend could help the girl.

The dolls were given as a form of curse by the mother to her only surviving daughter. You have noticed there are five. Five sisters and brothers who were killed. The sixth was Inez. The mother was disowning her in the imagery of the dolls. On no account should they be given to Inez. In fact, I strongly suggest you ask Dr. Simpson to destroy them.

Please let Dr. Simpson know. Send me his address, and I will write him directly.

Oh god. Inez.

"Why didn't you destroy them, Michael? Or let Jerry know, or any of us know what happened to Inez —"

"I let Jerry know about the dolls and why they were anathema to Inez. But do you see, now, why I never would have shown them to her? I knew what they could do to her. She was in my care, Caitlin. Do you think I'm some kind of monster?" His eyes reflected the light of the silver nymph on the table beside him.

I didn't know what to believe. His outraged tone sounded authentic, but I still had Inez's voice, Michael's voice, ringing in my ears. *Look at them; go on, look at them, Inez!*

"If you told Jerry, why didn't he tell me?"

"I'm sure he would have. If there'd been time. Look at the date. The letter came right before he died. I didn't … I —"

"You never told *me*, even after Jerry died, you never told me anything about what had happened to Inez. *You never mentioned it at her trial.*" I took a step towards him. "How could you?"

"It wouldn't have made any difference, Cat. She was found not guilty. The letter would only have confirmed that."

Watching him sit back, crossing his St. Laurent clad legs and steepling his manicured hands, made me want to hit him. "But you didn't know that, Michael. You didn't know what the verdict would be. What if she'd been found guilty? What then?"

"Then I would have come forward with the letter."

"Why wait?"

"I can't explain it to you, Caitlin. I was distressed beyond belief. I ..." He leaned his elbows on his knees, his brow furrowed and his red lips twisted in a mockery of concern.

"You didn't want to get involved, did you? You didn't want anyone connecting those dolls to you —"

"That wasn't it, Cat. I told you I can't explain."

I tried a different tack. "Why did you write to Fernandez? How did you find him?"

"It wasn't difficult. I knew the name of the town. I sent it to Dr. E. Fernandez, Panajachel, Guatemala. *Poste restante.* It means it goes to the post office, where people pick up their mail. They don't have delivery like we do here. It reached him."

"But we got no response when we tried to contact him the same way."

"He moves around a lot now, to avoid the soldiers. He never mentioned hearing from you. Perhaps your letter was intercepted."

"But why did you write?" The chair on its steel perch creaked as I leaned forward to pin Michael with my eyes.

"To ask what he knew about dream dolls. Jerry told me they were all broken in the same place. I knew he had already been warned by Fernandez that there might be some dark meaning to that. I wanted to see if I could find out more about them. Inez was my patient. I needed to learn all I could about her. I contacted him initially to ask about his examination of her. Then I mentioned the dream dolls."

He continued to deny that he'd shown them to Inez. "What do you think I am? A monster?" he repeated. "I couldn't do that to her. Why would I, Caitlin? Think about it. I had no reason to hurt her."

He was right. He had no reason that I knew of. But he also had no good reason that I could see to keep quiet about that letter.

———

Immediately after I arrived home, I invited Margaret over and told her everything.

"He says he didn't show Inez the dolls," I said.

"Do you believe him?"

"I heard Inez, and so did you. She was speaking in Michael's voice. How can I trust what he says, especially after reading that letter? All the same, I can't quite believe he would be so cruel. Why would he want to hurt her?"

"Michael Doherty is not someone I trust." Margaret's voice was chilly. "He's too smooth, and he's always in some kind of trouble about money —"

"Is he?" It made sense. That huge house, those designer clothes … "How do you know?"

"He and Jerry used to talk about it. It wasn't a big secret; I was often there when the topic came up. They also used to discuss Dr. Whitfield. Jerry was afraid the man was hurting his patients. Michael agreed, but they didn't know what to do about it."

Amazing what living with someone made you privy to. It was freakish finding out things I didn't know about Michael through Margaret, though I could see why Jerry never mentioned them to me. I was already prejudiced against the man, and he considered him a friend.

I knew about Jerry's problems with Whitfield, but I was surprised he'd told Michael. "But Michael and Whitfield are as thick as thieves!"

"They weren't then."

This was too much to think about at once. "How did the dolls get back in Jerry's study? Why were they out in the open?"

"I don't know."

Michael had come over the day prior to Jerry's death. I knew because of the investigation. He'd come to drop off something he'd borrowed, he said, and hadn't stayed long. The neighbours had seen him, both coming and going. They'd seen Jerry open the door to him and walk with him to the street on his departure.

He'd likely returned the dolls at that time. But why hadn't Jerry put them away?

"You're sure," I said to Margaret, "that Jerry knew there was something wrong with the dolls?"

"Yes, he told me he'd thought at first that he'd broken them accidentally by carrying them around in his pocket, but that Fernandez told him there might be more to it than that, because they were all broken in the same place, in the same way …"

"But do you think Michael told him about the letter, where there was no question the dolls would do harm to Inez?"

"That I don't know, Cat. I never heard them discussing it, but that doesn't mean it didn't happen."

"Even without the letter, why didn't Jerry throw the dolls away, or at least hide them right when he got them back?" I said.

Margaret shook her head. "I don't know."

"Did Michael tell the police it was the dolls he returned?"

"Not that I know of. I remember some mention of an analytic journal, but not dolls. But I was not his confidante, ever, and I wasn't there every time he spoke to the police." Margaret twisted a red curl so tightly round her finger that the tip blushed crimson.

"Somehow I doubt that he did. How are we ever going to find out what happened?" After all this time, I was still asking the same damn question, as though I had a manic woodpecker pounding away inside my skull. "Maybe we should confront Michael," Margaret said.

"I don't think that's good idea right now."

There was something I needed to look into before contacting Michael again.

"I'm going to phone Alita," I told her. "Remember her? It was her Guatemalan shawl that freaked Inez the day Michael brought her back to us in such a state. Supposedly."

"Supposedly?"

"We'll see."

I knew Alita was a model, so I contacted all the agencies in town until I found her. I left my name and invited her to call me, which she did.

"I wanted to check something," I said after the preliminaries. "You know that I just got back from visiting Inez? She got extremely upset when she saw some Guatemalan dream dolls I took with me, and it reminded me of her reaction to your Guatemalan shawl —"

"*What* Guatemalan shawl?"

I filled Margaret in as soon as I could.

"Alita never even saw Inez that day," I said to her over coffee in my kitchen. "She doesn't even own a *rebozo*."

We looked at each other over the plain pine table. The aroma of the rich brew jarred my senses. It was too deliciously comforting to fit the situation.

"Now what, Margaret?"

"Are you thinking what I'm thinking? *Something* freaked Inez that day —"

"— and Michael had already borrowed the dolls," I finished for her.

Margaret frowned and fiddled again with a loose strand of

hair. "He could have left them out by mistake and not been able to admit what he'd done."

"And a horse might lay an egg." I rubbed my mouth with my hand. "I don't understand."

"Let me get this straight." Margaret folded her arms and leaned into the table. "First, Michael borrows the dolls. Then he offers to treat Inez for free, when I know he's desperate for money. Gambling debts," she said in response to my quizzical look. "Threats. And a fierce coke habit. The man lives way beyond his means. Something is not right here. And I'll bet it has to do with Dr. Whitfield."

This was too sudden a jump for me. "A coke habit? What threats?"

"Michael was addicted to coke. Didn't you know? He and Jerry began by studying entheogens together, then Michael went too far and started dabbling in drugs that had nothing to do with therapy, though he said he was doing research, at least at first. Jerry was trying to help, but the man was beyond it, I think. He was being hounded by people he owed money to. Tough people."

How could I have missed all this? At least I knew about Whitfield's negligence. "Why do you think this has anything to do with Whitfield?"

"Michael knew Jerry was thinking of exposing Whitfield. I was there when they discussed it."

"Jerry and I talked about it, too," I said. "Jerry told me he didn't think he could do anything because it was only hearsay, then he found a patient willing to make a formal complaint. He was getting everything ready to take it to the Society. He was all torn up about it. But Margaret, how does this connect to Michael and Inez?"

Her eyes narrowed. "I wouldn't be at all surprised if our man didn't see an opportunity to make good on his debts."

I stared, speechless.

"What if Michael contacted Whitfield," she went on, "told him what was up, and offered to help him, in return for a large sum of money? Whitfield's loaded."

"What kind of bargain would they have struck?"

"Michael could have offered to discredit Jerry, Caitlin. Think about it. If it looked like Jerry had badly mishandled a patient, no one was going to listen to him or the patient he'd found to complain about Whitfield. They'd think he was just trying to cover his ass."

I was remembering the plagiarism charge that had been haunting Jerry, and the fact that he'd been passed over as a training analyst for the second time. All that made him vulnerable to being discredited. I wondered, too, if "all that" hadn't also been part of the plan.

It was no more than a hunch of Margaret's, with no proof to back it up, but she knew so much more than me about Michael's debts and drug addiction, I had to take it seriously. "You mean Michael cared so little for Inez he was willing to damage her just to save himself? And cared so little for Jerry he was willing to risk Jerry's life?" I was still trying to take it in.

Margaret shook her head. "I could be wrong about the whole thing ..."

"Wait," I said, "why would Michael tell Jerry about his debts if he was planning to get money from Whitfield? Why let Jerry in on it at all?"

Margaret gave me a look. "Jerry already knew about the coke, Cat. And before he knew about Whitfield — well, Jerry was a source of funds ..."

"He helped him?"

"He was already trying to help him get off coke. And he felt sorry enough for the guy that he loaned him money, not to gamble or buy drugs, but to get him out of the hole he'd dug himself into."

Goddamn Michael! He'd played on Jerry's goodheartedness in a way that disgusted me.

Margaret put a hand on my arm. "Like I say, I may be wrong about all of it. But if I'm not, I doubt Michael could ever have thought that Inez would kill Jerry. Why would he? I suspect things got out of hand. Discrediting Jerry to save his and Whitfield's necks — yes, I believe Michael Doherty is fully capable of that. But I doubt he meant Jerry to die."

Chapter Thirty-Six

Caitlin's Story

I went to Michael's again that night. I knew I shouldn't go alone, but I'd concocted a plan that wouldn't work in company. It was a simple plan, perhaps too obvious, but I thought it worth a try. If he wasn't guilty, we'd be no worse off than we'd been before. If he was, it might pay off. Unless Michael got violent. Unless he was coked up.

I pushed the thought to the back of my mind and knocked on his front door.

He opened up after what seemed an interminable wait, peering at me out of bloodshot eyes.

"What's up, Caitlin? It's late ..."

I could tell from his breath that he'd been drinking. It was something I hadn't dared to hope. I knew his fondness for liquor, and I'd brought a bottle of expensive Scotch to loosen his forked tongue. The fact that he'd gotten a head start on the alcohol meant my task would be a lot easier. "Yes, it's late."

"Well, it's, ah, nice of you to drop by."

"Can I come in?"

"It's late ..." he said again.

"I know, but this is important. I've something to say that you need to hear."

"Can't you just tell me?"

I held out the bottle of Scotch. "Over drinks?" I said.

He stood back from the door. "All right then."

This time, he led me downstairs. That put me on edge, so as soon as we sat down in his luxurious basement studio, I asked for two glasses and poured us both a drink. "On the rocks?" I said, and he agreed.

I let him savour his drink for a few moments, then I hit him between the eyes before I could lose my nerve. I told him that Alita had said she didn't own a *rebozo*.

His eyes grew wide, then hooded, as though he had a cowl at his disposal. He let out a breath that made his lips vibrate then leaned forward, like he wanted to tell me something, but instead ran a hand over his mouth.

"It's okay, Michael," I said, forcing kindness into my voice. "Whatever was going on, I don't believe you meant it to go that far."

His eyes were everywhere except on me. "Go what far? I don't know what you mean."

"You took the dolls back to Jerry's, didn't you?"

He didn't deny it. He just sat there with his bottom lip hanging low enough to trip a Basset hound.

"You put them in Jerry's office when he wasn't looking —"

"No ..." he began, half rising from his chair, then sank back down.

"Yes, I think so, Michael. Why? It's something to do with Whitfield, isn't it? You told Whitfield Jerry was on to him —"

He narrowed his eyes. I knew he was assessing me, hoping to find weak spots. "I told Dr. Whitfield *we* were aware that all was not well with him," he said righteously after a few moments, but he was looking past me, as if to some distant ideal. "I wanted to give him a chance to reform, you see. He *is* our president, after all."

"Is that right, Michael? How noble of you. Was it then he offered you money to discredit Jerry, or did you make that suggestion yourself?"

I clutched the arms of my chair, afraid the ammo I'd launched would ricochet off Michael and strike me through the heart.

His eyes glittered the way they had when I'd confronted him before. He was calculating something, I was sure. When he raised a palm like a stop sign or a white flag and lowered his head, I took a deep breath and leaned into my elbows where they rested on my knees.

I had to draw him out, keep his guilt strong, address his need to tell the truth. I had to be both good cop and bad cop, with a dash of therapist and a *soupçon* of understanding friend, but I was sweating and felt weak all over.

I deliberately thought back to Tommy's death, the guilt I'd felt afterwards, and how I ultimately had to forgive myself in order to carry on with my life. I needed to do this, so that what I said next would at least have a fighting chance of sounding genuine.

When he put his face in his hands, my confidence grew just enough for me to begin, softly, "I can't blame you for what you did. That may seem strange to you, but I do understand. We all have a survival instinct, we all behave terribly under stress. But then we regret it, and we want to make amends. It's the only way past the guilt and the grief. Especially when things go wrong. I know you didn't intend for Jerry to die. He was your friend. You must have suffered a lot over discrediting him; but you were trapped …"

He dropped his hands from his face. I couldn't quite believe it, but his cheeks looked wet. "I didn't ..." He waved his hands helplessly in the air and shook his head, opened his mouth and let it hang.

"Didn't what?" I almost breathed it.

He waved me away.

Didn't do it, or didn't mean it? Was he in denial or, like a cheating husband who needs to ease his guilt, ripe for disclosure?

"It's okay, Michael, I know." I got up and poured him a double shot of whiskey, straight up. "You didn't mean to hurt Inez that badly, either." I handed him the glass, and he took it, staring at me out of his handsome, blade-like face, like he was thinking things over.

That scared me. He was a calculating man, and he could be recovering himself. Maybe he'd find his courage in drink, and part of my plan was a bust before it began.

He tossed the whiskey back in a single gulp and shook his hair out of his eyes. "You don't know what you're saying, Cat." His pupils looked like black stones, and his voice had lost the scraped sound I'd heard in it moments before.

I thought fast. "Yes, I do, Michael, and so do you." I took a threatening step towards him, knowing that whatever I said next had to frighten him or I'd lose the game outright. "I know what you did. I have proof. Don't mess with me."

He jumped to his feet, brushed me aside, and went to the bar to pour another whiskey. After downing it, he swivelled round to face me, his hair once again falling into his eyes, his cheeks flushed. "How would you know anything about it, Cat? You've got it all wrong."

"Is that why Inez told me how you shoved the dolls in her face and demanded to know what she'd done?"

He paled, but one vermillion lip lifted at the corner. "Inez doesn't exactly speak, now does she?"

"She's started to, Michael. She should be quite the conversationalist soon. And she's always been able to imitate and repeat." Then I said the words Inez had used, words I knew originated with Michael, and added, "She's a brilliant mimic. She said that in your voice."

His breathing quickened, and he swept his hair off his forehead and parted his lips, but before he could say anything, I said, "Margaret Richards was with me. She heard every word. That's two strikes against you, right there." The words shot out of me like bullets. "You made a big mistake, Michael, showing me that letter. I know what you did, and now I've got you for obstructing justice, withholding evidence as well —"

"Shut up, Cat! Just shut up!" He slumped down into his chair.

I poured him another double; a stiff one for myself, too.

"I know you didn't mean it, Michael." Good cop again. "I'll bet it's been eating at you." The booze gave me a warm buzz I could ride on, like a glider on a carrying wind.

He downed the drink I'd handed him, went to the bar again, came back with the bottle of whiskey. He took a slug then put the bottle down beside his chair. "If you're not looking for a confession, why did you come?" The words came out slowly, as if it was a struggle for him to locate them in his head, let alone say them, and I could tell he was smashed.

"Just to talk," I said. "You were Jerry's friend. You did Inez a lot of good. I can't believe you meant either of them any real harm. I just wanted to know what really happened. And I wanted to hear you say that you didn't mean to hurt either of them."

"Why?" He was squinting at me the way drunks do when they are finding it hard to focus and concentrate at the same time.

"So I can move on. Forgive you. It matters to me."

"You mean, if I talk, you won't go to the police with what you have?"

It didn't even cross my mind to tell the truth. "Of course I won't. What good would it do? You didn't kill Jerry. If you're genuinely sorry for what happened, that's all I care about." I was counting on his extreme drunkenness to fuddle his brain. My main worry was that he would pass out before telling me what happened.

He stared at the carpet.

"All right then," I said after the silence had gone on long enough for me to become aware of his furnace kicking in. "I gave you a fair chance. I'm going now." I got up and gathered my things.

He looked up, startled, making it obvious he'd lost the thread of the conversation in an alcoholic haze. "What? To the police? Why?"

"Because I need you to tell me what happened."

His face cleared, and he looked straight at me. For the first time, I saw what I thought was violence in his eyes.

"If you hurt me, Michael, it will be the last thing you do." I picked up a large lamp from the end table closest to me.

It was the right weapon to choose. His eyes widened. "Okay. No. Wait. Put it down — I didn't ... mean it to happen." He sucked another slug from the bottle, still watching me, but now his eyes had slithered away behind a whiskey fog.

I moved in close and squatted beside him. "Tell me what you *did* want to happen." I put my hand over his where it rested on the arm of the chair.

His legs were splayed out in front of him. His head lolled against the chair back. He ran the fingers of his free hand clumsily through my hair. "I figured Inez would regress, Jerry would look bad, and I'd get that bastard Whitfield off my back." He was looking at me amorously now. I could hardly believe it.

For the only time since Jerry died, I was glad I'd been drinking to excess. It meant I knew firsthand what too much drink could do, and it seemed Michael was the same kind of drunk I was. Sloppy and sensual, with an angry undercurrent.

"What about the money?"

He shook his head disgustedly, though it bobbled a bit. His fine red lips twisted in an expression of contempt. "Look around you, Cat. Do I look like I need money? If I were desperate enough, I could sell all this ..." He opened his arms to indicate his domain.

So you hit up Jerry for money just so you could maintain your lifestyle, I thought bitterly. Why hadn't Jerry seen through it? Just too damned kind.

"I only asked Jerry for loans," he said as if he'd seen inside my head, "to tide me over so I didn't have to give anything up. I always paid him back. I was a lucky gambler for the most part."

I forced myself not to pull away, moved in closer instead, leaned my head against his knee. "Well, I knew you didn't want to hurt anyone ..."

"I didn't."

What had it all been about then? I decided not to press him. He was sliding into a confessional mood, and I had only to play my part, and wait.

"I almost didn't go through with it, Cat."

A hopeful note had sprung into his voice, and I turned my face slowly upwards without pulling it away from his knee, to gauge his expression. I caressed his hand.

"Showing Inez the dolls scared her so much it shook me. It really did. I did care about her."

Then, I wanted to say. *You cared about her* then. *But things changed, didn't they, Michael? And there's no one as important as you in the whole, wide world.* I waited for him to go on.

"I couldn't back out, no matter how much I wanted to. And believe me, I wanted to." He looked down at me as if I was to take this admission as proof of his good character and kiss him. When I didn't, he said, "Whitfield hated Jerry, and he knew I was into coke. Did *you* know that, Cat? That I was into coke?" He was beginning to emphasize random syllables they way people do when they've drunk so much, they can barely force the words past their swollen tongues.

I didn't answer.

"Whitfield could have taken away my medical *li*cense in a heartbeat. And I knew he would. It was so unfair! I'm a good *ana*lyst, always have been, and the coke never interfered. I wouldn't let it. Whitfield is a *terrr*ble analyst. Just terrrble. He came to me. He wanted Jerry de*stroy*ed, not just discredited."

"Why?"

"Your *part*ner was never the most diplomatic of men." The words were coming with many pauses now, and I wished I could jab him with something sharp to hurry him up. "He was careless enough to show our … fearless leader … up at a few important meetings, put him on the *spot*. He also argued with him about his approach. Whitfield is an egomaniac. He did not take kindly to it. Jerry made it clear he had no … respect … for him. Whitfield wants re*spect*. Whitfield de*mands* respect." He was wagging his finger at me like a teacher admonishing a pupil. "He *hated* self-psychology, just *hated* it, and Jerry championed it. He was winning a lot of us *o*ver, and Whitfield … couldn't stand that."

I was struggling hard not to cry. I had loved Jerry for his lack of diplomacy, his courage.

"I was screwed. I had no wiggle room at all. I tried, but Whitfield — that bastard was determined. Besides …" He lifted his head and flipped his glossy hair off his face. "I knew Jer would get his rep back. He was a damn good *ana*lyst. It was only a matter of time. And Inez —" He broke off abruptly, his top lip disappearing in an upward curl against his teeth.

"I knew she'd get better eventually, like she did the first time. In the meantime, Jerry would look bad. I ..." Right before his eyes closed and his jaw slackened, he shrugged.

I wanted to punch him or shatter every glass object in the room over his head. I'd seen the black hole inside him that sucked up all his good qualities whenever he was threatened. Doubtless something bad had happened to him. In his child-hood. It always came back to one's childhood. I couldn't have cared less. "Yes. After all, you helped her before, didn't you?" I kept my voice soft with an effort. "Did you show her the dolls? Michael?" I nudged him gently.

He nodded so briefly I barely caught it.

"Then you showed them to her again?" I spoke softly. "That day."

"Yes. The day after I returned the journal I'd borrowed."

Now I could move in. "What you did was very clever. I've always thought you were a smart man. How did you get them onto Jerry's desk without him seeing them?"

He made an effort to rouse himself from his drunken stupor, collecting his features into a reasonable facsimile of sobriety. "I told Jerry I'd like to see Inez," he said. "Jerry went to get her, and I spread the dolls out on the desk."

Already his face was starting to revert to the melting snow-man look it had worn earlier. His eyes blurred.

"What, Michael? Can you sit up?" I hauled him up in the chair, massaging his shoulders.

"The desk faces the door, but you know that," he said, giving his head a shake. "As soon as Jerry opened it, I handed him some papers, to distract him."

I rubbed his forehead.

"Thash nice, Cat. You're a good person. I wish I was good like you." He was slurring his words.

How revolting, I thought. *What a sloppy drunk.* I despised people who did not have the courage to admit to or reform their miscreant selves.

"I was hoping Inez would see the dolls." Michael sniffled. "She did. She went berserk. As planned." He looked up at me imploringly. "I wasn't going to say he did it purposely. I would jush im*ply* it, leave it hanging. I'd have told about the letter then, and what it said about the *dolls*. I'd let people know the dolls were on his desk that day. Then I'd claim I didn't know why, that Jerry told me he hadn't meant to, and I be*liev*ed him. It would still be seen as a *ma*jor therapeutic error. Major. I'd be the nice guy, the friend who tried to cover for a friend. And Whitfield would leave me alone. Mmm, is nice, Cat, keep doing that."

I couldn't believe how out of it he was.

"We both went to calm her down. Well, Jerry went to do that, I went with him." The words were coming ever slower, and he was slurring them even more. I dug my thumbs into his forehead. "Oww. Go easy. What were we talking about?"

"How Jerry died."

"Oh. Right. O*kay*. I walked towards Inez. On the way, I looked back at the dolls. 'My god,' I said. Something like that. '*Who* put these *here?*' Inez started thrashing around, and Jerry held on to her. When he saw the dolls, he let go and bent over them, to pick them up, I think. I went to Inez. She picked up the lamp and headed for the dolls — and me. I ducked, and ... Jerry took the blow." He raised his hands in the air as if helpless. His bloodshot eyes were wide. "I ... ran. I didn't know he was dead, I swear."

My mind was in chaos. Inez hadn't meant to kill Jerry. Immediately after the first flush of relief, I was hit by the horror of what Michael had done. "You left him there with Inez? What if he was just hurt? What if he died because you left him there?"

When he started making horrible sucking noises and blubbering, I stepped away and wiped my hands on my skirt.

You were there, you bastard, I thought. *You were there. All this time you've known what happened, known what I've been going through. And Inez too.*

"Where you going, Cat? Don't go."

"You went back the day after you returned the journal you'd borrowed," I said, turning around. "You were seen then. Why didn't anyone see you that day?"

"I was lucky ... Margaret was away. The neighbours work. I knocked at the patients' door in back. I didn't care if anyone saw me. I didn't plan for him to die."

His voice was getting stronger, and I figured I'd better get out of there fast. I only needed the answer to one more question. "It's okay, Michael. I know how sorry you are. What was your plan if Inez hadn't killed him?"

He slid down in his chair. "I was going to act understanding about it, like I said. See, he didn't *know* I'd put the dolls there. Wouldn't even think of it. My *friend.* If I had to ... planning ... blame *Mar*garet."

I couldn't take much more. I plied both of us with one last drink to distract myself from sticking a knife through his chest. You can hear the splashes of liquor and the tinkling of ice on the tape I had running. I didn't turn off my mini-recorder until I was almost home, because I was so rattled by everything that happened I forgot I had it with me.

The tape had been an afterthought. I didn't expect it would hold up in court, and what he'd told me could be used against him without it, anyway. There's nothing more natural to a journalist than recording the spoken word, though, so I had taken it along just in case. I'm surprised still that Michael didn't suspect I might.

I wanted out of there, but Michael wasn't finished. "Whitfield was out to get Jer, *big*time, Cat. Thing is, I'm not sure he needed … involve Inez at *all*. Teresa Prialo could have been e*nough*, if … played his cards right."

"Teresa?" I went so cold, my hands felt numb and heavy.

"The *su*icide," said Michael, as if I might not have heard. "Made Jerry — self-psychology — look pretty bad, all on its own."

"All on its own?" I repeated stupidly, not yet ready to admit the thought that was lurking inside my head.

Michael nodded. "Yes. Even without a little help …" He left the remark hanging.

"A little help …" Again, I couldn't quite allow my mind to make connections.

"From Whitfield?" I said at last.

"Mmmhmm." He was wagging his head up and down like a marionette. "Poshibly. *Quite* poshibly. I know Whitfield talked to Teresa. I don't know what he *said*, but I do *know* they were in contact." He reached again for the bottle.

I gaped at him in horror and backed towards the door, grabbing my purse as I went.

He struggled up. "See you *out* …" He staggered towards me for a few steps then collapsed onto his sofa. I stared at him briefly before closing the door behind me. I remember hoping he'd puke on himself or, at the very least, pee like a waterlogged horse inside those designer pants.

On my way home, hugging my purse with the tape recorder inside to my chest, I came across a small boy walking alone.

I followed him, with the vague idea of seeing him safely home, but near my apartment, he stopped and looked back at me with the face of my dead brother.

"Stop following me," he said. "I don't need you."

I watched as he went up a driveway to a red brick bungalow, then I continued on my way.

When I got home, I collapsed across my bed into a drunken sleep and woke hours later to throw up in the bathroom.

After the professionals got a chance at Michael, I learned that the episode with the dolls was part of a larger plan, set in motion before Inez had arrived on the scene.

The plagiarism accusation originated with Michael, as I'd suspected. He had also told outright lies about Jerry to the senior analysts who make decisions about who can become a training analyst, something Jerry coveted. Jerry had given Michael's name as a reference, I remembered him telling me about it. But the *coup de grâce* was Teresa's suicide. It went beyond Whitfield's wildest hopes. Poor, crazy Teresa. Soon Whitfield planned to let it slip that he knew all along Jerry had been mistreating Teresa, using self-psychology inappropriately, that he'd tried to intervene, told the woman to discontinue therapy, but he was just a little too late.

Who would believe a discredited analyst accusing the President of the Analytic Institute of unethical behaviour, especially one who turned the tables on him as Whitfield had? Even with a patient as a witness, Jerry would not be believed. Analysts know how easily patients can be influenced by doctors. Put that together with Whitfield's power over everyone's livelihood, and Jerry was a dead duck.

The man was a total prick, and I couldn't wait to go after him.

As for Michael, he had intentionally set out to destroy Jerry's good reputation and endanger Inez's sanity.

And for what? To protect his career. When I thought about that, it made me blind with rage and sorrow. There had to have been another way. For such a stupid thing, for such a stupid, stupid thing, he'd killed my lover. I thought the tidal wave of grief would knock me down and drown me.

The fact that Michael never intended Jerry to die didn't redeem him in my eyes. He deserved his guilt and his remorse. Why should he escape suffering for what he'd done to Jerry, Inez, and me? I regretted the little compassion I'd allowed myself to feel, regretted the mercy I'd shown him, however manipulative, regretted I hadn't killed him in revenge.

What court would find him guilty of murder? None. But I would pursue justice all the same, because that and only that would set Inez free.

And bring the truth about Whitfield to light.

I'd let Jerry down. I'd let myself down. I was an investigative journalist, and when he'd told me about Whitfield, I should've been on it like a vampire bat. If I'd backed him more strongly, if I'd drawn him out and learned more about how Whitfield was treating him, quite apart from his patients, he might have blown the whistle before any of this happened, and he would still be alive.

And Inez? Sad, beautiful, tragic Inez. How would she ever come to live with herself? To forgive herself? What could her future hold, after all that had happened?

Why had she keened so loudly that she drew the soldiers to her family? I could only guess she had no control over herself at that time, didn't understand what she was doing.

But she understood now and likely had for a long time. Her mother had made sure of that. Shut away in her box, what else was there for Inez to think about? If she hadn't been insane to begin with, that alone could have driven her mad.

And yet sometimes, like an old soul, she gave the impression of being in touch with things — wonderful things — the rest of us were not.

———

That night, I dreamt that Jerry and Inez were in a private compartment on an old steam train. He was holding her face in his hands and looking into her eyes. "*Ich liebe dich*," he said. The ticketa/tacketa of the train was a love song more haunting than any I'd ever heard awake.

I was woken by the same female voice I'd heard after Jerry died, a voice that for some dream-reason made me think of him. This time it called, "Caitlin, Caitlin. There are angels."

I saw a dark shape standing at the foot of my bed. And I thought "Jerry" and the figure became Jerry, fully clothed this time, still dark, still shadowy, still real. The features of his face were distinguishable from the other shadows, lighter, brownish, his thick hair falling over his forehead.

Drunk again, I said to myself, before I remembered I hadn't touched a drop since that night with Michael. A deep ache spread through my chest and up into my head. "Oh, Jerry."

Whatever vision I was projecting outward from the inside of my head was smiling, wearily, I thought.

What did it mean, I said to him inside, *that voice?* "There are angels"?

It was then I remembered that Inez had said the same words the night we made angels in the snow.

My throat felt dry, my head and my heart ached, but as Jerry faded from view, I was carried with him to a place where the air was so pure, it made me think of butterfly wings. I wanted to stay there forever.

Back on earth, I remembered that Inez was in the prison of her own traumas, and I'd done little but make that worse.

Now, at least, I had a fighting chance to set things right.

Chapter Thirty-Seven

Caitlin's Story

The moment I could, I gave Gretchen the tape, and she handed it over to the police. She was excited but warned me taped confessions were not as cut-and-dry as I might think, given the possibility they could be faked or edited. She said it was a huge breakthrough, though, and with Alita's testimony about the shawl, and mine and Margaret's about the dolls, things looked extremely bad for Michael — and good for Inez.

Knowing that Inez was completely innocent of malice towards Jerry, let alone of murdering him, was the most wonderful feeling in the world.

When I got home from Gretchen's, I took out the only picture I had of her, the black and white photo in Jerry's box of things, just so I could look at her and imagine her set free.

Before putting it away, I had to turn it over.

Ich Liebe Dich.

On the Vision Quest, I'd had to admit to myself that Jerry could have been in love with Inez. It was hugely easier to live with than if he had abused her sexually. Even so, I clutched the photo to my chest and sobbed.

It wasn't that I didn't understand. Through the dull walk of days comes a being of beauty, sorrow, innocence, and light. Who wouldn't want to go with her? Even I long to inhabit the place she seems to embody at her happiest moments, a world where it is still possible to feel the exquisite wonder of things, the place where light shines into the darkness. I am a little in love with her myself.

It's hard to say, though, exactly what Jerry sought from her.

Inez had suffered more than anyone we had ever encountered. Instead of totally destroying her, it seemed to have given her a rare purity of heart. Jerry, with his respect for suffering and his belief that emotional extremes were the gateway to growth, would doubtless have felt that more strongly than I.

Even so, I think being in love with her would have tormented and confused him. With us, expressing and receiving love through the body was part of who we were. Knowing that physical love between him and Inez would destroy them both goes a long way, in my opinion, towards explaining his sometime reluctance to make love to me after she came into our lives. Instead of something joyful and meaningful, sex might have become a question in his mind, something to brood over and analyze.

In my darkest hours, I wonder if Jerry sensed his death at Inez's hands, and it was part of her allure. A man so drawn to suffering and so beset by troubles could perhaps have seen death as a longed-for rite of passage, one final way to grow.

But what I remember best is a man I would wake to find stroking my cheek, a man who told me that when things went well with me, he had never been in a better place, that I had given him "the best and most unusual bedtimes" of his life. I also remember sitting with him at a picnic on his lawn and seeing him gaze at Inez with a mixture of confusion and longing.

I continue to believe that the true fruition of his yearning was finding his way back to what we had, and trusting in it. All the same, I reserve the right to be in error. If I've learned nothing else, I've learned not to put faith in every thought that goes through my head. I'm simply glad that I've faced up to all eventualities.

Perhaps our wonderful gift came too easily, so that in time we both discounted it and began looking in tougher places for transcendence — me through meditation and him through the beautiful, damaged, spiritually gifted young Mayan woman who killed him.

At that same picnic, Jerry had turned from Inez to me. "Enduring love," he'd said and twirled a lock of my hair around his finger. "Or was it 'endless'? There's a poem by Delmore Schwartz, where he talks about either enduring or endless love, but I can't remember it exactly."

"*How could I think the brief years were enough / To prove the reality of endless love?*" I quoted.

Jerry smiled and touched my hair again.

He was the only man who could make me believe in it, no matter who else he may have loved as well.

Inez has slowly made gains after the disastrous night of the dolls in the snow. Margaret and I stayed away from Great Northern for months; we had to. We would only have made her worse.

Dr. Peterson directly oversaw her care, and he was marvelous. I was surprised, of course, but not totally. I'd learned he had a human side, and perhaps, like me, he has become a better person through knowing Inez.

She's started to come back to us, he wrote a few months after we left, *and to smile again.*

He had arranged for a female doctor to treat her, someone who specialized in "ethnic" cases and was sensitive to cultural differences. She wasn't Guatemalan, she was Somali, but she learned as much Kaqchikel as she could and has concentrated on teaching Inez more English.

One day not long ago, Peterson called and invited us to visit Inez. "I think she's ready," he said, and when I asked why he thought so, he said her doctor had advised it.

"Does she understand that killing Jerry was not her fault?" I asked, and he told me that her doctor had worked with Inez but did not yet know whether she had buried the memory again or had in fact come to terms with it.

"And what about what happened in Guatemala?"

"Ah," he said. "We think she has definitely put that to the back of her mind again. She looks frightened if any mention of soldiers or her family is made. Dr. Mahad says it is too soon to press the issue, but that ideally she should be treated eventually by a Guatemalan, one who understands Kaqchikel, because otherwise it is impossible to reach her on the deepest level, which she needs."

Then he added, "But how likely are we to find someone like that? A Guatemalan psychiatrist, preferably a woman, who is fluent in a language spoken only by a few Mayan tribes?" A sigh travelled down the phone lines.

I thought of Jacinta Barrera then, but I didn't say anything. I knew she wasn't a therapist and also that she was not available to Inez. But we'd kept in touch, and I thought at least I might persuade her to visit, and I would find a way to help her with the fare. She knew Kaqchikel, and in my last letter to her I had asked her about "nu bi."

Yes, she had written back, *It does mean "I am." It is a very good sign that this girl knows who she is at last. You must tell me more things she says, and I will help you understand, and I will help you learn the language, if you like.*

Peterson added that Dr. Mahad had reported some success with Inez when she mentioned the names of Mayan deities to her. Inez did not shy away from these; in fact, she smiled, and when pictures were shown to her of these gods and goddesses, or of the churches of her homeland, or of Christ, she seemed eager to speak of these things. Dr. Mahad said that she had picked up English vocabulary very quickly after they were shown to her.

It had never occurred to me that Inez might be religious, despite the fact that, early on, she'd painted what looked like Mayan gods. Just another of my stupidities when it came to her. After all, why wouldn't she be? Jerry had told me of the religious icons, some Christian, some Mayan, in her parents' home. Agnosticism is largely a Western trait, and I have since learned how the Maya mix their ancestral religion with the Catholicism imported by the Spanish, and how rituals and worship remain central to their lives.

When Margaret and I went north again, Inez seemed happy to see us. At least she did not recoil or scream or cry. We've spent many hours in her company since then. She still does not speak often, but when she does, her command of English astonishes me. I love to watch her as she moves through the small world of the visiting room, gently touching the gifts I bring for her, or placing her palm, fingers spread, on the window, looking out. During our times outdoors, she plays with the snow as she did before, throwing it up in the air in glistening bursts or, when everything is frozen solid, she glides over the ice like a dancer.

Every gesture she makes has grace. She's like Molly in that, Molly at her best. The sweet purity of Inez's face is something I can believe in again. Dr. Mahad, when I met her, reminded me that Inez is capable of violence, for though she did not deliberately kill Jerry, she did raise the lamp against Michael, with intent to hurt. "There is darkness in her," she said, "which to me seems natural, given what she has been through. But we must work with that, not deny it."

When Inez's eyes cloud over, as they will do now and again, and she disappears inside herself, my heart aches for her.

I know something of how it feels to believe yourself responsible for the death of a sibling, but I can only imagine how terrible it would be to be viciously raped over and over again when you are still a child. Somehow we must bring Inez to realize that she is different through no fault of her own. The doctors now believe she may have suffered a brain injury near birth or early in her life. X-rays show old skull fractures. They are not sure, but it is possible she may have been unusual from a very early age.

I hope one day she is able to see that what happened to Jerry, though terrible, was in no way her fault, that the horror she gave a voice when the soldiers came for her again was not something she could control, nor could she have known that making noise would get her siblings killed. Inez, so childlike, might not have fully understood the permanence of death. She also had no reason to believe that a mother who was always trying to silence her was actually demanding something that for once made sense.

When Inez is released, it will be into Margaret's custody. Margaret would like to adopt her, though it's unclear whether this is possible, given the girl's age and with her father likely still alive but unreachable. Margaret says Inez is the answer to something she was looking for when she took the job with Jerry.

Margaret has already made contact with an organization that helps victims of torture, and also with Latin American groups in Toronto. So far, no one speaks Kaqchikel, but there are those who know of others who speak that language, some of whom are refugees from Guatemala. They are not doctors, but they are good people who will understand what she has been through. In time, Margaret will introduce these people to her. In the meantime, Molly, without whom none of these wonderful things would have happened, is eager to stay involved, to help Inez with her art.

I too considered adopting Inez because of the maternal feelings she aroused in me, but my feelings for her are more complex than that, and I know I'd never be able to relate to her only as my child, but she is my special friend.

I hope to be there for her whenever she needs me. It's hard to predict how my life will go, whether I'll stay where I am and still be able to see her regularly. But I'm committed to helping her understand I don't blame her for Jerry's death, and that I need her, too, that she has enriched my life in ways I could never have imagined. I've even learned I'm capable of writing a book, on which I soon plan to put the final touches. I love her for being the marvelous creature she is, and I believe that Jerry, wherever he is, and whatever he has become, loves her still.

This will be the last entry in my journal, but not the final chapter in my book. Once I have put it all together, I intend to give that opportunity to someone who can speak for herself at last.

Chapter Thirty-Eight

Inez

Inez *nu bi.*
I am I.
I did not know.
Many things.
Only warmth and cold, *c'aaten, tew*, darkness, light.
There is more light now, and more things I know.

My name is Inez.
I am from the lake. *Ya* Atitlan.

To my mother, I was *nagual.*
She who could become an animal.

Before the dark place, my father
told me that everything in all the world
has a song, but that only our people can hear it.
Even the dark place, even the soldiers,

each had their song.
And Lord Jesus, the Sun God,
who loves us, who forgives us.
And Itzamna, who made all things.
They sang to me often there and in
the white temple.

Inez *nu bi.*
I am I.

I will go back, *Ya* Atitlan,
when Ix Chel, the lady rainbow,
She who heals
is done with me
to the place of the deep waters where I was born.
I will listen for your song, Atitlan.
And I shall sing my song for you.

Acknowledgements

Thanks are due to the following people (in no particular order), who provided suggestions, encouragement, and/or information in a variety of ways:

Sylvia McConnell, for taking a chance on me once again; along with Allister Thompson, who did a sensitive and remarkably painless edit, and Emma Dolan for picking a cover I love; Paula Costa-Kuswanto; Guy Saville; Dr. Peter C. Thompson, for being a shining example of The Good Analyst; Prof. John C. Meagher, for his astute stylistic suggestions and clever conversation; Mark Bogumill, for his knowledge of autism; Vercingetorix (you know who you are); Roisin Moriarty; Caroline Kellems, for her input on Guatemala; Linda Hutsell-Manning; Claire Hoekstra; Pamela Moriarty; Heidi Woodhead; Mary Conybeare, Carlyle Clark; Suki Michelle; Sharon Stewart; Katerina Fretwell; Alexa DeWiel for a place to write undisturbed; and to my many reviewers on two Internet writing sites, The Next Big Writer, and You Write On; and the Amazon Breakthrough Novel Award contest.

I hope those I have forgotten will forgive the vagaries of my memory. Thank you all with all my heart.

Final Analysis by Jeffrey Masson (1990) was a useful source of information on the darker side of the psychoanalytic profession.

MORE GREAT FICTION FROM DUNDURN

Providence Island
by Gregor Robinson
9781554887712
$21.99

Returning to Ontario's northern lakes as an adult to bury his father, Ray Carrier is taken back not only to a tangled romance in that green paradise but also to the forests and lonesome swamps that have haunted his dreams. As a teenager, Ray was enchanted by the grace and privilege of the Miller family on Providence Island, part of the wealthy resort community up the road from the farm where Ray and his widowed father spent their summers. Ray's father had always said that he was too impressed by money, but it was more than that. But something happened near the abandoned railway tracks long ago — something that shattered Ray's illusions of love and money. And now something must be settled before Ray can achieve peace and let go of Providence Island and the Millers once and for all.

Six Metres of Pavement
by Farzana Doctor
9781554887675
$22.99

Ismail Boxwala made the worst mistake of his life one summer morning twenty years ago: he forgot his baby daughter in the back seat of his car. After his daughter's tragic death, he struggles to continue living. A divorce, years of heavy drinking, and sex with strangers only leave him more alone and isolated.

But Ismail's story begins to change after he reluctantly befriends two women: Fatima, a young queer activist kicked out of her parents' home; and Celia, his grieving Portuguese-Canadian neighbour who lives just six metres away. A slow-simmering romance develops between Ismail and Celia. Meanwhile, dangers lead Fatima to his doorstep. Each makes complicated demands of him, ones he is uncertain he can meet.

Available at your favourite bookseller.

What did you think of this book?
Visit www.dundurn.com for reviews,
videos, updates, and more!